The Best American
Mystery Stories 2012

D0193622

GUEST EDITORS OF
THE BEST AMERICAN MYSTERY STORIES

The Best American Mystery Stories™ 2012

Edited and with an Introduction by **Robert Crais**

Otto Penzler, *Series Editor*

DISCARD

A MARINER ORIGINAL

HOUGHTON MIFFLIN HARCOURT

BOSTON • NEW YORK   2012

Copyright © 2012 by Houghton Mifflin Harcourt Publishing Company
Introduction copyright © 2012 by Robert Crais
ALL RIGHTS RESERVED

The Best American Series® is a registered trademark of Houghton Mifflin Harcourt Publishing Company. *The Best American Mystery Stories*™ is a trademark of Houghton Mifflin Harcourt Publishing Company.

No part of this work may be reproduced or transmitted in any form or by any means, electronic or mechanical, including photocopying and recording, or by any information storage or retrieval system without the proper written permission of the copyright owner unless such copying is expressly permitted by federal copyright law. With the exception of nonprofit transcription in Braille, Houghton Mifflin Harcourt is not authorized to grant permission for further uses of copyrighted selections reprinted in this book without the permission of their owners. Permission must be obtained from the individual copyright owners as identified herein. Address requests for permission to make copies of Houghton Mifflin Harcourt material to Permissions, Houghton Mifflin Harcourt Publishing Company, 215 Park Avenue South, New York 10003.

www.hmhbooks.com

ISSN 1094-8384
ISBN 978-0-547-55398-6

Printed in the United States of America
DOC 10 9 8 7 6 5 4 3 2 1

These stories are works of fiction. Names, characters, places, and incidents are products of the authors' imagination or are used fictitiously. Any resemblance to actual events, locales, or persons, living or dead, is entirely coincidental.

"The Hit" by Tom Andes. First published in *Xavier Review*, Vol. 31, No. 1. Copyright © 2011 by Thomas Andes. Reprinted by permission of the author.

"The Bridge Partner" by Peter S. Beagle. First published in *Sleight of Hand*, March 2011. Copyright © 2011 by Avicenna Development Corporation. Reprinted by permission of Avicenna Development Corporation.

"Filament" by K. L. Cook. First published in *One Story*, No. 147. Copyright © 2011 by K. L. Cook. Reprinted by permission of K. L. Cook.

"The Funeral Bill" by Jason DeYoung. First published in *New Orleans Review*, 37.1. Copyright © 2011 by Jason DeYoung. Reprinted by permission of the author.

"Fifty Minutes" by Joe Donnelly and Harry Shannon. First published in *Slake: Los Angeles*, No.2: Crossing Over. Copyright © 2011 by Joe Donnelly and Harry Shannon. Reprinted by permission of *Slake* / Joe Donnelly and Harry Shannon.

"Man on the Run" by Kathleen Ford. First published in *New England Review*, Vol. 31, No. 4. Copyright © 2012 by Middlebury Publications. Reprinted by permission of *New England Review*.

"The Other Place" by Mary Gaitskill. First published in *The New Yorker*, February 14 & 21, 2011. Copyright © 2011 by Mary Gaitskill. Reprinted by permission of Mary Gaitskill.

"Safety" by Jesse Goolsby. First published in *The Greensboro Review*, Fall 2011. Copyright © 2011 by Jesse Goolsby. Reprinted by permission of Jesse Goolsby.

"Trafficking" by Katherine L. Hester. First published in *storySouth*, No. 31. Copyright © 2011 by Katherine L. Hester. Reprinted by permission of Katherine L. Hester.

"Soul Anatomy" by Lou Manfredo. First published in *New Jersey Noir*, November 2011. Copyright © 2011 by Lou Manfredo. Reprinted by permission of Akashic Books.

"The Good Samaritan" by Thomas McGuane. First published in *The New Yorker*, April 25, 2011. Copyright © 2011 by Thomas McGuane. Reprinted by permission of The Wylie Agency, LLC.

"Looking for Service" by Nathan Oates. First published in *The Antioch Review*, Vol. 69, No. 2. Copyright © 2012 by Nathan Oates. Reprinted by permission of Nathan Oates.

"Dog on a Cow" by Gina Paoli. First published in *Ellery Queen's Mystery Magazine*, February 2011. Copyright © 2012 by Gina Paoli. Reprinted by permission of Gina Paoli.

"Vic Primeval" by T. Jefferson Parker. First published in *San Diego Noir*, May 2011. Copyright © 2011 by Akashic Books. Reprinted by permission of the author.

"Hard Truths" by Thomas J. Rice. First published in *The New Orphic Review*, Vol. 14, No. 1. Copyright © 2011 by Thomas J. Rice. Reprinted by permission of Thomas J. Rice.

"Local Knowledge" by Kristine Kathryn Rusch. First published in *Ellery Queen's Mystery Magazine*, November 2011. Copyright © 2011 by Kristine Kathryn Rusch. Reprinted by permission of Kristine Kathryn Rusch.

"Icarus" by Lones Seiber. First published in *Indiana Review*, Summer 2011. Copyright © 2011 by Lones Seiber. Reprinted by permission of Lones Seiber.

"Trafalgar" by Charles Todd. First published in *The Mammoth Book of Historical Crime Fiction*, September 2011. Copyright © 2011 by Charles Todd. Reprinted by permission of Charles Todd.

"Half-Lives" by Tim L. Williams. First published in *Ellery Queen's Mystery Magazine*, March/April 2011. Copyright © 2011 by Tim L. Williams. Reprinted by permission of Tim L. Williams.

"Returning the River" by Daniel Woodrell. First published in the book *The Outlaw Album* by Daniel Woodrell. Copyright © 2011 by Daniel Woodrell. Reprinted by permission of Little, Brown and Company, New York, NY. All rights reserved.

Contents

Foreword

HAVING WRITTEN AND SPOKEN about mystery fiction frequently (some ungenerous soul might say ad nauseam) through the years, I have maintained that one of its appeals is that it is a literary presentation of a fundamental life force: a battle between those who value Good in opposition to the spear carriers of Evil.

Ruminating on it recently, however, I came to think this may be less true at this time than it was when I first became interested in crime fiction. As character and psychological elements of a story have transcended plots and clues, as the reason *why* a murder was committed has transcended the question of *who* committed it or *how* it was done, it seems to be that the two omnipresent factors in contemporary crime fiction are Death and Sin.

Death appears to provide the minds of readers with a greater fund of innocent amusement than any other single subject except love, but of course in crime fiction they are not mutually exclusive components of a novel or short story. Furthermore, when Death is accompanied by Sin in its most repugnant shapes, the fun increases exponentially. Some readers prefer the intellectual cheerfulness of a detective story while others have a taste that runs more to noir fiction, but in either case the story generally requires at least one dead body and at least one very wicked person for it to provide that frisson of pleasure that may be had while viewing horrible events from a safe distance.

Here, then, in the sixteenth volume in this distinguished series, is a collection of stories nearly all of which are about Death and Sin, with plenty of dead bodies and an abundance of wicked people. They are designed, albeit unconsciously on the most part, to make you feel that it's good to be alive and, while alive, on the whole, to be good.

It should be noted, in a parenthetical aside, that mystery writers are, with (truly) few exceptions, good. It is fundamental to their jobs to be aware of the fact that your sins will be discovered, no matter how clever you think you are. This is why, it should be further noted, mystery fiction is such a good influence in an increasingly degenerate world, and why it is so popular with academics, lawyers, politicians, and others who have reputations to protect; reading mysteries improves their morals and keeps them out of excessive mischief.

While it is redundant for me to write it again, since I have done it in each of the previous fifteen volumes of this series, I recognize the lamentable fact that not everyone has read every one of those books, nor memorized the introductory remarks, so it falls into the category of fair warning to state that many people regard a "mystery" only as a detective story. I regard the detective story as one subgenre of a much bigger genre, which I define as any work of fiction in which a crime, or the threat of a crime, is central to the theme or the plot. While I love good puzzles and tales of pure ratiocination, few of these are written today, as the mystery genre has evolved (or devolved, depending on your point of view) into a more character-driven form of literature, as noted previously. The line between mystery fiction and general fiction has become more and more blurred in recent years, producing fewer memorable detective stories but more significant literature. It has been my goal in this series to recognize that fact and to reflect it between these covers. The best writing makes it into the book. Fame, friendship, original venue, reputation, subject—none of it matters. It isn't only the qualification of being the best writer that will earn a place in the table of contents; it also must be the best story.

As frequent readers of this series are aware, each annual volume would, I am convinced, require three years to compile were it not for the uncanny ability of my colleague, Michele Slung, to read, absorb, and evaluate thousands of pages in what appears to be a nanosecond. After culling the nonmysteries, as well as those crime stories perpetrated by writers who may want to consider careers in carpentry or knitting instead of wasting valuable trees for their efforts, I read stacks of them, finally settling on the fifty best—or at least my fifty favorites—which are then passed on to the guest editor, who this year is the creator of Elvis Cole and Joe Pike, Robert Crais. Coincidentally, but generously, he began writing the introduction to this volume on the same weekend that his most recent novel, *Taken*, hit the number-one spot on the *New York Times* bestseller list.

My sincere thanks go to this supernaturally gifted author, as well as to the previous guest editors, who helped make this series so successful: Robert B. Parker, who started it all in 1997, followed by Sue Grafton, Ed McBain, Donald E. Westlake, Lawrence Block, James Ellroy, Michael Connelly, Nelson DeMille, Joyce Carol Oates, Scott Turow, Carl Hiaasen, George Pelecanos, Jeffery Deaver, Lee Child, and Harlan Coben.

While Michele and I engage in a relentless quest to locate and read every mystery/crime/suspense story published, I live in fear that we will miss a worthy one, so if you are an author, editor or publisher, or care about one, please feel free to send a book, magazine, or tearsheet to me c/o The Mysterious Bookshop, 58 Warren Street, New York, NY 10007. If the story first appeared electronically, you must submit a hard copy. It is vital to include the author's contact information. No unpublished material will be considered, for what should be obvious reasons. No material will be returned. If you distrust the postal service, enclose a self-addressed, stamped postcard.

To be eligible, a story must have been written by an American or a Canadian and first issued in an American or Canadian publication in the calendar year 2012 with a 2012 publication date. The earlier in the year I receive the story, the more fondly I regard it. For reasons known only to the blockheads who wait until Christmas week to submit a story published the previous spring, holding eligible stories for months before submitting them occurs every year, which causes much gnashing of teeth while I read a stack of stories as my wife and friends are trimming the Christmas tree or otherwise celebrating the holiday season. It had better be a damned good story if you do this. Because of the very tight production schedule for this book, the absolute deadline is December 31. If the story arrives one day later, it will not be read. Sorry.

O. P.

Introduction

THE TIME: edging past midnight.

The place: a suburban neighborhood where a quarter moon casts pale light across sleepy trees, tailored lawns, and darkened houses; the camera that is our mind's eye floats past these houses until it comes to rest on a window lit from within . . . which happens to be *your* window.

We now drift closer, where we find . . . me (aka Robert Crais, the coeditor of this book, along with the esteemed Otto Penzler) and author of this introduction), giggling like a goblin in the midnight shadows beneath the eaves of your roof, hanging in the darkness as I peer with cat-slit eyes into your bedroom. (Creepy, yeah, but *not* for deviant criminal purposes!)

I am watching you read this book.

I am giggling because you have plunked down hard cash for this book (*maybe* because my name is attached!), and I am having a blast and a half watching you enjoy this wonderful collection of short stories.

Because, good readers, this book is all about you enjoying yourselves and finding new authors to love, else my name would not be on it.

Short stories were my first love. Though I have published eighteen novels at this point in time, I began as a writer of short fiction and dearly love the form. For one, short stories are short. Poe famously defined a short story as a story one could read in a single sitting. I'm not sure that that is necessarily the case, but most of us can suck up a three-thousand-word short story in a sitting, and do, and that is part of the fun. You get the beginning, the middle, and the payoff all in a single gulp, and because of this, short stories are like peanuts—you probably won't eat just one.

A good reader might be able to plow through a novel in three or four nights, relishing the immersion in the novel's reality for a sustained period, but short stories allow the reader to sample many realities in that same period of time. I love checking out a contents page for the familiar names of writers I know I'll enjoy, and also the exploratory adventure of discovering new writers whose names are unknown to me, which is the joy of an anthology such as this. Here you'll get quick hits of superstars such as Peter Beagle and Thomas McGuane and Kristine Kathryn Rusch, as well as of writers whose work you might not yet have discovered.

With a collection like this, you get it all, and if you are like me, friends, you *want* it all!

Now that I've said this, make no mistake: short fiction should not be dismissed as a literary quickie, having no more importance than, say, stopping by McD's for a burger to go. The best short stories can linger. Salinger's "A Perfect Day for Bananafish," Hemingway's "The Short Happy Life of Francis Macomber," and Chandler's "Red Wind" all haunt me years after I first read them. In fact, the brevity of a short story often lends to its power.

Mr. Penzler and I have tried to provide something for everyone, from surprising amusements to complex character studies to noir pieces as desperate as a death row inmate's heart. The key to a great short story collection is diversity. These stories do not all feature private investigators or college professors or retired FBI agents or criminals doing crime. They are not all grim noir etchings, not all laugh-out-loud giggles, and do not all have snappy twist endings. This is by design, but regardless of your personal preferences and tastes, these stories all have one thing in common—they are the best of their American kind yer 'umble editors could find, and personally, I am most excited for you to sample the type of story you ordinarily *don't* read.

So explore. Taste new flavors, smell new aromas, and run your fingers across the textures of authors you haven't known before. Let Mr. Penzler and me be your guides.

The place: this book.

The time: now.

The mission: lose yourself in these dark dreams, and enjoy.

I am outside your window. Watching.

ROBERT CRAIS

The Best American Mystery Stories 2012

TOM ANDES

The Hit

FROM *Xavier Review*

THE GUY LOOKED like an off-duty cop. Even Marsh could see that. For a terrible moment, when the door swung open as if torn from its hinges, when the lumbering shape waddled in, blotting out the sunlight from Irving, Marsh thought he'd been set up. He pictured himself hauled off in cuffs, his name splashed across the *Examiner*'s afternoon edition; he pictured Gina's tears and the confused faces of their children, and something reared up inside him, an impulse toward self-destruction he didn't know he possessed.

"You were supposed to be here by eleven o'clock," he squawked, in the same petulant tone he reserved for his children, for the parolees they hired to scour pots at the hotel.

He didn't know what he'd been expecting—someone more like Pacino in *Scarface*, with a little 007 thrown in for good measure; someone with at least a good head of hair. Mickey's distended gut spilled out from under a dirty sweatshirt that said *Property of the San Jose Sharks*, and he was wearing shorts.

"All right, take it easy, will you?" the guy said finally, and Marsh knew what he was going to say before he said it—the parking, the traffic, stuck on the Bay Bridge for an hour and a half. "I've been driving circles around the block for half an hour looking for a place to park."

His voice was soft, and it rose to a lilting crescendo that might have been funny, under different circumstances. He stood six feet, and Marsh would have said six across, too. He moved slowly, as if conserving his strength or impaired by his hulking physique, or as if he were in a great deal of pain. With the few pale wisps of blond hair standing up on the pink dome of his head, he looked like a toddler with a thyroid problem, but the threat of physical harm seemed to lurk just behind his every gesture, and Marsh recoiled in spite of himself, bumping into the empty barstool behind him.

"Come on," Mickey said in a stage whisper, glancing around the bar. "I don't think we should talk about this here."

Outside, the sun was like a spear driven through an iron patchwork of cloud, refracted into needles of light in the low-lying haze. The two and a half drinks Marsh had managed to choke down while he was waiting worked in his system, a fire that seemed to sap his extremities of warmth, numbing the tips of his fingers even as it raged in his belly, as if the heat were being drawn inward, sucked violently to his middle, by a bellows. When the wind gusted, it brought tears to his eyes, and at his side the briefcase hung a dead, leaden weight, as if he'd managed to stuff their history, the long and tortured declining curve of their failed marriage, twenty-two years, the bitterness, the venom, rows cataclysmic and inconsequential, in there, along with the banded piles of unmarked, nonconsecutive $20 bills.

He thought the guy was limping, and he was—drawing up short every time he stepped on his left foot. But he was moving quickly, and Marsh had to hurry to keep up.

He trailed at a few dozen paces as the guy walked down Lincoln, waited for a break in traffic, and lumbered across, and they dodged joggers on JFK, now crossing the rolling, windswept green of the park. Down on the grass, a gaggle of children ran screaming after a tennis ball, and a few sunbathers were sprawled on blankets at the edges of the fields, stretched out as if on display. They turned finally onto one of the innumerable hiking trails that webbed the park like capillaries, Marsh straggling now, his face flushed, his sides slick with cold sweat. An enclave of kids were lounging in the bushes alongside the crooked path, passing a bottle, and Marsh caught a whiff of what might have been marijuana smoke, but the wind took it away. Cresting a hill, they clambered through a copse of jack pines, the tops of the trees roiling above them, tossing crazily in the wind. Marsh caught his foot on one of the roots that elbowed up through the topsoil and nearly went sprawling, saving himself at the last minute by catching one of the low branches.

When they finally emerged onto another bright swath of grass, the sounds of the city had receded, a distant hum punctuated now and again by the faraway bleat of a car horn. Variegated bunches of green showed all around, clusters and copses of trees, heather gray and a deep, piney green. All angled spastically in the wind, curling like strange, drunken dancers.

Several trails converged on a duck pond bordered by an asphalt lane. The ducks bobbed uncertainly on the surface of the gray water, as if anticipating some massive upswell. They pitched from side to side as the wind razed through the trees and muted the sound of their chatter. They beat their wings on the water, striking up silvery flares.

A lone bench stood by the water's edge. The light was an opaque gray wash, as if the whole thing were being shot from some remote vantage and the atmosphere were disturbed between the camera and the action taking place.

Marsh licked his lips. With a trembling hand, he extracted the creased snapshot from his coat pocket and held it, fluttering on the wind. He knew he should be drunk, but he couldn't feel it anymore at all. Adrenaline, he supposed; he was buzzing with it.

"Your wife," the guy said, in a way that irritated Marsh, as if he'd seen it a million times, as if the whole thing were something squalid, some oft-repeated tragedy. Mickey sighed. "All right," he said, looking off at the slight milky haze lowering across the western sky. He looked at Marsh. "What did she do? Is she cheating on you? She's running around on you and you just can't take it anymore? What is it?"

Marsh began sputtering, unable to answer.

"No," he said finally. "Nothing like that." What was the man doing, trying to talk him out of it? "The car," he said, as if that explained everything. "Do you think you could spare the car?"

"What?" Mickey loomed over him.

"She drives a Mercury Sable. Last year's model. I was hoping you could avoid—you know. Damaging the car."

What happened next happened quickly, and while it was happening the one thing that occurred to Marsh, crowding out all other thoughts or considerations, was that he was being mugged. Mickey told him to drop the briefcase, and when he failed to do this, struck him a resounding blow with a large, pinkish fist that seemed to materialize out of thin air, the row of swollen and meaty knuckles making contact with the bridge of his nose. He heard a sharp crack, a ringing in his ears, and when he came to, he was flat on his back in the mud at the foot of the park bench, and several ducks were honking in his ear and padding about on their webbed feet in the mud not far from his head.

The briefcase, the snapshot, the money—all gone. Even his wallet, and yes, his Rolex. He'd been cleaned out, and his suit, $450 before alterations, was ruined. He felt frantically in his pockets for his keys and found them, thinking at least something had gone right. But forty-five minutes later, when he finally found his way out of the park, he could see the bright orange ticket fluttering under his windshield wiper as he approached the Jag. He screamed, not caring who gawked or shook his head. On 19th Avenue, passersby turned their faces away, as if his particular insanity could be transmitted by no more than eye contact, and he stumbled along in the thickening, dusky light.

2

They had a place in South San Francisco, a two-story walkup that sat in a row of identical walkups in what passed for a quiet neighborhood among the sprawl and the clutter of city life. They were still paying for the house, but they'd bought before the latest boom, and when she heard what the other houses on the block were going for these days, she gasped. Sometimes she thought they should sell, treble their money and get out, but she didn't want to uproot the kids halfway through their schooling. Her father—the Colonel—had dragged her from Illinois to Taiwan to Corpus Christi, Texas, before she was twelve, and she had sworn above all else that she would not do the same thing to Todd and Jaime.

They had a lawn, a twelve-foot-by-four-foot patch of grass she watered and fertilized and guarded jealously against the neighborhood dogs, who were always doing their business there.

They had a two-and-a-half-car garage, a thing that struck her as funny in a vague way, in the sense that two point five children might have been funny.

She watched him come tramping across the lawn, the shit, in what must have been a state of extreme drunkenness if he thought he was going to get away with it—trampling the hyacinths, tripping over the rhododendron along the brick walk, all but tearing the philodendron bush out by the roots as he stumbled coming up the steps. She'd had the feeling this was coming, though she couldn't have said just what *this* was yet. She'd sensed impending calamity, sniffing it on the breeze the way you would a coming storm, bracing herself for impact even as she dug in her heels and refused to let the smallest thing go. A tiny exhilaration blossomed inside her at the foretaste. She would have felt entirely justified stabbing him with the garden shears.

Drunk as a sailor. She pitied the creature she'd married.

"If you think," she said, bits of hamburger clinging to her fingers, on him before he'd set foot in the door, her voice carrying shrilly across the hall, "if you think you can come in here any goddamn way you please, mister, you'd better think again, because you've got another thing coming. I spent three and a half hours out there today, and look, would you just look at what you've done to my garden? Henry, goddammit, what the hell do you have to say for yourself?"

Then she saw his face.

His nose seemed to be screwed on sideways, as if it had tried to escape but had become confused and tried to go in two different directions at once. Purple bruises bloomed under his eyes, and wads of spittle clung to the corners of his mouth. He stunk like a barroom, the cheap, lowlife smell of booze and cigarette smoke clinging to his suit and wafting into their home. A sense of shock mitigated her horror, and then the whole thing suddenly became funny, and she collapsed against the wall, covering her mouth with the back of her wrist and giggling, aware even as she did of the cruel edge to her laughter, of the pleasure she took in seeing him disgraced.

Jaime had come halfway down the steps and stood there arrested, like a piece of garden statuary. Todd came running from the den, as if he sensed whatever drama was unfolding in the foyer of their home beat out *Judge Judy* or *The People's Court*. He stood in the doorway, elfin, his hair sticking out at the sides. His mouth hung agape, his tongue playing in the space where one of his front teeth had been. He took one look at his father, then he turned and fled.

"Jesus, Dad," the girl said. She was wearing some witchy, clinging thing that made of her budding curves a shapeless swell and made her entire shape that of a bell. She grinned uncertainly, showing the metal bands around her teeth, taking such obvious delight in her father's suffering that for the moment she was entirely unselfconscious. "You look like the Elephant Man," she said.

"Jaime," Gina remonstrated. She had a feeling her daughter's guidance counselor was going to hear about this, and she wanted to mitigate whatever damage had already been done, to keep the situation from escalating any further than it already had. She stanched wounds, bandaged knees, commiserated with Jaime over boys; she was all the children had in this world, the sane center of their lives. And someone had to protect them from their father.

"Go to your room," he said, his voice cracking. "You go to your fucking room right now. You little slut, you're lucky we even let you out of the house."

"Mom," the girl said, her face a shattered window, like someone had pitched a rock through it. "Something's wrong with Dad," and she retreated, backing up the stairs.

"You come back down here and there'll be something wrong with you," Henry said. "Things are changing around this house, and they're changing right now. First thing is, you're going to listen to your father, and if you don't, by God, you'll look like this by the time he's through with you. I will not be treated like an asshole in my own home."

He balled his fists. His face flamed, a sea of broken capillaries. "And you," he said, turning on his wife.

It took one well-placed blow with the blunt edge of the paperweight they kept on the end table by the front door to quiet him. She dragged him by the wrists into the tiny bathroom under the stairs and left him there, sprawled out next to the toilet. She could already see the child custody people sweeping down, a SWAT team surrounding the house, helicopters buzzing outside their bedroom window. Principal Dryer would call again on Monday, vague threats lurking as always behind his measured, even tone. Maybe this time he really would report them to CPS. This was bad.

But by the time she called the kids down for pancakes and Hamburger Helper, her thoughts had already turned to the sale starting Saturday at Saks.

"Where's Dad?" Jaime asked, picking at her food.

"Don't you worry about your father," she said. "He's sick, Jaime. I put him to bed, and all we can do is hope he'll feel better when he wakes up."

"I want a hot dog," Todd said, thrusting his plate away from him. He got up without asking to be excused and left, and a moment later she heard his bedroom door slam at the top of the stairs.

Two days later she noticed the car.

At first she thought she'd imagined it. But twice on Sunday morning and once in the afternoon she saw the beige Pontiac lumbering along like a dinosaur behind her. It kept two or three car lengths back, weaving through traffic, running a red light to follow her when she made an abrupt left without signaling, one headlight winking in the rearview mirror as the sun crept down in the sky and the day stretched on into evening.

It occurred to her, of course, that she should have been scared. She should have been, but strangely, she wasn't. She'd always known it would happen like this. The sudden appearance of the Pontiac confirmed something. It augured cataclysm, the great upheaval she'd been anticipating all her life. It made real the fear and suspicion she'd been living with since she could remember, drawing the blackout curtains her father insisted on hanging everywhere they lived at night, hiding under the bed in the dark and reading comics guiltily by flashlight, hoping she wouldn't be the one who got them all killed. The feeling something exceptional was happening to her now braced her immeasurably. She was jealous of the people who went on the talk shows claiming to have been abducted by aliens in New Mexico. She only wished something like that would happen to her, something to blast away every trace of her ordinary experience and make her life a dream. If the bluish shape massed behind the Pontiac's windscreen was the shape of her destiny, she welcomed it.

It occurred to her, of course, that they might be from CPS, whoever was in the Pontiac, tailing her, waiting for an opportunity to swoop into her life and take her children. But she felt such kinship with that eddying shape, almost a sisterhood, that she dismissed the idea summarily.

The next day, kids in maroon private school uniforms were playing by the bus stop on the corner. One of them was bouncing up and down on a pogo stick, and it made a sawing noise that cut through the afternoon air. You never saw kids playing in the street anymore, and it comforted her, in a vague way.

She watered the rhododendrons under the gunmetal sky, letting the machine take the calls and listening to the messages at her leisure.

"And I think that if this is happening repeatedly, as it seems to be, there may be some cause for alarm," Principal Dryer said, his altogether too friendly voice carrying through the empty house on Monday afternoon. He cleared his throat. "Habitual truancy often indicates trouble in the home, something the parents may not even be aware of. If you or Mister Marsh could give me a call in my office anytime during the week, I would greatly appreciate it. I'm sure we all want whatever is best for Jaime."

He hung up.

Deceitful turd, she thought. Cruddy administrators. The lines were being drawn in the sand.

Someone named Reardon called for Hank a few minutes later, and she listened to him speak into the machine, wrote his name down, and erased the message. Hank had disappeared sometime during the night on Friday. Lying awake in their bed, she'd heard the front door ease shut, wondered where he was going, and she had decided that she didn't care. She found herself hoping she'd killed him when she'd brained him with the paperweight. She thought there must have been something good in him once, but she didn't know anymore when he had ceased to be her husband, or even a man.

Her life no longer seemed to be happening to her but to someone else.

She ran a bubble bath before the kids got home, luxuriating in the folds of steam, scraping the dead skin from the balls of her feet. The flakes drifted away on the water, softened to opacity. She wondered what her life would seem like if it were on television, what some anonymous viewer in a faraway living room or den would think. She felt alienated from her own experience, atomized, like the molecules of steam rising from the water in the tub.

3

"Sushi?" Karyn said. "I'm impressed, Dad. This isn't your style at all."

She was majoring in graphic design at City College, she didn't wear makeup, and she never seemed to have a boyfriend. But

there were men in her life, he was sure there were, and he admired whatever it was that kept her from getting stuck.

She had her mother's eyes and her mother's hair. Only the dimple on her chin was his, and it was his favorite feature, incongruous, stamped there like an afterthought. She had her mother's way
about her, the sardonic smile and the jaw that tapered to a point,
always disapproving, like someone had pinched it while she was
still being formed in the womb. She might have been pretty if she
wasn't so serious. But the steely thing in her, the thing that had en-
abled her to survive her childhood, it had marked her somehow,
and Mickey didn't know whether to feel sorry for her or happy that
she was that much stronger than he'd ever been.

She winked back at him, and she seemed content to let him be
her dad for the evening. They assumed their roles, and as long as
she assumed hers and let him play his, they'd have a good time.
She even laughed at his jokes, and her mother had stopped doing
that before the honeymoon was over.

"We were just kids, you know. We had no business having kids of
our own."

"Stop it, Dad."

She ordered a California roll. She ordered the salmon and the
tuna, and the eel for herself. He watched her trying to pronounce
the Japanese from the menu, and he could picture her doing her
math homework at the table in the kitchen in their apartment on
Post Street all those years ago, her legs still too short to touch the
floor while she sat in the chair, her hair already that fine shade of
black. She'd been too serious even then, committing her multipli-
cation tables to memory while he'd argued with Sue, nearly coming to blows over the balance in the checkbook.

Japanese music lilted from the speakers in the corners of the
room, and an aquarium bubbled by the door. He sipped his tea,
scalding his upper lip, and cursed, setting the cup down angrily.
He thought for the hundredth time that day that all he wanted was
a beer, but as he'd discovered the other night, the Kolonopin the
court-appointed psychiatrist had given him didn't mix well with
beer. A woman in a kimono brought miso soup, seaweed and tofu
afloat in the cloudy broth. She bowed politely at them, demure,
self-effacing, made up like a porcelain doll. When she moved away,
Mickey realized she'd forgotten to bring spoons.

"Your nose looks better," Karyn said, and she sipped her soup, which answered that question. She prized out a piece of tofu with her chopsticks. "How's your side?"

"Better. Those fucking kids. I'm still a little sore. I can't take it like I used to. I swear to God, honey. I feel like I got old overnight."

"Hey, Dad? Do you think they have places like this in Japan? I mean with the costumes and the music and everything?"

"I think they all eat McDonald's over there," he said.

She got a kick out of that, and he felt better about everything for the moment. When the woman brought the sushi, he watched Karyn stir the wasabi into a tiny dish of soy sauce with her chopsticks, and he thought she looked like some kind of lesser samurai, diligently observing a time-honored ritual. She ate carefully, using her chopsticks. He used his hands. He scarfed tempura, crunching steamed asparagus, feeling the wasabi clear his sinuses.

"So you're in trouble again, huh, Dad?"

"Nothing I can't handle, sweetie. I'm just taking a little vacation. I'm gonna get out of the city for a while."

"Uh-huh," she said, nodding, and that was all they said about it.

He walked her back to the car and kissed her on the cheek. He could feel the hardness through her jacket, and she pulled away from him even as she nestled in his arms. Sunlight slanted across the tops of the houses on Twin Peaks, bathing them in pastel light, etching doors and windows in sharp bas-relief. Through layers of cloud, the radio tower pricked glumly at the sky.

"'Bye, sweetie."

"Yeah. Hey, see you, Dad. You take care of yourself, okay? And thanks for dinner."

As the sun slanted down and the sky turned from pink to cobalt blue, he sat behind the wheel of the Pontiac and dug the crumpled snapshot from his shorts pocket. He pressed it flat against the steering wheel. He didn't even know the woman's name. She stared up at him with panicked eyes, crow's feet etched into their corners, her smile bright and hysterical, as if the expression of connubial bliss pained her somehow. She was wearing a mohair sweater, and her skin had an eerie luminescence, a metallic sheen acquired from too many deep pore cleansers, facial rinses, and mud masks. Her hair was pulled back in a way that made her forehead seem too wide, and her eyebrows arched sharply, identical and neatly plucked works of art. She wasn't exactly catwalk material, Mickey thought. But she was still a hell of a good-looking woman.

He'd lost control in the park. He knew that. It seemed to happen more often these days. What did it mean when you quit drinking and you were even meaner than before? Like when those kids had jumped him the other night. He didn't remember half of that. They'd circled him up, and the next thing he knew, he was on the verge of beating one of them to death with his bare hands. In the park it was the same. He hadn't wanted to kill anybody, but he'd seen the guy standing there in his expensive suit with his gold-plated Rolex, and it was like the ghost of every CO, every commissioner or DA who'd reprimanded him for the last twenty years had reared up on him suddenly, and before he'd even known what he was doing, the guy was flat on his back, out cold with one punch.

He figured Reardon was probably going to be pissed. Whatever angle he was playing, Mickey had blown it for him. And if he had enough money in the briefcase he'd taken from Marsh to pay off his debts and put himself in the clear, his instincts still told him to take the money and run, hotfoot it for the airport before everything started to catch up with him.

But another voice whispered at him through those luminous brown eyes in the photograph. They were crazy eyes, he realized; something was missing in them, something was fractured. It wasn't lust they stirred in him. More like some deep and inexpressible desire to make good on his life after throwing forty-three years away. What was the point in running away from San Francisco? Here the battle lines had been drawn, and here he would make his stand. Only he didn't know yet what he was fighting—or what he was fighting for. He'd lost Sue years ago, and he didn't know if it was too late even to win Karyn back.

He let it all tick over in his mind as he started the car, meandering out toward the Great Highway as the last of the day's light burned out over Ocean Beach.

She was much smaller in person than he'd expected. She couldn't have been more than five feet tall. And Christ, the woman could shop. He tailed her to the malls, the department stores, the high-end places downtown. She took it seriously. Like some people take food or professional sports seriously. She stalked the aisles like a big-game hunter, shrewd eyes goggling out of her childish face. He watched her trying on a diamond tiara at Saks on Saturday, twisting from side to side in front of the mirror in her designer jeans, and he thought of Wonder Woman.

He staked out the house. He kept vigil. He hadn't realized how much he'd missed being a cop. However cynical you became, however arbitrary the designations seemed, by virtue of the uniform, you became one of the good guys. And you believed in it because it was all you had, because if you weren't one of the good guys, the only thing left for you was to be one of the bad.

Those days seemed simple to him now. It seemed to him they'd all been playing dress-up, like playing cops and robbers when they were kids. How many of his friends from the neighborhood had he put away over the years? And why them, when he was no different?

He had the feeling he was broaching new territory, entering uncharted waters. If he no longer wore the uniform, if he no longer had the force of the law at his back, how could he know what was right any longer?

He wasn't going to kill her. He knew that now. He'd known it from the first, from the moment he'd set foot in the bar and seen Marsh slouched there in his custom-tailored suit. And before, when Reardon had called. He'd known he wasn't going to be able to go through with it, even then.

The house might have gone for a hundred grand five or six years ago, but if he had to hazard a guess, Mickey would have said half a million by now. It looked just like every other house on the block, and they were all butted right up against one another, one house stacked on top of the other like Dixie cups in a line all the way to the top of the street and the dun-colored hills beyond.

If you wanted to know what kind of parents they were, all you had to do was look at the kids. The girl was your typical tortured adolescent—combat boots that reached her knees, hair dyed black with a flaming red stripe down one side. She carried a lunchbox to school, and Mickey wondered if he hadn't done all right by Karyn after all. As for the boy, Mickey just felt sorry for him. He was a chip off the old block, that was for sure. He already looked like his father—of whom, Mickey remarked, there had been no sign.

He ate fast food and slept in the car. After three days he could smell himself. He'd blown his tail on Sunday, he was sure of that, running a red light on Geary, and good sense told him to clear out before he got himself arrested. He didn't know what he was waiting for. For the clouds to part and reveal the firmament—he didn't know. He thought he'd figure it out when the time was right.

4

Henry Marsh checked into the Airport Hilton with a change of socks, a toothbrush, and a pint bottle of Jack Daniel's. He needed some time to think.

First thing Saturday, he called in sick for the week. He had AIDS, the Ebola virus. He'd come down with the bubonic plague. There was a family emergency, his grandmother was flooded out of her house in Mississippi, there was a war starting up in Bosnia again—whatever. He wasn't going back to work, not for as long as he lived. His last official act as assistant general manager of the Radisson Hotel in downtown San Francisco was canning Tommy Reardon.

"He's been late every day for a month. I think something's going on. I caught him drinking during his shift twice last week, and I think he's sniffing cocaine at work, too. He looks all bug-eyed and paranoid."

The open line hummed. He could hear Robert "Call-Me-Bob" Zimmer, the bar manager, making little clicking noises with his tongue.

"I tried to give him a chance," Marsh said. "I've been telling him to clean up his act. But I think it's time something was done about it."

"Where are you, Henry?" Zimm said finally. He was a big, poker-faced man with a dry sense of humor and an easy way with people. Everybody he worked with liked him. Marsh had been trying to get him fired for years. "People have been talking," he said. "They're worried about you. There's been some concern. They say you're showing all the signs of a real crack-up."

"San Diego," Marsh said. "We're waiting for a flight. It's Gina's mother. She's in the hospital again. Leukemia or something. Look, our flight's boarding. I've got to go."

"If anyone asks, Henry, you didn't hear it from me, all right? But people are talking."

"Thanks, Zimm. Just take care of Tommy for me, will ya?"

"Call me Bob," Zimm said, and he hung up.

Time folded in on itself after that. He finished one pint, went across the street for another. When he finished that one, he went back out and bought a fifth. He passed out sometime around noon, and when he woke up, it was dark again.

He watched *Saturday Night Live,* flipping channels with the bottle balanced precariously on his stomach. He watched Jenny Jones and thought about his wife. The thing was, he hadn't expected the guy to show. Never in a million years did he think there were people who did this kind of thing for money. He hadn't been prepared. The Cub Scout motto came back to him, and he remembered his father, a remote, congenitally disturbed man plagued by a host of neuroses who had deferred in all matters to his wife, Henry's mother, a woman whose overweening influence had driven him, Henry, to the far ends of the earth—to California—to escape, to make a life for himself, to raise his children where the woman could not smother them as she had smothered him. But curse of curses, fate of fates, he had married his mother, or a woman just like her, a woman who seemed in every way different from her but who had, in fact, turned out to be so much the same he could no longer separate the two in his mind, and the bitches at his back had become one.

Had she cheated? She'd lost interest in him sexually years ago, but then she'd never been much interested in sex. Still, he remembered times when it was free and easy between them. Certainly they'd fornicated once—twice, if they'd conceived the two brats, the bloodsuckers, and he wondered if that was when it had ended, when the first or the second of the kids had popped out, if that was the precise moment when the gates had swung closed, when the dream of better things and better times had died, stillborn. They—she and the children—had made his life a prison.

Sunday morning he washed his socks and his underwear in the sink. He found a Chinese takeout menu in the drawer by the bed, tucked into the obligatory Gideon's, and he ordered spareribs and egg rolls for breakfast. He drew the curtains and paced the room naked. He stood under the shower until it ran cold. He passed out again in the afternoon, and when he woke, it was a quarter of two and he had fifteen minutes to haul himself out of bed and across the street to the store for another bottle.

5

The girl crept downstairs after dark. The television was blaring in her parents' room, an apocryphal white noise, a bluish blush of light showing under the door. It gave the impression of something trying to get out, something she'd seen in a hundred horror movies, but it was only her mother in there, hiding away.

The lights in the hall burned like sentries and made her think of Bedouin fires in the desert, something she'd seen in *National Geographic,* though it was the words that came to her and not the image. *Like Bedouin fires,* she thought. The house was dark, as still as a mausoleum.

She'd just reached the front door when the noise from the television upstairs died and her mother's voice carried shrilly down the hall.

"Where are you going at this time of night, Jaime?"

The woman had some kind of sixth sense; she had sonar like a bat's.

"I'm just going for a walk, Mom. I'll be back in a while."

Her mother didn't say anything for a few seconds.

"Well, okay, sweetie. But you be careful, will you? I hate to think about you walking around out there all by yourself after dark. I know it's a good neighborhood, but don't be long. I can't stand to think about it."

The girl rolled her eyes.

"Then don't think about it, Mom."

She didn't wait for her mother to answer.

Outside was the roiling sky, the moon like a hole punched in the clouds, and the faint taste of the ocean on the air. She took it for granted they were near the water, although she couldn't see it from the house. When they'd gone to Sacramento to see her grandparents, she'd missed it. She'd felt some nameless dread, an anxiety she couldn't place until they'd come back across the San Mateo bridge, and she'd realized it was the ocean she missed all along.

She felt reflexively in her pocket for her keys before she pulled the door shut and stood on the front step for a minute, looking up and down the quiet street, the starlit confines of her world. A couple walked slowly past, dappled in shadow. They were climbing the hill, leaning into the grade, and they were maybe a few years older than she was. Moonlight glinted off the boy's glasses, and the girl's face shone, her lips parted in an expression that was at once abject and leery and was somehow frightening on both accounts. The boy was neat, clean-cut, and maybe a little embarrassed. He held her hand awkwardly, as if unsure what to do with it.

Boys were puzzling, Jaime thought, only in the depths of their stupidity.

A man went quickly past on the other side of the street, ducking under the trees, his face hung in shadow. His jacket flashed like a warning signal, bumblebee yellow, and the girl hesitated, letting him dart past before she came down the steps and crossed the lawn, turning up the hill toward the bus stop. Her mother's paranoia was rubbing off on her. But if she'd married her father, Jaime thought, she'd probably be stark raving mad by now, too.

She waited until the end of the block to light a cigarette, although she couldn't figure out how her parents hadn't caught on by now, seeing as she'd come in reeking like a cigarette every day for almost a year. If they knew, they weren't saying any-thing—maybe hoping she'd give it up if they just acted like they didn't notice—and she didn't see any reason to rub their noses in it.

The first few drags made her woozy, an ephemeral wooziness she wanted to hold on to for as long as it lasted and that was gone too quickly. The bus stop sat crookedly like a chess piece at the top of the hill, webbed in a skein of gauzy light from the street lamp, the opaque siding pitted and scarred. A dark-skinned woman in a rain jacket who was as wide as she was tall was waiting under the shelter, and she turned her eyes on Jaime as if some vague animal instinct had registered an incursion.

But there was no threat, no reason whatsoever to be alarmed, and she seemed smug then, sitting primly on the tiny seat, glanc-ing quickly at Jaime out of the corner of her eye and looking away as she folded her arms across her chest.

She didn't wear black for the sins of the teeming world, and not because she was obsessed with sex or with death or because she wanted to die, although she thought about it—with sex, it was the other great mystery—and not even because she came from what she considered the archetype of the dysfunctional family. Even Reynaldo, the Spanish exchange student who'd been trying to get in her pants for the last six months, seemed to think it meant there was something wrong with her. "It says to me you have great sadness," he said, in that ridiculous accent that made everything he spoke seem a come-on. But then Reynaldo thought Americans were all head cases anyway, and there were things she couldn't explain to him. There were things she couldn't explain to anyone, not to her friends or her boyfriends, not to her parents or the endless procession of guidance counselors and psychologists they were always sending her to at school. Not to Principal Dryer, who'd taken an almost fawning interest in her, whose wife was cheating on him with Jaime's math teacher. But she'd never questioned her own capacity to survive, and she knew something inside her would persevere. She'd made that decision a long time ago, without ever knowing she was making it, and she would not become crazy like her mother, she would not die inside like her father, who she half expected to find waiting at the breakfast table with a loaded gun one of these mornings. She didn't know if Todd was going to make it, but she'd take him with her if she could, and she knew that one way or another, come what might, she'd survive them all with her soul intact.

One cigarette led to another. She had a relationship with the things that had power over her; there was a give and a take. Things like Reynaldo, who was always pushing the envelope, always asking—begging—for a little bit more. She said, "Don't, goddammit," and he only laughed. But if she ever let him have what he wanted, he'd disappear. She intuited this the same way she intuited he was lying when he said he wasn't a virgin. He talked about the girls he'd had in Spain, and she wondered if they were real or not, or if he was only making them up. He was terrified of the world waiting between her legs, and the power that gave her over him gave her an almost sexual thrill that was far more exciting than his anxious, inept fumbling. And that thrill in turn, that feeling that he didn't even know he was giving her and wouldn't understand if he did, it held sway over her.

She took all responsibility. She had to handle him with kid

gloves. And if she ever let him have his way, she'd ruin it. He'd never look at her again.

The world was a matrix of power relationships. Love and pity, tolerance and kindness—sometimes she wondered if those entered into the equation at all. In her estimation, God was a bleak thing, a cold, clear eye watching with dispassion.

The bus rolled to a stop with a hissing of air brakes, the door opened, and the woman got on, giving Jaime a look over her shoulder. She sat a while longer before she started back down the hill, and it occurred to her as she passed the Parsons' place that she'd seen the beige Pontiac across the street the night before. She thought it had been sitting there the night before that, too. And that might not have struck her as out of the ordinary, if not for the fact someone was sitting in the car, a shape massed behind the wheel, under the galaxy of reflected light. She walked quickly, not wanting to sprint for the front door but having to fight to keep from doing just that, all her cool thrown off for the moment, fumbling with her keys for what seemed an eternity, hands trembling, the hackles rising on the back of her neck. She could feel him watching her.

"Jaime? Is that you?"

"Yes, Mom." She slammed the door and fell against it. She twisted the deadbolt and peered around the curtain. There was no movement outside.

"Don't slam the door, Jaime."

"Mom, I think there's something going on. There's a guy sitting in a car across the street. It's kind of creepy."

The pause before her mother answered alerted the girl to her mother's complicity, to a web of knowledge and causality that stretched far past where she was standing now.

"Stop it. Jaime, you stop it right this minute. You're scaring me half to death. You know how I am."

"Yeah, Mom. I do." It occurred to her then that she ought to leave well enough alone, that she was going to become as crazy as her mother if she wasn't careful.

The kitchen was a wreck. Pots and pans were climbing out of the sink, and the gray, stagnant water smelled like roadkill. A week's worth of plates and dishes were stacked on the counter. And her father hadn't been home in three days. He'd called her a slut, which was so far from the truth, she wanted to laugh. If her father only knew how hard she'd worked to curb her desire, to preserve the upper hand.

She managed to clear off a corner of the counter, enough room to make herself a peanut butter and jelly sandwich, and she poured herself a glass of the chocolate soymilk they bought just for her before she carried her sandwich upstairs on a paper towel.

6

He'd finally decided he was going to have to take matters into his own hands. That had been his only mistake. Trusting anyone else to do his dirty work, to take care of his business.

After three days, he'd sobered a little. Enough. The idea came with sudden, vicious clarity. He hadn't wanted to get blood on his hands, but life was like that. Sometimes you had to do things you didn't want to do. He thought of Clint Eastwood; he thought of Sean Connery; he thought again of Pacino in *Scarface*. They were cowards, weak men. Then he thought about Smilin' Jack in *The Shining*. Now there was a man who could take care of business.

He left his dirty socks in the sink. He didn't bother to check out. He wasn't coming back, but he guessed they'd figure that out soon enough. Walking through the lobby, he saw the implements arrayed beside the fireplace, which was nonfunctional, strictly ornamental. There was the shovel; there, the broom. There were the giant tongs, and yes, the poker. The kid behind the desk was staring at his computer like he'd been shot up with Thorazine—eyes glassy, jaw slack. Probably stoned, Marsh thought. It was impossible to find reliable help anymore.

He swooped through the lobby like a bird of prey, catching hold of the poker as he passed the hearth and whisking it from the rack, carrying it out the door like a cane. The kid didn't look up. Marsh started laughing. His breath came in whinnies and grunts, hurting his side. He swung the poker once, twice, listening to the whistling sound it made on the chilly air. The elderly couple coming in the door steered clear, giving him wide berth. He made a beeline for the car, stopping only once, to vomit.

7

He scarfed a cold cheeseburger from the glove box. He had three more; he could make it another night. They weren't so bad once you got used to them. He washed it down with some flat Pepsi and belched, tasting pickle.

The girl started up toward the corner at a quarter of ten. She did it every night. Up to the bus stop before ten, and she'd sit there and have two, maybe three cigarettes, then she'd walk back.

The car stunk. It smelled like French fries and animal fat, like dirty sweat socks and musty sneakers, like unwashed, unshaven Irish ex-cop. After three days of sleeping behind the wheel and waking in his clothes, three days of waiting for the answer, he was through. Nothing had come to him, and nothing, so far as he could tell, had happened. And nothing, he'd decided, was going to happen, either. He considered ringing the doorbell, but dismissed the idea as soon as it occurred to him. He didn't know which was worse—stalking the woman, staking out her house and scaring her children half to death, or ringing her doorbell and announcing himself: *I know you don't know me, Mrs. Marsh, but my name is Mickey Walsh, and your husband hired me to kill you.*

If he thought his life was in the shitter a week ago, he could just imagine. He'd go from metro section to the front page.

He realized he'd been expecting something to happen, that he'd been keeping his vigil half hoping and half fearing Marsh would turn up and try to do the deed himself. If it came down to his word against Marsh's, he knew where he stood. Even with twenty years on the force, he'd be on the losing end, and that seemed to him the story of his whole sad and shoddy existence on the earth, all forty-three years of it. What would he do if Marsh came home? Was he protecting the woman? Did he need to? He didn't know. Should he have gone to the departmental psychiatrist years ago like everyone had told him to? Probably.

He'd gone through his life doing whatever the crowd did. When they rode around in squad cars looking for drunks to roll, he'd done it. When they'd gone whoring, when they'd beaten up the homeless or the Mexicans or rousted the blacks for conglomerating on street corners, he'd done that, too. On his own, he didn't know the first thing. He didn't even know how to behave around his wife or his daughter.

He started the car. The old Pontiac still turned over on the first try. He had $125,000 in a briefcase in the trunk, and he was going to South America. He'd read it in a book. That was what people did when they wanted out—out of the country, out of the life. He was taking early retirement, a permanent vacation.

He'd just put the Pontiac in gear when the green Jaguar came screaming around the corner at the top of the hill, hopping the curb and narrowly missing the bus shelter on the corner. Marsh swerved across his lawn and plowed into the side of his wife's Mercury. He lurched out of the car, waving something in his hands. Mickey reached over, fumbling in the glove box, digging under the cold cheeseburgers for the .38 he'd been carrying for twenty years, since he was a rookie on the force, the spare piece he'd carried for two decades without firing it. Once he'd thought about using it to plant on a suspect. Now, watching Marsh stumbling across the moonlit yard, hacking at the philodendron bushes as he tottered up the steps to his front door, Mickey only hoped it still worked.

PETER S. BEAGLE

The Bridge Partner

FROM *Sleight of Hand*

I WILL KILL YOU.

The words were not spoken aloud, but silently mouthed across the card table at Mattie Whalen by her new partner, whose last name she had not quite caught when they were introduced. Olivia *Korhanen* or *Korhonen,* it was, something like that. She was blond and fortyish—Mattie was bad with ages, but the woman had to be somewhere near her own—and had joined the Moss Harbor Bridge Group only a few weeks earlier. The members had chosen at the very beginning to call themselves a group rather than a club. As Eileen Berry, one of the two founders, along with Suzanne Grimes, had said at the time, "There's an exclusivity thing about a club—a snobby, elitish sort of taste, if you know what I mean. A group just *feels* more democratic." Everyone had agreed with Eileen, as people generally did.

Which accounted, Mattie thought, for the brisk acceptance of the woman now sitting across from her, despite her odd name and unclassifiably foreign air. Mattie could detect only the faintest accent in her voice, and if her clothes plainly did not come from the discount outlet in the local mall, neither were they so aggressively chic as to offend or threaten. She had clear, pleasant blue eyes, excellent teeth, the delicately tanned skin of a tennis player—as opposed to a leathery beach bunny or an orange-hued tanning bed veteran—and was pleasant to everyone in a gently impersonal manner. Her playing style showed not only skill but grace, which Mattie noticed perhaps more poignantly than any other member of the Bridge Group, since the best that could have been said for

Mattie was that she mostly managed to keep track of the trumps and the tricks. Still, she knew grace when she saw it.

I will kill you.

It made no possible sense—she must surely have misread both the somewhat long, quizzical lips and the intention in the bright eyes. No one else seemed to have heard or noticed anything at all unusual, and she really hadn't played the last hand as badly as all that. Granted, doubling Rosemarie's bid could be considered a mistake, but people make mistakes, and she *could* have pulled it off if Olivia Korhonen, or whoever, had held more than the one single miserable trump to back her up. You don't *kill* somebody for doubling, or even threaten to kill them. Mattie smiled earnestly at her partner, and studied her cards.

The rubber ended in total disaster, and Mattie apologized at some length to Olivia Korhonen afterward. "I'm not really a good player, I know that, but I'm not usually that awful, I promise. And now you'll probably never want to play with me ever again, and I wouldn't blame you." Mattie had had a deal of practice at apologizing, over the years.

To her pleasant surprise, Olivia Korhonen patted her arm reassuringly and shook her head. "I enjoyed the game greatly, even though we lost. I have not played in a long time, and you will have to make allowances until I start to catch up. We'll beat them next time, in spite of me."

She patted Mattie again and turned elegantly away. But as she did so, the side of her mouth repeated, clearly but inaudibly—Mattie could not have been mistaken this time— *"I will kill you."* Then the woman was gone, and Mattie sat down in the nearest folding chair.

Her friend Virginia Schlossberg hurried over with a cup of tea, asking anxiously, "Are you all right? What is it? You look absolutely *ashen!*" She touched Mattie's cheek, and almost recoiled. "And you're *freezing!* Go home and get into bed, and call a doctor! I *mean* it—you go home right now!" Virginia was a kind woman, but excitable. She had been the same when Mattie and she were in dancing school together.

"I'm all right," Mattie said. "I am, Ginny, honestly." But her voice was shaking as much as her hands, and she made her escape from the Group as soon as she could trust her legs to support her. She was grateful on two counts: first, that no one sat next to her on the bus; and, secondly, that Don would most likely not be home yet from the golf course. She did not look forward to Don just now.

Rather than taking to her bed, despite Virginia's advice, she made herself a healthy G&T and sat in the kitchen with the lights on, going over and over everything she knew of Olivia Korhonen. The woman was apparently single or widowed, like most of the members of the Moss Harbor Bridge Group, but judging by the reactions of the few men in the Group she gave no indication of being on the prowl. Seemingly unemployed, and rather young for retirement, still she lived in one of the pricey new condos just two blocks from the harbor. No Bridge Group member had yet seen her apartment except for Suzanne and Eileen, who reported back that it was smart and trendy, "without being too off-puttingly posh." Eileen thought the paintings were originals, but Suzanne had her doubts.

What else, *what else?* She had looked up "Korhonen" on the Internet and found that it was a common Finnish name—not Jewish, as she had supposed. To her knowledge, she had never met a Finnish person in her life. Were they like Swedes? Danes, even? She had a couple of Danish acquaintances, a husband and wife named Olsen . . . no, they were nothing at all like the Korhonen woman; one could never imagine either Olsen saying *I will kill you* to so much as a cockroach, which, of course, they wouldn't ever have in the house. But then, who *would* say such a thing to a near stranger? And over a silly card game? It made no sense, none of it made any sense. She mixed another G&T and was surprised to find herself wanting Don home.

Don's day, it turned out, had been a bad one. Trounced on the course, beaten more badly in the rematch he had immediately demanded, he had consoled himself liberally in the clubhouse; and, as a consequence, was clearly not in any sort of mood to hear about a mumbled threat at a bridge game. On the whole, after sixteen years of marriage, Mattie liked Don more than she disliked him, but such distinctions were essentially meaningless at this stage of things. She rather appreciated his presence when she felt especially lonely and frightened, but a large, furry dog would have done as well; indeed, a dog would have been at once more comforting and more concerned for her comfort. Dogs wanted their masters to be happy—Don simply preferred her uncomplaining.

When she told him about Olivia Korhonen's behavior at the

Bridge Group, he seemed hardly to hear her. In his usual style of picking up in the middle of the intended sentence, he mumbled, ". . . take that damn game so damn seriously. Bud and I don't go yelling we're going to kill each other"—Bud Gorko was his steady golf partner—"and believe you me, I've got reason sometimes." He snatched a beer out of the refrigerator and wandered into the living room to watch TV.

Mattie followed him in, the second G&T strengthening a rare resolve to make him take her seriously. She said, "She did it twice. You didn't see her face." She raised her voice to carry over the yammering of a commercial. "She *meant* it, Don. I'm telling you, she *meant* it."

Don smiled muzzily and patted the sofa seat beside him. "Hear you, I'm right on it. Tell you what—she goes ahead and does that, I'm going to take a really dim view. A dim view." He liked the phrase. "Really dim view."

"You're dim enough already," Mattie said. Don did not respond. She stood watching him for a few minutes without speaking, because she knew it made him uncomfortable. When he got to the stage of demanding, "What? What?" she walked out of the room and into the guest bedroom, where she lay down. She had been sleeping there frequently enough in recent months that it felt increasingly like her own.

She had thought she would surely dream of Olivia Korhonen, but it was only in the sweet spot between consciousness and sleep that the woman's face came to her: the long mouth curling almost affectionately, almost seductively, as though for a kiss, caressing the words that Mattie could not hear. It was an oddly tranquil, even soothing vision, and Mattie fell asleep like a child, and did not dream at all.

The next morning she felt curiously young and hopeful, though she could not imagine why. Don had gone off to work at the real estate office with his normal Monday hangover, pitifully savage; but Mattie indulged herself with a long hot shower, a second toasted English muffin, and a long telephone chat with a much-relieved Virginia Schlossberg before she went to the grocery store. There would be an overdue hair appointment after that, then home in time for *Oprah*. A *good* day.

The sense of serenity lasted through the morning shopping, through her favorite tea-and-brioche snack at La Place, and on to her date with Mr. Philip at the salon. It ended abruptly while she was more than half drowsing under the dryer, trying to focus on *Vanity Fair,* as well as on the buttery jazz on the PA system, when Olivia Korhonen's equally pleasant voice separated itself from the music, saying, "Mrs. Whalen—Mattie? How nice to see you here, partner." The last word flicked across Mattie's skin like a brand.

Olivia Korhonen was standing directly in front of her, smiling in her familiar guileless manner. She had clearly just finished her appointment: the glinting warmth and shine of her blond hair made that plain, and made Mattie absurdly envious, her own mouse-brown curls' only distinction being their comb-snapping thickness. Olivia Korhonen said, "Shall we play next week? I look forward so."

"Yes," Mattie said faintly; and then, "I mean, I'm not sure—I have things. To do. Maybe." Her voice squeaked and slipped. She couldn't stop it, and in that moment she hated her voice more than she had ever hated anything in the world.

"Oh, but you must be there! I do not know anyone else to play with." Mattie noticed a small dimple to the left of Olivia Korhonen's mouth when she smiled in a certain way. "I mean, no one else who will put up with my bad playing, as you do. Please?"

Mattie found herself nodding, just to keep from having to speak again—and also, to some degree, because of the genuine urgency in Olivia Korhonen's voice. *Maybe I imagined the whole business . . . maybe it's me getting old and scared, the way people do.* She nodded a second time, with somewhat more enthusiasm.

Olivia Korhonen patted her knee through the protective salon apron, plainly relieved. "Oh, good. I already feel so much better." Then, without changing her expression in the least, she whispered, *"I will kill you."*

Mattie thought later that she must have fainted in some way; at all events, her next awareness was of Mr. Philip taking the curlers out of her hair and brushing her off. Olivia Korhonen was gone. Mr. Philip peered at her, asking, "Who's been keeping *you* up at night, darling? You never fall asleep under these things." Then he saw her expression and asked, "Are you okay?"

"I'm fine," Mattie said. "I'm fine."

After that, it seemed to her that she saw Olivia Korhonen everywhere, every day. She was coming out of the dry cleaners' as Mattie brought an armload of Don's pants in; she hurried across the street to direct Mattie as she was parking her car; she asked Mattie's advice buying produce at the farmers' market, or broke off a conversation with someone else to chat with Mattie on the street. And each time, before they parted, would come the silent words, more menacing for being inaudible, *"I will kill you."* The dimple beside the long smile always showed as she spoke.

Mattie had never felt so lonely in her life. Despite all the years she and Don had lived in Moss Harbor, there was no one in her local circle whom she could trust in any sort of intimate crisis, let alone with something like a death threat. Suzanne or Eileen? Out of the question—things like that simply did not happen to members of the Bridge Group. There was Virginia, of course . . . Virginia might very well believe her, if anyone did, but would be bound to fall apart under the burden of such knowledge. That left only going further afield and contacting Patricia.

Pat Gallagher lived directly across the bay, in a tiny incorporated area called Witness Point. Mattie had known her very nearly as long as she had known Virginia, but the relationships could not have been more different. Pat was gay, for one thing; and while Mattie voted for every same-sex-marriage and hate-crimes proposition that came up on any ballot, she was honest enough to know that she was ill at ease with homosexuals. She could never explain this, and was truly ashamed of it, especially around someone as intelligent and thoughtful as Pat Gallagher. She found balance in distance, only seeing Pat two or three times a year, at most, and sometimes no more than once. They did e-mail a reasonable amount though, and they talked on the phone enough that Mattie still knew the number by heart. She called it now.

They arranged to meet at Pat's house for lunch on the weekend. She lived in a shingly, flowery, cluttery cottage, in company with a black woman named Babs, an administrator at the same hospital where Pat was a nurse. Mattie liked Babs immediately, and was therefore doubly nervous around her, and doubly shamed, especially when Babs offered in so many words to disappear graciously, so that she and Pat could talk in private. Mattie would have much preferred this, but the very suggestion made it impossible. "I'm sure there's nothing I have to say to Patricia that I couldn't say to you."

Babs laughed. "That you may come to regret, my dear." But she set out second glasses of pinot grigio, and second bowls of Pat's minestrone, and sat down with them. Her dark-brown skin and

soft curly hair contrasted so perfectly with Pat's freckled Irish pink-
ness and they seemed so much at ease with one another that Mattie felt a quick, startling stitch of what could only have been envy.

"Okay," Pat said. "Talk. What's got you scared this time?"

Babs chuckled. "Cuts straight to the chase, doesn't she?"

Mattie bridled feebly. "You make it sound as though I'm a big
fraidy cat, always frightened about something. I'm not like that."

"Yes, you are." The affection in Pat's wide grin took some of the
sting from the words. "You never call me unless something's really
got you spooked, do you realize that? Might be a thing you saw
on the news, a hooha with your husband, a pain somewhere there
shouldn't be a pain. Maybe a lump you're worried about—maybe
just a scary dream." She put her hand on Mattie's hand. "It's fine,
it's you. Talk. Tell."

She and Babs remained absolutely silent while Mattie told them
about the Bridge Group, and about Olivia Korhonen. She was
aware that she was speaking faster as the account progressed, and
that her voice was rising in pitch, but all she wanted was to get the
words out as quickly as she could. The words seemed strangely
reluctant to be spoken: more and more, they raked at her throat
and palate as she struggled to rid herself of them. When she was
done, the roof of her mouth felt almost burned, and she gratefully
accepted a glass of cold apple juice from Babs.

"Well," Pat said finally. "I don't know what I expected to hear
from you, but *that* was definitely not it. Not hardly."

Babs said grimly, "What you have there is a genuine, certified
stalker. I'd call the cops on her in a hot minute."

"How can she do that?" Pat objected. "The woman hasn't *done*
anything! No witnesses, not one other person who heard what she
said—what she keeps on saying. They'd laugh in Mattie's face, if
they didn't do worse."

"It does sound such a *silly* story," Mattie said wretchedly. "Like
a paranoiac, somebody with a persecution complex. But it's true,
I'm not making it up. That's just exactly the way it's been happening."

Pat nodded. "I believe you. And so would a jury, if it ever came
to that. Anyone who spends ten minutes around you knows right
away that you haven't the first clue about lying." She sighed, refill-
ing Babs's glass and her own but not Mattie's. "Not you—you have

to drive. And we wouldn't want to frustrate little Ms. What's-her-face, now would we?"

"That's not funny," Babs interrupted sharply. "That's not a bit funny, Patricia."

Pat apologized promptly and profusely, but Mattie was absurdly delighted. "You call her Patricia, too! I thought *I* was the only one."

"Only way to get her attention sometimes." Babs continued to glower at an extremely penitent Pat. "But she's right about the one thing, anyway. Even if the cops happened to believe you, they couldn't do a damn thing about it. Couldn't slap a restraining order on the lady, couldn't order her to stay *x* number of feet away from you. Not until . . ." She shrugged heavily, and did not finish the sentence.

"I know," Mattie said. "I wasn't expecting you two to . . . fix things. Be my bodyguards, or something. But I do feel a bit better, talking to you."

"Now, if you were in the hospital"—Babs grinned suddenly and wickedly—"we really *could* bodyguard you. Between old Patricia and me, nobody'd get near you, except for the surfers we'd be smuggling in to you at night. You ought to think about it, Mattie. Safe *and* fun, both."

Mattie was still giggling over this image, and a couple of others, when they walked her out to her car. As she buckled her seatbelt, Pat put a hand on her shoulder, saying quietly, "As long as this goes on every day, you call every day. Got that?"

"Yes, Mama," Mattie answered. "And I'll send my laundry home every week, I promise."

The hand on her shoulder tightened, and Pat shook her a little more than slightly. "I mean it. If we don't hear, we'll come down there."

"Big bad bull dykes on the rampage," Babs chimed in from behind Pat. "*Not* pretty."

It was true that she did feel better driving home: not at all drunk, just pleasantly askew, easier and more rested from the warmth of company than she had been in a long time. That lasted all the way to Moss Harbor, and almost to her front door. The *almost* part came when, parking the car at the curb, she heard a horn honk twice, and looked up in time to see an arm waving cheerfully back to her as Olivia Korhonen's bright little Prius rounded a corner.

Mattie sat in her car for a long time before she turned off the engine and got out.

Is she watching my house? Was she waiting for me?

She did not call Pat and Babs that night, even though she lay awake until nearly morning. Then, with Don gone to work, she forced herself to eat breakfast, and called Suzanne for Olivia Korhonen's home telephone number. Once she had it in hand, she stalled over a third cup of coffee, and then a fourth, before she finally dialed the number and waited through several rings, consciously hoping to hear the answering machine click on. But nothing happened. She was about to break the connection when she heard the receiver being picked up and Ms. Korhonen's cool, unmistakable voice said, "Yes? Who is this, please?"

Mattie drew a breath. "It's Mattie Whalen. From the Bridge Group, you remember?"

If she has the gall to even hesitate, stalking me every single day . . . But the voice immediately lifted with delight. "Yes, Mattie, of course I remember, how not? How good to hear from you." There was nothing in words or tone to suggest anything but pleasure at the call.

"I was wondering," Mattie began—then hesitated, listening to Olivia Korhonen's breathing. She said, "I thought perhaps we might get together—maybe one day this week?"

"To practice our bridge game?" Somewhat to Mattie's surprise, Olivia Korhonen pounced on the suggestion. "Oh, yes. That would be an excellent idea. We could develop our own strategies—that is what the great players work on all the time, is it not? Excellent, excellent, Mattie!" They arranged to meet at noon, two days from that date, at Olivia Korhonen's condo apartment. She wanted to make cucumber sandwiches—"in the English style, I will cut the crusts off"—but Mattie talked her out of that, or thought she had. In her imagining of what she planned to say to Olivia Korhonen, there would be no room for food.

On the appointed day Mattie woke up in a cold sweat. She considered whether she might be providentially coming down with some sort of flu, but decided she wasn't; then made herself a hot toddy in case she was, ate Grape-Nuts and yogurt for breakfast, went back to bed in pursuit of another hour's nap, failed miserably, got up, showered, dressed, and watched *Oprah* until it was time to go. She made another hot toddy while she waited, on the off chance that the flu might be waiting, too.

The third-floor condo apartment turned out as tastefully dressy as Eileen and Suzanne had reported. Olivia Korhonen was at the door, smilingly eager to show her around. The rooms were high and airy, with indeed a good many paintings and prints, of which Mattie was no judge — they *looked* like originals — and a rather surprising paucity of furniture, as though Olivia Korhonen had not been planning for long-term residence. When Mattie commented on this, the blond woman only twinkled at her, saying, "The motto of my family is that one should always sink deep roots wherever one lives. Because roots can always be sold, do you see?" Later on, considering this, Mattie was not entirely certain what bearing it had on her question; but it sounded both sensible and witty at the time, in Olivia Korhonen's musical voice.

Nevertheless, when Olivia Korhonen announced, "Now, strategy!" and brought out both the cards and the cucumber sandwiches, Mattie held firm. She said, "Olivia, I didn't come to talk about playing cards."

Olivia Korhonen was clearly on her guard in an instant, though her tone remained light. She set the tray of sandwiches down and said slowly, "Ah? Ulterior motives? Then you had probably better reveal them now, don't you think so?" She stood with her head tipped slightly sideways, like an inquisitive bird.

Mattie's heart was beating annoyingly fast, and she was very thirsty. She said, "You are stalking me, Olivia. I don't know why. You are following me everywhere . . . and that *thing* you say every single time we meet." Olivia Korhonen did not reply, nor change her expression. Mattie said, "Nobody else hears you, but I do. You whisper it — *I will kill you.* I hear you."

Sleepless, playing variations on the scene over and over in her head the night before, she had expected anything from outrage and accusation to utter bewilderment to tearful, fervent denial. What happened instead was nothing she could have conceived of: Olivia Korhonen clapped her hands and began to laugh.

Her laughter was like cold silver bells, chiming a fraction out of tune, their dainty discordance more jarring than any rusty clanking could have been. Olivia Korhonen said, "Oh, I did wonder if you would ever let yourself understand me. You are such a . . .

such a *timorous* woman, you know, Mattie Whalen—frightened of so very much, it is a wonder that you can ever peep out of your house, your little hole in the baseboard. Eyes flicking everywhere, whiskers twitching so frantically . . ." She broke off into a bubbling fit of giggles, while Mattie stared and stared, remembering girls in school hallways who had snickered just so.

"Oh, yes," Olivia Korhonen said. "Yes, Mattie, I will kill you—be very sure of that. But not yet." She clasped her hands together at her breast and bowed her head slightly, smiling. "Not just yet."

"*Why?* Why do you want . . . what have I ever, *ever* done to you?"

The smile warmed and widened, but Olivia Korhonen was some time answering. When she did, the words came slowly, thoughtfully. "Mattie, where I come from we have a great many sheep, they are one of Finland's major products. And where you have sheep, of course, you must have dogs. Oh, we do have many wonderful dogs—you should see them handle and guide and work the sheep. You would be so fascinated, I know you would."

Her cheeks had actually turned a bit pink with what seemed like earnest enthusiasm. She said, "But Mattie, dear, it is a curious thing about sheep and dogs. Sometimes stray dogs break into a sheepfold, and then they begin to kill." She did not emphasize the word, but it struck Mattie like a physical blow under the heart. Olivia Korhonen went on. "They are not killing to eat, out of hunger—no, they are simply killing blindly, madly, they will wipe out a whole flock of sheep in a night, and then run on home to their masters and their dog biscuits. Do you understand me so far, Mattie?"

Mattie's body was so rigid that she could not even nod her head. Olivia's softly chiming voice continued. "It is as though these good family dogs have gone temporarily insane. Animal doctors, veterinarians, they think now that the pure *passivity*, the purebred *stupidity* of the sheep somehow triggers—is that the right word, Mattie? I mean it like *to set off*—somehow triggers something in the dog's brain, something very old. The sheep are blundering around in the pen, bleating in panic, too stupid to protect themselves, and it is all just too much for the dogs—even for sheepdogs sometimes. They simply go mad." She spread her hands now, leaning forward, graceful as ever. "Do you see now, Mattie? I do hope you begin to see."

"No." The one word was all Mattie could force out between freezing lips. "No."

"You are my sheep," Olivia Korhonen said. "And I am like the dogs. You are a born victim, like all sheep, and it is your mere presence that makes you irresistible to me. Of course, dogs are dogs—they cannot ever wait to kill. But I can. I like to wait."

Mattie could not move. Olivia Korhonen stepped back, looked at her wristwatch, and made a light gesture toward the door, as though freeing Mattie from a spell. "Now you had better run along home, dear, for I have company coming. We will practice our strategy for the Bridge Group another time."

Mattie sat in her car for a long time, hands trembling, before she felt able even to turn the key in the ignition. She had no memory of driving home, except a vague awareness of impatient honking behind her when she lingered at intersections after the traffic light had changed. When she arrived home she sat by the telephone with her fingers on the keypad, trying to make herself dial Pat Gallagher's number. After a time, she began to cry.

She did call that evening, by which time a curious calm, unlike any other she had ever felt, had settled over her. This may have been because by then she was extremely drunk, having entered the stage of slow but very precise speech, and a certain deliberate, unhurried rationality that she never seemed able to attain sober. Both Pat and Babs immediately offered to come and stay with her, but Mattie declined with thanks. "Not much point to it. She said she'd wait . . . said she *liked* waiting." Her voice sounded strange in her own ears, and oddly new. "You can't bodyguard me forever. I guess *I* have to bodyguard me. I guess I just have to."

When she hung up—only after her friends had renewed their insistence that she call daily, on pain of home invasion—she did not drink any more, but sat motionless by the phone, waiting for Don's return. It was his weekly staff-meeting night, and she knew he would be late, but she felt like sitting just where she was. *If I never moved again, she'd have to come over here to kill me. And the neighbors would see.* The phone rang once, but she did not answer.

Don came home in, for him, a cheerful mood, having been informed that his supervisor at the agency, whom he loathed, was being transferred to another branch. He had every expectation of a swift promotion. Mattie—or someone in Mattie's body, shap-

ing words with her still-cold lips—congratulated him, and even
opened a celebratory bottle of champagne, though she drank
none of her glass. Don began calling his friends to spread the
news, and Mattie went into the kitchen to start a pot roast. The
steamed fish with greens and polenta revolution had passed Don
quietly by.

The act of cooking soothed her nerves, as it had always done;
but the coldness of her skin seemed to have spread to her
mind—which was not, when considered, a bad thing at all. There
was a peculiar clarity to her thoughts now: both her options and
her fears seemed so sharply defined that she felt as though she
were traveling on an airplane that had just broken out of clouds
into sunlight. *I live in clouds. I always have.*

Fork in one of his hands, cordless in the other, Don devoured
two helpings of the roast and praised it in between calls. Mattie,
nibbling for appearances' sake, made no attempt to interrupt; but
when he finally put the phone down for a moment she remarked,
"That woman at the Bridge Group? The one who said she was going to kill me?"

Don looked up, the wariness in his eyes unmistakable. "Yeah?"

"She means it. She really means to kill me." Mattie had been
saying the words over and over to herself all afternoon; by now
they came out briskly, almost casually. She said, "We discussed it
for some time."

Don uttered a cholesterol-saturated sigh. "Damn, ever since you
started with that bridge club, feels like I'm running a daycare center. Look, this is middle-school bullshit, you know it and she knows
it. Just tell her, enough with the bullshit, it's getting real old. Or
find yourself another partner, probably the best thing." He had
the cordless phone in his hand again.

The strange, distant Mattie said softly, "I'm just telling you."

"And I'm telling you, get another partner. Silly shit, she's not
about to kill anybody." He wandered off into the living room, dial-
ing.

Mattie stood in the kitchen doorway, looking after him. She
said—clearly enough for him to have heard, if he hadn't already
been talking on the phone—"No, she's not." She liked the sound
of it, and said it again. "She's not." Then she went straight off to
bed, read a bit of *Chicken Soup for the Soul,* and fell quickly asleep.

She dreamed that Olivia Korhonen was leaning over her in bed, smiling widely and eagerly. There were little teeth on her tongue and small, triangular teeth fringing her lips.

Mattie got to the Bridge Group early the next afternoon and waited, with impatience that surprised her, for Olivia Korhonen to arrive. The Group met in a community building within sight of the Moss Harbor wharf, its windows fronting directly on the parking lot. Mattie was already holding the door open when Olivia Korhonen crossed the lot.

Did she look even a little startled—the least bit taken aback by her prey's eager welcome? Mattie hoped so. She said brightly, "I was afraid you might not be coming today."

"And I thought that perhaps *you* . . ." Olivia Korhonen very deliberately let the sentence trail away. If she had been at all puzzled, she gathered herself as smoothly as a cat landing on its feet. "I am glad to see you, Mattie. I had some foolish idea that you might be, perhaps, ill?"

"Not a bit—not when we need to work on our strategy." Mattie touched her elbow, easing her toward the table where Jeannie Atkinson and old Joe Booker were both beckoning. "You know we need to do that." It was a physical effort to make herself smile into Olivia Korhonen's blue eyes, but she managed.

Playing worse than even she ever had, with foolish bids, rash declarations of trumps, scoring errors, and complete mismanagement of her partner's hand when Olivia Korhonen was dummy, she worked with desperate concentration—manifesting as lightheaded carelessness—on upsetting the woman's balance, her judgment of the situation. How well she succeeded, and to what end, she could not have said; but when Olivia Korhonen mouthed *I will kill you* once again at her as she was dealing a final rubber, she fought down the ice-pick stab of terror and gaily said, "*Ah-ah*, we mustn't signal each other—against the rules, bad, bad." Jeannie and Joe raised their eyebrows, and Olivia Korhonen, very briefly, *almost* looked embarrassed.

She left hurriedly, directly after the game. Mattie followed her out, blithely apologizing left and right, as always, for her poor play. At the car, Olivia Korhonen turned to say, evenly and without expression, "You are not spoiling the game for me. This is childish, all this that you are playing at. It means nothing."

Mattie felt her mouth drying and her heart beginning to pound. But she said, keeping her voice as calm as she could, "Not everybody gets to know how and when they're going to die. If you're really going to kill me, you don't get to tell me how to behave." Olivia Korhonen did not reply, but got into her car and drove away, and Mattie walked back to the Bridge Group for tea and cookies.

"One for the sheep," Pat said on the phone that night. "You crossed her up—she figured you'd be running around in the pen, all crazy with fear, bleating and blatting and wetting yourself. The fun part. And instead you came right to her and practically spit in her eye. I'll bet she's thinking about that one right now."

On the extension, Babs said flatly, "Yes, she sure as hell is. And *I'm* thinking that she won't make that mistake again. She's regrouping, is what it is—she'll be coming from another place next time, another angle. Don't take her lightly, the way she took you. Nothing's changed."

"I know that." Mattie's voice, like her hands, was unsteady. "I wish I could say *I've* changed, but I haven't, not at all. I'm the same fraidy cat I always was, but maybe I'm covering it a little better, I don't know. All I know is I just want to hide under the bed and cover up my head."

Pat said slowly, "I was raised in the country. A sheep-killing dog doesn't go for it just once. This woman has killed before."

Babs said, "Get in close. You snuggle up to her, you tail her around like she's been tailing you. That's not part of the game, she won't like that at all. You keep *coming* at her."

Pat said, "And you keep calling us. Every day."

It took practice. All her instincts told her to turn and run the moment she recognized the elegant figure on the street corner ahead of her or heard the too-friendly voice at her elbow. But gradually she learned not only to force herself to respond with equal affability, but to become the one accosting, waving, calling out—even issuing impromptu invitations to join her for tea or coffee. These were never accepted, and the act of proposing them always left her feeling dizzy and sick; but she continued doggedly to "snuggle up" to Olivia Korhonen at every opportunity. Frightened and alone, still she kept coming.

She had the first inkling that the change in her behavior might be having some effect when Eileen mentioned that Olivia Korhonen had diffidently sounded her out about being partnered with a more skilled player for the Group's upcoming tournament. Eileen had explained that the teams had already been registered, and that in any case none of them would have taken kindly to being broken up and reassigned. Olivia Korhonen hadn't raised the subject again, but Eileen had thought Mattie would want to know. Eileen always told people the things she thought they would want to know.

For her part, Mattie continued to make a point of chattering buoyantly at the bridge table as she misplayed one hand after another, then apologizing endlessly as she trampled through another rubber, leaving ruin in her wake. She announced, laughing, after one particularly disastrous no-trump contract, "I wouldn't blame Olivia if she wanted to strangle me right now. I'd have it coming!" Their opponents looked embarrassed, and Olivia Korhonen smiled and smoothed her hair.

But once, when they were in the ladies' room together, she met Mattie's eyes in the mirror and said, "I will still kill you. Could you hand me the tissues, please?" Mattie did so. Olivia Korhonen blotted her lipstick and went on, "You are not nearly so bad a player as you pretend, and you have not turned impudently fearless overnight. Little sheep, you are just as much afraid of me as you ever were. Tell me this is not true."

She turned then, taking a single step toward Mattie, who recoiled in spite of her determination not to. Olivia Korhonen did not smile in triumph, but yawned daintily and deliberately, like a cat. "Never mind, dear Mattie. It is almost over." She started for the restroom door.

"You are not going to kill me," Mattie said, as she had said once before in her own kitchen. "You've killed before, but you are not going to kill me." Olivia Korhonen did not bother to look back or answer, and a sudden burst of white rage seared through Mattie like fever. She took hold of Olivia Korhonen's left arm and swung her around to face her, savoring the surprise and momentary confusion in the blue eyes. She said, "I will not let you kill me. Do you understand? I will not let you."

Olivia Korhonen did not move in her grip. Mattie finally let her go, actually stumbling back and having to catch herself. Olivia Korhonen said again, "It is almost over. Come, we will go and play that other game."

That night Mattie could not sleep. Even after midnight, she

felt almost painfully wide awake, unable to imagine ever needing to sleep again. Don had been snoring for two hours when she
dressed, went to her car, and drove to the condominium where
Olivia Korhonen lived. A light was still on in the living room window of her apartment, and Mattie, parked across the street, could
clearly make out the figure of the blond woman moving restlessly
back and forth, as though she shared her observer's restlessness.
The light went out presently, but Mattie did not drive home for
some while.

She did the same thing the next night, and for several nights
thereafter, establishing a pattern of leaving the house when Don
was asleep and returning before he woke. On occasion it became
a surprisingly close call, since whether the light stayed on late or
was already out when she reached the condo, she often lost track
of time for hours, staring at a dark, empty window. She continued to check in regularly with Pat and Babs in Witness Point; but
she never told them about her new nighttime routine, though she
could not have said why, any more than she could have explained
the compulsion itself. There was a mindless peacefulness in her
vigil over her would-be murderer that made no sense, and comforted her.

From time to time, Olivia Korhonen came to stand at her window and look out at the dark street. Mattie, deliberately parking
in the same space every night, fully expected to be recognized and
challenged; but the latter, at least, never happened.

She took as well to following Olivia Korhonen through Moss
Harbor traffic whenever she happened to spot the gleaming Prius
on the road. In an elusive, nebulous way, she was perfectly aware
that she was putting herself as much at the service of an obsession
as Olivia Korhonen, but this seemed to have no connection with
her own life or behavior. She could not have cared less where the
Prius might be headed—most often up or down the coast, plainly
to larger towns—or whether or not she was visible in the rearview
mirror. The whole point, if there was such a thing, was to bait her
bridge partner into doing something foolish, even coming to kill
her before she was quite ready. Mattie had no idea what Olivia
Korhonen's schedule or program in these matters might be, nor
what she would do about it; only that whatever was moving in her
would be present when the time came.

When it did come, on a moonless midnight, she was parked in

her usual spot, directly across the street from the condominium. She was in the process of leaving a message on Pat and Babs's answering machine—"Just letting you know I'm fine, haven't seen her today, I'm about to go to bed"—when Olivia Korhonen came out of the building, strode across the street directly toward her, and pulled the unlocked car door open. She said, not raising her voice, "Walk with me, Mattie Whalen."

Mattie said into the cell phone, as quietly as she, "I'll call you tomorrow. Don't worry about me." She hung up then, and got out of the car. She said, "The people I was talking with heard your voice."

Olivia Korhonen did not answer. She took light but firm hold of Mattie's arm and they walked silently together toward the beach, beyond which lay the dark sparkle of the ocean. The sky was pale and clear as glass. Mattie saw no one on the sand, nor on the short street, except for a lone dog trotting self-importantly past them. Olivia Korhonen was humming to herself, at the farthest rim of Mattie's hearing.

Reaching the shore, they both took their shoes off and left them neatly side by side. The sand was cold and hard-packed under Mattie's feet, this far from the water, and she thought regretfully about how little time she had spent on the beach, for all the years of living half a mile away. Something splashed in the gentle surf, but all she saw was a small swirl of foam.

Olivia Korhonen said reflectively, as though talking to herself, "I must say, this is a pity—I will be a little sorry. You have been . . . entertaining."

"How nice of you to say so." Mattie's own odd calmness frightened her more than the woman who meant to kill her. She asked, "Weren't any of your other victims entertaining?"

"Not really, no. One can never expect that—human beings are not exactly sheep, after all, for all the similarities. Things become so *hasty* at the end, so hurried and awkward and tedious—it can be very dissatisfying, if you understand me." She was no longer holding Mattie's arm, but looking into her eyes with something in her own expression that might almost have been a plea.

"I think I do," Mattie said. "I wouldn't have once." They were walking unhurriedly toward the water, and she could see the small surges far out that meant the tide was beginning to turn. She said, "You're more or less human, although I've had a few nasty dreams about you." Olivia Korhonen chuckled very slightly. Mattie said,

"You feed on the fear. No, that's not it, not the fear—the *knowl-edge*. Fear makes people run away, but *knowledge*—the sense that there's absolutely no escape, that you can come and *pick* them, like fruit, whenever you choose—that freezes them, isn't that it? The knowing? And you like that very much."

Olivia Korhonen stopped walking and regarded Mattie without speaking, her blue eyes wider and more intense than Mattie had ever noticed them. She said slowly, "You have changed. I changed you."

Mattie asked, "But what would you have done if I *had* run? That first time, at the Bridge Group, if I had taken you at your word and just packed a bag, jumped in my car, and headed for the border? Would you have followed me?"

"It is a long way to the border, you know." The chuckle was deeper and clearer this time. "But it would all have been so messy, really. Ugly, unpleasant. Much better this way."

Mattie was standing very close to her, looking directly into her face. "And the killing? That would have been pleasant?" She found that she was holding her breath, waiting for the answer.

It did not come in words, but in the slow smile that spread from Olivia Korhonen's eyes to her mouth, instead of the other way around. It came in the slight parting of her lips, in the flick of her cat-pink tongue just behind the white, perfect teeth; most of all in the strange way in which her face seemed to change its shape, almost to fold in on itself: the cheekbones heightening, the fore-head rounding, the round chin in turn becoming more pointed, as in Mattie's dreams.

. . . and Mattie, who had not struck another person since a re-cess fight in the third grade, hit Olivia Korhonen in the stomach as hard as she possibly could. The blond woman coughed and doubled over, her eyes huge with surprise and a kind of reproach. Mattie hit her again—a glancing blow, distinctly weaker, to the neck—and jumped on her, clumsily and impulsively. They went down together, rolling in the sand, the grains raking their skins, clogging their nostrils, coating and filling their mouths. Olivia Korhonen got a near stranglehold on a coughing, gasping Mattie and began dragging her toward the water's edge. Breathless and in pain, she was still the stronger of the two of them.

The cold water on her bare feet revived Mattie a moment be-fore her head was forced under an incoming wave. Panic lent her strength, and she lunged upward, banging the back of her head into Olivia Korhonen's face, turning in the failing grip and pulling her down with both hands on the back of her neck. There was a moment when they were mouth to mouth, breathing one another's hoarse, choking breath, teeth banging teeth. Then she rolled on top in the surf, throwing all her weight into keeping the struggling woman's bloody face in the water. The little waves helped.

At some point Mattie finally realized that Olivia Korhonen had stopped fighting her; she had a feeling that she had been holding the woman under much longer than she needed to. She stood up, soaked and shivering with both cold and shock, swaying dizzily, looking down at the body that stirred in the light surf, bumping against her feet. There was a bit of seaweed caught in its hair.

In a while, in a vague sort of way, she recognized what it was. Something glinted at the edge of a pocket, and she bent down and withdrew a ring of keys. She walked away up the beach, stopping to slip on her shoes.

She did not go back to her car then, but went straight to the condo and walked up the stairs to the third floor, leaving a thinning trail of water behind her. Entry was easy: she had no difficulty finding the right key to open the doorknob lock, and Olivia Korhonen had been in too much of a hurry to throw the deadbolt. Mattie wiped her shoes carefully, nevertheless, before she went inside.

Walking slowly through the graciously appointed apartment, she realized that it was larger than she recalled, and that there were rooms that Olivia Korhonen had not shown her. One took particular effort to open, for the door was heavy and somewhat out of alignment. Mattie put a bruised shoulder to it and forced it open.

The room seemed to be a catchall for odd gifts and odder souvenirs—"tourist tchotchkes," Virginia Schlossberg would have called them. There were no paintings on the walls, but countless candid snapshots, mostly of women, though they did include a handful of men. Their very number bewildered Mattie, making her eyes ache. She recognized no one at first, and then froze: a photo of herself held conspicuous pride of place on the wall facing her. It had obviously been taken by a cell phone. Below it, thumbtacked to the wall, was a gauzy red scarf that she had lost before Olivia Korhonen had even joined the Moss Harbor Bridge Group. Mattie pulled it free, along with the picture, and put them both in her pocket.

All of the photographs had mementos of some sort attached to them, ranging in size from a ticket stub to a pair of sunglasses or a paper plate with a telephone number scrawled on it in lipstick. None of the subjects appeared to be aware that their pictures were being taken; each had a tiny smiley face drawn with a fine-tipped ballpoint pen in the lower right corner. An entire section of one wall was devoted to images of a single dark-eyed young woman, taken from closer and closer angles, as though from the viewpoint of a shark circling to strike. These prints were each framed, not in wood or metal, but by variously colored hair ribbons, all held neatly in place by pushpins of matching hues. The central photo, the largest, was set facing the wall; there were two ribbons set around it, both blue. Mattie took this picture down, turned it around, and studied it for some while.

Hurt, still damp, bedraggled, she was no longer trembling; nor, somehow, was she in the least exhausted. Still cold, yes, but the coldness had come inside; while a curious fervor was warming her face and hands, as though the pictures on the walls were reaching out, welcoming her, knowing her, speaking her name. Still holding the shot of the dark-eyed girl, she moved from one new image to the other, feeling with each a kind of fracturing, a growing separation from everything else, until the walls themselves had dimmed around her and the photos were all mounted on the panelings of her mind. She was aware that there were somehow more there than she could see, more than she could yet take in.

The police will come. They will find the body and find this place. They'll call her the Smiley Face Killer. The photographs were pressing in around her, each so anxious to be properly savored and understood. Mattie put the dark-eyed victim into her pocket next to her own picture, and reached out with both hands. She did not touch any of the pictures or the keepsakes, but let her fingers drift by them all, one after another, as in a kind of soul-Braille, and felt the myriad pinprick responses swarming her skin, as Olivia Korhonen's souvenirs and trophies joined her. It was not possession of any sort; she was always herself. Never for a moment did she fancy that she was the woman she had killed on the beach, nor did any of this room's hoarded memories overtake and evict her own. It was rather a fostering, a sheltering: a full awareness that there was more than enough room in her not for Olivia Korhonen's life, but for what had given that life its only true meaning. Aloud, alone in that room filled with triumph and pride, she said, "Yes, she's gone. Yes, I'm here. Yes."

She walked out of the room, leaving it open, and did the same with the apartment door rather than pull it shut behind her.

Outside the stars were thin, and there were lights on in some of the neighboring condos. Mattie got in her car, started the engine, and drove home.

As chilled as she still was, as battered and scratched, with her blouse ripped halfway off her shoulder, there was a lightness in her, a sense of invulnerability, that she had never felt in all her life. The car seemed to be flying. With the windows down her damp hair whipped around her face, and she sang all the way home.

Reaching her house, she ran up the steps like an exuberant child, opened the door, and stopped in the hallway. Don was facing her, his face flushed and contorted with a mixture of outrage and bewilderment. His pajama jacket was buttoned wrong, which made him look very young. He said, "Where the fuck? Damn it, where the *fuck*?"

Mattie smiled at him. She loved the feel of the smile; it was like slipping into a beautiful silk dress that she had never been able to afford until just now, this moment. Walking past him, she patted his cheek with more affection than she had felt in a long while. She whispered, hardly moving her lips, *"She killed me,"* and kept on to the bedroom.

K. L. COOK

Filament

FROM *One Story*

WHEN SHE WAS SEVENTEEN, Loretta discovered that she was pregnant with Blue Simpson's child, a shame really. Not because Tildon turned out to be a bad son. (In fact, he would do quite well, thirty-two years later, buying and operating a chain of successful southern fried chicken franchises.) It's just that Loretta's future seemed genuinely promising before this turn of events. She'd graduated high school as the valedictorian when she was sixteen. Granted, this was in Honey Grove, Texas, so there were not that many students, certainly not that many bright ones, but she had nonetheless impressed her teachers enough to skip a couple of grades, and then went off to college in Denton on a full scholarship to study journalism. In Denton, she met Blue, a strawberry-headed pipe fitter and apprentice welder from Bug Tussle who liked to two-step. At the beginning of her sophomore year, he took her dancing every night for three straight weeks. By the end of that time, Tildon was conceived. Blue and Loretta hastily married during a freakish October snowstorm, and she gave up her academic pursuits and, until after Blue's death, her dream of becoming a reporter.

Tildon arrived the following spring, followed by two miscarriages that left her depressed and wishing she could return to the promising trajectory of her old life. But then Melinda was born, and Tanya soon after. They'd moved to Charnelle in the Texas Panhandle, where they lived in a too-small, too-hot cinderblock house near the drive-in. On summer weekend nights, she and the kids and Blue would climb up to the flat, pebbly roof, set up folding chairs and a blanket, and watch the double feature for free. Those nights—as the Panhandle dusk turned a velvety blue, as the kids fell asleep in their sleeping bags, as she and Blue sipped beers and she nestled in the crook of his arm with a blanket wrapped around them, and, on one occasion, they actually made love, quietly, thrillingly, during the final fifteen minutes of *Double Indemnity*—those nights were, Loretta would reflect much later, the best times of the marriage.

Blue worked at Charnelle Steel, and Loretta stayed home in the cramped house and cared for the children. She gradually realized, too late, that she had no special knack for mothering. It wasn't that she felt a particular animosity toward her children, but rather against motherhood itself. At first she was ashamed of this epiphany, but after a few years, she no longer tried to deny it. She didn't confess it to others, certainly not to Blue or the children. People tended to harbor a grudge against mothers who seemed to dislike their own, even though, from what she could tell, it was a common enough occurrence. To acknowledge her feelings, to herself at least, eased her conscience a little and rekindled the sense of disciplined observation and fidelity to truth, no matter how unpleasant, that had made her want to pursue a life in journalism. The effort to be kind and compassionate also demanded from her a rigorous testing of her spirit that was, she felt, not unlike prayer, even though she didn't consider herself a religious woman.

Loretta believed she would have adapted just fine to this situation if matters had not taken a turn for the worse in the eighth year of her marriage, when a minuscule filament of hot steel wedged itself in Blue's left eye. The accident ironically had not taken place at work, so Charnelle Steel claimed no responsibility. Nearly blind in that eye, Blue returned, after surgery and a month and a half of recuperation, to work, but his disposition soured with the disfigurement, the now endless medical bills, and the bad luck of getting an injury that, if he'd been more fortunate, could have resulted in a handsome settlement and perhaps a semi-comfortable life of early retirement.

Most mornings he left for work by five and didn't return until six-thirty or seven, later if he happened to stop off at the Armory for drinks and to shoot a little pool, at which he was deceptively skilled, despite his bad eye. When he arrived home on these nights to the house that never seemed to stay clean or uncluttered, the dust growing like moss on the furniture, he often felt the walls squeezing him, a claustrophobic bitterness puddling like acid in his stomach. His wife had grown too thin, with a hostile little smirk nestled in the corners of her mouth, though she wasn't even thirty yet. She'd always been smart, and perhaps that was the real problem. He'd wooed her away from college. He knew she held against him the life he'd provided for them. But that had been as much her fault as his, if fault was to be found. It seemed unjust the way her lips drew tight like a purse string, the way she seemed to hold him responsible for her regrets, without ever acknowledging that he was the one with the goddamn bad eye, who had to work seventy, sometimes eighty hours a week, relegated to the shitty welding jobs rather than the custom work he'd been trained and paid well to do, and still *could* do if just given half a chance. Entering the house, he often felt as if he'd been lit on fire, as if his whole body was a breeding ground for army ants, a feeling exacerbated by the holes in his shirt and little blisters and pockmarks beneath the holes where the torches had burned and reburned his forearms and neck and wrists.

Loretta understood how his predicament might embitter him, but it didn't seem right that he'd sometimes take it out on her and the children, shouting for them to *shut up, shut up, just for holy chrissakes shut the fuck up,* and after the injury, occasionally and then more routinely striking Loretta, once even with his brown leather belt, the buckle of which left a puncture in her hip that had become infected and never completely healed. A blistered scab chafed under the elastic waistband of her slip.

After these incidents, he would leave, setting out for the Armory or, in lonelier moods, on long drives to the nearby lakes or to the Waskalanti Creek, where he'd get out, take off his shoes and socks, cuff his jeans, and wade into the cold running water, the smooth pebbles caressing his feet. He'd wait for the train to roll across the wooden bridge at five minutes past midnight. Pressing his hands against the posts when the train passed, he would feel the trestle shake and the surprising heat shimmy to the bottom of the foundation. Standing in the cold water and touching those warm vibrating wooden posts soothed him.

After he returned, calmer, contrite even, he'd sometimes take his guitar from the closet, wake the children, and sing to them, ballads he'd learned before he was married, when he dreamed of traveling with a band from dancehall to dancehall all the way to Nashville. Tildon, Melinda, and Tanya warily appreciated this part of the evening and came to recognize it as a prelude to quieter months before their father's dangerous sap would rise again.

Later, in bed with Loretta, he'd stroke her stomach as he kissed the places where he'd bruised her, and then he'd make love to her with a tenderness that she relished, even if she didn't like the road by which they'd arrived at this place, nor did she want any more children, and had taken to cleansing herself afterward, once Blue'd fallen asleep, with a foul-smelling potion that she purchased from Maria Fernandez, the midwife who lived in what was back then called Mexican Town on the east side of Charnelle.

The next morning she would stir into a cup of hot tea a yellow powder, also provided by Maria Fernandez, that tasted like formaldehyde smelled. Then she'd spend the rest of the day in the bathroom vomiting and sometimes spotting, even if it wasn't her time of the month. It seemed to her a heavy price to pay for an hour of tenderness, but she did not want to imagine another child in this house.

On March twenty-second of the twelfth year of their marriage, Blue came home late with more burn holes in his shirt than normal. He'd been to the Armory, where he'd drunk six shots of tequila and lost $28 on a double-or-nothing rack of nine ball. When he arrived, at nearly midnight, he struck Loretta twice across the face and then drove to the Waskalanti Creek and stood under the trestle in the ice-cold water, waiting, but the train never came. He'd missed it. After a while he felt soothed just the same by the hooting of the owls, out now for spring, and the purr of the tequila in his body, which rendered him, as it often did, feeling more alert than sleepy, though he knew even in his drunkenness that he might not remember a damn thing the next day. He drove home and woke the children, who patiently listened to him strum a song he'd written himself years ago called "Long Train Rolling," followed by a particularly soulful rendition of "Blue Moon of Kentucky," and then he kissed them and carried Tanya to bed, nearly toppling over the nightstand in the children's room.

"I love you," he said, and lingered by the door.

After a long pause, Melinda said, "I love you, too, Daddy," though Tildon remained quiet, feigning sleep. Tildon knew what his father wanted, but he could not bring himself to appease the man's wish to be forgiven.

Blue shut his bedroom door, shed his clothes into a puddle, and stretched out over his wife and began to kiss her. She pushed him away.

"I'm sorry, honey, I'm so sorry," he said, and then wept for a good ten minutes. "I'm a sorry bastard, I know. Sorry sorry sorry."

She remained unmoved. He pried her knees open, cooing into her ear. She felt and then, surprising even herself, acted upon an impulse to claw his back and his face. He cuffed her clumsily across the temple, but she didn't make a sound. He held her arms down, and they wrestled on the bed until Tildon knocked on the door, tentatively whispering, "Is everything all right?"

Tildon's words provoked a momentary truce, both of them unsure what to do next. Blue said, "Get on back to bed, son."

"Mom?" Tildon said, and Loretta heard, alongside her son's fear, his desire to help her. *Please,* he seemed to be telling her, *please please tell me what I should do, and please don't have me do a thing.* That voice broke her heart.

"Mind your father," she said as lightly as she could.

They heard him retreat, and then, without resistance, she let Blue finish what he'd started, holding the headboard so that it wouldn't thump against the wall and alarm the children any more than they were already alarmed. It was over in a matter of minutes. She pushed him off her. He rolled over and fell asleep.

She opened the door. Tildon and Melinda sat huddled in their pajamas outside, their backs against the wall.

"Everything's okay," she said. "Go on to bed." They didn't move at first, but then she said, "Hurry up, now. It's late." Her voice pacified them, and they obeyed her.

She went to the bathroom, where she cleaned herself and doctored her face, and then returned quietly to the children's room to make sure they were asleep. The girls were both out, but Tildon was merely pretending. She didn't question him, though, just kissed all their foreheads. She whispered in his ear, "Don't you worry." And then she left the room, closing the door behind her.

She started to go back to her bedroom, but couldn't bring herself to do it. She shuffled into the dark living room and lay on the sofa, where she just wanted to close her eyes for a few minutes and collect herself. The house was silent except for the whisper of branches brushing against the window. She rose and went to the kitchen, where she thought about administering Maria Fernandez's remedies. She knew that she would begin vomiting in an hour or so if she did, so she decided to wait. After pulling her favorite cast-iron skillet from the cabinet, she shifted it from hand to hand, feeling its familiar heaviness. She drank a glass of water slowly, rinsed the glass, put it in the drainer, and then carried the skillet back to the bedroom.

She shut the door and pulled the cord on the lamp so that a yellow glow enveloped the bed, where her husband lay, his mouth agape, his naked body sprawled over the tangled sheets. He looked like a dead man, limp and pale, splotched with blisters at his neck and wrists. Holding the cool and slightly greasy handle, she raised the skillet and hit him across his face, the flat bottom covering his nose and right eye socket. She heard bone crack and felt his blood spray her arm and the hollow of her throat.

Immediately, she knew that she hadn't hit him as hard as she had wanted to. She had wanted to crush his skull, and she felt she would have been justified in doing so, but at the last second she'd held back just enough so that only his nose and perhaps his cheek appeared to break. He did not move, though, and she was unsure whether or not she had, despite her failure of courage, killed him.

For a solid sixty seconds she watched him, counting each second. He still didn't move. She sat down on the chair next to the bed and studied, with the skillet in her lap, the shape of his body.

Tentatively, she put her hand on his chest, searched for the *thump-thump* of his heartbeat. She tipped his chin away from her and inspected the broken part of his face. His nose and cheekbone were starting to swell and appeared pulpy. The dried blood from the scratches created a black line running from his temple to his jaw, another one on his forehead. Fresh blood from his nose trickled over his upper lip. She reached over to the dresser and pulled a clean handkerchief from the top drawer and dabbed gently at his face until the white cotton turned red.

*

When he woke forty minutes later, she was holding a cloth full of
ice against his nose and cheek. Groggily, still in shock, he asked,
"What happened?"

"The dresser tipped over onto the bed. We're lucky it didn't kill
us both."

She could tell he didn't believe her. In all this time of waiting,
she hadn't given one thought to what she would say to Blue when
he woke. She was surprised by the words that came out of her
mouth. It seemed outlandish even to her, but she decided, out of
curiosity, to leave it at that, to offer nothing else in order to see
how he'd respond. She was even more surprised that he didn't
challenge her story, just lay there, limp and swelling. He pulled the
sheet up over his exposed body.

When he said nothing, she felt some crucial element of power
in her marriage shift.

At five-thirty, he went to work with his nose bandaged, the cuts
on his face beginning to harden, his good eye as threaded with
broken blood vessels as his bad one had been several years before.

When Tildon and the girls woke, shortly after their father left, they
studied their mother's face, but she understood that they didn't
really want her to tell them anything. The inner life of a marriage must be kept hidden from children. She knew that much.
Loretta made them oatmeal and toast, fixed their lunches, and
hurried them off to the bus stop, and then she bathed quickly.
She remembered that she hadn't taken Maria Fernandez's powder.
Maybe it wouldn't make her vomit this time. Maybe she had built
up immunity, like a person who is bitten several times by snakes becomes snake-proof. But when she went to the pantry and opened
the tin can on the top shelf where she kept the powder hidden,
she found it empty. She would deal with that later. Right now she
needed to remain as clearheaded as possible. She put on her nicest
wool skirt and dark purple sweater and walked down to the courthouse.

"I want a divorce," she told the clerk, Gail Weathers, a man
who'd lost all four fingers of his left hand in the war.

"Why?" he asked.

"I don't love my husband anymore."

"That ain't a good enough reason for the state of Texas."

She pointed to her bruised face, and when he still seemed unconvinced, she discreetly rolled back the waistband of her skirt and slip to reveal the belt buckle puncture, a halo of swollen pink flesh surrounding the still-infected hole. This got Weathers's attention, mainly because of the audacity of the revelation rather than the impressiveness of the wound. But he didn't show his surprise, just continued chewing on an already gnawed toothpick.

"Guess you should talk to Hef Givens," he said.

She walked over to the office of Hef Givens, one of only two lawyers in town.

"A divorce'll cost you more than it's worth," he said. "And you can be sure Blue won't take it well."

Hef Givens and Blue Simpson sometimes hunted deer together. He was not excited about being enlisted as the attorney in a divorce proceeding against his friend.

"Here," Loretta said, handing Hef Givens $25 for his retainer, money she had been hoarding the past year by shaving a couple of dollars off the grocery bill each month. "That's all I have right now."

These were not, despite postwar prosperity, exactly fat times in Charnelle, but Hef Givens was doing well enough. He did not need to take on this case. But his own father had been a thief who sometimes savagely beat his mother and him and then deservedly spent seven years in jail for armed robbery—a time of poverty for Hef and his mother, yet also a period of relative safety and occasional happiness, especially after they moved to Charnelle to live with his grandparents.

Hef looked at Loretta, an intelligent but sullen woman, and saw in her bruises and resolve a refracted portrait of his own mother's life. "Okay, then," he said, without touching the money. "Here's the first order of business."

She returned home, as Hef Givens instructed her to do, and packed Blue's personal belongings into two boxes, which she placed on the porch, along with a suitcase filled with his clothes. She took the children to Carol Lippincott's house. Then she called the sheriff and requested that a deputy be sent to escort Blue away when he arrived home.

The sheriff's office had already received a call from Hef Givens, and no one there relished this assignment. They didn't appreciate domestic situations, since those were often the only dangerous ones in Charnelle. Not many people were injured with criminal intent in the county unless, experience had taught Sheriff Britwork, they were on the receiving end of a love gone sour. In 1949 there was very little by way of criminal activity at all in Charnelle, so Sheriff Britwork and his four officers spent most of their time at the Ding Dong Daddy Diner, drinking coffee and munching onion rings, or hanging out at the high school football and basketball games to prevent adolescent brawls, or cruising through Mexican Town to make sure the residents knew that someone was keeping a suspicious eye on them. There were also no divorces recorded in Charnelle during the previous six years, even if a majority of marriages, by Britwork's estimation, were not happy ones. Sometimes a couple would separate temporarily, or a man would run off with a mistress for a while, or a wife would run off with her husband's best friend, only to return a few days or weeks later. These incidents seldom resulted in divorce. Acrimony, certainly, and a malignant resentment. Sometimes shots were fired or knives wielded or suicides threatened. But seldom divorce.

The sheriff sent Fortney Nevers, the pudgy twenty-year-old deputy, out to the Simpson home to oversee the proceedings. This wasn't a kind assignment on the part of the sheriff, but Britwork had a root canal performed that very morning—the fourth of what would eventually be six surgeries—and he was not in a generous mood. He didn't want to be the one dealing with a marital dispute, especially between Blue and Loretta Simpson. He had known them since they first moved to Charnelle. The sheriff and his wife had even played pinochle with the Simpsons a time or two before both couples were besieged by children. Britwork would now and again shoot a game of pool with Blue down at the Armory, but since Blue's accident a few years ago, the two families seldom saw each other, and that was just fine with the sheriff. Blue Simpson carried his misfortune and self-pity around like a virus, and the sheriff didn't want to catch it.

Besides, it would serve Fortney Nevers right. The young deputy annoyed the sheriff. The boy's fatness was particularly galling to Britwork, a man with the metabolism of a greyhound, who harbored an unreasonable prejudice against the portly.

"Nevers ain't old enough," Britwork once told his other officers, within earshot of the deputy, "to have earned the right to be fat."

The sheriff had been forced to hire the twenty-year-old because Fortney's uncle was the Honorable Cleavis Nevers, the county judge. Given the irritable mood the root canal had fostered in Britwork, he half hoped that Blue Simpson might beat the shit out of the young deputy—not badly enough to inflict serious injury, of course, but enough to persuade the pudgy kid to give up on police work.

Months later, at Fortney Nevers's trial, the sheriff would change his tune. He would testify that the deputy was a model policeman, and that he had been confident Fortney could handle the assignment when he sent him to the Simpsons' house that day. The sheriff would tell the court that he was sure the boy had warned Blue Simpson not to take another step, and that he had fired the shot only to scare the man. The jury would acquit Fortney Nevers, in large part because of their fondness for Hef Givens, who had agreed to represent the young officer, and out of deference to Judge Nevers, who reluctantly recused himself from the case but sat on the front row, directly behind his nephew, and stared solemnly at the jury members, as if issuing his own verdict. Sheriff Britwork would emerge as the incompetent one, the person in fact most culpable for the tragedy, a courtroom performance that would result in the loss of his job in the next election.

Blue was already in a surly mood when he left for home. His eye itched and watered. His nostrils had swollen shut during the day, forcing him to breathe through his mouth, and now his throat was raw. He'd gobbled down aspirin every two hours to diminish the pain of his swollen nose and cheek and the scratches on his face and back, but it didn't seem to help much. To make matters worse, he'd had to field the same questions a dozen times from his coworkers about how his face had become mangled.

He repeated what Loretta had told him—that the dresser had fallen on him while sleeping. It had knocked him out and broken his nose, maybe busted his cheek. His coworkers' arched eyebrows and smirks reinforced the suspicion he'd already had that such an accident was unlikely at best and preposterous at worst. Moreover, he didn't have a good excuse for the scratches on his face, not to mention the unseen ones on his back and shoulders, and couldn't come up with any better story. He didn't tell them he'd gone a little nuts himself last night, drunk too much tequila, lost too much shooting pool, and did what he always regretted doing when he drank more than three shots and lost more than $20. Nor did he tell them that he didn't really remember much after that, except that he woke in the morning with his face swollen and aching, his nose broken, his eyes black.

"That dresser must've had some pretty sharp fingernails," Melvin Doogle said. The other men snickered in such a way that Blue understood he'd been and would continue to be the butt of jokes for days, maybe weeks, to come. It didn't help that at four o'clock that afternoon, lightheaded and then dizzy, hyperventilating, he'd collapsed on the floor of the shop and had been forced to breathe into a paper bag that Bean Peterson, the foreman, put over his mouth.

How could the day be any more miserable? But then he arrived home to find a police cruiser parked on the curb, two boxes and a suitcase on the front porch, the door locked.

Blue rapped on the door, but no one answered. He didn't have his key. They never locked the house, except when they went for Christmas every other year to Bug Tussle and Honey Grove. He knocked again and heard footsteps on the other side, but no one answered.

"Open the damn door," he said.

"Take your things and leave," Loretta answered.

He pressed his cheek, the one that was not bruised, against the wood and could hear his wife breathing on the other side, her face just inches from his.

"Open it!"

"No."

"I don't mind breaking this fucking door down." He said this flatly, without malice, which was a kind of victory, though he regretted the profanity. He didn't usually swear at his wife unless he'd drunk too much tequila, and he'd sworn off tequila soon after he'd become lightheaded today and found himself on the floor with a paper sack over his face.

The deadbolt was thrown. He waited a few seconds and then opened the door to find Loretta standing on the other side of the room, near the fireplace.

"What are you doing?"

"Stay there," she said. There wasn't any alarm in her voice. In fact, he wondered if this might be an elaborate joke.

His sinuses throbbed, and he felt again the wooziness he'd experienced just moments before he'd passed out earlier in the day. He touched his nose. It felt tender and swollen—and he imagined that it was already turning a darker shade of blue. Both his good and bad eye began to itch and water, but he knew enough not to scratch that itch. It would only make things worse. He blinked a few times to clear his vision. A chubby boy in a uniform suddenly emerged from the bathroom.

"Who are you?" Blue asked.

"Deputy Nevers?" the boy said, his voice going up at the end so that his answer sounded like a question.

"You related to Judge Nevers?"

"I'm his nephew," Fortney said, almost embarrassed. He had arrived at the Simpson home shortly before five-thirty and had been waiting for nearly an hour, wishing all the while that he'd urinated before he left the station because he didn't want to be stuck inside the Simpson bathroom with his penis in his hand when Blue showed up. Fortney had inherited a weak bladder from his father's side of the family, complicated by a serious kidney infection when he was a boy, and consequently he had to piss eight to ten times a day and often twice during the night. When he was nervous, he sometimes lost continence, which was not advantageous for a young man, especially a deputy—a predicament that forced him to order double-padded underwear from Montgomery Ward. This solution minimized but did not entirely eliminate his worry and shame.

"Get out," Loretta said. "This officer will follow you to the Charnelle Inn or wherever you want to go. But you *must* leave. Now."

"What're you talking about?" Though Blue assumed that whatever he'd done last night could not have been good, given the state of his own face and hers, he didn't expect such immediate nor dire consequences for his actions. He just wanted, for now, to lie down in his own bed and sleep for about twelve hours.

"Blue. Now."

"Where're the kids?"

"Out," she said. Blue wasn't sure if she was referring to the children or issuing him another order. He breathed deeply through his mouth, having forgotten again, in the confusion of the moment, that this was the only way he *could* breathe. Dizziness seemed ready to engulf him.

"Come with me, Mr. Simpson," Fortney said nervously. "I'll help you load your things."

"Loretta," Blue said. He could hear a whine in his own voice, which surprised and embarrassed him.

"Go, Blue," she said, quieter now. He detected a trace of pity, a tenderness that he thought he might leverage to his advantage.

"Let's just you and me have a glass of tea and talk about it." He sat down in the chair closest to the door.

"No, Blue. You have to go."

"I don't feel so good, you know. It's been a hard day, Loretta. I need to rest."

"Sir," Fortney said, "I'm afraid you have to leave. I'll help you."

"You'll be hearing from Hef Givens in the morning," Loretta said.

"Hef Givens?"

"My lawyer."

"Hef? What do you mean Hef Givens is your lawyer? Hef is *my* friend."

He remembered suddenly, vividly, the last time he and Hef had gone hunting, both of them squatting in the bushes, the predawn light shrouding them, their breaths misting in the November air, both of them waiting, waiting, waiting for the bucks to appear on the meadow by the lake. He loved such moments, rare though they were, when he and another man, who also understood the dignity and beauty and suspense of such stillness, crouched together, watching and waiting patiently.

"It's over," she said.

"Come along, sir," the deputy said, his voice rising again in a way that reminded Blue of Tildon. *Where was Tildon? Where were the girls?*

Fortney put his hand on Blue's arm, a place where Blue had blistered himself that very day when he dropped the torch as he fell to the concrete floor. Blue knocked the boy's hand away and stood up.

"Mr. Simpson," the deputy said, unsnapping the button on his holster. Later he would swear under oath that he didn't aim for the man's back but for the fireplace, though after the trial he would sometimes remember or, in a feverish night sweat, dream it differently, would see his revolver pointed at a spot just below Blue Simpson's left shoulder blade, would feel again his finger squeezing the slightly oily steel of the trigger. But right now Fortney only saw Blue glance down at the front of his pants. A small dark circle growing wider and wider. The man's swollen lips seemed to curl with the dismissive contempt Fortney had put up with his whole damn existence. Blue shoved him aside and took two long strides toward his wife.

It was now dusk, and the lights were not yet on in the house. Loretta was surprised when her husband moved toward her, suddenly blocking the window. The shadowy outline of him suddenly reminded her of the young man—not even twenty, with a thin fuzz of reddish blond scruff on his chin and jaw—who had charmed her when she was at college in Denton. The night they'd met, Blue was standing on the edge of the dance floor. He'd offered his hand. She'd taken it, and he twirled her quickly through a double-time waltz, and she'd smiled, thanked him for the dance, and started away, but then the next song began—a slow melancholy number, evocative, lovely—and he'd pulled her close, held her against him, and they'd moved in slow, swaying circles, and just like that he'd kissed her on the lips, a feather touch, then leaned back and smiled.

As he crossed their living room now, Blue seemed impossibly young again and determined to claim Loretta's last dance. But then she saw his face clearly. That left eye disfigured. She could see again the filament of steel lodged in the iris—like a tiny jagged flower. There it was, and then gone. She heard the sound of the shot, which echoed in the small room and kept ringing in her ears days later. Then she no longer saw Blue's features, just his distinct silhouette falling toward her, eclipsing the fading sun.

JASON DeYOUNG

The Funeral Bill

FROM *New Orleans Review*

AT ONE TIME the landlord Jeffers had been a busy person, but not anymore. Now he had time to think, and he had recently decided that he was going to die. His stomach was no longer the taut paunch it had been. Food passed his tongue joylessly. He no longer lusted. His feet and legs often went numb, and he'd taken to massaging isopropyl alcohol on them to regain some feeling. The smoke from his pipe remained one of the only things that seemed right—perhaps the craving for vice was the last thing to leave a person. Just before his mother passed away she would only eat soft candies. Jeffers's death wouldn't be immediate: he wouldn't pass away today or tomorrow. It just landed upon him, pressed upon him, that his own passing was imminent, and he had no idea what to expect in the afterward.

Alone on the front porch in a frayed and stretched lawn chair, eyes closed, he imagined funerals. His tenant's wife had died a few days ago. He pictured her supine like all bodies he'd seen in a coffin—clenched eyes, somewhat enlarged nostrils, mouth gently closed as if asleep. Peaceful rest. He remembered the summer evening years before when he'd had a body removed from Ashcross. The renter's daughter draped across her father's swollen body, weeping "Daddy . . . Daddy." Her little fists sinking into her father's stomach, her fingers groping at his shirt. The mortician's assistant, grinding his teeth, pulled the little girl off the body, rending the moist stitching around the shirt's collar. The renter didn't appear as if he slept. In the near-subterraneous light, gape-jawed with eyes half closed and unfocused, his waxy face was constricted into a rictus articulating the ineffable of the beyond. Or perhaps the lack thereof. He didn't look heaven-bound. If Jeffers had not gone when the rent stopped coming in, he wondered how long the kid would have stayed there, caring for her father's decomposing body.

Jeffers envied those who had seen a person die. He believed they understood what he didn't—what death brought. He asked the renter's little girl what had happened when her father passed. Without a tear in her eye, she said she didn't know. She hadn't seen it.

This envy had taken root when his son, James, witnessed his mother pass away while Jeffers was out making a deal with a man named White who was ignorant enough to believe a handshake was still as good as a notarized contract. For James, watching his mother's passing had been such a powerful thing he'd gone into the seminary. He now ran a church out of the storefront of an old third-rate grocery in the lower part of the state; its sanctuary still smelled of hoop cheese and day laborers. (Jeffers thought his son would have been better off reopening the grocery.) But James had witnessed many of his parishioners die, some of old age, others from disease. Each time his son told him of another death, Jeffers's resentment grew. He never asked his son what it was like, afraid he'd get an earful of capricious religious nonsense, a tangle of words that would make him feel stupid.

He opened his eyes to stop the images and looked at the clear plastic freezer bags filled with water and four pennies hanging from the upper porch railings. Craziest thing he'd ever heard—a suggestion from James, an article he'd sent Jeffers on how to ward off flies. It said to hang plastic freezer bags with pennies and water outside to keep flies away. It worked. But as the sunlight shot through them, casting a liquid-copper glow, he thought of the coins once used to cover the eyes of the deceased. He spat over the porch railing. He put his unlighted pipe in his mouth.

He tried to recover his mind, replacing contemplating death with what to do about the Ashcross property, in which—he'd been told—a set of kids were now squatting. He'd let the place go to seed since the renter died in it nearly three years ago. Its roof and plumbing leaked, its walls drilled out by all manner of nest-build-ers, but he couldn't abide the squatting. But apathy or something like it had gotten hold of him; it had embraced him at the same time the numbness started creeping into his legs. In quiet times such as these, something in the boredom and the numbness and the nature of age drew back like a bow and twanged when he tried to move, and a misdirected laugh or, on occasion, a hiccuplike cry sprang from his mouth. He didn't understand it. But it locked him in his chair, kept him from getting anything done.

He tapped a wooden, bald-headed match on the arm of the chair while trying not to look at the pennies. But images of edemas, time at work, wasting disease, null and vacant and quicklime-covered faces impinged upon his concentration. His pipe hung limply from his lips. He sucked on the raw tobacco packed inside it to get a hint of sweetness mixed with a burned residue.

Jeffers saw the tenant who lived across the street walking up the driveway. As he walked, he smacked at the ash-brown leaves of the spent okra that framed one side of the property.

Jeffers dropped the unlighted match in his palm.

The tenant stopped at the porch steps. A scrawny man with brow-darkened eyes and a fresh crookedness barbing his face as if he'd been howling or banging his head against the wall.

"RD, what's ailing you?"

"We buried LaRae this morning," RD said, closing his eyes.

"I was sorry to hear about LaRae," Jeffers said. He looked down at RD, who shifted his weight between his feet like a child needing to pee. He patted the porch railing, causing it to wobble. "It's a hard thing to lose a wife," Jeffers continued, to fill in the silence. He pictured his two wives in his mind, pondered which one might meet him in heaven, if there was a heaven. Age had made him hopeful again that there was such a place. Experience made him doubtful. "I've lost two myself."

RD nodded thoughtfully at the bottom of the porch steps. He shifted his weight and squinted at the pennies and water bags.

Jeffers studied RD. He knew little about him. Looked mid-thirties, but Jeffers had stopped believing he could guess a person's age a long time ago. A quiet tenant—paid his rent. But RD had a bottom-of-the-litter look, runtish, forgotten. He looked given to schemes. He might have been the skinniest *grown* man Jeffers had ever seen—his shoulders angled like those on a starved child.

He'd known scrounging for sure. RD and LaRae had come from Tennessee.

"She saw haints, you know," RD said.

"Haints?"

"Ghosts."

"Ghosts?"

RD nodded and splashed a brown vein of spit into the grass. A wind buffeted his face, and he looked a slight better to Jeffers, who supposed the little man had come over just to talk out his sadness. Jeffers struck the match, sheltered its flame, and pressed it to the tobacco while making gentle, moist pops to pull the fire into the pipe.

"In that house of yourn," RD said.

"What's that?" Jeffers said.

"Haints in your house."

"This house?"

"No, ourn. The one you lettin us have."

Jeffers lowered the pipe and shook out the match. "Rent."

"Yep. Haints in that house you lettin us rent."

Jeffers leaned forward and looked across the porch where he could see through a stand of weather-broken pines the squat gables of the house RD rented. Below the boundary of trees, a graying neighborhood dog was working over roadkill flattened on the unlined blacktop that split the properties.

"I'll be damned." Jeffers looked back at RD, who had climbed the first step and was leaning toward the porch as if he wanted to come up. He was almost panting.

"Them haints killed LaRae."

Jeffers leaned back in his chair and drew on his pipe. The spirit of the tobacco warmed his mouth as he considered his next words. RD climbed another step. He shuddered and proffered a what-are-you-going-to-do-about-it glare. Behind the spindly man, the sun was low and the sky bloodied in a balsam light.

Jeffers took the pipe down. "I am sorry about LaRae. But what do you want me to do about a ghost? I cain't charge it rent."

"You could pay for LaRae's buryin expense, that's what, since it was your haints that killed her."

"How you figure they're mine?"

"It was in your house."

"Well, they could have come with you from Tennessee. I've had untold number of folks live in that house. Not one of them complained of *'haints.'*"

RD squinted, catching the sarcasm in Jeffers's voice. He quivered.

"If there are haints in that house, as you say, RD, they must've come to roost the same time you did. And that house is only supposed to be occupied by two people. The way I see it, you might owe me money, housing your haints, when your lease says only two shall live there." Jeffers drew on his pipe, satisfied with himself. He felt a pleasant jolt of blood and adrenaline shock his body.

"That house killed her."

"House or haints?"

RD chewed the inside of his cheek. The broad outlines of his skull were visible. He reminded Jeffers of the half-fed prisoners who worked chain gang years ago.

"RD, how do you make money? You work?"

RD, leering, backed down a step.

Jeffers held his gaze wide-eyed until he squinted from the falling sun breaking from the clouds. If this was a scheme, Jeffers thought, it's awfully weak.

"Before LaRae passed, she told me that you would take care of her funeral bill. She said it was your wives who told her that you'd cover it."

Jeffers peered unblinkingly through white smoke.

"You going to pay?"

"What do you think?" Jeffers said.

"I think you will."

For a brief moment he considered giving in before a surge of meanness rose up. "Get the hell off my porch 'fore I throw you off."

RD stood up straight and a haughty tic ran through his shoulders. He turned and headed back in the direction he'd come from.

Jeffers called to RD when the little man was equidistant between the porch and the road: "If you see them haints, send them my way."

RD didn't respond. As he passed the old dog in the road, he stopped to stare at it, and then for no reason scared it off its tire-mangled dinner.

Jeffers spat a long silvery streak into his boxwoods. He relaxed and puffed, satisfied. But the reminder of LaRae's passing made him think again about his own shortening time, of what was to come. He lowered the pipe and leaned once more to see the house across the road, looking for the little, dissatisfied man, angry with him for his audacity and privation and for his existence, which Jeffers suddenly considered unearned.

The little spat with his tenant left Jeffers wanting some more excitement and so he went to the Ashcross property to run the squatters out. He found no one there. They had trounced the weeds around the house, creating a cowpath to a five-gallon bucket simmering with turds and urine. In the long-untended shade tree hung wispy catfish skins. Several catfish heads had been hammered into the tree's trunk and their husky mouths and eyes gawked in bewilderment. Redneck trophies, Jeffers thought.

Standing on the Ashcross porch, Jeffers recalled the last time he'd been inside the house, holding the little girl by the shoulder, quizzing her on her father's death, and her dry eyed answers. Her little fingernails had been chewed to the quick.

His remembrance was broken when he glimpsed a young pregnant woman walking down the road, her hair a freak of colors—yellow, red—her stomach full and hanging low. Jeffers thought for a moment she was the squatter, but she passed the weed-lined driveway as if she were headed elsewhere. And then Jeffers felt a twinge of lust, something he hadn't felt in a while. He stifled a half-laugh. If asked what he thought of the young woman, he would have ranted over her hairstyle and clothes—he knew a slut when he saw one! But in truth she was lovely, and her pregnancy made her all the more so. What if she had been his squatter? Could he have thrown her out? He'd never felt sorry for squatters. One winter he had thrown a whole family out, and learned later that one of their children died of pneumonia. Still he thought he'd made the right decision. He was well-off and thought it was because he'd made good decisions. These people had to earn their place; they couldn't just take. Wanting something for nothing, that was the problem.

He still liked to brag that he had once held over a million dollars in his hands. It had come from the sale of the White property, which he considered bad luck, seeing as how he got it the same day his first wife died. His second wife came with property but she died within a year of when they married. Her kids had taken her away from Jeffers, back to her home state, to care for her. He'd given all of her property to her children. It seemed the right thing to do. And after she passed, he sold off several large sections of his holdings. But he wished he had it all back now. It worried him how easily he'd accepted age, how he'd told himself he was getting old and selling off his properties was a good idea. At one time he'd owned twenty-one rental properties, most of them run-down farmhouses in which he installed young couples and hard-working hillbillies. Grief-pierced, he yearned to have it all back. Now he just had the house next to his own to give him his pocket money, and the Ashcross place.

James wanted Ashcross to put a church on, and he wanted Jeffers to donate it. But there was promise still in the property and money to be made. He needed to get the squatters out, and install fresh tenants. It was also that his son wanted the plot so bad that Jeffers couldn't let it go; he couldn't let his son take the last of his holdings, leaving him with just the squat-gable home. In his imagination, Jeffers saw his son holding the hands of a dying parishioner, whispering that the man who had owned the property had donated it, just gave it up. The face of the imagined parishioner looked up with a wink and smirked. And Jeffers saw that this was where his son would bury him, too—under a light-gray headstone carved with his birth and death and ASHCROSS UNITED METHODIST CHURCH BENEFACTOR.

The young woman passed behind some trees. His lust abated, the numbness in his feet stretched out as if originating from inside the bones. The numbness, the age. There would be a time soon when he wouldn't be able to care for himself. He wouldn't be able to rise from a chair, wouldn't be able to put himself to bed, wouldn't be able to cook or attend to his own needs. Perhaps giving the land to his son would be a good thing, and then James would have no choice but to make it his duty to devote himself to Jeffers. But what he really wanted was someone who would care for him without demand. He would pay for that.

That night Jeffers dreamed of LaRae. He dreamed of going over to the little house with pockets full of cash. He found her there with a baby up to her breast while she smiled brightly at him. He looked down at the baby, its jaw fluttering, gnawing. Unhealthy, pallid, the child unmistakably RD's: they shared the same sunken cheeks. LaRae draped a frayed copper-colored shawl over her chest and tugged the baby from her nipple as if to show Jeffers the infant, and the child gave out an insufferable squall, bile resembling doused ash dribbled from its mouth. Its cry wasn't like any infant's he'd heard before, and Jeffers woke to hear that the sound wasn't the child's at all but was coming from something else nearby. He sat up in bed, switched on the bedside lamp.

The painful howl went up again.

His feet and shins were numb, as they often were when he woke. He slipped on his yard shoes and tried to stand. He sat down on the bed and then stood up again. It felt as though he was walking on peg legs. He stumbled across the room. Another wail went out. He forwent his pants. He went to the closet, held on to the doorjamb, his leg muscles smarting and stinging. He pulled out his pistol. He tromped down the hall in his boxer shorts and undershirt; he said a prayer that his varicose legs wouldn't give out and that he'd have sense enough to protect himself. He looked out the living room window and saw nothing. He eased his front door open, his pistol pointed in the direction he imagined the sound was coming from, his lips parted, ready to receive a breath of cool air.

The outdoor lamp washed everything in a plaintive white or buried it in shadow. At the far end of his yard, a quaking silhouette crouched under a pecan tree. He walked slowly over to it—his face jutted trying to see what it was. His pistol lowered.

The old dog moaned as Jeffers approached. Its gut had been slit open. Blood adorned its fur in black blotches.

He heard rustling in the pine trees that flanked his property. He kept the pistol lowered and listened. He called for the cutthroat to come out. He called again. The base of the pine trees were bleached white from the lamp's light and between their trunks Jeffers could see only darkness.

He looked down at the dog. One visible eye glinted in the sparse light. Jeffers looked back at the stand of pine trees before gripping the barrel of the pistol. He brought its handle down swiftly on the dog's skull to avoid firing a bullet in the middle of the night, which would bring the curiosity and ire of neighbors. And there was the cost of the bullet to consider.

He hit it again—and then a third time. After each strike,

he glanced back at the trees and saw only rib-white pine trunks and night. Jeffers peered down at the extinguished dog before limping back to the house, knowing the man in the pines was watching.

His sleep was chancy these days. Many nights he sat up, the vapors from the isopropyl alcohol rising from his feet, a subsuming numbness creeping further up his legs. He often mapped its ascent, trying to sense the true direction of the numbness, what area it would covet next, whether it had or would enter his spine or some other territory. When would it be too late to ask for help? When would the numbness settle in his stomach and make it impossible to eat? Or would it skip his stomach and spine and ground itself with fresh purchase in his heart? And then what? Death.

But this night Jeffers sat at his kitchen table, puffing on his pipe, replaying the events. He figured it was RD who had gutted the dog. He imagined the two, both lean and dirty animals—RD with the upper hand only because he had sense to bait the scrawny thing and could wield a knife.

Just before light, he went out with a shovel to remove the dog from the yard. Taped to the door was a list of LaRae's burial expenses written in an untrained hand. At the bottom, beneath the tally, was the message "You O me that much RD."

It was unlike Jeffers to befoul one of his properties and he wished he hadn't. He knew he might suffer for the considerable effort it took to carry the animal up a ladder, but he was angry and dropping the dog's gut-slung body down RD's chimney made him feel young, as if he were playing some outlandish prank. He knew the dog would get stuck in the flue and create an unbearable stink. But it had felt good, his legs felt strong.

Seated on his porch, a warm breeze eased him. Numbness slowly budded in his toes. Soon it would blossom up his legs, and then like vines it would gather around his waist and approach his back. Unrelieved numbness: faintly its tendrils would furl the base of his spine. He knew paralysis would take soon. He looked up at the bags of pennies and water. Such a simple measure, and a small cost to keep the flies at bay. With lips folded between teeth, he squelched a whimper.

As the numbness grew, he pondered over the list of expenses RD had tacked to his door. He thought of his own wives. One was buried in the city's cemetery and the other was buried in North Carolina. Even though it had been almost a decade, he knew by the tally tacked to his door that he'd spent more, given more respect, to his wives than RD had to LaRae.

He saw RD coming up the driveway, gripping something nearly hidden in his hand.

"Ain't you got business?" Jeffers blurted.

"I'm here on business. I've been to the funeral home."

He gazed down at RD, who was dressed in a shirt Jeffers wouldn't have used for a rag—threadbare in the chest, as if it belonged to a man who itched a lot. He noticed that RD was petting a rabbit's foot in his left hand, part of a keychain. "You bring that for luck?"

"Hell, I don't need no luck."

"You need something. You've eaten or buried the best part."

"You get my note."

"Yeah, I got your duns."

"I told them at the home you'll pay for it."

"You kill that dog?"

"LaRae said it was your wives that haunted her. Said you beat 'em."

"I never struck them."

"That's not what they said."

"You kill that dog?" Jeffers asked again.

"Said you should have to pay."

"You kill that dog?" Jeffers leaned forward, puffed smoke.

RD gnawed at the inside of his cheek. "Why don't you give me a smoke and I'll knock off a few dollars on that bill."

"You kill that dog?"

"I know who did. I'll tell you for ten dollars."

"So you know it's dead."

"I know you been asking about a dead one, and that one's been lately put out of its misery."

Jeffers shot a gleaming stream of spit at the little man without hitting him. "I didn't cause its misery."

"But you killed it."

"I put it down."

"Then why are you ragging on me about killing a dog?"

"Cause you're the one who gutted it to start with."

"I don't know about that," RD said.

"You don't know you gutted a dog?"

"I didn't."

Jeffers was silent.

Looking at the spit webbed across the parched green leaves of the boxwoods, RD said, "What's that dog mean to you?"

"Nothing. Having it slaughtered on my property does mean something."

"Well, I'll help you look for your dog-gutter if you pay for LaRae."

Jeffers felt the slight palpation of his heart. "I'm not paying you for a goddamn thing."

"You will."

"Why do you think I'll pay?"

"You want peace, don't you?"

Jeffers legs were numb, up to his stomach. At that moment, he wanted more than anything to chase RD down and beat him senseless.

Slightly hunched, RD eased up onto the porch as if he sensed weakness. He stood up and reached for one of the Ziploc bags of pennies and plucked it down from its nail. Jeffers's head twitched and he ground his teeth. There was no feeling whatsoever in his legs, as if he were dead from the waist down.

RD turned and walked down the steps.

"Hey," Jeffers called. "Come get this." Jeffers held up the funeral bill.

RD stood in the yard, with a big smile on his face, danced a burlesque and mocked masturbation and then spat a reddish brown streak. He wiped his chin. "You can knock four cents off that bill," he said. He turned and walked out of the yard, disappearing behind the trees.

His Sunday evening phone calls with James were little more than reminders—for James it reminded him that his father was still alive, and for Jeffers that his son was little more than a beggar, begging for a donation. Tonight James called asking about some article he'd sent Jeffers regarding blood circulation. Poor circulation: that was what was wrong with Jeffers, according to James.

They sat in silence, Jeffers listening to his son's breath and the hum of foreign ambience at the other end of the line. He yawned. He flicked off the lamp beside the chair and sat in the dark so he could see through the window to the little, unlighted house across the road. He opened his shirt and put a hand to his chest, his heart. His feet were cold in his bedroom shoes.

"Any more thought given to what you're going to do with the Ashcross place?"

"Some," Jeffers said.

"I spoke to the United Methodist Ministries. They said if I could get the land, they'd help me with the church."

"That so?"

"Yes."

James called it a perfect little hill to build a church upon. For Jeffers, property had to be earned. He *had* earned it, bought with monies he got paid from other lands, which he bought with monies he earned originally from labor in a dust-filthy mill. Everything he owned he'd earned. He wanted his son to earn it. James prated on about church, but Jeffers couldn't listen to him. He was angry with RD, angry with himself. He was going to have to get rid of the little man, evict him.

"Anything else going on up there?" James asked.

"Nothing."

"Did you get the squatters out of the house?"

"Not yet."

"You can't do anything with the place until you get them out."

Jeffers let out a meek *huh,* which his son didn't respond to. He flicked the light back on and saw himself in the blackened window with a hand across his chest as if he were taking a pledge. His face was sullen. He smiled at himself, mirthless, false. When he stopped smiling the leaden expression returned. His son wasn't speaking. Who was his confidant? Jeffers wondered.

"Don't make any decision about that place before talking to me," James said.

Jeffers didn't respond.

James sighed on the other end and told his father goodnight.

Jeffers got up the next morning surprised he'd had a good night's sleep. His feet were warm and when he stood he could feel them—he could feel the coolness of the floor. He was still angry, but he felt good and up to running off squatters. He would have to deal with RD soon, and getting Ashcross taken care of would be one less thing to worry about. He'd foregone calling the police.

In years past, just telling the squatters to leave did the trick. Sometimes he'd flash his pistol.

When he got to Ashcross he knocked on the front door and a young woman with a gaudy bloom of red- and yellow-dyed hair answered. She was very pregnant, and she smiled so brightly that Jeffers couldn't help thinking of a flower he wished he could pick. The young woman said her name was Lucinda, but that everyone called her Panky.

He didn't mention that he'd seen her before. He began by telling her that she was a squatter and that the property belonged to him. If she didn't clear out immediately, he would have her arrested for trespassing and demand back rent by garnering future earnings.

The young woman stood quietly as Jeffers finished speaking. After a few moments she spoke. "Someone told me and Toby it was empty and we could just stay a while until Toby got a job."

"I am the landlord. I charge rent on the people who live here."

"But it's been empty for a long time."

"That doesn't mean anything."

"But we have nowheres to go."

He'd never felt sorry for squatters or tenants, but Panky's festival hair, spray of freckles across her nose—her belly—released an unexpected shock of tenderness in his chest. He looked away, toward the trees and the catfish heads, as she continued to talk about their plucky intentions to stay briefly, have the baby, find a job for herself, find a better place. She just needed a little more time.

He hustled his pants around his haunchless hips. The weight of the pistol tugged on his trousers. His feet were going numb.

She was silent for a moment, and he looked back to see why she'd stopped talking. Then she said, "We could do some repairs on the house. Toby's good with that. Let us stay here and we'll fix it."

He hustled his pants again. He felt squirmy. His legs were being subsumed. His mind snarled with untethered thoughts. The woman before him, unpleasantly steady, continued to plead for more time. Her words became senseless in his ears.

He needed her. Or someone like her. This sudden upstroke of clarity frightened him. He needed someone to relieve him of the unrelenting loneliness of the last few years, someone to care for him. He was going to need care. He was dying and she was about to give life. She couldn't help it. Panky carried it inside her freely. He saw that.

Jeffers's mouth palsied inward before he stammered, "Do I look sick to you?"

Panky took a step back. "Maybe a little."

Jeffers stumbled forward. "How little?"

"Your face."

"What about my face?" He took another, cautious step forward. She parried his gaze and reached back for the doorknob.

Something uncoiled itself within his body. For a moment, he believed he might have pissed himself, and he patted his crotch, checking for dampness. He took another step toward Panky. He murmured—he wasn't sure what he had intended to say. He reached for his crotch, still not convinced that he hadn't soiled his trousers. He felt his mouth gape inexplicably. Panky blurted, "Mister, I don't know what you want." He stumbled forward and clasped his hand on her shoulder. She smacked at his hand. His thumb bit into the meat between her collarbone and rib cage. Panky grimaced and threw Jeffers's hand away.

He lurched forward. "I want you to tell me what I look like."

"You look sick. Like an old man," she said, swatting his hand as it reached out again.

"I am sick."

"Do you need me to get help?"

"Yes. Yes." He then turned and left the porch—Panky already behind the door. Jeffers heard scraping as if heavy furnishings were being drawn to block entry.

He cranked the truck and drove out of the pea-gravel drive. He wanted to howl or squall. He sensed he was running out of something. He gripped the steering wheel so tightly he felt the rubber give loose of the wheel inside the tubing.

He clenched his jaw until his partial denture bit into his gums and he could taste blood. He belched a laugh, or maybe it was a cry. He was stunned by how empty he felt. His crotch wasn't wet, but the numbness swarmed his legs and was advancing upward, a gripping numbness combined with a pressure that seemed to gnaw at the bone. He could no longer sense how deeply he pressed the accelerator or the brake. He let out a yowl and then wondered for a half second if there was someone else in the pickup with him. And then he did it again.

When he got home, RD was on his porch steps, smoking a pipe. Jeffers hissed.

He pulled his truck into the yard, coming as close to the porch as he could, got out, with the pistol in his hand, and walked slowly, purposefully, painfully the few steps to where RD sat, puffing, his lips drawn into a mirthful grin. All the bags of pennies were gone.

"That yours?" Jeffers asked, snatching the pipe out of RD's mouth.

"Just smoking a little. There's a god-awful smell over there and just wanted to smell something sweet for a little bit." RD cocked his head at the pistol. "That's a nice one."

"Maybe it's that haint of yours stinking up the place. Is it house-trained?"

"Where you been, landlord? You do some shooting?"

"What do you want, RD?"

"Money."

"Charity?"

"Call it what you like. It's all the same to me."

Jeffers collapsed in his porch chair, put the pistol across his lap, and cleaned RD's spit off the mouthpiece of the pipe with a handkerchief.

"Smells like something died over there, Jeffers."

"Well, she did." Jeffers swatted at a fly that had landed on his arm.

RD looked at him darkly. "Something new."

"Maybe you ought to clear out then, RD. Maybe it's that haint. Or it might be my wives wanting the house for themselves. Maybe they're tired of your laying about."

"Maybe." RD turned to leave. He spat a brown streak of spit in the yard. "When you're ready to settle up, you know where I live."

When RD was behind the pines, Jeffers exhaled a short strangled laugh, and then another, but it was more like a gasp. He placed the pistol on the little table beside him. His right leg twitched, his left crackled as if its very veins and capillaries were bursting. He rapped the pipe on the porch railing to clean out the tobacco RD had been smoking. He took out his pocketknife and scraped the chamber clean; he lighted a match and burned the mouthpiece a little. He sighed and let his body rest for a few moments.

He reached under the chair where he kept a pack of tobacco. Its weight was wrong—too light. Jeffers spread the bag open. Dust, ash, dirt? He wasn't sure. He leaned over and poured out the contents. Teeth fell out. Fragments of bone. The dog's? LaRae's? Another copy of the funeral bill lined the bottom of the tobacco bag. A small deduction had been made for the tobacco RD had smoked and the pennies.

A fly landed on his hand.

By the time he walked to the squat-gable house, he was sweating and quaking with a chill. The numbness in his legs scoured him bone to flesh. He didn't know why he hadn't driven the short distance. Impatient with RD's games, he'd gotten out the lawn chair and shoved his pistol in his right front pocket and descended the porch steps half blind with anger.

He entered the front door with his own key and limped into the tiny living room, bare except for a tattered recliner and an empty TV stand with a midden of chicken bones and stale French fries littered across it. The smell of the dog was monstrous.

In the kitchen, empty bean cans lined the counter and most of the cabinet doors hung open. A spoon, crusted and unpolished, reclined in the sink. Jeffers could hear RD moving around in the back of the house. He listened for a few moments before continuing down the hall. He passed a slender closet, empty except for a lone, bent coat hanger. He passed the bathroom, darkened and faintly urinous.

When he reached the bedroom, he was surprised by the vision of RD seized in a blade of dust-speckled sunlight—shirtless, his bones seemingly lifted to just under his skin. It was as if Famine itself stood before Jeffers in a swirl of ash and red-brown light. RD smiled at him.

As if heat lightning passed through the little house, he glimpsed a future and past. He reimagined the death rictus of his Ashcross renter long ago. His first wife's closed coffin. He saw his own death—the paralysis, the absolute loss of modesty. His son, robed, offering up thanks to heaven for his father and for land. Jeffers removed the pistol from his pocket, pointed it at RD, and pulled the trigger. The little man snapped up in the dusty air and landed on his back.

He looked down upon the little man gasping, observed his twitching, witnessed a tiny spring of blood bubble up and then flow. RD grasped at his chest, his breath already shortening.

"What do you see?" Jeffers demanded.

"What?" RD spat.

Jeffers crouched over RD and moved in close enough to feel the other's moist breath. "What do you *see?*"

A half smile, half grimace palsied RD's face. "I see you." He rolled over and tried to stand.

Jeffers shoved RD back to the floor. He stepped to the window and drew the copper-colored curtains.

"You goin to get me some help?"

Jeffers turned from the window and in the cheap light raised the pistol and shot RD again. A shallow splatter of blood leapt from RD's chest, a near-inaudible grunt left his mouth. Jeffers resumed his position over RD's face.

"And now, do you see anything?"

RD squinted. "You got to help me."

"What do you see?" Jeffers roared.

"You don't have to pay that bill."

Jeffers stepped away from the spread of blood. He pointed the pistol at RD again, but then didn't shoot. He thought he saw some change in the little man. "What do you see?"

"You," RD gasped. "I see you. Help me."

Jeffers asked him again and again what he was seeing, but it didn't change. Jeffers was in disbelief that he was awaiting a man so given to lies as RD to tell him the truth. RD tried to crawl. Jeffers struck him, and then again, thrashing like a man at labor. The little man curled tighter and clutched his head after each blow.

Finally both men were still. Jeffers leaned in. He turned RD's head and held his crumpled cheek tenderly as a nurse might do. "What's there? What do you see?"

There was no answer. RD was dead.

Jeffers sat for a spell in the recliner. With his index finger he pushed at the pile of dry chicken bones and withered fries. He could no longer smell the stench of the dog rotting in the chimney. He could feel his legs and feet, but knew it wouldn't last long.

He could sense the numbness creeping in again, and he removed his shoes and socks so he could rub his toes. *We are perched atop nothingness,* Jeffers thought, *we make up heavens, but we are atop nothing.* He didn't want to go home. He called his son.

They took his pistol, his belt, and the laces of his shoes and put him in the back of the patrol car. His son was running his mouth to the police. He couldn't hear what was being said. He wanted his pipe, which still rested on the porch railing where he'd left it.

He was numb up to his waist.

As Jeffers began to close his eyes, the glimpse of a specter stopped him. In the distance, crouched between pine trees, he saw something beautiful. She was unmistakable, with an ornate flourish of hair, her round pregnant belly. She had come to his house, had come to see him, to help him. Jeffers stared at her, hoping that she would turn and look his way, see him behind the glass, give some forgiveness. He needed that gift. But she looked past him, watching James and the police. He wept dryly, knowing that he had earned nothing today. She turned to walk back into the pines. Jeffers watched the disappearing carnival of hair and the bubble of a cry burst from his lips.

JOE DONNELLY AND HARRY SHANNON

Fifty Minutes

FROM *Slake: Los Angeles*

THE CLIENT IS a balding, sunburned man with soft, forgettable features. Running late, he enters the office at 7:02 p.m. and nearly knocks a small Buddha statue from its wooden base. He closes the waiting room door behind him and pauses, unsure of the protocol. From behind his desk, Dr. Bell watches intently. Experience has taught him that a new client will give you 90 percent of what you need just walking through the door. Dr. Bell sees that Mr. Potter is mildly agitated—perspiration rings the armpits of his Hawaiian-print shirt and his breathing is rapid. Not unusual for a first-timer, Dr. Bell thinks. The psychotherapist smiles wryly and motions for Potter to sit on the green couch. Mr. Potter collapses into the cushions and sets his leather shoulder bag in front of him. His khaki slacks are a size behind the times.

"How long does this last?" Mr. Potter asks. "An hour?"

"Fifty minutes," Dr. Bell says pleasantly.

The new client stares at Dr. Bell for a moment, takes a deep breath, and pulls a small-caliber pistol from under his shirt.

"Fine," Mr. Potter says, waving the gun at Dr. Bell. "Then you have fifty minutes to live."

An aluminum taste floods Dr. Bell's mouth. Trauma patients have told him this is what true fear tastes like, but until now he'd never taken them literally. Sure, every shrink has stories about unhinged patients. A client in the middle of a manic episode once threatened to scratch out Dr. Bell's eyes with her car keys if he didn't introduce her to her soul mate, Johnny Depp, but nothing has prepared him for this.

Coherent thoughts vanish in the vacuum of fear. Struggling to find a way back, Dr. Bell takes a quick inventory. The landline is across the room on an end table, and besides, what would he do with it? Propped against the wall, also out of reach, is his souvenir baseball bat, a gift from a professional ballplayer Dr. Bell helped get back on track after he washed out on coke and hookers. *Should I yell, scream, lunge for the gun? Or can this guy be reasoned with?* Dr. Bell wonders. Despite the beads of sweat on Mr. Potter's upper lip, he appears relatively stable. His eyes aren't darting and he's not pumping his legs. His resolve appears to be genuine, possibly deadly. Dr. Bell tries to remain calm and go with what he knows. Talking.

"Clearly, you're quite upset. I'm sorry."

"You are?"

"I don't like to see anyone in pain."

"Really, Dr. Bell? Is that so?"

Dr. Bell looks into Mr. Potter's eyes, trying to project empathy.

"Yes. I believe that's why I chose this profession, Mr. Potter, and why, I suppose, I'm so highly regarded in my field." Dr. Bell thinks he sees Mr. Potter relax just a bit. He presses on. "May I call you by your first name?"

"No, you may not," Mr. Potter says firmly. "I know what you're trying to do. It won't work. I hated seeing her in pain, too, Dr. Bell."

"Who, Mr. Potter?"

"You know."

"Forgive me, I don't believe I do. And needless to say, for the purposes of this discussion, that places me at a serious disadvantage. Please, tell me who you are talking about."

Mr. Potter crosses his legs and his pants ride up too high, revealing short black socks. Dr. Bell can see that his new client's shin is badly bruised and a bandage covers a fresh wound. Dr. Bell takes a long look at the man's shoulder bag. A slot on the front flap has a laminated name tag of the sort frequent fliers fill out. Mr. Potter glances at his watch, purses his lips as if about to give the time, but says nothing. Dr. Bell tells himself to stay in control of the situation.

"Okay, Mr. Potter," he says, as evenly as possible. "Let me try a different question. Why do you want to kill me?"

"Oh, I think you know."

"I really don't, and I must confess I have little experience with this. No one has ever threatened to kill me before. At least not seriously."

"There's always a first time, yes?"

"Mr. Potter, did you make this appointment in order to kill me?"

Mr. Potter does not answer.

He's giving me a blank screen, no expression, no emotion, Dr. Bell thinks. *Perhaps he's imitating a trained therapist, maybe a therapist who has something to do with why he's here? A bit of a reach, but . . .*

"May I ask who referred you to me, Mr. Potter—another professional?"

"I'm not the type who feels the need to talk incessantly about his feelings, Dr. Bell. You're the last therapist I expect to see in my life. And the clock, as they say, is ticking."

It suddenly comes to Dr. Bell that Mr. Potter must have booked this appointment, the last available on a Friday, at least a week ago. He's planned this well. A joke about needing to better screen first-time clients sweeps through Dr. Bell's brain like a tumbleweed. He thinks better of sharing it. He has to crack Mr. Potter's shell delicately, if it is in fact a shell. Fifty minutes isn't a lot of time to do it. But Dr. Bell is starting to realize his life depends on it.

The second hand on the grandfather clock ticks away and Mr. Potter seems to grow larger, more intimidating. Despite the urgency of the situation, Dr. Bell knows it is imperative not to let the clock rule him. *He wants more than to just kill me or he'd have done that already. Let him have his theatrics for now. The need to speak will build. He'll tell you why he's here eventually. He'll have to, or what's the point?*

Dr. Bell flashes back to his student days, when a gifted supervisor used father transference to reduce him to a whimpering puddle. Dr. Bell crosses his legs, struggling to appear above it all, but his knees feel weak and his fingers tremble slightly.

"Forty-six minutes," Mr. Potter announces, "and seven seconds."

Dr. Bell takes a deep breath and releases the air quietly, allows himself a thin smile. His stomach settles. He holds the smile as best he can and tries to affect something just shy of disdain. "Okay, then. This is your time, as we say. What do you want to talk about?"

"I don't want to talk about anything. I want you to do all the talking."

"What is it that you want me to talk about?"

"You know, Dr. Bell."

"No, I don't, Mr. Potter, and I fear that our time will go by in silence if it's left up to me to guess why you came here, other than to threaten to kill me. But maybe that's the best place to start. Why don't you tell me why you believe you want to kill me?"

"Because you're a fraud, Dr. Bell."

"Why do you think so, Mr. Potter?"

"I think you know."

"I really don't, and we're in danger of getting stuck in this circular dialogue, but let me try something else. Let's presume that I am a fraud, which we all are to some degree. What does that mean to you?"

"It means that I'm going to kill you."

"Do you kill all frauds, Mr. Potter, or is it just me for whom you reserve that honor?"

"Maybe I'm starting with you."

"So what comes next? Politicians, CEOs, clergymen . . . Jodie Foster? Is someone speaking to you, Mr. Potter, telling you that you've been chosen to do these things?"

"No, Dr. Bell, I'm not schizophrenic, paranoid or otherwise. I haven't lost my job, my home, my standing in society. I'm not mad at the world. I'm an average man, Dr. Bell. But sometimes average men have to do extraordinary things."

Mr. Potter raises the gun. The barrel is a deep, dark well. Dr. Bell's bowels suddenly stir. He notices Mr. Potter's hand is not trembling.

"One shot through the front of your skull and you're done, Dr. Bell. I understand you fancy yourself a Buddhist. What do you imagine occurs next? Will it be a joyful reconnection with the one consciousness? Or perhaps just zip, nada, nothing? Tell me, I'm curious. You see, this is not really my fifty minutes, it is yours."

Dr. Bell tries to process quickly. *"I understand" you fancy yourself a Buddhist. Not "I see" you fancy yourself one. He's either done his research or heard about me through someone else. He mentioned a woman earlier, having seen her in pain. His wife? His girlfriend? His mother?* Dr. Bell struggles to think of a female patient with the same last name. Too many faces, too many names. *Someone terminal, perhaps? Someone from the cancer ward?* He draws a blank. *The years of practice are callusing me. The faces and names and problems and patterns are all running together.*

If he's realized anything over the years, it's that each and every one of his patients is sure that he or she occupies a new and entirely unique spot at the center of the universe and Dr. Bell has become all too aware of how crowded it is at that spot. Did he believe anything was different from one week, month, year, or life to the next with his patients? Did he even care anymore? Every week they pay their $150 a session to say and hear the same things, and every week they leave satiated like crack addicts, only to come back with that hungry, desperate look in their eyes realizing they need another fix.

Mr. Potter lowers the weapon. "Where did you go just now?" he asks, leaning forward, but not in a threatening manner. "When I did that with the gun, what did you see? Feel? I'd really like to know."

Dr. Bell swallows. "Mr. Potter, you just mentioned putting a bullet through my skull. You're pointing a gun at me. So, naturally, I felt afraid. Buddhist or not, I'm not looking forward to dying here, today, and in this way. Understandable, yes?"

"Yes, quite understandable. But we don't always have a say in what happens to us, do we, Dr. Bell?"

"You're speaking of karma?"

Mr. Potter shrugs.

Dr. Bell tells himself to keep Mr. Potter talking. *Get him to give you his first name. Make yourself a human being. It's easy to hurt an object or a symbol, but not so easy to hurt another human being.*

"Of course the world is often a random place. That fact does not prove or disprove the idea of karma," says Dr. Bell. "But that's a moot point right now, for this isn't at all random. You came here with a purpose. I'm trying to figure out what brought you to this place. What drove you to come here and terrorize me in this way?"

Mr. Potter scratches his nose with the barrel of the gun.

"Tell me your first name," Dr. Bell says. "I'd like to be less formal, especially under the circumstances."

Mr. Potter stands up and shakes his head. "Just keep talking," he says, pacing in front of the green couch.

"Okay, I'm thinking that if you came here just to kill me, you would have done it by now. So why don't you tell me what else it is that you're looking for? You said I'm a Buddhist. Who told you that? And does this person have something to do with why else you're here?"

"You know who that person is, Dr. Bell, and you now have forty-one minutes and thirty-two seconds to tell me why you did it."

Dr. Bell feels his forced calm giving way to a tempest of frustration, his anxiety flaring into anger. He shakes inside with as much outrage as fear. Dr. Bell has to fight his urge to charge the man with the gun, to do violence to Mr. Potter for the way he is being violated. But he knows that could be a fatal mistake. Mr. Potter seems to register this wave passing through Dr. Bell. He takes half a step back and levels the gun. He finds the edge of the couch with one hand and sits down. Smiles.

Dr. Bell takes a deep breath and reminds himself not to telegraph his feelings. "So we know someone in common. Or you think we do. Is that correct?"

"Yes, Dr. Bell. It is. Continue . . ." Mr. Potter takes another theatrical look at his watch. "Time, after all, isn't on your side."

"Was this someone a patient of mine?"

"She was. Her name was Katherine Cook."

"Katherine Cook. I don't recall seeing anyone named Katherine Cook."

"Try harder. She sometimes went by Katie."

"Can you describe her to me?"

"She was beautiful . . . beautiful, and full of life. Until she met you."

"So you say. A young woman named Katie Cook. How long did she see me, for how many sessions?"

"Long enough to be destroyed."

"By me, I assume, in your worldview, which I'm beginning to think of as increasingly aberrant. Tell, me, Mr. Potter, what happened to your leg?" Dr. Bell scowls, framing the question just shy of an accusation.

The sudden change of topic confuses Mr. Potter. He glances down at his bruised leg and the small bandage, clearly startled. His gun hand goes lax and Dr. Bell thinks it's now or never if he's going to go for the weapon. But before he can make his move, Mr. Potter pushes down his pants leg, his face flushed, and regains himself.

Something is there, thinks Dr. Bell.

"I want you to tell me precisely what happened," Dr. Bell says. "Did you hurt someone?"

Mr. Potter purses his lips like a goldfish at the edge of the bowl. He struggles for breath. His face reddens, tics associated with shame and anxiety, clearly a regressive response. Dr. Bell knows it's time to play his highest card.

"What have you done, Martin?"

The sudden use of the man's first name peels back another layer of defense. Mr. Potter's composure melts, his face is that of a scared child. Dr. Bell reminds himself that he's walking a fine line. Children are easy to break down, but they also act impulsively and without thought of consequence. And this one is carrying a gun. Dr. Bell eases up a little.

"It's there on your name tag," Dr. Bell says evenly. "Martin Potter, 3712 Moorpark Street, Apartment 11, North Hollywood . . . I can't quite make out the Zip Code."

Dr. Bell hopes this traditional disarming move, using Mr. Potter's first name, placing him at his address, identifying him as a person with a life outside this office, will blunt his aggressiveness, give Dr. Bell the room he needs to exploit Mr. Potter's insecurities. Clearly Mr. Potter exhibits signs of regret. But where has this taken him? Is he suffering from a character disorder, severe perhaps? Is he projecting his own guilt onto Dr. Bell—reaction formation? Dr. Bell softens, leans forward, and lowers his voice.

"I'm sorry if I snapped at you, Martin," he says. "I'm deeply worried, and not just about my own safety. About you as well. Have you perhaps already hurt someone else?"

Mr. Potter stares back dully, traumatized. His fingers loosen a bit and the gun sags in his hands as if it's suddenly a great weight. Dr. Bell again considers going for it, but he's making progress breaking Mr. Potter's resolve. Best to stick with it.

Mr. Potter falls back into the couch, which nearly consumes him. "I haven't hurt anybody, Dr. Bell. In fact, I'm pretty sure you'll be the first. And you can call me Mr. Potter, if you don't mind. We're not ever going to be on a first-name basis."

"Fair enough, Mr. Potter. Why don't you tell me about what happened to your leg, then?"

Mr. Potter pauses, takes a deep breath. He regains some of his composure. "Very well, Dr. Bell, I will, since it does concern you and not indirectly."

"It does?"

"Yes. You see, Dr. Bell, I hurt my leg when I walked into Ms. Cook's apartment last Tuesday and found her . . ."

Mr. Potter's voice trails off, his eyes close.

Dr. Bell tries to wait him out, a game of chicken played in tense silence. He is surprised to find his own nerve fails first. "You *found* her?"

Mr. Potter's eyes snap open like a man tied to train tracks who hears a loud whistle. "I didn't do anything. I didn't hurt her. It was you, I know it was you."

"Ms. Cook. Tell me what happened to Ms. Cook," Dr. Bell presses.

Mr. Potter grows more agitated. He waves the weapon like a dowsing rod and Dr. Bell flinches involuntarily.

"I found her that way. Hanging there. From one of those pull-up bars you put in a doorway? She'd tied the sash of her robe around her neck and . . . or so it appeared . . . Maybe someone arranged it to look that way." Mr. Potter lowers his head.

"Go on, Mr. Potter," Dr. Bell says, voice thickening. "How did you happen to be at Ms. Cook's apartment—were the two of you . . . friends?"

"I didn't know her. But I loved her." Mr. Potter's eyes cloud and he looks close to crying. "It was an awful thing to see."

Dr. Bell says nothing, waits for more. Mr. Potter wipes his eyes and nose on his right sleeve. He looks up, angry now, and points the gun once more in Dr. Bell's direction. Dr. Bell recoils.

"I know what you're thinking, but it wasn't like that," Mr. Potter says. "I really did love her. From afar, yes, but it was pure and true."

Bell takes a shot. "You've been following her?"

Mr. Potter reddens again. "Yes, yes. I followed her. I saw her in that supermarket at Burbank and Laurel Canyon, buying vegetables. She looked familiar, and then I realized I'd seen her in a commercial, the one for cat food."

He waits for Dr. Bell to register a sign of recognition.

"I'm sorry, Mr. Potter. I haven't seen it. I don't watch much television, and when I do it tends to be CNN or MSNBC. I don't recall seeing this cat-food commercial."

"Ms. Cook was wearing a long-sleeved sweater," Mr. Potter continues, as if Dr. Bell had said nothing, wasn't even there. "It was beige, almost the color of her hair, and a pair of worn jeans. Those big blue eyes . . . I wanted to say something right away, but I was too shy. So I followed her to her car and watched her load the groceries. I knew it wasn't right, but what was the harm so long as I didn't harass her? Lots of men look at someone like that, all day long I'm sure."

Dr. Bell just stares back, regaining some leverage.

Mr. Potter looks away again, flustered. "Well, I went back to the grocery store the next day at the same time, and there she was again," he continues, looking beyond Dr. Bell into some darkened corner. "At first I just followed her around the store, watching her and wondering what it would be like to be with her . . . you know, shopping with her. Going through a day with her."

Dr. Bell sees an opening. "But that's not where it stopped, is it, Mr. Potter?"

"No, it's not," Mr. Potter says, mostly to himself. "I looked her up on the Internet, found her on IMDb, familiarized myself with her background. She grew up in Ohio. Went to NYU, where she studied theater. Came out here to follow her dreams, like a lot of us do, right, Dr. Bell?"

"Would you say this was a healthy fixation, Mr. Potter?"

"Is love a fixation, Dr. Bell? I suppose it might be. But I did hope to talk to her one day, so why wouldn't I be prepared? I went back to the supermarket every day at the same time and saw her there. She only ever picked up a few things. Sometimes it seemed like she just did it for the routine. Routines can be comforting, Dr. Bell."

"They can be, Mr. Potter, but some are more appropriate than others. Did you ever speak to Ms. Cook?"

"I was too shy to approach her in the grocery store. I didn't want to seem like . . . well, I didn't want to intrude. Finally I did follow her to her apartment building—"

"You followed her home?" Dr. Bell cuts in, accusingly.

"Yes, I did, but only because I was so enchanted. I watched her unload the bag of groceries. I sat in my car, telling myself to leave, that this was silly, but then she came right back out again and got in her car."

Mr. Potter stops, raises his head again, and stares directly at Dr. Bell. "She drove here, to your office, Dr. Bell."

"So you say, Mr. Potter," Dr. Bell says, turning in his chair, putting his back to Mr. Potter, "but why should I believe any of this?

I don't know you. I don't know this woman you speak of. You're obviously going through something and I'd like to help you—"

"Please face me, Dr. Bell. I can shoot you just as well through that chair and I'll be inclined to do it sooner than later if you don't turn around so I can see you."

Dr. Bell takes a deep breath and turns back around to face Mr. Potter.

"Okay, Mr. Potter. You say this woman, Ms. Cook, came here?"

"Yes, here. I followed her here."

"What day was that, Mr. Potter?"

"Tuesday . . . of last week. She was here for nearly two hours," Mr. Potter says, fondling the gun. "Yet these appointments last fifty minutes, yes?"

"But I don't have a client named Katie Cook. There was no Katie Cook here last Tuesday. I'm positive, but if it makes a difference, I'll check my appointment ledger."

Dr. Bell flips backward through his calendar to the date in question and runs his index finder down the page. "No, no Katie Cook, or Katherine Cook, Mr. Potter. I'm sorry to disappoint you."

"But you have an appointment booked with someone named Katherine, don't you, Dr. Bell? Didn't you? Goddammit, didn't you!"

Dr. Bell tells himself to stay calm, show nothing.

"Yes, Mr. Potter. I did book a double appointment, with a woman named Katherine Friedman, a relatively new client. I was just getting to know her. She double-booked because she was going to miss the following week, going to Hawaii or something. Patients do that all the time, book double appointments. You understand, right?"

"I understand that you're telling your story, Dr. Bell. I also understand that Katie Cook was Katherine Friedman's stage name, but I'm sure you know that, don't you?"

"No, Mr. Potter, I don't know that. I don't know anything you're talking about. All I know is that someone whom I suspect is delusional is pointing a gun at me and talking in riddles."

"What about that night, Dr. Bell? What happened later that night?"

"I don't know," Dr. Bell replies, feeling an icy ripple up his spine, "but I'm afraid you do."

"I waited outside in my car," says Mr. Potter, pointing his gun toward the window facing the street, "for two hours, Dr. Bell, while she was in here with you. Then I followed her home. I parked outside her apartment. I tried to get the courage to walk up and introduce myself but just couldn't do it, you know? I just couldn't. I'm shy around pretty girls. Lots of men are."

Dr. Bell could see Mr. Potter getting more excited, his pupils dilating now, his hands wavering, one foot tapping steadily. *He's coming down from some kind of meds,* Dr. Bell thinks. *He may already be having some auditory or visual hallucinations.*

"May I change the subject for just a moment, Mr. Potter? If you don't mind my asking, are you, or have you been, on psychotropic medication? Are you taking anything for stress, anxiety, PTSD?"

Mr. Potter sneers and grips the gun tightly. "You shrinks are all alike. Don't try to twist things around. That's not going to work with me."

"I'm sorry I interrupted," Dr. Bell says soothingly. "Please continue. You were parked on the street outside when Ms. Friedman, or shall we say Ms. Cook, came to see me?"

The door to the waiting room opens, a buzzer sounds. Dr. Bell stiffens in his chair. Mr. Potter raises the gun.

"Wait," Dr. Bell says. "I haven't scheduled anyone else."

"Send whoever it is away or I'll kill you," Mr. Potter says under his breath, leaning forward but not standing.

"If you kill me there will apparently be a witness."

"You are the murderer," Mr. Potter hisses. "You killed a patient. How could anyone blame me for killing you?"

"I've killed no one," Dr. Bell replies with as much even-voiced authority as he can muster. "I'm so sorry, but whatever you're going through here, it has nothing to do with me other than the fact that I happened to treat Ms. Friedman the day you followed her home. They call that stalking, Mr. Potter. Let me help you. Perhaps I can prescribe something that will give you some rest."

"No more pills!" Mr. Potter yells, almost infantile in his fury. "I'm tired of the damn pills. You guys have a pill for everything. *I saw you.*" Mr. Potter's lips curl and quiver. "I saw you go into that girl's apartment. I saw you run out a few minutes later and drive away. Something about the way you left made me fear for her safety. So I went to Ms. Cook's apartment and found her. You tried to make it look like a suicide, but I know the truth, I know you killed her.

What happened, did she threaten to take you to the professional board, cost you your license, tell your wife?"

Dr. Bell rises from his chair, puts his hand on his desk, and speaks slowly. "I honestly don't know what you're talking about, Mr. Potter. *Mr. Martin Potter,* of 3712 Moorpark Street, Apartment 11. But I do know you're very upset right now, and that things feel like they have gone . . . out of focus. Please don't do anything rash when an event such as this is taking place. You're not stable. During these . . . these breaks, things that seem certain to you are not at all what you think. The subconscious is out on parade in full daylight and the normal consciousness—reality, as it were—is in the shadows. Do you understand, Mr. Potter? Do you realize you're just passing through something that won't be here when you come back?"

"No, no. It's not like that. It's not how you say. I have proof. I'm not crazy, Dr. Bell."

Mr. Potter reaches inside his pants pocket. Dr. Bell clenches and retreats to his chair.

"Proof? Proof of a manic episode?" protests Dr. Bell.

"You were there," Mr. Potter says. "See?"

Mr. Potter holds up his cell phone, which is playing a short clip of video. Dr. Bell squints. "That simply isn't me," he says. "You have a blurred image of someone my general size and weight, Martin." He pauses for a moment. "Wait, and how did you think you knew what I looked like in the first place?"

"You walked her to the outside door, Dr. Bell. I saw you say goodbye to Katie Cook," Potter says triumphantly. "You hugged her."

"I often hug my patients, Mr. Potter. It's not something the board necessarily approves of, but it is a natural human response to a developing connection and not out of the ordinary with relatively new clients. Empathy, nothing more. And I resent the implication I'd get romantically involved with someone such as poor Ms. Friedman, or Cook as you know her."

"Sure. Protest all you want. *I know.*"

Dr. Bell leans forward. "Mr. Potter, what I know is that you are off your meds, you've been stalking a beautiful young woman, and that you're at minimum hiding valuable information from the police. Perhaps this was a suicide. If not, you may even be implicated in a murder. And I still want to know what happened to your leg."

"Never mind my leg. Dr. Bell, why don't you tell the truth? Your fifty minutes are just about up."

"I've told you the truth, Martin. I can't tell you any more. I had a new client who fits your description. She booked a double appointment last week before she was to go away on business. And now you say this woman is dead and you are the only person who we know was at the scene of the death and you've admitted to me that you've been stalking her. I'm sure if I wanted to, I could go to the board and find a record of your psychiatric treatment."

"Wait, wait, you're turning this around on me." Mr. Potter looks drained, his composure gone. "You, you're the one. I know it." Mr. Potter raises the gun with trembling hands. It wavers in front of him for what seems like an eternity. Something in Dr. Bell tells him this is it. He ducks behind his desk. A shot rings out and the bullet thumps into the wall above his head. The sound is dull, lifeless, like a staple gun shooting into a piece of wood. It's not at all what he would have expected. Dr. Bell stays down and waits. But there is nothing more, only the sound of Mr. Potter running out the door.

Dr. Bell holds still for a minute. Silence. He thinks about what to do next. Gingerly he opens the door to the waiting room and finds a kid there cowering on his couch, looking like he'd seen a ghost.

"Who are you?" Dr. Bell asks.

"Look . . . I'm, I'm just here to sell magazine subscriptions. What . . . what just happened?"

"Wait here," Dr. Bell says, locking the front door. "I'm calling the police. Did you get a good look at the guy? Could you describe him? He may be a murderer."

"Yeah . . . yes. I think I so. Yes," the kid stutters.

Dr. Bell goes back into his office and picks up his phone to call the authorities. But first he erases the message from Katherine Friedman, the actress who goes by the stage name Katie Cook, the one who'd left yet another rage-filled outburst on his office voicemail in which she said that they must speak about what was going on with them, how she'd had enough of his empty promises, how she was going to Hawaii for a couple weeks, and how she expected him to have told his wife by the time she got back or she didn't know what she would do, maybe *she'd* tell his wife, or maybe she'd kill herself; there was also something else about how the board might be interested in his methods . . . Dr. Bell hadn't listened all the way through. He was familiar enough with these rants by now, familiar enough to know these were no longer idle threats.

All that was left to do now was call the police. Then he could, for the first time in fifty minutes, thank god, or whatever you want to call it, for Mr. Martin Potter.

KATHLEEN FORD

Man on the Run

FROM *New England Review*

Ithaca, New York, 2003

"This isn't the first time the McGuires have taken in a man on the run," Rosemary said to the imaginary crowd beyond the stove. She loved the drama in her words, even though they weren't exactly true. She and her sister hadn't taken in a man but a woman, and the woman wasn't running from the law but from a boyfriend. Still, the situations weren't entirely different. When the crowd roared, Rosemary took the wooden spoon out of the oatmeal, whacked it on the rim of the pot, and waved it at them. Then she shuffled to the hall and looked up the stairs to where the poor girl was sleeping.

Last night, after the battered girl climbed the stairs, Rosemary had called to her to ask if she could see the lake. "Sorry, Aunt Rosemary," the girl answered. "It's pitch black." Rosemary rested her forehead on the newel post, remembering how the upstairs windows turned into shiny black mirrors, and how, when she stood in front of them, she felt she was inside a glass ball.

Francis, Rosemary's husband, had wanted curtains, but Rosemary loved the bare windows. She loved looking out to the water and the wide stretch of lake, and besides, she always told him, there wasn't any need to cover the windows because no one could look inside. A pine grove stood at the front of the house and a brush-covered hill was at the back. The hill fell away as sharply as a sliding board, and at its base was Cayuga Lake—a lake so deep the water never froze.

*

Hours before, when Rosemary first woke, she'd gripped the hand-rail and hoisted herself up the steps. She thought that by using her hands, she'd spare her hips, but she hadn't taken her upper body into consideration. She hadn't considered how she'd get down the stairs either. Frightened and wobbly, she'd bounced down on her backside, so now, in addition to the usual aches in her hips and knees, her elbows and shoulders were throbbing.

Even so, it had been worth it. It was worth a million aches to see the sleeping girl's hair spilled out like golden seaweed. Rosemary's brothers and sister had been blessed with that same glorious hair, while Rosemary had been cursed with hair like the strings on a coconut. But in the next generation, the injustice was righted and the honey-colored hair passed only to Rosemary's daughter, Moira. And now, here it was in still another generation. Linda—the girl with the bruised face and swollen lips—was the granddaughter of Rosemary's oldest brother.

When Rosemary's daughter was a toddler, strangers would stop to ask if they could touch her hair. By age six, Moira gave permission herself. The girl's nod told people she understood her own beauty—her blue eyes and perfect features, her black eyebrows and golden crown. When she became a teenager, Moira rinsed her hair with lemon juice and brushed it every night. On winter nights, her hair came alive and threw sparks in the air. At age twenty, when Moira lay in her coffin, her face as smooth and peaceful as an angel's, people leaned over to touch her hair.

Rosemary turned when the water began its whistle. She was ninety-one, but her hearing was sharper than a guard dog's. She could hear the drip of water in the basement washtubs and the crunch of gravel in the neighbor's drive. She could hear the beating of birds' wings as they flew to and from their nests in the fir trees. And lately, after determining that the scratching sounds weren't branches brushing against the house, she could hear the scurrying of squirrels in the attic. Once she identified exactly what the noise was, it was easy to picture the dirty pests nibbling away at her papers. Just thinking about the nasty rodents made her stiff with fury. She dreamed of firing Mike's pistol into the rafters and leaving poisoned chestnuts in the eaves, but she had as much chance of getting to the attic as of landing on the moon.

Rosemary shut off the teakettle and tilted her head. Ordinary creaks came from the second floor while a whine like a pipe organ came from Betty's room off the kitchen. Rosemary was used to her sister's snoring. Betty was up half the night going back and forth to the bathroom, then she slumbered the morning away.

In the sitting room, Rosemary pressed the back of her knees against the cushion and sank faster than she planned. She folded her hands and smiled at the memory of the golden hair. "May perpetual light shine upon her, O Lord," she whispered, "and may her soul, and the souls of all the faithful departed, rest in peace." Rosemary had prayed for the repose of Moira's soul for fifty years, and for fifty years she'd regretted being talked into a home wake.

Rosemary didn't believe it was natural for a mother to want her daughter to be put in the earth, but with every moment Moira's body remained unburied Rosemary feared for her daughter's soul. Throughout the days of waking, when Moira lay in her coffin on the table in the front room, Betty never stopped talking. The mourners came and went, filling and emptying the rooms, but Betty rattled on, explaining how the poor girl had taken Rosemary's car even though she'd been warned the brake lights weren't working.

Rosemary, numb with shock, understood that Betty kept telling the story about the broken brake lights in order to shield her from blame. But every time Rosemary heard the story, she felt only guilt—for being too weak to insist that the car was unfit to be driven.

*

"Is Linda awake?" Betty said, coming into the sitting room in her red quilted robe.

"Not yet," Rosemary answered.

Betty sank to the sofa. "Well, now we have proof, if we ever needed it."

"Proof?"

"Of the power of prayer."

"What are you saying, Betty?"

"My prayers have been answered."

"Betty, what are you talking about?"

"Ever since Mike graduated, I've been praying that someone would come to help us. When Al told us he was moving, I really stormed the heavens with my prayers, and now, here she is—a girl to help us."

"You think this poor girl is an answer to your prayers?" Rosemary stared at her sister, but Betty looked away.

It was true that they'd been in a fix since Mike moved back to Texas, but back then Rosemary hadn't realized how bad their situation really was. She'd assumed another Cornell student would take Mike's place in the neighbors' basement apartment, and that this other young person would be happy to make some money running errands. She hadn't thought that the neighbors would lock up the house and go on sabbatical. She hadn't thought that the other students on Mike's list would be busy. Then, in what turned out to be an even bigger surprise, Al Murphy—the son of one of Francis's old colleagues—announced that he was retiring. Al said he needed the sun; he was moving to Florida.

Rosemary and Betty were on a church list for a driver and errand-runner, but so far no one had turned up except Gladys O'Farrell, a seventy-year-old woman who took them to Sunday mass. On the way home from church, Gladys sometimes let Betty go into the store for milk or eggs, but usually Gladys was in a hurry to drop them back home.

Every few weeks, Betty called a cab to go to the hairdresser. The taxi wouldn't come down the sloped driveway the way Gladys did and that meant Rosemary couldn't go at all.

"Our situation," Rosemary had said two weeks ago, when she looked at the dwindling supply of canned soup and tuna fish, "isn't good. You might even say it's desperate."

"I'll pray to Saint Jude," Betty had said.

Rosemary put her hands on the armrests and tried to lift herself, but her elbows screamed and she fell back. Meanwhile, Betty, whose face was settled comfortably in a smug smile, was swinging her left leg like a beauty queen. "Little Miss Muffet sits on her tuffet," Rosemary mumbled.

Rosemary didn't believe having a grandniece beaten up by someone described as a "psychopath" was the answer to any prayers, and no one, no matter how desperate, would pray that a young woman would have to change her whole life around to avoid what Joanne, Linda's sister, had called "a control nut."

When Joanne phoned to ask if Linda could stay with them, she said that Linda needed a safe place where Tommy wouldn't think to look. "He's a real psychopath, Aunt Rosemary," Joanne added, her voice thick with worry. "And I'm sure he'll keep stalking her if she stays in the city."

"Stalk." The word made Rosemary think of big-game hunters. She actually pictured a man in a jungle carrying a rifle and wearing khaki shorts and a pith helmet.

"He's a control nut," Joanne said. "He knows all Linda's friends and the places she'd hide. He'll come to my apartment the minute he finds out she's gone, and with my kids here, I can't take a chance."

"Of course not." Rosemary remembered something about Joanne's marrying and having children, though she couldn't recall if she and Betty had been invited to the wedding or if they'd sent a gift. "We'd love to have Linda stay with us. Tell her to take a taxi when she gets to the bus station. Aunt Betty and I will be waiting up for her."

"I've given her some clothes and money," Joanne said, "but I'll get to the bank tomorrow and send more."

Rosemary stared at her sister, who'd fallen back to sleep. Rosemary had always wished she could sleep late and doze off at odd hours, but she was the nervous sort like their father, though now, thinking back, she had to admit that even their father could take it easy. Every now and then he'd sprawl in his club chair, his feet crossed at the ankles, smoke curling up from a cigar between his fingers.

"Doesn't all this remind you of Daddy and de Valera?" Rosemary said, watching as Betty opened her eyes and wiggled a throw pillow behind her back. A moment later, Betty plunked her feet onto the padded footstool as if it were as easy as dropping a spoon.

"What?"

Betty's hearing wasn't as sharp as it should be, and Rosemary had to work on holding her temper. "EAMON DE VALERA!" Rosemary shouted. "THE MAN ON THE RUN! WE TOOK HIM INTO THE BROOKLYN HOUSE IN 1919."

"De Valera? What about him?"

"I said having Linda here, running away from the boyfriend, reminds me of the time Daddy took in de Valera."

"I was too young," Betty said. "I don't remember."

"You certainly *do* remember! We've talked about it a hundred times." Rosemary couldn't bear it when her sister acted dumb. She knew it was just because Betty didn't want to think hard.

"Well, I don't remember the way you do. I was only five years old."

Rosemary was seven when de Valera came and she remembered everything—how her father brought the family into the parlor and said a great honor had befallen them—that they'd been asked to open their home to one of the greatest Irish patriots who ever breathed God's air.

"A 1916 man," James McGuire had said. "He gave proof of the faith that was in him." It was an expression Rosemary's father used for the men of the Easter Rising.

Rosemary's father told them that although de Valera would be raising money and trying to get America to recognize an independent Ireland, they weren't to tell anyone they had a guest, or who he was.

"Didn't Daddy make us promise not to tell anyone de Valera was staying with us?" Betty asked, as if reading Rosemary's mind.

"That's right."

"What was all the secrecy about anyway?" Betty asked.

Rosemary couldn't believe her sister had forgotten. For over eighty years they'd talked about that visit. They'd discussed the vow of secrecy their father had made them take hundreds of times.

Rosemary took a deep breath and counted to five. "If the authorities found out *when* de Valera arrived, they'd know which ship he'd been on. And if they knew which ship, then they'd know who'd given him help, and the people who helped him would have been in trouble. De Valera and his friends would have lost an important link to America."

"Huh?" Betty said.

Rosemary narrowed her eyes. "He had to stay quiet before meeting the public. That meant we had to stay quiet, too."

"He was a stoker on the ship, wasn't he?"

"That's what Daddy said." Rosemary tried to lift her feet, but her hips wouldn't allow it. The old newspaper next to the chair reminded her of the newspapers her mother had saved from de Valera's visit. Rosemary had taken dozens of boxes of old papers when her mother died, and she was sure she'd had them when she married Francis and moved to Ithaca. Were those old newspapers

still somewhere up in the attic? Was it possible that at this very
minute they were being eaten by squirrels?

"You made that big pot of porridge?" Betty said.

"Oatmeal. And it will wait."

"I'm hungry. Do we have to wait?"

Rosemary held up a hand when the floorboards creaked. Half
a minute later, when the toilet flushed, she managed to right herself. She had to stand a full minute while the pain in her hips subsided. Meanwhile, Betty, nimble as a cat, bolted up from the sofa
and practically ran to the kitchen.

Betty had the bowls on the table and was pouring milk into a
pitcher when Linda came into the kitchen wrapped in a turquoise
robe. The left side of her face was the color of an eggplant; her
right eye was a slit in her cheek.

"Oh, dear heart," Rosemary said, feeling pain in her own face.
Last night, the girl's face hadn't seemed quite as bruised or swollen.

"I'm all right," Linda said through cracked lips. Her eye began
to run with tears. "I slept like a log for the first time in months."

"We're very glad we could help," Betty said. "Rosemary made
some porridge."

"I wonder if you should see a doctor," Rosemary said, remembering that over seventy years ago, she'd taken a friend to a doctor
after a beating. The friend had sat beside her on the trolley, her
head wrapped in a shawl, her hand squeezing Rosemary's wrist.

"Joanne looked me over," Linda said. "She's a nurse, you know."

Rosemary couldn't remember if she ever knew Joanne was a
nurse. The only thing Rosemary was sure of was that Linda and
Joanne's parents—Rosemary's nephew Jimmy and his wife—had
been killed in a hotel fire.

When Betty brought the tea to the table Rosemary made sure
she dipped her toast into the mug so Linda would follow her example. The girl couldn't put a cup to her lips, but she needed
nourishment. She was a stick under that beautiful head of hair.

Rosemary tried to picture what Linda would look like without
the bruises, but with all the swelling it was hard to imagine. She
didn't have Moira's widow's peak or blue eyes, and the one eye
Rosemary could see was green. Still, the hair was the same; if anything, Linda's mane was thicker than Moira's had been.

Moira would be seventy now, Rosemary thought. She forced

herself to picture a seventy-year-old woman. All that came to mind was a plump woman with florid cheeks and thinning hair. The woman, Rosemary realized, was Gladys O'Farrell.

When Linda bent her head and began crying, Rosemary leaned toward her and touched her shoulder.

"I'm so ashamed," Linda said.

Rosemary's friend on the trolley had used the same word. Rosemary hadn't known how to help her friend—hadn't even advised her to leave her husband, though she was sure she'd known her friend had done nothing to be ashamed of.

"Why do you say that, dear heart?" Rosemary asked.

"I let it happen," Linda said. "Almost like I was punishing myself."

"But you did nothing wrong."

"Oh, everything will be just fine," Betty piped up. "You'll get yourself back together in no time." She sounded as breezy as a summer wind. "And would you refill the pitcher, Linda dear?" Betty pointed to the counter where the milk carton stood.

Linda struggled out of her chair, and in that moment Rosemary was sure the girl was as bruised under her robe as on her face. Rosemary was furious that she hadn't told Betty to get the damn milk herself.

Betty dished out her third bowl of oatmeal, then sprinkled it with two spoonfuls of sugar.

Linda dabbed her bruised cheeks with a napkin. "Joanne gave me medicine so I could sleep. She gave me stuff for the swelling, too."

"Well, you go upstairs and rest," Rosemary said. "I'm just sorry we can't bring a tray to you, but neither of us can climb the stairs."

"Please don't worry. I'll be all right. You're wonderful for taking me in."

After the girl had gone, Rosemary went to the sitting room to finish her shopping list. Al had told them he could make one more shopping trip before his move, and Rosemary had already filled two pages. Now she added ice cream, cookies, and packaged cakes. On a separate piece of paper, she wrote, "Rat Poison." Al wouldn't be too happy to go to the hardware store, but Rosemary felt that because there was a girl there with workable legs, she might as well get the damned squirrels out of the attic.

*

At four in the afternoon, Linda was still sleeping. It was dark enough to put on the back porch light, and when Rosemary flipped the switch she wondered when they'd have their first snow. Last year it had come the week before Thanksgiving, but she knew it could be as early as October. Still, the air wasn't quite cold enough. She looked through the window, angry that she couldn't see the water. She used to be able to see a decent sliver of lake from the bottom panes of the first-floor windows, but the underbrush now blocked the view. Seeing the water had always given Rosemary a peaceful feeling. Francis used to say that she looked drugged when she watched the water. Rosemary would tell him she was simply relaxing. But the truth was, the sight of water *did* put her in a stupor. It brought a calm feeling to every part of her body.

She'd probably inherited her love of the water from Nonny, her maternal grandmother. Nonny had lived all her life on Tralee Bay. Ma had said Nonny could read the ocean waves as well as the priest could read his prayer book. Ma swore that as a young woman Nonny had seen the Phantom Islands—the underwater home of the spirits. "And after she saw those islands, she told everyone she met that there was no reason to fear death."

Rosemary tapped the window. Even if the man at the bank told her she couldn't afford it, she was going to call the tree man in the spring and have him clear out her view.

When Betty finished watching her game shows and began saying her rosary, Rosemary wandered into the living room. The man at the bank said she had to protect the investment in her house, so last year she'd had the roof patched and the chimneys repointed, even though she rarely saw the roof and never used the fireplaces. After spending the money for the outside, there was nothing left for the inside, where she might have enjoyed the improvements. Large plaster cracks crisscrossed the ceiling, and sheets of wallpaper pulled away from the walls. The windows that fronted on the porch were thick with grime, and Rosemary deliberately didn't look too closely in the corners of the room. On her last inspection, she'd found cobwebs as long as Spanish moss.

A moment after turning to the back of the house, Rosemary heard a snap coming from the front porch. Next the porch floor creaked. A second later there was a knock at the door. The mailman always came before one o'clock, and he knocked only when the mail wouldn't fit through the letter slot. Al Murphy came to the back door, and Gladys O'Farrell, who'd never come anytime other than Sunday morning, always tooted the horn from inside her big car.

"Just a minute," Rosemary called, turning on the lamp on the hall table. She went to the door and switched on the light. When she looked through the glass panel on the side of the door, she didn't see anyone. Then, just as Mike had instructed her when he'd installed the chain, she checked to see it was securely attached before unlocking the bolt.

"Who is it?" she called. "Is anyone there?"

Just then, like a jack-in-the-box, a large man popped up in front of her. He pulled off his watchman's cap and his hair fell forward in dark coils. "I'm sorry if I scared you," he boomed. "I'm looking for Linda McGuire."

"Linda?" Rosemary said after a second. Her heart had jumped to her mouth and was beating behind shaky lips.

"She's here, isn't she?"

"Who?"

"Linda McGuire," the man said, coming so close to the chain Rosemary could feel his breath in her face.

"McGuire," Rosemary said as if she'd never heard the word.

"I know she's here," he whispered softly.

"There's no Linda here," she said. She needed to get to the telephone and call the police. This was a stalker. This was a psychopath and a control nut.

"You know who I want," the man said. "She's here. I found out from a reliable source."

"I'm sorry I can't help you," Rosemary said, pressing her body against the door.

"You'll help me," he said, the second before Rosemary got the door closed and bolted. She made it to the sitting room as fast as she could.

"Betty." Rosemary was breathless from fear and from moving quickly. "He's here. The boyfriend who beat Linda is on the porch."

"What?" Betty said, waking from a sleep. The silver rosary beads, blessed by the pope, were on her lap.

"The stalker is on the porch! I'm calling the police."

Betty kept a startled look on her face while Rosemary went to the desk and picked up the phone. "Jesus, Mary, and Joseph help us," Rosemary said, pressing the phone button.

"Who did you say was here?" Betty said.

Rosemary pushed the button over and over, but she couldn't get a dial tone. She rushed into the hall.

Frustration about her body's limitations made her pound the newel post. If only she could run up the stairs or dash out the back door. If only she could get to the road and hail a passing car. "Linda!" she yelled. She yelled three more times before shifting her eyes from the stairwell to the front door. The porch light was still on, and so was the lamp. Anyone watching from outside could see her.

"What?" Linda said, coming down the stairs. "What's the matter?"

"He's here," Rosemary said. "He came to the door. I tried to call the police but the phone is broken."

"Tommy is here?"

Rosemary grabbed her grandniece's hand. "What will he do?"

"He won't hurt you, I promise."

A loud crash came from the dining room. "Linda," Tommy called, over a tinkling sound.

Rosemary took two steps and twisted her head until she saw him cracking off shards of glass from the window frame.

"I need to talk to you," Tommy called.

Rosemary felt the heat leave her body. A second later, Linda whispered in her ear. "I'll try to get rid of him. See if you can get the police on the phone."

Rosemary, as petrified as a fossil, watched Linda go into the dining room. She listened as Tommy said, "Don't you ever run away from me."

"Tommy," Linda said, "please calm down. We can talk."

"Defend us in battle," Rosemary whispered. She'd learned the prayer to Saint Michael over eighty years ago. "Be our protection against the malice and snares of the devil."

Rosemary made her way to the sitting room and found Betty asleep on the sofa.

"Thrust into hell Satan and the other evil spirits who roam through the world seeking the ruin of souls." Rosemary couldn't stop the words from shooting into her head. She went to the phone and lifted the receiver. Nothing. She clicked the button again and again, but there was no dial tone.

She padded her way to the kitchen and from there to the threshold that led to the dining room.

"You can't leave me," Tommy growled. "I'd rather see you dead."

"Please, Tommy," Linda said.

"No!" he shouted, and from the loud thump, Rosemary guessed he'd slammed his fist on the table. "Now get dressed. I've got a car."

"Okay, it's okay," Linda said. "Would you wait outside? There are two old ladies here and they're very scared."

"Get dressed."

Rosemary retraced her steps through the kitchen as fast as she could. Linda was already there, hugging her shoulders in the passageway between the kitchen and the sitting room. "Did you get the police?" she whispered into Rosemary's ear.

"No dial tone."

"I'll have to go with him," Linda said.

Rosemary put her hand on Linda's shoulder and the girl leaned forward so her wild hair brushed Rosemary's cheek.

After Linda went upstairs, Rosemary stood stock-still. She knew Tommy was in the house but she hadn't heard him. She thought he was still in the dining room. "Be our protection against the malice and snares of the devil . . . ," she began again, her terror growing with each second.

"Hey," Tommy said. He'd come around through the kitchen and was looming behind her. He was even bigger than she first thought. In the kitchen light there seemed to be oil on his face and in his dark eye sockets. She had to speak, if only to prove that she could. "How did you find her?"

"Joanne goes out but leaves the address right on the refrigerator. Not too smart." He went to the refrigerator and grabbed the orange juice container. He took a long drink from the cardboard spout before opening the drawers.

Rosemary looked at the oatmeal pot, filled with soapy water and sitting on the counter. She made herself think about what would happen next. *He'll need to stop us from reporting him,* she thought, a second before he found the knives. He looked them over but left them in the drawer.

"Are you Linda's old granny?" he asked, opening the drawer where they kept the table mats and napkins.

"Great-aunt," Rosemary said. Tommy looked at the bottles of pills they kept on a tray near the sink.

"What have you got here, anything good?"

Rosemary heard Linda on the stairs, but she didn't turn. She wanted the girl to run out the front door. She sent Linda a message by closing her eyes and thinking the words, "Save yourself!" In grade school, she'd learned that the first duty of a Catholic was to save his own soul.

When Rosemary opened her eyes Linda was standing beside her, dressed in the black pants and purple sweater she'd worn the night before. "I'm ready," she said. "Let's go."

"What about the old ladies here? One is asleep in the next room, but we got this one—the Big Defender. What's she gonna do? Report the broken window?"

"She won't do anything," Linda said. "Let's go."

"I want to think first," Tommy said, opening the cabinet that held the silver candlesticks. As he reached for the silver from the cabinet, Linda kissed Rosemary's cheek. Rosemary put her hand on Linda's back and felt the girl's bones. She was as delicate as a bird, more delicate than Moira. "I'm going to check the broken window," Rosemary said; her voice was trembling and she wasn't sure Tommy or Linda heard her. She turned and headed back to the hallway. As she moved, she thought how scared she was and how she despised her fear. It made her legs and arms tremble and it made her feel she was suffocating. Fear had plagued her her whole life; it had pulled her back and stopped her from taking action. It had made her weak and indecisive, and had caused her the deepest sorrows.

Entering the dining room, she wondered if she'd have the strength. She'd only have a minute before Tommy would come to see what she was up to, but a minute would be enough if she was going to do it.

She went to the left side of the buffet table and slid open the drawer. Mike had said the gun wasn't any good if she couldn't get to it, or if it wasn't fully loaded. He'd shown her the safety, and how to take it off. She released it now before lifting the gun from the drawer. It wasn't as heavy as she remembered, but she held it in both hands pointing downward as she walked.

"Thrust into hell Satan and the other evil spirits who roam through the world seeking the ruin of souls," she whispered. The words in her head were louder than the pounding in her heart. At the entrance to the kitchen, she stopped. Linda was standing where she'd been before, but Tommy was leaning with his back against the sink, facing her.

"Oh, the old granny's got a weapon," he said, straightening up. He took a step forward as Rosemary raised the gun in the way Mike had shown her. "Help me," she said. She squeezed rather than pulled the trigger and heard the loud explosion. The smell and the smoke surprised her, but nothing was more surprising than the look on Tommy's face. He stood still, staring at her, as his eyes went from wide to narrow.

Rosemary squeezed again, this time aiming higher. Blood sprayed the kitchen.

Linda held both hands to the sides of her head as if she needed to suppress her unruly hair. Betty, her mouth open, stood in the doorway.

Rosemary saw them but couldn't hear them. She looked at Tommy on the floor. His head was gushing blood. The smell of fire filled her nose and the taste of ashes was in her mouth, but no noise reached her ears. She thought maybe the gun had made her deaf, and that probably the deafness was temporary, the way everything was.

Stillness filled her chest, and the muscles in her neck and shoulders eased. A deep peacefulness spread through her body, and she felt as she did when she stared at the water. It was the same feeling, she now knew, that her grandmother must have had when she saw the Phantom Islands and knew there was nothing to fear.

MARY GAITSKILL

The Other Place

FROM *The New Yorker*

MY SON, DOUGLAS, loves to play with toy guns. He is thirteen.
He loves video games in which people get killed. He loves violence
on TV, especially if it's funny. How did this happen? The way everything does, of course. One thing follows another, naturally.

Naturally, he looks like me: shorter than average, with a fine
build, hazel eyes, and light-brown hair. Like me, he has a speech
impediment and a condition called "essential tremor" that causes
involuntary hand movements, which make him look more fragile
than he is. He hates reading, but he is bright. He is interested in
crows because he heard on a nature show that they are one of the
only species that are more intelligent than they need to be to survive. He does beautiful, precise drawings of crows.

Mostly, though, he draws pictures of men holding guns. Or men
hanging from nooses. Or men cutting up other men with chainsaws—in these pictures there are no faces, just figures holding
chainsaws and figures being cut in two, with blood spraying out.

My wife, Marla, says that this is fine, as long as we balance it out
with other things—family dinners, discussions of current events,
sports, exposure to art and nature. But I don't know. Douglas and
I were sitting together in the living room last week, half watching
the TV and checking e-mail, when an advertisement for a movie
flashed across the screen: it was called *Captivity* and the ad showed
a terrified blond girl in a cage, a tear running down her face. Doug
didn't speak or move. But I could feel his fascination, the suddenly
deepening quality of it. And I don't doubt that he could feel mine.
We sat there and felt it together.

And then she was there, the woman in the car. In the room with my son, her black hair, her hard laugh, the wrinkled skin under her hard eyes, the sudden blood filling the white of her blue eye. There was excited music on the TV and then the ad ended. My son's attention went elsewhere; she lingered.

When I was a kid, I liked walking through neighborhoods alone, looking at houses, seeing what people did to make them homes: the gardens, the statuary, the potted plants, the wind chimes. Late at night, if I couldn't sleep, I would sometimes slip out my bedroom window and just spend an hour or so walking around. I loved it, especially in late spring, when it was starting to be warm and there were night sounds—crickets, birds, the whirring of bats, the occasional whooshing car, some lonely person's TV. I loved the mysterious darkness of trees, the way they moved against the sky if there was wind—big and heavy movements, but delicate, too, in all the subtle, reactive leaves. In that soft, blurry weather, people slept with their windows open; it was a small town and they weren't afraid. Some houses—I'm thinking of two in particular, where the Legges and the Myers lived—had yards that I would actually hang around in at night. Once, when I was sitting on the Legges' front porch, thinking about stealing a piece of their garden statuary, their cat came and sat with me. I petted him, and when I got up and went for the statuary, he followed me with his tail up. The Legges' statues were elves, not corny, cute elves but sinister, wicked-looking elves, and I thought that one would look good in my room. But they were too heavy, so I just moved them around the yard.

I did things like that, dumb pranks that could only irritate those who noticed them: rearranging statuary, leaving weird stuff in mailboxes, looking into windows to see where people had dinner or left their personal things—or, in the case of the Legges, where their daughter, Jenna, slept. She was on the ground floor, her bed so close to the window that I could watch her chest rise and fall the way I watched the grass on their lawn stirring in the wind. The worst thing I did, probably, was put a giant marble in the Myers' gas tank, which could've really caused a problem if it had rolled over the gas hole while one of the Myers was driving on the highway, but I guess it never did.

Mostly, though, I wasn't interested in causing that kind of problem. I just wanted to sit and watch, to touch other people's things, to drink in their lives. I suspect that it's some version of these impulses that makes me the most successful real estate agent in the Hudson Valley now: the ability to know what physical objects and surroundings will most please a person's sense of identity and make him feel at home.

I wish that Doug had this sensitivity to the physical world, and the ability to drink from it. I've tried different things with him: I used to throw the ball with him out in the yard, but he got tired of that; he hates hiking and likes biking only if he has to get someplace. What's working now a little bit is fishing, fly-fishing hip-deep in the Hudson. An ideal picture of normal childhood.

I believe I had a normal childhood. But you have to go pretty far afield to find something people would call abnormal these days. My parents were divorced, and then my mother had boyfriends — but this was true of about half the kids I knew. She and my father fought, in the house, when they were together, and they went on fighting, on the phone, after they separated — loud, screaming fights sometimes. I didn't love it, but I understood it; people fight. I was never afraid that my father was going to hurt her, or me. I had nightmares occasionally, in which he turned into a murderer and came after me, chasing me, getting closer, until I fell down, unable to make my legs move right. But I've read that this is one of those primitive fears which everybody secretly has; it bears little relation to what actually happens.

What actually happened: he forced me to play golf with him for hours when I visited on Saturdays, even though it seemed only to make him miserable. He'd curse himself if he missed a shot and then that would make him miss another one and he'd curse himself more. He would whisper, "Oh, God," and wipe his face if anything went wrong, or even if it didn't, as if just being there were an ordeal, and then I had to feel sorry for him. He'd make these noises sometimes, painful grunts when he picked up the sack of clubs, and it put me on edge and even disgusted me.

Now, of course, I see it differently. I remembered those Saturdays when I was first teaching Doug how to cast, out in the backyard. I wasn't much good myself yet, and I got tangled up in the bushes a couple of times. I could feel the boy's flashing impatience; I felt my age, too. Then we went to work disentangling and he came closer to help me. We linked in concentration, and it occurred to me that the delicacy of the line and the fine movements needed to free it appealed to him the way drawing appealed to him, because of their beauty and precision.

Besides, he was a natural. When it was his turn to try, he kept his wrist stiff and gave the air a perfect little punch and *zip*—great cast. The next time, he got tangled up, but he was speedy about getting unstuck so that he could do it again. Even when the tremor acted up. Even when I lectured him on the laws of physics. It was a good day.

There is one not-normal thing you could point to in my childhood, which is that my mother, earlier in her life, before I was born, had occasionally worked as a prostitute. But I don't think that counts, because I didn't know about it as a child. I didn't learn about it until six years ago, when I was thirty-eight and my mother was sick with a strain of flu that had killed a lot of people, most of them around her age. She was in the hospital and she was feverish and thought she was dying. She held my hand as she told me, her eyes sad half-moons, her lips still full and provocative. She said that she wanted me to know because she thought it might help me to understand some of the terrible things I'd heard my father say to her—things I mostly hadn't even listened to. "It wasn't anything really bad," she said. "I just needed the money sometimes, between jobs. It's not like I was a drug addict—it was just hard to make it in Manhattan. I only worked for good escort places. I never had a pimp or went out on the street. I never did anything perverted—I didn't have to. I was beautiful. They'd just pay to be with me."

Later, when she didn't die, she was embarrassed that she'd told me. She laughed that raucous laugh of hers and said, "Way to go, Marcy! On your deathbed, tell your son you're a whore and then don't die!"

"It's okay," I said.

And it was. It frankly was not really even much of a surprise. It was her vanity that disgusted me, the way she undercut the confession with a preening, maudlin joke. I could not respect that even then.

I don't think that my mom's confession, or whatever it may have implied, had anything to do with what I think of as "it." When I was growing up, there was, after all, no evidence of her past, nothing that could have affected me. But suddenly, when I was about fourteen, I started getting excited by the thought of girls being hurt. Or killed. A horror movie would be on TV, a girl in shorts would be running and screaming with some guy chasing her, and to me it was like porn. Even a scene where a sexy girl was getting her legs torn off by a shark—bingo. It was like pushing a button. My mom would be in the kitchen making dinner and talking on the phone, stirring and striding around with the phone tucked between her shoulder and her chin. Outside, cars would go by, or a dog would run across the lawn. My homework would be slowly getting done in my lap while this sexy girl would be screaming "God help me!" and having her legs torn off. And I would go invisibly into an invisible world that I called "the other place." Where I sometimes passively watched a killer and other times became one.

It's true that I started drinking and drugging right about then. All my friends did. My mom tried to lay down the law, but I found ways around her. We'd go into the woods, me and usually Chet Wotazak and Jim Bonham, and we'd smoke weed from Chet's brother, a local dealer named Dan, and drink cheap wine. We could sometimes get Chet's dad to give us a gun—in my memory he had an AK-47, though I don't know how that's possible—and we'd go out to a local junkyard and take turns shooting up toilets, the long tubes of fluorescent lights, whatever was there. Then we'd go to Chet's house, up to his room, where we'd play loud music and tell dumb jokes and watch music videos in which disgusting things happened: snakes crawled over a little boy's sleeping face and he woke up being chased by a psychopath in a huge truck; a girl was turned into a pig and then a cake and then the lead singer bit off her head.

You might think that the videos and the guns were part of it, that they encouraged my violent thoughts. But Chet and Jim were watching and doing the same things and they were not like me. They said mean things about girls, and they were disrespectful sometimes, but they didn't want to hurt them, not really. They wanted to touch them and be touched by them; they wanted that more than anything. You could hear it in their voices and see it in their eyes, no matter what they said.

So I would sit with them and yet be completely apart from them, talking and laughing about normal things in a dark mash of music and snakes and children running from psychos and girls being eaten—images that took me someplace my friends couldn't see, although it was right there in the room with us.

It was the same at home. My mother made dinner, talked on the phone, fought with my dad, had guys over. Our cat licked itself and ate from its dish. Around us, people cared about one another. Jenna Legge slept peacefully. But in the other place, sexy girls—and sometimes ugly girls or older women—ran and screamed for help as an unstoppable, all-powerful killer came closer and closer. There was no school or sports or mom or dad or caring, and it was great.

I've told my wife about most of this, the drinking, the drugs, the murder fantasies. She understands, because she has her past, too: extreme sex, vandalizing cars, talking vulnerable girls into getting more drunk than they should on behalf of some guy. There's a picture of her and another girl in bathing suits, the other girl chugging a beer that is being held by a guy so that it goes straight down her throat as her head is tipped way back. Another guy is watching, and my smiling wife is holding the girl's hand. It's a picture that foreshadows some kind of cruelty or misery, or maybe just a funny story to tell about throwing up in the bathroom later. Privately, I see no similarity between it and my death obsession. For my wife, the connection is drugs and alcohol; she believes that we were that way because we were both addicts expressing our pain and anger through violent fantasies and blind actions.

The first time I took Doug out to fish, it was me on the hot golf course all over again. As we walked to the lake in our heavy boots and clothes, I could feel his irritation at the bugs and the brightness, the squalor of nature in his fastidious eyes. I told him that fly-fishing was like driving a sports car, as opposed to the Subaru of rod and reel, I went on about how anything beautiful had to be conquered. He just pulled down his mouth.

He got interested, though, in tying on the fly; the simple elegance of the knot (the "fish-killer") intrigued him. He laid it down the first time, too, placing the backcast perfectly in a space between trees. He gazed at the brown, light-wrinkled water with satisfaction. But when I put my hand on his shoulder, I could feel him inwardly pull away.

As I got older, my night walks became rarer, with a different, sadder feeling to them. I would go out when I was not drunk or high but in a quiet mood, wanting to be somewhere that was neither the normal social world nor the other place. A world where I could sit and feel the power of nature come up through my feet, and be near other people without them being near me. Where I could believe in and for a moment possess the goodness of their lives. Jenna Legge still slept on the ground floor and sometimes I would still look in her window and watch her breathe, and, if I was lucky, see one of her developing breasts swell out of her nightgown.

I never thought of killing Jenna. I didn't think about killing anyone I actually knew—not the girls I didn't like at school or the few I had sex with. The first times I had sex, I was so caught up in the feeling of it that I didn't even think about killing—I didn't think about anything at all. But I didn't get sex much. I was small, awkward, too quiet; I had that tremor. My expression must've been strange as I sat in class, feeling hidden in my other place, but outwardly visible to whoever looked—not that many did.

Then one day I was with Chet's brother, Dan, on a drug drop; he happened to be giving me a ride because his drop, at the local college, was on the way to wherever I was going. It was a guy buying, but when we arrived, a girl opened the door. She was pretty and she knew it, but whatever confidence that knowledge gave her was superficial. We stayed for a while and smoked the product with her and her boyfriend. The girl sat very erect and talked too much, as if she were smart, but there was a question at the end of everything she said. When we left, Dan said, "That's the kind of lady I'd like to slap in the face." I asked, "Why?" But I knew. I don't remember what he said, because it didn't matter. I already knew. And later, instead of making up a girl, I thought of that one.

I forgot to mention: one night when I was outside Jenna's window, she opened her eyes and looked right at me. I was stunned, so stunned that I couldn't move. There was nothing between us but a screen with a hole in it. She looked at me and blinked. I said, "Hi." I held my breath; I had not spoken to her since third grade. But she just sighed, rolled over, and lay still. I stood there trembling for a long moment. And then, slowly and carefully, I walked through the yard and onto the sidewalk, back to my house.

I cut school the next day and the next, because I was scared that Jenna had told everybody and that I would be mocked. But eventually it became clear that nobody was saying anything, so I went back. I looked at Jenna cautiously, then gratefully. But she did not return my look. At first this moved me, made me consider her powerful. I tried insistently to catch her eye, to let her know what I felt. Finally our eyes met, and I realized that she didn't understand why I was looking at her. I realized that although her eyes had been open that night, she had still been asleep. She had looked right at me, but she had not seen me at all.

And so one night, or early morning, really, I got out of bed, into my mother's car, and drove to the campus to look for her—the college girl.

The campus was in a heavily wooded area bordering a nature preserve. The dorms were widely scattered, though some, resembling midsized family homes, were clustered together. The girl lived in one of those, but while I remembered the general location, I couldn't be sure which one it was. I couldn't see into any of the windows, because even the open ones had blinds pulled down. While I was standing indecisively on a paved path between dorms, I saw two guys coming toward me. Quickly, I walked off into a section of trees and underbrush. I moved carefully through the thicket, coming to a wide field that led toward the nature preserve. The darkness deepened as I got farther from the dorms. I could feel things coming up from the ground—teeth and claws, eyes, crawling legs, and brainless eating mouths. A song played in my head, an enormously popular, romantic song about love and death that had supposedly made a bunch of teenagers kill themselves.

Kids still listen to that song. I once heard it coming from the computer in our family room. When I went in and looked over Doug's hunched shoulder, I realized that the song was being used as the soundtrack for a graphic video about a little boy in a mask murdering people. It was spellbinding, the yearning, eerie harmony of the song juxtaposed with terrified screaming; I told Doug to turn it off. He looked pissed, but he did it and went slumping out the door. I found it and watched it by myself later.

*

I went back to the campus many times. I went to avoid my mother as much as anything. Her new boyfriend was an asshole, and she whined when he was around. When he wasn't around, she whined about him on the phone. Sometimes she called two people in a row to whine about exactly the same things that he'd said or done. Even when I played music loud so I couldn't hear her, I could *feel* her. When that happened, I'd leave my music on so that she'd think I was still in my room and I'd go to the campus. I'd follow lone female students as closely as I could, and I'd feel the other place running against the membrane of the world, almost touching it.

Why does it make sense to put romantic music together with a story about a little boy murdering people? Because it does make sense—only I don't know how. It seems dimly to have to do with justice, with some wrong being avenged, but what? The hurts of childhood? The stupidity of life? The kid doesn't seem to be having fun. Random murder just seems like a job he has to do. But why?

Soon enough I realized that the college campus was the wrong place to think about making it real. It wasn't an environment I could control; there were too many variables. I needed to get the girl someplace private. I needed to have certain things there. I needed to have a gun. I could find a place; there were deserted places. I could get a gun from Chet's house; I knew where his father kept his. But the girl?

Then, while I was in the car with my mom one day, we saw a guy hitchhiking. He was middle-aged and fucked-up-looking, and my mom—we were stopped at a light—remarked that nobody in their right mind would pick him up. Two seconds later, somebody pulled over for him. My mom laughed.

I started hitchhiking. Most of the people who picked me up hitchhiking were men, but there were women, too. No one was scared of me. I was almost eighteen by then, but I was still small and quiet-looking. Women picked me up because they were concerned about me.

I didn't really plan to do it. I just wanted to feel the gun in my pocket and look at the woman and know that I *could* do it. There was this one—a thirtyish blonde with breasts that I could see through her open coat. But then she said she was pregnant and I started thinking about what if I was killing the baby?

Doug had a lot of nightmares when he was a baby, by which I mean between the ages of two and four. When he cried out in his sleep, it was usually Marla who went to him. But one night she was sick and I told her to stay in bed while I went to comfort the boy. He was still crying "Mommy!" when I sat on the bed, and I felt his anxiety at seeing me instead of his mother, felt the moment of hesitation in his body before he came into my arms, vibrating rather than trembling, sweating and fragrant with emotion. He had dreamed that he was home alone and it was dark, and he was calling for his mother, but she wasn't there. "Daddy, Daddy," he wept, "there was a sick lady with red eyes and Mommy wouldn't come. Where is Mommy?"

That may've been the first time I truly remembered her, the woman in the car. It was so intense a moment that in a bizarre intersection of impossible feelings I got an erection with my crying child in my arms. But it lasted only a moment. I picked Doug up and carried him into our bedroom so that he could see his mother and nestle against her. I stayed awake nearly all night watching them.

The day it happened was a bright day, but windy and cold, and my mom would not shut up. I just wanted to watch a movie, but even with the TV turned up loud—I guess that's why she kept talking; she didn't think I could hear—I couldn't blot out the sound of her yakking about how ashamed this asshole made her feel. I whispered, "If you're so ashamed why do you talk about it?" She said, "It all goes back to being fucking molested." She lowered her voice; the only words I caught were "fucking corny." I went out into the hallway to listen. "The worst of it was that he wouldn't look at me," she said. I could almost hear her pacing around, the phone tucked against her shoulder. "That's why I fall for these passive-aggressive types who turn me on and then make me feel ashamed." Whoever she was talking to must've said something funny then, because she laughed. I left the TV on and walked out. I took the gun, but more for protection against perverts than the other thing.

*

I gave my boy that dream as surely as if I'd handed it to him. But I've given him a lot of other things, too. The first time he caught a fish he responded to my encouraging words with a bright glance that I will never forget. We let that one go, but only after he had held it in his hands, cold and quick, muscle with eyes and a heart, scales specked with yellow and red, and one tiny fin orange. Then the next one, bigger, leaping to break the rippling murk—I said, "Don't point the rod at the fish. Keep the tip up, keep it up"—and he listened to me and he brought it in. There is a picture of it on the corkboard in his room, the fish in the net, the lure bristling in its crude mouth. I have another picture, too, of him smiling triumphantly, holding it in his hands, its shining, still living body fully extended.

She was older than I'd wanted, forty or so, but still good-looking. She had a voice that was strong and lifeless at the same time. She had black hair and she wore tight black pants. She did not have a wedding ring, which meant that maybe no one would miss her. She picked me up on a lightly traveled 45-mile-an-hour road. She was listening to a talk show on the radio and she asked if I wanted to hear music instead. I said no, I liked talk shows.

"Yeah?" she said. "Why?"

"Because I'm interested in current events."

"I'm not," she said. "I just listen to this shit because the voices relax me. I don't really care what they're talking about."

They were talking about a war somewhere. Bombs were going off in markets where people bought vegetables; somebody's legs had been blown off. We turned onto a road with a few cars, but none close to us.

"You don't care?"

"No, why should I? Oh, about this?" She paused. There was something about a little boy being rushed to an overcrowded hospital. "Yeah, that's bad. But it's not like we can do anything about it." On the radio, foreign people cried.

I took the gun out of my pocket.

I said, "Do you have kids?"

"No," she said. "Why?"

"Take me to Old Post Road. I'm going to the abandoned house there."

"I'm not going by there, but I can get you pretty close. So

why do you care about current events? I didn't give a shit at your age."

"Take me there or I'll kill you."

She cocked her head and wrinkled her brow, as if she were trying to be sure she'd heard right. Then she looked down at the gun and cut her eyes up at me; quickly, she looked back at the road. The car picked up speed.

"Take the next right or you'll die." My voice at that moment came not from me but from the other place. My whole body felt like an erection. She hit the right-turn signal. There was a long moment as we approached the crucial road. The voices on the radio roared ecstatically.

She pulled over to the shoulder.

"What are you doing?"

She put the car in park.

"Turn right or you die!"

She unbuckled her seat belt and turned to face me. "I'm ready," she said. She leaned back and gripped the steering wheel with one hand, as if to steady herself. With her free hand she tapped herself between the eyes—bright, hot blue, rimmed with red. "Put it here," she said. "Go for it."

A car went by. Somebody in the passenger seat glanced at us blankly. "I don't want to do it here. There's witnesses. You need to take me to the place."

"What witnesses? That car's not stopping—nobody's going to stop unless the emergency lights are on and they're not, look."

"But if I shoot you in the head the blood will spray on the window and somebody could see." It was my own voice again: the power was gone. The people on the radio kept talking. Suddenly I felt my heart beating.

"Okay, then do it here." She opened her jacket to show me her chest. "Nobody'll hear. When you're done you can move me to the passenger seat and drive the car wherever."

"Get into the passenger seat now and I'll do it."

She laughed, hard. Her eyes were crazy. They were crazy the way an animal can be crazy in a tiny cage. "Hell, no. I'm not going to your place with you. You do it here, motherfucker."

I realized then that her hair was a wig, and a cheap one. For some reason that made her seem even crazier. I held my gun hand against my body to hide the tremor.

"Come on, honey" she said. "Go for it."

Like a star, a red dot appeared in the white of her left eye. The normal place and the other place were turning into the same place, quick but slow, the way a car accident is quick but slow. I stared. The blood spread raggedly across her eye. She shifted her eyes from my face to a spot somewhere outside the car and fixed them there. I fought the urge to turn and see what she was looking at. She shifted her eyes again. She looked me deep in the face.

"Well?" she said. "Are you going to do it or not?"

Words appeared in my head, like a sign reading I DON'T WANT TO.

She leaned forward and turned on the emergency flashers. "Get out of my car," she said quietly. "You're wasting my time."

As soon as I got out, she hit the gas and burned rubber. I walked into the field next to the road, without an idea of where I might go. I realized after she was gone that she might call the police, but I felt in my gut that she would not—in the other place there are no police, and she was from the other place.

Still, as I walked I took the bullets out of the gun and scattered them, kicking snow over them and stamping it down. I walked a long time, shivering horribly. I came across a drainage pipe and threw the empty gun into it. I thought, *I should've gut-shot her—that's what I should've done. And then got her to the abandoned house. I should've gut-shot the bitch.* But I knew why I hadn't. She'd been shot already, from the inside. If she had been somebody different I might actually have done it. But somehow the wig-haired woman had changed the channel and I don't even know if she'd meant to.

The fly bobbing on the brown, gentle water. The long grasses so green that they cast a fine, bright green on the brown water. The primitive fish mouth straining for water and finding it as my son releases it in the shallows. Its murky vanishing.

The blood bursting in her eye; poor woman, poor mother. My mother died of colon cancer just nine months ago. Shortly after that, it occurred to me that the woman had been wearing that awful wig because she was sick and undergoing chemo. Though of course I don't know.

*

The hurts of childhood that must be avenged: so small and so huge. Before I grew up and stopped thinking about her, I thought about that woman a lot. About what would've happened if I'd gotten her there, to the abandoned house. I don't remember anymore the details of these thoughts, only that they were distorted, swollen, blurred: broken face, broken voice, broken body left dying on the floor, watching me go with dimming, despairing eyes.

These pictures are faded now and far away. But they can still make me feel something.

The second time I put my hand on Doug's shoulder, he didn't move away inside; he was too busy tuning in to the line and the lure. Somewhere in him is the other place. It's quiet now, but I know it's there. I also know that he won't be alone with it. He won't know that I'm there with him, because we will never speak of it. But I will be there. He will not be alone with that.

JESSE GOOLSBY

Safety

FROM *The Greensboro Review*

NICHOLLE, MY NEWLY MINTED serious girlfriend, hails from southern Alabama. The first time I meet her family, her brother, Dub, takes me to his swimming hole. Just before we splash in the muddy river he slaps my back and says, "Watch fer moccasins and snappers." Sure enough, we're neck-deep under the hazy summer sky when I spot a black snake enter the water. I have no idea what kind it is, and I quickly lose sight of it. Dub, this crazy bastard, is unaffected by my update. I don't want to be scared, but I've reached my breaking point and hurtle myself toward the bank. There's a ways to go and every water ripple grows a tail and fangs. Behind me I hear Dub laughing at my terror.

When it's all done and I sit at the dinner table with Nicholle, Dub, and her parents, I wonder if there's anything in my northern New Mexico upbringing that would scare Dub, and although I search hard, all I recall is a harmless bluegill fish attached to my pinkie when I'm eight. I look across the table at Nicholle's mother, a cheerful, plump lady who, if I unfocus my eyes enough, could be Nicholle in thirty years. Her father smiles approvingly at me, so at least I have that going. I'm nervous as hell, but I still feel for Nicholle's thin legs underneath the table. She swats me away.

Dub scares me a little. His hair is cut at varied lengths and there appears to be a knife scar across his cheek. After dinner, he asks me if I've ever been waterboarded. I tell him no, and he says he hasn't either.

"But," he says, "I beat up a homeless guy. Dumbass didn't even fight back, just laid there."

"Thanks for that, Dub."

"I've seen some shit," he says. He's out of high school, probably eighteen or so, but has an enthusiasm and weakness of intellect that makes eighteen hard to swallow. "Nicholle don't know this, but I can count cards. I act broke, but there's ten thou in my room. Swear."

"Okay," I say while fingering my chin, "cool."

I have no idea why I say "cool," can't think of anything else, and even Dub looks at me curiously.

"You count cards?" he asks.

Actually, I do, but I'm not interested in where the conversation will go or what I'll be invited to do. "You mean like gambling?" I say.

"Jesus," he says, laughing. He shakes his head. "Gambling."

What Dub doesn't know, and what I never plan on telling Nicholle, is that I do gamble. It's not bad: local games with friends. I bring what I can lose and that's it.

I do have the bad type of secrets. At the top of the list is a night in Los Alamos, New Mexico, just after dusk. I was late to a no-limit game across town, and I decided to cut through the Woodmen Pointe subdivision. I was up to 40 miles per hour on the straightaway near the end of a row of tan stucco homes. I never saw the girl scatter from the shadows, never heard her over the radio. I only felt the bump of her body, like running over a small dog. And before I could think about anything, the Jeep stopped, my fingers strangled the wheel. I closed my eyes. For a weightless moment only sound: Tom Petty, the idling four-cylinder, a slight breeze whistling the aspen. When I opened my eyes, no one was outside to scream and rush forward and finger me. No cars approached the other way. There was just a motionless girl in my rearview mirror, basking in the filtered red brake light. She wore torn pink sweatpants, and the soles of her tiny shoes were brand-new white. I saw my arm reach out and turn off the radio, then put the Jeep into first. My eyes swung back to the rearview mirror just in time to see her legs jolt once, then calm. Was she dead or just now dying? I drove away. I could still see her through the suffocating air, now quiet as a napping child.

Later that night I huddled in my shower, replaying images of the jolting pink legs. I tried to convince myself that she'd live, that a doctor would find her, that she'd suffer a little—a lifelong limp,

perhaps—and there would be a recovery, but her death was on
the news and in the paper the next morning. It was a hot story
in Los Alamos for two weeks, until the wildfires took over. Even
the big station in Albuquerque carried it. On the telecast the an-
chors reported the event and begged people to call in with any
information on the assailant. They showed her family huddled
on their front yard in front of microphones, their faces falling
apart.

I don't know where my belief in a just universe comes from, but
it's there, and one day, be it snake or other ailment, I know my
time will come. I can't get it out of my head. The worst part is that
it's a waiting game, and so I wait and feel the possibility of justice
hovering over me, pausing until the time is right.

The night I call Nicholle's father to ask for his daughter's hand in
marriage he cries. Gravel dances in his throat. "I couldn't be hap-
pier," he says. "I'll let you talk to Karen." There's silence while he
passes the phone, but his voice comes through again. "Two things,
son." It's the first time he's called me son. "One. I'll only loan you
money if Nicholle asks. Two. If you don't have a gun, get one." A
pause. I smile. "Three. You're a Tide fan when you visit. Four. I'll
give you a nickname which you probably won't like. Just smile.
Five. We've loved you for a while now. Good luck."

After I ask Nicholle to marry me under a flowering dogwood,
she makes me call Dub.

"Know where I been?" Dub says after telling me good job on the
proposal. I tell him no, I don't know where he's been. "Riverboats,
man. Rivers are international waters. No rules, buddy. State, government, can't touch 'em."

"Okay," I say.

"Should get married on a riverboat. There's one called the
Gypsy."

"We'll consider it, Dub."

"Love you, man," he says, like he means it.

I pass the phone to Nicholle, who's all smiles. "The *Gypsy*?" she
says while I shake my head next to her. She gives me a look. It
means that Dub is off-limits.

During our engagement, Nicholle and I pick up books about marriage. We open our favorite one, *The Questions You Should Ask Before*

"I Do," whenever we Sunday-drive from Knoxville, where we both work. I learn that Nicholle would never adopt, thinks sex three times a week is enough, hates cats, wants to visit Mongolia ("Just to say I've been"), doesn't mind if I have to travel for work, dreams of performing on Broadway if she could sing, is scared of getting her mother's cheeks, and doesn't like it when I say, "Ya know what I'm saying?" when trying to prove a point.

She learns a lot about me as well, at least the stuff I want her to know, but her face goes to stone when I tell her my number-one pet peeve is when people praise God only for the good things in life. "If God is so great," I say, "what the hell is up with cancer and dropped touchdown passes? No one points to the sky when a pass slips through their fingers." We go at it pretty good when I think, *If you're smart, you'll never say these things again,* but I know I will. All this learning about each other is fine, but the great stuff comes out when we sit in a tan stucco courtyard on our honeymoon in Savannah. We are waiting for our food, sipping on red wine, when Nicholle asks me the worst thing I've ever considered doing to someone else, even if it was just for a split second. I consider taking my hit-and-run and forming a hypothetical, just to see the reaction, but all that comes to me are the girl's spotless white shoes. I feel my stomach clench and push the image away. I search my mental catalogue for relief, and it doesn't take me long to sift through the feeble mock threats and momentary revenge wishes to a wooded mountainside near my childhood town.

I was twelve, cutting down dead white pine with my father in the backcountry. I'd taken a break, leaning against the old red Dodge truck, and in a bizarre mental pulse I thought of taking the chainsaw and hacking my father. I imagined the roaring saw, the blood and limbs mixing with the sawdust, the dumbfounded look in his eyes before the spinning hot teeth bit. Even in that moment I remember being ashamed and frightened of my own psychological capacity.

Now in the Italian restaurant courtyard, I hold the saltshaker in my hand and avoid Nicholle's brown eyes. I don't know if the words have come out right. Can those words come out right? "It's crazy," I say. I feel heavy and place my hands in my lap. "I don't know what I'm saying. Ya know what I'm saying?" I steal a glance. She's wearing my favorite sundress, a white number with small red and yellow flowers. She's tan and has her hair pulled back. There's a large party in the courtyard clinking wineglasses and talking over one another. We're all visitors.

"Stealing a baby," Nicholle says. "I don't know where it comes from. But there it is. I'd planned names, escape routes from the hospital, everything. I didn't care if it looked like me. I even thought it might be easier to take a year-old, not a newborn. They'd be eating solids."

The food arrives. I cut the veal with my knife. I take another bite and watch Nicholle move her bare arms as she negotiates her utensils into her pasta, then grabs for her wineglass and gulps. We should laugh. I think of laughing.

"So," I say. "I'm glad we're the normal ones."

We move into a nice rolling subdivision in Knoxville called Hawks Landing. Lo and behold, about a month into our stay, two hawks make their nest in a giant ponderosa in our front yard. The place is spacious and we have privacy on almost an acre. The neighbors are fine, but there's a guy around the corner who lets his dog shit in our yard. One Sunday morning, as I trim the flowering bushes in the front, he comes around with the dog and waves friendly to me before the dog scampers ten feet onto the grass and does his business. I don't have the balls to say anything. I'm out-of-shape thin and believe there's a hovering fistfight in every confrontation. He's a big guy, brick shoulders, looks like he wouldn't mind a fight, win or lose. Sometimes I see both him and the dog rolling around on his front yard when I come home from work. I stay clear. Besides that, life is great. Nicholle and I join a coed softball league, help clean up the local park, and make church about a third of the time. I like the routine. We break it up just enough to keep everything interesting. Nicholle steals $400 worth of tile from a local hardware store. Just walks out. It's in our bathroom on a diagonal. I lie to my boss most days about where I am, the hours I put in, but I work hard enough that he never questions me. I'm a Tennessee fan now, but Nicholle is Alabama all the way, so we have one of those stupid house-divided license plates, half orange, half crimson. We have lots of friends and a few enemies, but it's a healthy proportion.

Dub calls one night and talks to Nicholle for an hour. This is not normal.

"He needs money," Nicholle says. My head is already in my

hands. "Five thousand." We don't have $2000. "He'll pay us back. He says he'll pay us back. I know what you're going to say. He wouldn't ask unless he needed it." I'm not going to say a thing. "He's desperate and we can cash bonds if we have to. Say something. We need to be together on this."

She's near tears. It's breaking her heart. She knows we'll never see a penny back, knows we can't afford it, knows I despise her for asking, and yet here she is. It's her brother. I tell her I want him to drive up so I can see him face-to-face when I hand him the check. Everyone agrees, but two weeks later Nicholle puts the money in the mail and talks to me about the price of gasoline.

Nicholle and I think we'll get pregnant right away. We're both healthy, but after six months we're still not pregnant. We lie to the doctors, tell them it's been a year, but they say nothing's wrong. Nicholle and I fight and stress, and making love morphs into an exercise of hopelessness over the next two years. I change jobs and become a rep in a pharmaceutical company selling erectile dysfunction drugs. The money is good, but I'm on the road every other week. I'm outside a Taco Bell in Jacksonville when Nicholle calls me. I shift the greasy bag to my right hand and answer the phone.

"You're going to be a father," she says.

"Okay," I say. "Really?"

She loses it and I want to, but I can't cry. Of all things, I imagine the drive home from the hospital with our newborn child in the back seat. I think of all of the new drivers, the drunk drivers, the red-light racers.

"We need a car seat," I say.

"I love you," Nicholle says through the sniffles.

I love her, too, but I say, "Does this mean we don't have to steal a baby?"

Four weeks later I'm outside the VA hospital in Charlotte when she lets me know the pregnancy is ectopic. It's July, and dust swirls in the empty sky. I think of our growing child in Nicholle's right fallopian tube, budding bigger and bigger, slowly killing my wife, but she says the doctors are going to take care of everything the next day, and they do. I fly home and sit in our living room, Nicholle's head in my lap as she rubs at her legs. There's nothing I can say, so we're mostly quiet.

She says, "We have to wait three months."

The ceiling fan spins above us, and Nicholle's hair brushes at my legs. I study her body from her head down to her hips and bent knees and tucked feet. Very slowly, she uncoils. She hasn't told her parents yet, but as she heads upstairs and closes our bedroom door I know she's going for the phone. I hear her muffled voice through the ceiling. She's not crying yet. There's nothing her mother can do from that distance, but there's a safety in that bond that I'll never be able to join. The fan does little to help with the thick humidity. I wonder, is all of this part of my penance? A life for a life? Am I even with the universe? Still, the pain of losing something sight unseen seems like an easy sentence. Is this just the beginning? I see the Los Alamos girl curled up like an embryo. My heart was exploding and my hands pounded as they shifted the Jeep into first gear and released the clutch. I pressed the gas. I named the girl long ago, and tonight I hear it in my ears: Courtney. It's not the name said in the television reports in the aftermath, but I don't care. I haven't met a Courtney since. She's the only one.

In early September, just as we find our voices again, we watch television clips from New York City of people jumping from the buildings. I've never considered choosing between flame and gravity, and later, when the photos come out in magazines showing the bodies falling to their deaths, I am certain gravity would be the answer if given the choice.

After another miscarriage, Nicholle becomes pregnant. She's seven months along, a big, beautiful belly with a dark line bisecting her bulge. We ride in a bus. I can't stop touching her. Across from us sit four men that resemble the plane hijackers. I'm educated. Logically, I know these aren't terrorists. They ride the public bus downtown. They're happy and joking with one another. They speak a mix of English and something else. But one of them looks over at us, looks at Nicholle, at her belly, and stares. His brown face goes slack, his entire countenance trancelike. Am I due? Will this be it? The man will make a move toward us. His friends will hold me down while he struggles with Nicholle. I may survive this attack, alone. When that image passes, I imagine him flying a plane, a little single-prop Cessna, over our neighborhood. The hawks are up and circling high in the sky. He brings the plane into a dive, tears up the birds, heads straight for our shingled roof, but before I can complete the daydream, Nicholle reaches for my clenched hand, unfolds it, and intertwines hers. The man stares unflinchingly.

"Soon," Nicholle says to the man, tilting her chin up. "Two months left." It takes a second for him to realize that she has spoken to him. The man breaks his stare. "Soon," Nicholle repeats.

The four of them become quiet. The man taps his brown shirt above his heart, taps his forehead, and circles his hand toward us. "Girl," he says.

The magnolias I planted bloom large white blossoms. I stare at them with a cup of coffee one Saturday morning when the neighborhood jackass brings his retriever by. Nicholle's parents are in town, and her father stands next to me as the dog unloads one on our driveway. I'm near my limit with no plan. He gives me enough time to say something, and when I don't he asks, "How often, Slim?"

"I only see them on the weekends," I say.

"That's not what I asked," he says, and looks at me as if I'm a whiny child.

Later in the week Nicholle's dad tells me the jerk works the midshift, that he must walk the dog when he gets home. I don't ask how he knows this. He steps into the den and calls someone on his cell phone. When he returns he says, "You'll have to help." He asks me to wait in the parking lot of the store, and comes out with a plastic bottle of antifreeze. Sparks fly around me, and before he gets in the car, I assign the guilt to him: his idea, his purchase. I can't take on this one as well. I've decided I won't say no as long as he pours it into the dog bowl. Nicholle's father sits down with a heavy exhale.

"Dub's done this a couple times," he says. "Says to mix in a little vinegar, helps it go down."

"Vinegar?"

"That's what he says. He sends his love. Wanted me to tell you."

The doctor makes me grab a leg before he tells Nicholle to start pushing. Emma arrives early, only three pounds, two ounces. This is what family means. Three days later Emma comes home. No man could endure Nicholle's schedule of no-sleep, all-go patience.

Emma has my blue eyes, and even though many children are born with blue eyes, hers are my blue. I see them under the oxygen mask she has to wear to keep her lungs full.

Eight weeks later Emma has some neck control. I've just returned from Lexington. She rests on my chest when I get a call.

"Kevin has died," Uncle Norv says.

Kevin, my cousin, died while trying to escape Paddy's Pub in Bali. After the call, I do a little research until I know the scene inside the pub: a small explosion flashed out of a backpack amid the music and drinks and sweat. Kevin joined the frantic swarm into the warm night, only to be greeted by a white Mitsubishi van loaded with explosives. It left a crater more than a meter deep. Later, as I consider the incident, I like to rewind a moment before the backpack detonation; where, in his midtwenties, Kevin swayed and bounced to the band in pure bliss; where the dreamlike Bali became real under a mix of alcohol and moonlight; where, for Kevin, time slowed just enough to pause.

I consider the end often. I always have after the hit-and-run. I tell Nicholle that if we played the percentages I'd go before her, most likely some kind of cancer. It's probably already started somewhere deep inside my slippery body. Sometimes I worry Nicholle might go first. When she's late getting home from a mom's night out, my mind allows about a thirty-minute cushion and then begins the murmurs of what-ifs. The whole scene flashes by: the dreaded call—auto accident, funeral, insurance money, my baby girl growing, me dating or not, the guilt of either, moving (would I have to move? yes, definitely), different career, Emma's wedding—but then the garage door grumbles open and Nicholle saunters in, because in the end, there's absolutely nothing wrong.

I'm back on the road now: a week away every other month. When I'm gone I call home at six-thirty their time every night. Emma has just finished her bath and Nicholle puts the phone up to her ear so she can hear my voice. Emma's only eight months old and already she plays with her first steps.

Whenever I'm in Memphis I play cards a couple blocks off the strip in a brick basement where there's a password. It's a thrill. I know most of the participants. We aren't thugs. When we lose money, it hurts. We have polo shirts and mortgages. This time I have a flush and a story starts up around the table about a guy who had his dick put in a vise. He owed money to the wrong people, the regular story. There's laughter. I stare at my spades, organized and lethal. I reach for chips.

"Named Dub," says Nick, the organizer of the game.

"Dub?" someone says. "Deserved it."

Jordan, a baker with nervous hands, asks if you could die from that—a dick in a vise.

A new guy, Alec, quiets everyone with his monotone. "Yes," he says. "If you leave 'em there, eventually they die of hunger."

How many Dubs can there be? I think of what I'll say to Nicholle. What do I ask? Water moccasin Dub, snapping turtle Dub. I see him laughing in the muddy water as I dry off on the bank, still unable to quiet my knees. I wait until the next day. It's 7 p.m. I've whispered to Emma, and Nicholle explains how she's considering going back to work, just part-time, over the summer. She's having trouble losing the last ten pounds of pregnancy weight.

"When's Dub going to come visit his niece?" I ask.

"I don't know," she says. "He's not coming with money."

Dub rolls his truck eight times on a Monday morning at 3 a.m. He's drunk and his face and chest are mashed up good. Nicholle's parents call. Her mother asks for our prayers. We pray. It's close for a few hours, but Dub pulls through. Nicholle's mother praises God and his mercy and his comfort. It's all she talks about. Dub drank a bottle of Jack and got behind the wheel. He forgot to put his seatbelt on, was ejected from the rolling vehicle, and landed on his back, his eyes looking up at dizzying stars. I want to ask Nicholle's mother if buckling in is the devil's work, but I never will.

Two months later Dub shows up at the house one evening, twenty pounds lighter, hands shaking. He smells like boiled cabbage and urine. He says he's been in the same clothes for a week, sleeping during the day, driving at night. He's out of money and in trouble. Says it's the kind of trouble you don't wake up from.

"Got to stay out of 'bama," he says.

Before I can wrap my head around the situation, Nicholle has invited him in and shown him to the guest room. He showers upstairs while Nicholle and I cuss and stomp. Before the water turns off we've come to a compromise. He has two weeks. After that, he's on his own. I know Nicholle won't kick him out at the deadline, but it's something.

A month later I make the morning hospital rounds in Little Rock. I'm not supposed to leave until the following day, but I think of changing my flight to get back to the girls and Dub that night. I hustle back to the hotel. I pick up the ringing hotel receiver just before I leave for the airport. It's Nicholle's voice, nervous and quick. She says there are two men, a tall one at the front door, the other standing at the side of the house. She's ignored them, but the man at the front door has stopped knocking and peers into the long, narrow window to the left of the door. Emma sleeps.

"Am I crazy?" she asks.

"Just wait a minute," I say. "Deep breaths. Are they in uniform?" I ask.

"No," she says, "Why? Did you schedule something?" But she doesn't let me answer. "Because it's been far too long, they've been here five minutes." She tells me that she can see the one at the front door glancing around, not into the house, but around and at the other houses in the neighborhood. I hear Dub in the background.

"Put Dub on." I wait for his voice and the pause stretches. I force myself to breathe.

"There's some shit," he says. "Damn. Damn. Nothin's gunna happen, man. Trust me."

"You son of a bitch. Handle this, Dub." There's no reply.

"Hello?" It's Nicholle. "The one on the side moved into the backyard," she says. I picture the spacious yard, the towering ponderosa and medium dogwoods. It is 3:15 my time, 4:15 there. "Dub left the damn truck in the driveway. Listen to me. Something's not right here."

I stand in the small hotel room, packed suitcase at my feet. "Go get Emma," I say.

Nicholle breathes heavy into the phone and she says, "My God." I trace her path in my head, down the long second-floor hallway, through the white door into the baby's yellow bedroom with pink block letters above the crib: EMMA.

"I'm back in our room. Emma's . . . They're in—" she says. "The other one is on the back porch and the man at the front door, he's knocking again."

"Lock the door and call 911," I say. "Do it now."

"Don't hang up, damn you."

"I don't hear Emma."

"She's here."

"Where's Dub?"

"He's down there. They're screaming."

It was $20 a month for the alarm, whose wires probably dangled unconnected. I picture its white box under the stairs. Then the blue safe under our bed.

"Get the gun," I say.

"I'm putting the phone on the bed." Over the line I can hear Emma's labored breathing. It sounds like she's trying to put the receiver in her mouth. She was born at thirty weeks, the size of my forearm.

"I have it," Nicholle says. "Okay, I have it." A pause. "They're fighting. God, they're fighting."

"Like we practiced. Put the magazine in. It should have rounds in it."

"Crashing downstairs."

"Pull the hammer back," I say.

"What? What's the hammer?"

"I mean the slide. Shit, the slide. We've practiced this. The top part, throw the slide back."

"It's sticking. On the stairs now," she whispers. "Up the stairs."

"Yell out to them, 'I have a gun.'" She does. "And again," I say. She says it again. "And I will shoot you." I hear her say it, and she says, "Motherfuckers." Emma cries.

"It's sticking," is all she says to me.

"Do you remember?"

"Yes," she says. "I know what to do, but it's sticking." Her pitch rises. No one is on their way to them.

"Got it," Nicholle says. Then, "They're talking on the stairs." And her voice lowers even more. "They said 'Dub.' My God, they know us."

"Say it again."

"What?"

"The gun," I say.

"I've got a gun," she yells.

"If they open the door, you shoot until the gun stops firing and then load the next magazine."

She must hear the finality in my voice because she says, "No."
I hear it right before I hang up and dial 911. I sling information
as fast as I can to the operator, and picture the safety on the gun
Nicholle holds, turned down, the red dot hidden. My sight goes
wavy, the ceiling lowers on me as I think of the locked trigger. I
hang up, call home, and the metallic tone pulses off and on until the answering machine engages. It's her slow morning voice:
"You've reached Nicholle and Keith Bailey," and my voice in the
background, "and Emma"—she's laughing—"We're not in right
now, but please leave a message and we'll get back with you. Thank
you." I listen to the entire thing and hang up and call back. She
won't be able to hear me, no matter what I say into the phone.
When I get the message again, I hang up immediately and call
back. This time I let the whole message play and sit with the phone
in my hand, a beam of light from the hotel window now in my
eyes. I close them. The silence through the line is muffled. It's
recording me listening, and I think there's a chance, if I'm loud
enough, Nicholle might be able to pick up one word, through
the drywall and beams and carpet, past Dub's body, through the
locked bedroom door, past the men with outstretched arms.

I breathe and scream, "Safety," over and over and over, until
there are no more words, just a machine recording my empty
lungs.

KATHERINE L. HESTER

Trafficking

FROM *storySouth*

As FAR AS James is concerned, the asphalted tongue of interstate between Houston and Baton Rouge will never end, and he's been driving it half his life. Having first taken it westbound to college; then backtracking along it every Christmas before his stepfather died, when his mother was still so fixed on the idea that the four of them—James and her; his stepfather and his stepfather's son, Moultrie—would some year shape themselves into a family.

But this time Baton Rouge is not exactly where he's headed. He may have driven grudgingly into Louisiana, where the car of choice seems to be a mud-spattered white Caddy, but no way does he have any allegiance to this place, where houses seem to be something to be carried along interstates by flatbed trailers and debris he keeps having to swerve to avoid litters the road.

"I'm not even related to him," he'd reminded his mother when she phoned, though it had wanted to come out of his mouth as *He ain't no real kin of mine.* In Houston he's careful about how he says things and is able to get away with claiming he grew up in Louisiana miraculously, without any accent.

"He's all the kin you've got," his mother had said with asperity. "You know none of those people he ran around with will ever be coming to see him." Her voice softened. "And there's something he says he wants to talk to you about. You know he's just no good at letters."

Letters that, James realizes—guilt being something his mother has always been especially good at—he probably wouldn't have answered, were they to have arrived in the first place.

Now, because of that same guilt, he is driving once more over the Atchafalaya Basin into that brief hollow space sandwiched between night and dawn, when the bonds that hold things together seem, mysteriously, either strongest or loosest. Beyond the vapor lights' wan glow, the darkness is rich, has *body*, is like some fine wine. It remains unpunctured. Once, this stretch of interstate arching over swamp, where when he was in high school someone either he or his stepbrother Moultrie knew always lost their life on prom night, signaled either the beginning or the end of his trips. This time, the pitch from elevated roadway down to solid ground just indicates that he still has farther to go.

The squatty cinder-brick houses that announce the outskirts of Baton Rouge are already bravely swathed with Christmas lights, but their red glow might as well be that of a cigarette tossed from a passing truck. The blue and green seem thoughtless to James, something that draws the wrong kind of attention to unguarded houses built too close to the roadway.

When his stepfather passed away and left his mother a widow, Moultrie had been the one to show up unannounced at her house with a stepladder under his arm, the one who good-naturedly hauled the artificial tree down from the crawlspace and outlined the windows and eaves with Christmas lights. Another of Moultrie's typical gestures, simple and perfect and something James would have thought of himself, if he hadn't been busy — *working*, unlike his stepbrother — in Houston.

Up until the very second when what Moultrie still refers to as his *misstep* occurred, he always claimed he got some sort of lenience. He was still in business because he had scruples and they knew it: if the sale of certain drugs was going to happen in Baton Rouge, they'd rather it be him that did it than anybody else, so they turned a blind eye. This logic seemed stupid to James, one of his stepbrother's wrongheaded assumptions that left him wondering how Moultrie had managed to survive life for almost forty years.

"Who's *they*?" he'd said a year ago at Christmas, the last time he actually saw Moultrie. "You're full of shit — you know that, don't you?"

It was always cold when James saw Moultrie, always Christmastime. When his mother started asking him in June if he'd be home in December, he always told her he wouldn't, but in the end, he always was. Driving along the holiday-dead streets to pick up Moultrie, whose cars were never running, and take him to their mother's, where they went through the motions: the midnight mass attended by a sparse group of elderly parishioners which it always startled James to realize included his mother; the forced cheer of unwrapping the small pile of presents; the drawn-out dinner of Coca-Cola-basted ham.

Everything had changed about Baton Rouge, except his stepbrother and the dirty houses he lived in and the way James always wound up sitting in the living rooms of them, drinking beer and staring out the window at the messy strands of Christmas lights that licked up and down the street, while Moultrie told James who'd moved where and who had divorced or died, and other things James said didn't matter but that bummed him out a little when he thought about them later.

The house Moultrie had lived in last year had been on a different questionable side of town from the one James remembered him living in the year before, but houses Moultrie rented always smelled the same. Of old, possibly faulty gas space heaters and cigarettes, not Moultrie's, because he didn't smoke, but those of his nervous customers; of potentially decent weed; of Moultrie's clothes, which he usually found at thrift stores.

"Who's *they*?" James had demanded last Christmas.

"The Dixie Mafia," Moultrie explained. "The police."

"The Dixie Mafia?" James repeated. "And who is that, exactly?"

Only Moultrie would believe he was still in business because the underworld and the law, working in some weird conspiratorial partnership, believed he was a scrupulous dealer. Although it was true enough that Moultrie had never once been caught holding any bag, not once in any of the years James knew of: through buying beer for him when he was still underage to selling pot to kids who halfheartedly attended the nearby junior college.

"The other shoe is going to drop down soon enough," James warned, taking a swig from his beer. "Get out while the getting's good."

"I'm careful," Moultrie said, but he wasn't. James knew he ought to stop coming by Moultrie's house, even if it was only once a year—to be there when the cops busted down the door wouldn't do him a bit of good. And in any case, he didn't want to be around, to have to be the one to break the news of Moultrie's latest bad luck to his mother.

When Moultrie had let him into his house, he hadn't even thought to lock the door behind them once he waved James through it; James had been the one who reached back and shot the probably useless deadbolt home, and he had hardly touched anything anyone could fault him for in years. If Moultrie got busted while James was sitting in his living room, James would end up downtown for questioning or as a witness at Moultrie's trial, forced to lie or tell the truth, or he'd have to make Moultrie's bail, and any of those things would solder him too tightly to this place. Which he prefers to visit for a day or so, then leave.

As soon as James makes it east of Baton Rouge, he has to remind himself to watch the road signs for I-12 as it branches away from 10 and slips above New Orleans, flat and even duller than the ground he's already covered. I-12's the comfortable sure shot, the choice of truckers and salesmen and the middle-aged, of those poor fools who hope to, or have to, make time. Ten's the party route, no reason to be on it but New Orleans, and for years he and Moultrie held anybody who'd choose I-12 instead of it in contempt.

The horizon beyond the windshield is brightening, degree by imperceptible degree, and some of the cars on the other side of the grassy median have already cut off their headlights. An oncoming car flashes theirs and his spirits lift. It seems like such a friendly gesture, as if the occupants of these cars streaming toward him—going where? home? to work? going somewhere—are well-meaning fellow travelers telegraphing to him the news that his long haul through the night is finally over.

In the grayish half-light, he takes his eyes from the road long enough to glance down at the piece of paper on the seat beside him. Moultrie's hand-drawn map contains a Kentucky Fried Chicken and a Home Depot as landmarks, and precise mileage. How can Moultrie know these details, when he hasn't ever had the opportunity to drive this particular route himself? Moultrie's handwriting is the sort of deliberate, flourished cursive James jettisoned in high school.

All in all this situation has given me time to reflect on my life and see my accomplishments and mistakes with open eyes, the last paragraph of the letter begins. It's hard to know whether this is a sentiment Moultrie actually wants to convey to James or it's for the benefit of someone else who reads his mail.

The postscript to the letter — and James has followed its instructions, even though it has always irked him to have Moultrie tell him what to do — is this: *Be sure to bring change for the vending machines, man.*

Moultrie's current predicament has cleared up several things James always wondered about: how elderly mothers can continue to love felon sons; how neighbors, unswayed by yellow webs of police tape and the eyewitness of the news, always swear that the quiet man who lived across the cul-de-sac from them just went hunting a lot and that was why his house contained so many guns. Moultrie is still the same person he always was. Besides, it's not as if he killed somebody, a fact that James's mother, of whom James expected more, has not yet tired of pointing out.

When Moultrie's father married James's mother, when James was fifteen and Moultrie was seventeen, Moultrie had been fairly circumspect, and at that point all he sold was pot. It wasn't until James started college that it occurred to him that it might have been more considerate of Moultrie to move out of his father's house rather than keep living in the basement rec room.

By last year, Moultrie had long since moved out and on, as had James. By last year, Moultrie had also taken to keeping much harder stuff — *his* stuff, swaddled as tenderly as babies waiting to be adopted and taken home by people James had known all his life and others he would never meet — stashed in empty Haagen-Dazs ice cream bar containers arrayed in a row in his freezer. It was the last place anybody would look, he told James. His electronic scale and stash of Baggies were hidden underneath the floorboards in the living room, and the phone rang nonstop while he showed James exactly how he measured things with the same pride in his craftsmanship as when he'd taken him, earlier, past the cabinet he'd built of scavenged heart pine.

"Such a worrier," he said, his fingers busy. "Be cool, man."

Now Moultrie is the one who worries. Which is as it should be, James thinks. As James's mother says, Moultrie *frets*. Every phone call he makes to what he now without even noticing calls the *outside* requires a catechism that no longer startles James when he picks up the phone to hear it — *press 1 to indicate that you understand this call has been initiated by an inmate of the Louisiana State Prison system; press the pound key if you are willing to accept these charges.*

Moultrie's called James just often enough that responding to the recorded request to pay for a call has become habit: once James even accepted the charges for what turned out to be a wrong number or misdial, some other poor fuck in some other prison hoping to get word of something to someone. *Tell Mama I'm in here,* the voice had wailed into his ear over the shriek of a prison common room, and there'd been nothing for James to do but gently replace the phone in its cradle.

And now Moultrie, mellow Moultrie — who used never to worry about much of anything and often slept, James remembers, past noon; Moultrie, who any afternoon in 1983 might have announced to an admiring James that pretty soon he'd be quitting one of the interchangeable menial jobs he held to go off to follow the Dead; Moultrie, who several summers after that would tap into something called the Rainbow Family Gathering, and even more recently hitchhiked all the way to Burning Man, threatening to stop in Houston on the way — now Moultrie, he frets. Apparently. He's called James twice — at least a five-dollar charge each time — to confirm the make, model, and tag number of the car James will be parking in the prison lot, and once more since then to make sure he's still planning to show up.

James hunches over the steering wheel, fumbling to turn on the windshield wipers, to swipe at the windshield with a bit of ragged Kleenex scavenged from underneath his seat. The difference between damp night and warmer morning has fogged the curving glass. His mother doesn't realize arriving in time for visiting hours meant he had to leave Houston in the middle of the night. Moultrie has no idea how what he did has aged her. James flicks on the radio, looks down at the passenger seat at Moultrie's carefully written directions, and noses the car into the exit lane.

It's that time, just pre–morning drive time, when in other circumstances James might be leaving a woman's apartment, shirt untucked, shoes off and in one hand so he doesn't wake her when he lets himself out of her apartment. The time of morning when there's still dew to spangle the windshields of all the recently waxed compacts in the parking lots and, once he slips behind the wheel of his car and turns on the radio, the DJs can play pretty much what they please, the flip sides of hits and songs that never made the top ten. This time of day always feels like a fresh start, and James wishes he had a better reason to have driven all this way.

It's approached so delicately, in code—Moultrie's situation. His misstep. He pled guilty to the charges against him in the hope he'd somehow beat the mandatory sentence and serve less than the three-plus-something years that trafficking—a felony, James would like to point out to both his mother and Moultrie, a federal crime—had meant. The fact that he didn't beat anything and 'll now be serving at least four years out of fifteen means he harbors great enmity toward his lawyer, one found by James's mother, who either failed or did not fail to live up to his end of the bargain and cost a sum she'll be struggling to pay off for the duration of Moultrie's sentence and probably past that—but Moultrie has never once admitted to *being* guilty.

All in all this situation has given me time to reflect on my life and see my accomplishments and mistakes with open eyes. Alone in the car, James allows himself to roll his eyes. This is not fucking *Oprah*—Moultrie was *busted.*

There's probably an actual town with a main street and square cached between the interstate and the state highway leading to the prison, but James will never come back here again. Sometime in the future he'll speed along I-12 past the signs indicating this exit and remember only the Kentucky Fried Chicken and Home Depot from Moultrie's map, and the deserted McDonald's playscape he just passed. The restaurant behind it is already open, circled by vehicles waiting their turn at the drive-through.

Three strikes and you're out, Moultrie reminded him over the phone. *I didn't even get one!* His tone had been righteous. Rapists were in and out in much less time that he'll be.

He'd just made a misstep.

The prison, or, as Moultrie labeled it so carefully on the return address of his letter, the *correctional facility,* turns out to be in a field that might've once grown corn or cotton. Its location falls somewhere between country and town, and it could be located anywhere, in fact probably is; there have to be a thousand places just like this all over the country. It could be a school or a sewage treatment plant or rehab facility or any of a number of vaguely institutional things. The gravel parking lot is already almost full by the time James pulls into it, a fact that reminds him this is podunk minimum-security stuff. He'd expected something more — the Big House and the Pen and cinematic lockdowns.

The line to check in at the guard box at the edge of the lot snakes back five yards or more, consists almost entirely of girls who look too young. Possibly too young to have finished high school, certainly too young to drink, or to possess the babies half of them hold in their arms. He takes his place in their midst, is surreptitiously looked over and then ignored. At the front of the line, the security wand dips and crackles, passing over the Baggie of change and car keys a girl with hair combed into an elaborate up-do clutches in one hand, then over the apparent self-portrait drawn in ballpoint on lined notebook paper she holds in the other. The envelope of photographs she also wants to bring in apparently will require permission from someone higher up, a sergeant.

"I'm going to have to wand you, little man," the guard says, bending toward the toddler who's wandering blithely toward and then away from the gate. The guard reaches out and tugs gently at the straps at the back of the little boy's overalls: the wand in his hand passes over the tiny tennis shoes, their laces tied in neat bows; over the dingy blue plush stuffed animal hugged in one hand.

James waits his turn, wondering if the real punishment of jail might lie in the complete tedium of it. *Everyone* is bored — the girls standing in line with their arms folded and their hips lazily cocked, some of whom holler across him about the Greyhound bus they took to get here; the guards, who over and over again in a monotone explain rules everyone already understands.

But everyone seems to know each other, and the guards are less uptight than Security at the Houston airport.

"How you doing, Miz Cantrell?" the guard in the booth says to the elderly woman in front of James. He extends his clipboard for her to sign. Everybody else knew to put their coins for the vending machines into Zip-loc Baggies, but James is going to have to toss his loose change into a bowl before he walks through the metal detector.

"Moultrie Woodruff," he announces when he gets to the window of the booth. It's so simple, like a password. One second, he's out in the free world, then the security wand blesses him with a flourish, and there he is—on the inside.

There's nothing high-tech about his entrance. He just signs in, walks the thirty feet into the squared-off cinder-brick building, is buzzed through one small waiting area and into the next like live-stock moving through a chute. Each group of guards waves him on with an astounding lack of suspicion; they don't even bother to prevent him from noticing, when he puts pen to paper at his second stop, that no one's been to see Moultrie in months. Some-where, behind another set of closed doors, he can hear a loud-speaker summoning his stepbrother.

Moultrie's long ponytail has been cut off; what's left of his hair has gone gray. All the other inmates being visited seem to be the same age as the girls who've come to see them—as far as James can tell, they're all mere babies being visited by babies.

"James, man," Moultrie says, moving forward.

James steps back.

"Hey, it's not like it's catching or something," Moultrie says, his voice loud. "Not like if you touch me they won't ever let you back out again." Their second try at an embrace dissolves into an awk-ward bumping of shoulders. "Let's just sit down, bro'," he says.

James realizes he'd expected—planned on—a pane of plastic between them. Where are the phones, the surveillance cameras? What the room resembles most is a school cafeteria, one where the folding chairs Moultrie indicates have been arranged in rows along the sides like bleachers. The vending machines are at the back.

"Can't sit facing each other," Moultrie explains as they sit down shoulder to shoulder. "You might pass something off to me. How are you?"

"Okay," James says. The wall in front of him looks mirrored, but he knows it's not, that there must be more bored-seeming, pokerfaced guards behind it. All around them, family groups have begun to settle in in a way that makes him realize they're go-ing to sit here like this for the entire five visiting hours, the long haul.

"What's up?" he says, hands on his knees, because it's what he has always said, since he was fifteen and his mother and Moultrie's father had just merged households and he used to get home from school and knock on Moultrie's bedroom door, and sometimes Moultrie would let him shake the seeds from the weed into the crease of *Quadrophenia*'s double jacket before he cleaned and bagged it. James asks it even though it feels like saying to some cancer patient *How are you?* The answer can't be good.

"Thanks for coming, man," Moultrie says formally beside him. "It's been a long time. Directions get you here okay?"

"Yeah." Had those directions been so detailed, and Moultrie's handwriting so careful, just because it was another way to fill up time? The five hours ahead of them stretch into eternity. Driving here, James had imagined he'd stay for an hour or two; that maybe he'd be able to make it back to Houston before midnight, only half his weekend wasted. What can they possibly *do* here?

"What's your day like?" he asks finally, clearing his throat.

Moultrie pauses. "I read," he says. "Read a lot. We got a group that reads the paper after dinner."

"There a decent library here? What kind of stuff are you reading?"

"Elmore Leonard. Tom Clancy. Lot of the guys read romance novels." Moultrie's lip curls. "But I just finished *Notes from Underground*. Dostoevsky. He's got it *down*, man."

"What down?" James asks.

"This." Moultrie waves an encompassing hand at the room. "Before that I read *The Fountainhead*. I keep to myself," he adds abruptly.

James sits back. Maybe *now* the prison movie he'd imagined will start, and Moultrie'll say something like *I keep my nose clean.*

"Got a job," he says instead. "Mom tell you?"

James remembers hearing something about work in the kitchen. Framed by his mother's eternally optimistic voice as something good, something Moultrie could use later. On the outside. She has always looked on the bright side, at least as far as Moultrie is concerned.

"That one didn't work out." Moultrie sighs. "I was real fucking depressed, those first few months, about my situation."

There it is: the situation. The reason James is sitting here, the reason he can't think of a single thing to say.

"I'm in the shop now," Moultrie says. He turns so he can look James full in the face, careful to keep both feet on the floor. He sounds awake for the first time since James arrived. "Painting signs."

"Signs?" James says. The clatter of chairs scraped back on the linoleum is threaded through with the wails of fretful kids and the thud of a soda can as it rattles into the chute in the vending machine. He feels defeated by the clamor of so much important information needing to be conveyed so fast—five hours isn't much, when you've got a life you're sealed away from and a family out there doing stuff they need to tell you about.

"You brought change, man?" Moultrie asks, interrupting himself hopefully. As early as it is, everybody around them's drinking Coke like coffee, even the guard sitting, yawning, by the door. "I could use something to drink."

"Sure." James digs in his pocket.

"You've got to go get it. We can't both go. You might be handing something off to me. You know."

"Oh," James says, disconcerted. "What do you want?"

A Coke, a Baby Ruth bar, some vinegar and salt potato chips, maybe some Twinkies. As Moultrie lists them, James realizes Moultrie didn't ask him to bring change because he wanted to be as much of a host as possible and have a way to offer *something*, but more because whatever James brings back from the machines will be out of the ordinary, an unexpected entertainment. What's it like to be bored so shitless?

"Yeah, I know," Moultrie says when he gets back. "I'm going to start working out again a couple of months before my date comes up." He peels back the wrapper on his candy bar.

"So you've got this job in the sign shop," James says. "You just going to let yourself turn to shit, man?"

"Huh? Like, you know, you've seen those signs they put up when there's going to be some kind of big meeting? About a piece of property? Like so somebody can make changes to it?"

"Oh," James says. "Like for zoning hearings."

"Yeah. And sometimes highway signs. You know, the big green and white ones."

"People paint those?"

James never thought about where they came from, had assumed they were printed somehow, stamped out by some giant machine, and this is Moultrie, for Chrissakes, who could've gone to LSU, who could've done anything.

"Yeah," Moultrie says simply. "I'm the best at it in here, so now it's mostly just me. Pretty cool. I get the shop to myself. There's a radio. Everybody else they tried at it, they just slopped the paint all over the place."

His obvious pride doesn't seem manufactured; besides, there's no way anybody else can hear them: the din's almost enough to stop their conversation in its tracks.

"Oh," James says.

Moultrie leans over. "Look at him," he whispers abruptly, with a jerk of his chin indicating a young guy sprawled out in a chair. The guy's girlfriend or wife or lady or whoever she is leans solicitously toward him. James recognizes her as the one at the front of the line who'd carried in the drawing that looked like something she'd done at her desk at the back of math class. The envelope of photos that held up the whole line must've made it through somehow, because she's handing each of them over and then taking them back like a handful of cards she's been dealt. *Bee-Bee, she say tell you hey,* she says. *Over there's La-Keisha.* The names ride the current of noise toward them. *Coconut cake for dessert,* she adds. *Wish I could've brung some.*

"Let me tell you, that fucker was *on* my ass when I first came in," Moultrie says. "This might as well be his living room or something. He'll be here his whole fucking life. In and out."

Unlike Moultrie, who just last Christmas looked mainly like some placid hippie type and now has lost it all—his supply, his beautiful long braid, his dirty house so comfortable for hanging out in—and doesn't even have anybody to visit him every weekend like these other guys do.

"What about you?" Moultrie says. "What's going on in Houston? Got a girlfriend?"

James shakes his head.

"What about that little brown-eyed girl, what was her name, that one you brought home that time us three drove down to New Orleans for the weekend?"

"May-Beth?" James says repressively. "You know her name, man. Shit, I ain't seen her in two years."

When May-Beth had come to Baton Rouge with him, she and James and Moultrie had stood in the wind on the observation platform at the top of the state capitol and stared at the muddy Mississippi. James still remembers the way her curly brown hair had escaped from its ponytail, the way she pushed it away from her face with her fingers.

"That's right," Moultrie says. "May-Beth."

Such a typical Moultrie move, to pretend he doesn't remember. May-Beth had joked that she wanted to touch her fingers to a bullet hole left from the barrage fired at Huey P. Long, so they'd taken the elevator, all three of them, down to the basement, and after that Moultrie had driven them on what he called his guided tour of the city, which consisted mostly of slowing the car at houses where he got stuff. That night, when May-Beth folded herself into the narrow twin bed in James's old bedroom with him, she'd sleepily pronounced Moultrie *a trip and a half,* and James should have known what was coming. The next night, she'd danced with them both in turn in the Quarter, Moultrie more than him. And then she had linked arms with them both as they stumbled their way back, tipsy, through the empty streets toward their car.

And that, as they say, had been that.

"So who all's come to see you?" James says pointedly. He knows from his quick glance at the guard's clipboard that the answer's *Nobody.*

A girl he'd been sort of dating when he went in, Moultrie says without much regret in his voice. She came once at the very beginning.

"I asked her to pack up the rest of my shit and get it to Mom. Did she do it? She hasn't ever wrote me."

"What shit?" James asks.

"Huh? I got somebody to hold on to all the furniture, but this was like, little things. Books and pictures. Stuff you could fit into a suitcase. You know."

"You didn't figure out what to do with it before? It's not like you didn't know you'd end up here."

"Mom," Moultrie says, ignoring him. "Mom was somebody who came to see me. I couldn't let her come again after the first time. Just couldn't take it, the way it made her so upset."

"That was nice of you," James says. "Of course it made her upset."

Moultrie takes a quick, furtive look around. "Hey, James, chill," he says. "I didn't think I was going to end up here."

"Where the fuck did you think you were going to end up?"
James hisses. "No way was some junkie ever going to pack up your
shit and get it to Mom's house."

"It wasn't like that," Moultrie says, looking affronted.

"Like what?" James says. "You mean it was all hearts and flowers?"

"Hey, James, take it easy," Moultrie says again, simply. He pauses.
"Let's not fight. You and Mom are just about all I got now."

"Cut the sad song and dance," James says, standing up. "I already know what you want to ask. Mom already said. How you
need me to tell the parole board I'll let you live with me once you
get out. That you've turned over some new leaf."

"Hey, calm down, it's cool, bro'," Moultrie says, looking stricken.

It's just another family squabble, business as usual for this place.
The girl who drew the portrait of herself in ballpoint pen is crying, fat tears running down her face. The scarred linoleum on the
floor beneath James's feet, the folding chair he's sitting on, the
thump and clank of the vending machines, all enrage him.

"Just admit it for once," he leans over and hisses to Moultrie.
"Okay? Just admit you were so fucking dumb you had a backpack
full of heroin lying there on your living room floor and the front
door unlocked. That's all I'm asking."

"Huh?" Moultrie says.

"Are you fucking deaf?"

"Yeah," Moultrie says simply. "A little. It gets to you, in here. The
noise."

"Jesus," James says. "Why bother lying to *me*? What's the point?"

"No," Moultrie says stubbornly. "I don't know how that stuff got
there."

He looks away.

Nobody here is guilty of anything. Everybody was just in the
wrong place at the wrong time. All it was was bad luck or circum-
stance. Connections that went bad, and deals that went sour.

"Aw, shit," James says. He sits back down. "You dumb fuck."

In the end, he retraces his steps out of the gravel lot and past the
field shored up with barbed wire. Past the stand of curving pines,
and then along the corridor of strip mall—Home Depot and the
KY Fry, and all the other buildings Moultrie hadn't listed in his
directions, a Citgo and a yogurt shop and a place for to-go Chi-

nese food. The road in front of James is glinting wet windshields from the afternoon rain. Everybody in this town seems to be going somewhere, and the wide flat lots in front of all the restaurants are starting to fill up. With couples, and families stopping for their big meal of the day, still so country that behind the big plate-glass windows they're clasping their hands and bending their heads to bless the food set on the plastic tablecloths in front of them.

The interstate is a looming comfort he can spot from the trajectory of the access road. The coffee he stops for at the last-chance McDonald's wedged into the on-ramp is hot enough to scald him back to Houston. It makes the car smell like home.

All the newness he remembers from the morning has burned off the day, and the two right-hand lanes are clogged with truckers, not a single good citizen among them. The trucks are all chrome and heat and glow, impatient to get somewhere before dark, and it's just as easy for them to box James in as not to.

All it was was a suitcase, Moultrie said when he turned to leave; and there were just a couple of places it might be.

These trucks are never going to let James merge without a fight; they'll never give him a courtesy blink to remind him that in the rain that's started beating down again he ought to put his lights on.

"So what am I looking for?" he'd asked, turning back to his stepbrother, jingling the change left in his pocket.

"Some other stuff's in there, too," Moultrie had said, looking pained. He cleared his throat. "If nobody found it. Just flush it."

The trucks press close on either side of James in a dangerous lumbering embrace. Green-and-white reflective signs Moultrie could've painted nudge at his right shoulder. He forces his way into the middle lane. How quick your reflexes have to be, he thinks as he merges, rejoicing. A moment's hesitation and all might be lost.

LOU MANFREDO

Soul Anatomy

FROM *New Jersey Noir*

IN CERTAIN PLACES there exists a permeating pointlessness to life, with an aura of despair so acute that its inhabitants come to be unafraid of or, at the very least, indifferent to the inevitability of death. Camden City is just such a place.

Camden is a torn-down, ravished ghost of a city, blighted by poverty and corruption, violence, drugs, and disease. Its residents wallow amid the decay which lies like a sickened, dying animal prostrate in the sun's heat.

Within this city, in stark and ironic contrast, the modern glass and steel complex of Cooper University Hospital rises awash in bright, artificial light, a towering monument to mainstream mankind's fierce desire to live. The hospital exists on sprawling acres of urban renewal, restored row houses lining its borders, a false oasis of promise in a true desert of desperation.

Frank Cash, senior partner of the distinguished Haddonfield law firm of Cash, Collings and Haver, slowly turned his shiny new BMW into the hospital's enclosed parking garage. He stopped just short of the barrier arm as the dashboard digital flickered: 4:01 a.m.

As the driver's window lowered silently, a cold dampness from the dark November morning intruded into the car's warm interior. Cash shuddered slightly against it, reaching a hand to the automated ticket machine and pressing a manicured finger against the glowing green button. He frowned unconsciously at the cheerful computer-generated male voice which accompanied the dispensed parking stub.

Welcome to the Cooper University Hospital parking facility.

Tucking the stub into his pocket, Cash swung the car left and accelerated quickly up the smooth concrete ramp of the nearly deserted garage. It occurred to him that perhaps it would have been more prudent to use the family minivan as opposed to his 750. He noted a small cluster of parked vehicles at level two, centered around the elevator bank. He parked quickly and strode to an elevator.

Ten minutes later he stood facing a window in a small consultation area located within the emergency room. He gazed out across Haddon Avenue and eyed a squat building in the near distance. Emblazoned across the top, the words *Camden Police Department* gave fair warning to anyone in and around the hospital to behave themselves. Cooper had been as effectively isolated from the surrounding city as possible, Interstate 676 and parkland to the east, police headquarters to the north, renovated housing used as residences for hospital staff and medical offices to the south and west.

It had been a rather profitable project, Cash mused as he scanned the scene, absentmindedly scraping a bit of soot from the sill before him, sleep stinging his eyes. Quite profitable.

As he waited, Cash's thoughts returned to the events of last evening: the quiet dinner with family in his sprawling Victorian home in Moorestown, some reading, the late-night news, sleep, and then the phone call.

"Hello?" he had whispered into the mouthpiece, glancing to his sleeping wife as she gently stirred beside him.

"Mr. Cash?" a tentative voice had begun. "It's Ken, sir, Ken Barrows."

Jesus Christ, Cash had thought, what could the most junior member of the firm possibly want at this hour? "What the hell, Barrows, it's almost three-thirty in the morning."

"Yes sir, I realize that. It's just that . . . well, I'm on call tonight. For the FOP, you know, the police union. It's my week to be on call."

Cash frowned into the mouthpiece, again glancing to his wife. She seemed resettled, her nightly sleeping pill working its wonder.

"And?" Cash asked harshly.

Barrows paused for a moment, perhaps suddenly rethinking the wisdom of the call. "There's been a shooting, sir. A fatal police shooting. One person is dead, but no police were injured. The union rep called me from the scene a few minutes ago. He wants me down there."

Cash's frown turned to a scowl. "Of course he does, Barrows. That's the purpose of having a lawyer on call twenty-four-seven. It's mandatory when you represent the unions. But why in God's name did you feel it necessary to—"

"I thought you'd want to know, sir," Barrows interrupted, a new confidence in his tone. "You see, the shooting was in Camden City. It was a white officer, the dead man is black. And the officer involved, the one who shot the perpetrator, was . . . it was that new officer." He paused here for effect. Barrows, despite his youth, was a good lawyer. "It was Anthony Miles." Another slight pause. "I thought it best you knew, sir. Of course, I can handle it if you'd like . . . but I thought you should know."

Now Cash sat upright, indifferent to whether or not the movement would further disturb his wife. "Oh," he said, his mind shifting sharply from disgruntled employer to defensive lawyer. "Oh," he repeated.

After a brief silence, he spoke again. "Call the union rep at the scene. Tell him to put Miles into a radio car and get him over to Cooper ASAP. I'll call ahead and get hold of whoever is in charge of the emergency room. I want Miles sedated. Tell the union rep to convince the kid that he's stressed out and needs to see a doctor. Once the doctors get a drug into him, the law says he can't be interviewed. It'll buy us some time. I can be at the hospital in less than thirty minutes."

"Yes sir, I'll call the rep. Shall I meet you there?"

Cash considered it. "No. Just make sure the rep gets Miles to the ER immediately. I'll grease the wheels. I don't want some intern refusing to sedate."

"Yes sir," Barrows said, his confidence even stronger now.

"You were right to call, Ken. It shows good presence of mind."

"Thank you, sir. I thought you should know."

Cash slipped out of bed, shaving and dressing quickly. He left a note for his wife and drove to Route 38, leaving the lush, manicured splendor of Moorestown for a twenty-minute drive to the desolate wasteland of Camden City. As the BMW cut rapidly through misty darkness, Cash thought about police officer Anthony Miles.

Miles had gone directly to the Camden Police Department after graduating from the County Police Academy. Like all rookies, he had been assigned to routine patrol duty with a senior training officer. In most such cases, no one in any remotely influential position would have cause to notice or care.

But Miles was different. Miles was the son of Curtis Miles, United States attorney to the State of New Jersey. The *Republican* United States attorney.

And Camden was ground zero for the Democratic machine that had maintained a strong and lucrative hold on New Jersey politics for more than two decades. Frank Cash, himself the son of a former county chairman, had lined his pockets and filled the coffers of his law firm with countless contracts, retainers, and fees financed with state and county tax dollars. Indeed, his firm's representation of every police union in South Jersey was merely one such plum.

So when Cash sat down to lunch some months earlier with the current county chairman, the implications had not been lost on him.

Officer Miles, the chairman had suggested, was no ordinary rookie. His father was an ambitious, driven man who had chosen a pragmatic approach to what he hoped would be an unlimited political future: he would dedicate himself to fighting corruption in New Jersey—particularly Democratic corruption.

"Like shooting fish in a barrel," the chairman said between forkfuls of shrimp. "If he's serious about it."

"Is he?" Cash asked.

The chairman laid down his fork, then patted his lips gently with a linen napkin.

"Yes, he is—it's his ticket to the governor's office."

Cash considered it. "What's our exposure?"

The chairman shrugged. "Any is too much. This young cop has his own political juice, courtesy of his old man. If becoming a cop was all he really wanted, his father could have gotten him assigned to bikini patrol in some shore town or crabgrass stakeout in our neck of the woods. Why would he want to go to Camden?"

"Maybe," Cash offered with little conviction, "he just wants to be a *real* cop."

"Yeah," the chairman said, reaching once more for his fork. "And I'm Harry fuckin' Truman." He leaned in across the table, speaking more softly. Cash had to strain his ears to make out the words. "Camden has about twenty-three hundred violent crimes per hundred thou population, compared to the national average of about four hundred fifty. It's been named the most dangerous city in the entire country time after time. The state had to take over the entire police department and school system because they're so fucked up. Tell me, why would the son of Curtis Miles, the guy who wants to be governor, maybe president someday, want to work in Camden? The kid's a Rider University graduate, for Christ's sake." The chairman sat back. "He's a fuckin' plant for his old man. You have any idea what motivated and hostile eyes can find in that environment?"

Cash sipped his wine before responding. "So you figure his father for a white knight sending his kid in to help?"

The chairman laughed. "White knight my ass. He's no better than anybody else. He's already greased some wheels for his son. The kid isn't on the job six months, and he's assigned to HIDTA already. The *worst* fuckin' place for him, far as we're concerned. No, Curtis Miles is no white knight. He's just so ambitious he's willing to throw his own son into the fire to help get him what he needs to nail Democrats."

Cash shook his head. "We've chosen a nasty business for ourselves."

"Yes. And that kid working High Intensity Drug Trafficking Areas can turn things even nastier."

"Why are you telling me all this?"

The chairman shrugged. "You're the union lawyer. Sooner or later, this kid will most likely wind up in your lap. I want you to understand what you'll be dealing with. I haven't survived in this shit all these years without learning to anticipate."

Cash drained his wineglass and reached for the bottle. "I understand."

Now, forty minutes after leaving his bed, Frank Cash stared out the hospital window into the Camden night and sighed. He remembered long-ago advice from his politician father. *There are winners and losers. Be a winner. It makes life bearable.*

He turned as the door to the small consultation room opened. It was the union representative, Peter Negron.

"Hello, Pete."

The man entered the room and closed the door softly behind him. "Hello, Mr. Cash. I didn't figure you'd come down personally."

"Yes, well, I have. Has Miles been sedated?"

"Yeah, the chief resident saw him soon as we got here. They jacked the kid up on Xanax. Five minutes later, two spooks from the county prosecutor's office showed up. I told 'em the kid was medicated and couldn't talk to them . . . They left, said they'd see him tomorrow. They seemed pissed off."

Cash grunted. "They'll get over it. We needed to buy some time so I can get a handle on this."

Negron nodded. "Okay. I was with Miles when the shooting went down. We were workin' HIDTA citywide, me and Miles and Sanchez."

"Where'd it happen?"

"Line Street, between South 6th and Roberts."

"Tell me what happened."

When Negron finished, Cash ran a hand through his hair thoughtfully. "Sounds pretty clean," he said. Then pointedly added, "*If* that's how it went down."

Negron smiled and raised his right hand. "I swear on my eyes, counselor, I ain't dumb enough to lie to the lawyer. 'Specially for this kid."

With their eyes locked, Cash nodded. "Go get him. Bring him to me."

Negron turned and left.

When Miles entered the room, Cash was immediately stricken by his youthful appearance. Although twenty-two, he looked seventeen. His black hair was long, unkempt. It spilled over the collar of the faded navy pea coat he wore. Dried vomit stained the front panel of the coat, its sour odor touching at Cash's nostrils. Dark blood was splattered across the left cuff and forearm. The young man's eyes were hollow and listless. A stubble of light whiskers covered his chin and cheeks, giving him a dirty, unpleasant look. While the clothing and grooming fit well with Miles's antinarcotic assignment, he seemed a little too comfortable in the outfit. Cash found a mild disliking begin to dawn.

"Have a seat, Miles," he said, and watched as the cop slid a chair back from the small, round table. Cash sat opposite him, folding his hands on the smooth plastic tabletop. How much bad news, he wondered, had been discussed in this very same room?

"All right," he said as Miles's eyes lifted to meet his own. "My name is Frank Cash. My law firm represents members of the local chapter of your union, the Fraternal Order of Police. I'm here to help you deal with all this."

Cash saw Miles's gaze fall away, dropping to the tabletop, his body shaking with a sudden chill. His appearance seemed to suddenly morph into that of a frightened boy caught in some youthful transgression and summoned to his father's study. Cash found his initial suspicions and dislike begin to waver. In all his fifty-one years, he had never taken a life, not even that of a small animal or rodent. And here was this boy, barely out of school, who had violently sent a man to hell in what surely must have been a horrifying, desperate moment.

"All right," Cash repeated, gentler this time, softer. "State, county, and city headhunters will be hounding you tomorrow, son. I need you to tell me what happened, *everything*, every detail. Get it straight in your head. Let's see where I can help. Just start from the beginning and go slowly. Tell me everything, even if it doesn't sound very good. It'll sound worse said cold tomorrow, believe me."

Miles raised his eyes. "Negron said he told you everything already."

Cash nodded. "Yes. He told me what *he* did and what he *thinks* he saw. I need *you* to tell me what you did. What you saw."

Miles's eyes filled with tears. "Yes. I understand."

The young policeman shifted himself in his seat, fixed an unblinking stare at the darkened window behind Cash, and began to tell his story.

"We were on patrol, the three of us, me in the front recorder seat, Negron driving, Sanchez in back behind me. It musta been about two in the morning. We were cruising known drug locales; just eyeballing. Cold, crappy night like this, most of the deals were going down indoors. Anyway, we wind up on Line Street, heading east, just rolling past the broken-down houses along there."

"Where is Line Street?" Cash asked.

Miles shrugged. "'Bout six, seven blocks south of here, just east of Broadway."

"What neighborhood is that?"

Another shrug. "I don't know. Whitman Park, I guess."

"Go on."

"So we're just rolling along, real slow—maybe ten, fifteen tops. The street is narrow, a few parked cars here and there, some just abandoned. So we cross South 6th Street heading toward Roberts. Northwest corner of Line and 6th is an empty lot where some condemned buildings got demoed. There's a fence around it, chain-link. Even though we're kinda looking around as we roll, none of us saw this old lady till she was right in front of us, like she just appeared out of the dark, you know? Negron almost ran her over. Well, she makes us for cops and starts banging on the hood of the car and screaming at us."

"Was she black? Hispanic, Caucasian, what?"

Miles glanced briefly at Cash. "Hispanic." He paused for a moment before continuing. "Anyway, she's all excited, so Sanchez gets out of the back seat and approaches her. He tins her and starts talking in Spanish, and she starts bawling and pointing to the only house on the north side of Line Street that's still standing. It was the house she had come out of."

"Had you seen her come out of it?"

"No, like one second the street was empty, the next second there she was, in front of the car." Cash noticed the trembling begin to intensify, apparently overcoming the dosage of Xanax the cop had received. When Miles spoke again, there was a rise of pitch in his voice. "So anyway, I get out of the car and Sanchez winks at me and makes a face, like he's saying, *Look at this old bitch, do you believe this?*"

"How old would you say she was?"

Miles shifted in his seat and leaned forward slightly, still directing his words at the black rectangle of the window. "Old. Pushing sixty. I don't know."

Cash smiled slightly. "Go on."

"So when I reach them, she starts speaking English, telling us there's a black guy up on the second floor of the house, been acting crazy all night, people coming and going and she was trying to sleep and told him something and he cursed her and tried to hit her, and she got scared and ran out and saw us. So by now Negron is standing there too, and he asks her if she called the cops. She says no, there's no phone in the house, no water, no electricity, nothing. We can see it's boarded up, abandoned, and we figure her for a squatter. She tells us the black guy deals H, sometimes crack, the building is his base, everybody is afraid of him and all this kind of shit. So Sanchez starts writing it down, you know, to sort of appease her a little. We figure maybe she's stoned, you know, old and stoned and half nuts. So then Negron says he feels like a little action, let's check it out. Well, I'm a little bored myself, it was a slow tour and I figure, what the hell. So Sanchez stays at the car with the old lady to call in our ten-twenty. Me and Negron start walking toward the house."

"Describe the house."

"Two-story brick, like all of them around there. Most of the windows boarded up. There was a narrow, covered front porch with side steps leading up to it. The front door was missing, it was just a dark open hole. The east side of the house was just like the west, another empty lot."

"All right. Go on."

"Well, me and Negron get to the house and I walk around the porch to the side steps. Just as I reach them, I hear Negron cursing. He stepped in dog shit. At least he *hoped* it was dog shit. The place really stinks—piss, garbage, shit, everything. The nearest streetlight is burned out, it's dark as hell . . ."

Now Miles's body seemed to tighten on itself, the trembling turning sharply into a steady shake. He tried desperately to moisten his mouth before speaking again.

"So, I'm laughing at Negron, he's wiping his shoe on the edge of the porch. I start up the steps."

"How many steps?"

"Four, maybe five."

"Where's your gun at this point?"

"Well, I have two guns on me. My Glock is in a belt holster under my coat, and a thirty-eight revolver is in the right coat pocket."

"Both regulation sidearms?"

"Yeah."

"Is your coat open or buttoned up?"

"Open. You know, it was warm inside the car, so it's open."

Cash glanced at the now tightly closed coat, the warmth of the room unable to reach Miles's chill. "Go on."

"The old lady told us this guy didn't have a weapon, none that she saw, anyway. We figured it for a dispute between two homeless squatters, we'd check it out and then leave. So while Negron is still scraping shit off his shoe, I go up maybe two, three steps and I hear something coming from inside the doorway."

"What did you hear?"

Miles's shoulders twitched and his right hand jerked out of his lap, fisting. "A sharp double metallic click. Like a weapon being locked and loaded. Negron heard it, too. He said *Fuck!* and I saw him duck in front of the porch and go for his gun. I just stood there, frozen."

Cash sat back in his seat, eyeing the young, trembling cop. "Go on," he said softly.

"All of a sudden this guy, this enormous fuckin' guy, is right there, right in the doorway, maybe eight, nine feet away from me. A huge, crazy-looking guy, and he's got a fuckin' rifle in his hands. A *rifle!*"

The words were pouring out now, and Cash held his questions. Let him spit it out, get it all out and over with. The details, actual or invented, could wait.

"I almost peed myself. I mean, this guy looked like a real maniac, sweating, cursing to himself, stepping out onto the porch and swinging that rifle back and forth." Miles spasmed slightly. He took a deep breath, held it briefly, then continued. "So I say, *Hey,* you know, like a fuckin' idiot, and the guy zeroes in on me, he don't hesitate for a second. I'm telling you he was *crazy,* and he starts yelling at me, something about his old lady, about his kid, something like that, and he's pointing the rifle at me and I know he's gonna kill me, and I've got my left hand on the banister, you know, I was climbing the stairs, and so I push myself backward. I don't know what the fuck I'm doing, just throwing myself down the stairs. Then I hear this tremendous explosion and there's a giant flash of light and I'm rolling down the stairs into the dirt, and Jesus Christ, I swear I did pee myself. I mean, I felt it, you know, the warm piss in my pants. I thought it was blood, I thought I was shot. Mr. Cash, I swear to God, I don't remember taking it out, but my thirty-eight was in my hands and I'm pointing it at the guy and he's swinging his aim over toward Negron, who's down behind the front of the porch yellin' something about us being cops, and the guy starts screamin' he's gonna kill us and he swings the rifle back at me, right at my fuckin' chest, and he jacks another round into the chamber and my gun goes off and the guy just blinks like bullets can't hurt him, and so I figure I missed. Then he fires again and I think I'm hit again, I'm going to die, and I start firing over and over. The last shot I see his shirt, he's wearing a T-shirt, and I swear to God I see the shirt tear. It's like slow motion. The shirt gets pushed in, like somebody poked him with a pencil or something, and then it pops out, out of the hole in his chest, and it's torn, you know, the shirt is torn and it's red with blood, and it just popped in, then out of his chest. Blood sprayed out of the hole—some of it hit me. It was like slow motion. Then he falls down, sits down actually. Negron goes rushing past me. The guy drops the rifle and it slides down the steps and Negron, he's all red and excited and he sticks his Glock in the guy's face and says, *You son of a bitch,* and the guy just plops onto his back and his head hits the porch, and that's it. That was it."

Cash let a few moments elapse before asking, "Would you like some water or something? Coffee? Maybe the doctor can give you something more to relax you."

"No, sir. No." Tears welled in Miles's eyes, and he wiped them quickly away. He sighed and looked down at the floor, his right leg shaking, anger and shame weighing heavily on him. The tears welled again, and Cash rose and turned to face the window, his back to the young man. Uneasy moments passed before he sat down again and spoke.

"What happened next?"

Miles shook his head clear. His voice was low, flat. "Sanchez came up and started running his hand over me. You know, I was down on the ground, the guy had fired right at me, so Sanchez figured I was hit. He kept saying, *Holy Christ, are you okay, are you okay?* I stood up. Sanchez took the gun out of my hand and put it in my pocket. We just stood there looking at each other. Then Negron said, *Come on,* and he ran into the house. There coulda been a second perp, we had to clear the place, so me and Sanchez followed him."

"Did you look at the body?"

"No."

"Go on."

"The old lady told us the guy's room was on the second floor. We went up. It was very dark. Then we saw an old kerosene lamp in what we figured was the guy's room, that was the only light. Negron and Sanchez went in. That's where they found the heroin on a small table against the wall. I just sorta wandered into the bathroom. And for the first time in my life, my mind was a total blank. I wasn't even thinking, *Hey, you're not thinking about anything.* It was just completely blank, empty. I had a pencil flash in my pocket. I took it out and turned it on. That's when I saw myself in the old mirror, in the bathroom, you know, and I started . . . I started crying. But it was crazy, like I was crying for no reason, because my mind was blank, totally blank. I was just looking at my reflection, then I started shaking like a leaf and threw up in the sink. Just like that, I puked, and I felt so embarrassed. Negron came into the bathroom, he had his light on, too. I don't know what he was saying, I felt so ashamed, and then he just went away and I was alone. I shut the door. I wanted to wash out the sink, clean myself up, but there was no running water. I didn't want to leave the bathroom. I was *embarrassed.*" Miles shook his head slightly. "Then it dawned on me, what the hell, I did my job, I've got no reason to be ashamed. Then, all of a sudden, I got real hostile . . . like I was thinking, *Fuck everybody, fuck them.* It was stupid, I guess."

Cash didn't comment. Instead he asked, "What happened next?"

"Sanchez came in, didn't knock or anything, just opened the door and walked in. He said he was going to seal the building and call for the detectives. I think that's when he told me they had found some crack, too, I don't remember for sure. Anyway, I walked out of the bathroom. There were uniformed cops everywhere. Sanchez had put out a *Shots fired — ten-thirteen.* I wandered off, went downstairs. Some neighborhood people were standing outside the house, a little crowd of them. I guess the radio cars woke 'em up. It was very weird, this deserted street all of a sudden with this crowd . . . They looked like . . . like zombies or something. Like it was Halloween. They were talking and looking at the dead body and having a good time. I think some of them made me for the cop who shot the guy. I got some dirty looks, you know, and some mumbles. Most of them didn't seem to care much, though. One old guy wanted to shake my hand, told me there were a few others around needed killing."

"Where was the woman who started the whole thing?" Cash asked.

"Some uniform was holding her in a black-and-white, waiting

for the detectives. Anyway, I went to look at the body. You know
. . ." He shrugged and let his voice trail off.

"You said the people were looking at the *dead* body. How'd you
know it was dead?"

This seemed to stun Miles. "I just figured. I don't know, he
looked dead."

"You said before you hadn't yet looked at the body, so how'd
you know it looked dead?"

Miles did not respond. Instead he seemed puzzled, confused.

Cash said softly, "Listen, Anthony, I'm only asking you what
others will ask. And you have to provide the right answers. Just
off the top of my head, you had better polish up your demeanor
and change some terminology about certain things when you're
speaking to the investigators. And you need to make eye contact with them, not stare out the window like somebody reciting
Hamlet's soliloquy. You can't say you responded to the call because Negron wanted 'action' or because you were 'bored.' You
can't say you didn't know what you were doing when you threw
yourself down the stairs, you can't say you don't know how your
weapon got into your hand. You can't say you felt hostile or pissed
off. Look, I'm not trying to put words in your mouth, Anthony,
but you need a tighter version, a neat, professional version. You
took the call because the woman made an official complaint, you
defensively threw yourself out of the way of the first shot, you
drew your weapon, and after Negron's shouted identification
as police officers and the perpetrator's second shot, you fired
that weapon. Your gun just didn't 'go off,' you fired in defense
of your life and the life of your partners. Now I'll ask you again,
how'd you know the man was dead before you looked at the
body?"

Miles was sweating heavily at this point and at last opened his
coat. He shifted in his seat and looked into the lawyer's eyes. "I
knew he was dead because . . . because Negron had examined the
body shortly after the shots were fired, and he told me that the
perpetrator appeared to be dead."

"All right," Cash said with a curt nod of his head. "And after
they sealed the house, what then? Did you speak to anyone? What
did you do?"

"Sanchez approached me. He told me not to talk to anybody,

not even another cop, until after Negron got ahold of the union lawyer. Then he slapped me on the arm and walked away; he was trying to disperse the crowd. In the meantime, more cops poured into the area. Negron was keeping guys away, you know, so they wouldn't mess up the scene. I just sorta got lost in the crowd."

"Is that when you looked at the body?"

Miles squirmed slightly in his seat. "Yeah. I walked over and there he was, just where he fell. His eyes were open."

"What did you think when you looked at the body? Did you think, *This guy almost killed me,* something like that?"

Miles hesitated. "Look, Mr. Cash, I didn't think anything like that. And what does it matter what I thought? Thoughts don't mean much. I had . . . I had crazy thoughts, but they weren't anything like you might think."

Cash smiled a thin, tired smile. "You're right, Anthony, most thoughts don't mean much. But tell me anyway. I need to get the whole picture in order to best protect you."

Miles looked pale. He was trembling more noticeably now and clasping his hands together in an attempt to steady them. He suddenly removed his pea coat, folding and dropping it neatly to the floor. He peered up at Cash. "All right," he said. "You want to hear it, I'll tell you. But like I said, it was a little crazy. I don't really understand it, but here it is. I went over and looked at the body. It seemed sort of . . . sort of fake, you know? Like a mannequin or a pile of laundry. It was like . . . like a machine that somebody unplugged. And then, all of a sudden, I started thinking about . . . about college. When I took an anatomy class, senior year. The professor I had was great, he made it very interesting, you know? We learned about the human body, the bones and muscles, the glands, the brain, the blood and heart, all functioning together, forming a human being. You know, it doesn't matter how smart you are, if you're rich or poor or whether you're good or evil, *everybody's* got the same stuff inside, like a computer or something. Your values, your personality, that's all secondary. What's important is your body, your *anatomy.* That's what I thought about when I looked at the guy. My anatomy elective."

Cash said nothing when Miles fell silent. Over the years he had interviewed enough people to know when to be silent and when to speak. He knew Miles would continue. Cash didn't care about body parts, he cared about the facts surrounding the shooting. And he was willing to let Miles digress for a while if that's what it took to gather those facts.

"Anyway," Miles continued, as though there had been no break in his narrative, "I just kept on thinking about anatomy and my professor. The human body was like God to him, he worshipped it. Like even though he spent years studying and teaching, he was still fascinated by it. Some of the students didn't give a damn, but I did. I found it all so amazing. I remember discussing it one day with some blonde who sat next to me in class. She said it was boring, she only took the course because it fit into her schedule and was offered as a pass-fail. I tried to explain why it was so fascinating, but she was completely turned off by it. Then she said something that had never occurred to me. And it all came flooding back into my head while I was looking down at the bloody hole in that guy's chest."

Cash found himself frowning. "And what was that?"

Now Miles raised his eyes to meet Cash's. "She said, *This guy,* meaning the professor, the one I figured was so cool, *This guy is a real cold bastard. He talks about people like they're meat. To him, there's no difference between anybody—just between dead and not dead.* That's what she said. At first it kind of pissed me off. But then after I thought about it, I began to see her point. And I had it filed away in my head all these years that she was right, you know? Like people really are more than just blood and veins and body parts. But when I looked at that body tonight, I realized the only difference between it and me was that it was dead and I wasn't. The *only* difference. Its systems were shut down, mine weren't. Its heart was stopped, mine was beating." Miles shrugged. "See? Crazy, right?"

"Yes, well . . . people have odd thoughts at times like that." Cash wanted more relevant information. "What about the perpetrator, Anthony? How many times had you shot him?"

"Well, there was the chest. There was also a side wound, the right side, by the ribs. And one of the bullets hit him in the hand. The EMT found that one. The detectives checked my gun. I had fired all six rounds."

Cash reached across the table and patted Miles's shoulder. "This sounds like a very clean shooting, son. If Sanchez goes along and the crime scene unit confirms those two rifle shots, you'll waltz through the mandatory grand jury inquest. You did what you were forced to do. You need to realize that, calm down a little."

Miles looked up at Cash, his sad eyes hooded. "Mr. Cash," he asked softly, "have you ever wept?"

The question surprised the older man. "Sure, son, everyone cries. Don't think because you're a man or a police officer that you're not allowed to cry."

Miles shook his head sharply and leaned forward in his seat. His tone implored Cash for understanding. "Not *cry*. I'm talking about *weeping*. When I looked at that guy, I sat down on the porch next to him and I wept. I mean, really *wept*. In my whole life I never did that; sure, I've cried—from pain, frustration, anger, sorrow, but I never wept. Not until tonight."

Cash straightened in his seat. Jesus, he thought, the kid was really taking this hard. All this crap about weeping and crying, as if there were some difference. "Look, son, it's tough, we all cry, and no cop who saw you will ever mention it. They know it could be them next time."

Miles reacted sharply, almost rising from his seat. "No, dammit," he said in a suddenly strong, clear voice. "It's not the macho thing, it's not about *crying*, it's about *weeping!* You don't understand. I didn't care about that guy, or his family, or his friends, nobody. I only cared about his *body*, his blood and his brain, his chemistry, his parts, his fuckin' anatomy. All that incredible machinery, broken, dead. I wept for *that*. Don't you understand? Nobody ever thinks about that or cares. But that's all there is, Mr. Cash, that's all there is to care about."

Cash leaned back in his seat. "Listen, Anthony, you're tired, you're upset. You're not making a hell of a lot of sense here, and tomorrow no one will appreciate that kind of talk. It doesn't sound . . . just doesn't sound right, do you understand?"

Miles shook his head and abruptly stood up. He was still trembling. He stepped around the table to the window. "I don't care how it sounds, it's true. Just look out there." He gestured at the window. Cash turned somewhat nervously, as much to keep his eye on Miles as to glance out the window. "Look out at Camden. Tell me, what value does a person have if he's a rapist, a murderer, a junkie? Or a liar or a cheat, or a mean bastard or skinflint for that matter? How many people out there fit that description, or part of that description? If some terrorist blew it all to hell, what would be said? All those poor people, those poor human beings, murdered. But they'd be talking . . . about something else, something totally different from what I'm saying. They wouldn't care about the *bodies*, the machinery. *That's* why I wept for that guy, because I destroyed his body. If his soul even existed, it wasn't worth a damn to him, me, or anybody else. Humans are pompous fools, they award themselves souls so they can look at a cow or a monkey and say, *I'm better than that, I'm a human being.* So what, Mr. Cash? How can anyone really give a goddamn?"

Cash rose from his chair and moved closer to Miles. He faced the window, speaking to his own reflection in the darkened glass. "Anthony, you killed a man tonight. When you took this job, you must have asked yourself at least one time, *Am I willing to chance being killed? Am I willing to chance killing someone?* Well, tonight it came to pass, son, and you did what had to be done. If you're going to get all philosophical about it, you'll only cause yourself a lot of grief. You wouldn't be so damn philosophical if you were lying in the morgue right now, or up in the OR with a bullet lodged in your spine. You killed a man; I don't give a damn if you think you killed his soul, his body, or his goddamned asshole. He's dead and you're not. So when you're interviewed tomorrow, you forget about all this bullshit and you talk facts; you talk distance in feet and inches, you talk lighting and visibility, and you talk police procedure. You talk it because that's what they want to hear. That's what they *need* to hear. If you have a problem with something, talk to a priest. If you can't handle it, go see a psychiatrist. This is a police shooting and we talk facts, not bullshit. Do you understand me, Anthony?" Cash turned and peered at the young officer. "Do you understand me?" he said into the bloodshot eyes glaring back at him.

"Yes, I understand. It's *you* who doesn't understand. You prove my point. Answer the questions, fill out the forms, toe tag the corpse, and shovel it under. Then on Sunday talk soul and spirit." Miles paused and returned to his chair. He sat down heavily and spoke softly: "I'm sorry. Maybe I don't know what I'm saying. Maybe you're right. Maybe any damn thing. It's dawn and I feel like I came to work a week ago. I'm exhausted. Can I go home now?"

Cash turned back to the window. "Where are your guns?"

"The detectives took them. They gave me a receipt." Miles produced the wrinkled paper and placed it on the table.

Cash glanced at it. "All right, put it away, hold on to it. You know procedure. You'll be reassigned to a desk job until you're cleared on the shooting. Tomorrow we'll talk again and cross the t's and dot the i's. Then you'll sit for your official interview. I'll be there personally to monitor things."

Miles stood up and began to leave the room.

"One more thing," Cash said to the man's back. "Stay home. Let Negron take you straight home and stay there. Don't speak to anyone about the shooting, not even Negron. I'll call you tomorrow."

Miles placed a hand on the doorknob and started out. Before leaving, he turned slowly and spoke softly: "Mr. Cash, I know what everybody thinks. I know what *you* think. Tonight, any other cop would have been assigned some lawyer right out of school. But because of my father, you showed up personally. And I'm sure you know how grateful he'll be for that."

Cash wore a neutral expression. "Yes," he said.

"I need you to understand something, though. I want everybody to understand something. The last thing in the world my father wanted was for me to become a cop. He tried his best to change my mind, and when he couldn't he tried to talk me out of working for Camden PD. But he couldn't do that, either. There are some good people in Camden, Mr. Cash. They're trying to make a life for themselves."

For the first time since entering the room, a small, tired smile touched Miles's face as he continued.

"I just wanted to help them do it. That's all I ever wanted. The other cops, they hardly talk to me. Negron and Sanchez have me for a partner because they pissed off the duty sergeant. But they've got me all wrong."

He turned back to the door, speaking as he left the room.

"I was just trying to help."

When Miles was gone, Cash turned to the window behind him, his cold gray eyes studying the early-morning light as it began to nudge against the slowly dying night sky.

He stood there alone for quite some time. He wondered why

Negron, from his position of cover behind the porch, had not fired.

He wondered why Sanchez had not fired.

And as the Camden sky grew brighter, he wondered about organs and brains, nerves and enzymes, anatomy and souls.

THOMAS McGUANE

The Good Samaritan

FROM *The New Yorker*

SZABO DIDN'T LIKE to call the land he owned and lived on a ranch—a word that was now widely abused by developers. He preferred to call it his property, or "the property," but it did require a good bit of physical effort from him in the small window of time after he finished at the office, raced home, and got on the tractor, or, if he was hauling a load of irrigation dams, on the ATV. Sometimes he was so eager to get started that he left his car running. His activity on the property, which had led, over the years, to arthroscopic surgery on his left knee, one vertebral fusion, and mild hearing loss, thanks to his diesel tractor, yielded very little income at all and some years not even that—a fact that he did not care to dwell on.

He produced racehorse-quality alfalfa hay for a handful of grateful buyers, who privately thought he was nuts but were careful to treat his operation with respect, because almost no one else was still producing the small bales that they needed to feed their own follies. They were, most of them, habitués of small rural tracks in places such as Lewistown or Miles City, owners of one horse, whose exercise rider was either a daughter or a neighbor girl who put herself in the way of serious injury as the price of the owner's dream. Hadn't Seattle Slew made kings of a couple of hapless bozos?

Szabo was not nuts. He had long understood that he needed to do something with his hands to compensate for the work that he did indoors, and it was not going to be golf or woodworking.

He wanted to grow something and sell it, and he wanted to use the property to do this. In fact, the work that he now did indoors had begun as manual labor. He had machined precision parts for wind generators for a company that subcontracted all the components, a company that sold an idea and actually made nothing. Szabo had long known that this approach was the wave of the future, without understanding that it was the wave of his future. He had worked very hard and his hard work had led him into the cerebral ether of his new workplace: now, at forty-five, he took orders in an office in a pleasant town in Montana, while his esteemed products were all manufactured in other countries. It was still a small, if prosperous, business, and it would likely stay small, because of Szabo's enthusiasm for what he declined to call his ranch.

It wasn't that he was proud of the John Deere tractor that he was still paying for and which he circled with a grease gun and washed down like a teenager's car. He wasn't proud of it: he loved it. There were times when he stood by his kitchen window with his first cup of coffee and gazed at the gleaming machine in the morning light. Even the unblemished hills of his property looked better through its windshield. The fact that he couldn't wait to climb into it was the cause of the accident.

The hay, swathed, lay in windrows, slowly drying in the Saturday morning sun. Szabo had gone out to the meadows in his bathrobe to probe the hay for moisture and knew that it was close to ready for baling. The beloved tractor was parked at the foot of the driveway, as though a Le Mans start would be required once the hour came around and the moisture in the tender shoots of alfalfa had subsided, so that the hay would not spoil in the stacks. Szabo, now in jeans, tennis shoes, hooded sweatshirt, and baseball cap, felt the significance of each step as he walked toward the tractor, marveling at the sunlight on its green paint, its tires nearly his own height, its baler pert and ready. He reached for the handhold next to the door of the cab, stepped onto the ridged footstep, and pulled himself up, raising his left hand to open the door. Here his foot slid off the step, leaving him briefly dangling from the handhold. A searing pain informed him that he had done something awful to his shoulder. Releasing his grip, he fell to the driveway in a heap. The usually ambrosial smell of tractor fuel repelled him, and the towering green shape above him now seemed reproachful. Gravel pressed into his cheek.

As he lay in recovery, the morphine drip only prolonged his obsession with the unbaled hay, since it allowed him to forget about his shoulder, which he had come to think of not as his but as a kind of alien planet fastened to his torso, which glowed red like Mars, whirling with agony, as soon as the morphine ran low. It was a fine line: when he wheedled extra narcotic, his singing caused complaints and he got dialed back down to the red planet. Within a day, he grew practical and managed to call his secretary.

"Melinda, I'm going to have to find somebody for the property. I've got hay down and—"

"A ranch hand?"

"But just for a month or so."

"Why don't I call around?"

"That's the idea. But not too long commitment-wise, okay? I may have to overpay for such a limited time."

"It is what it is," Melinda remarked, producing a mystification in Szabo that he ascribed to the morphine.

"Yes, sure," Szabo said. "But time is of the essence."

"You can say that again. Things are piling up. The guy in Germany calls every day."

"I mean with the hay."

Melinda was remarkably efficient, and she knew everyone in town. Her steadiness was indispensable to Szabo, who kept her salary well above temptation from other employers. By the next day she had found a few prospects for him. The most promising one, an experienced ranch hand from Wyoming, wore a monitoring ankle bracelet that he declined to explain, so he was eliminated. The next most promising, a disgruntled nursery worker, wanted permanent employment, so Szabo crossed him off the list, ignoring Melinda's suggestion that he just fire him when he was through. That left a man called Barney, overqualified and looking for other work, but happy to take something temporary. He told Melinda that he was extremely well educated but "identified with the workingman" and thought a month or so in Szabo's bunkhouse would do him a world of good. Szabo called Barney's references from his hospital bed. He managed to reach only one, the wife of a dentist who ran a llama operation in Bozeman. Barney was completely reliable, she said, and meticulous: he had reshingled the tool shed and restacked their large woodpile in an intricate pattern—almost like a church window—and swept the sidewalk. "You could eat off it!" she said. Szabo got the feeling that Mrs. Dentist had been day-drinking. Her final remark confused him. "Nobody ever did a better job than Barney!" she said, laughing wildly. "He drove us right up the wall!"

Szabo took a leap of faith and hired him over the phone. The news seemed not to excite Barney. "When do you want me to start?" he droned. After the call, Szabo gazed at his phone for a moment, then flipped it shut. His arm in a sling, his shoulder radiating signals with every beat of his heart, he returned to his office and stirred the things on his desk with his left hand. Eventually he had pushed the papers into two piles: "urgent" and "not urgent." Then there was a painful reshuffle into "urgent," "not that urgent," and "not urgent." Melinda stood next to him. "Does that make sense?" he asked.

Melinda said, "I think so."

"I'm going home."

Barney, who looked to be about forty, with a pronounced widow's peak in his blondish hair and a deep dimple in his chin, was a quick study, though it took Szabo a while to figure out how much of his instruction the man was absorbing. Barney was remarkably without affect, gazing at Szabo as he spoke as if marveling at the physical apparatus that permitted Szabo's chin to move so smoothly. At first Szabo was annoyed by this, and when Barney's arm rose slowly to his mouth to place a toothpick there, he had a momentary urge to ask him to refrain from chewing it while he was listening. It was the sense of a concealed smirk behind the toothpick that bothered Szabo the most. But once he'd observed Barney's efficiency Szabo quickly trained himself not to indulge such thoughts. Some of the hay had been rained on, but Barney raked it dry, and soon the shiny green tractor was flying around the meadows making beautiful bales for the racehorses of Montana. This gave Szabo something of a heartache, but he praised Barney for the job he had done so well. Barney replied, "That's not enough hay to pay for the fuel."

Szabo tried to ride his old gelding, Moon, a tall chestnut half-

Thoroughbred he had been riding for thirteen of the horse's sixteen years. One-armed, he had to be helped into the saddle. He could get the bridle over Moon's head and pull himself up from the saddle horn, barely, but the jogging aroused the pain in his shoulder so sharply that he quickly gave up. Barney looked on without expression. Szabo said, "I really need to ride him regularly. He's getting old."

"I'll ride him."

"That would be nice, but it's not necessary."

"I'll ride him. There's not much else to do."

Barney rode confidently but without grace of any kind. Moon's long trot produced a lurching sway in Barney's torso, exaggerated by the suspenders he always wore, that was hard for Szabo to watch. And it was clear from Moon's sidelong glances that he, too, was wondering what kind of burden he was carrying. But the sight of Barney's lurching exercise rides seemed a small price to pay for the skilled work he provided: repairing fences, servicing stock waterers, pruning the orchard, and even doing some painting on the outbuildings. One day, as he rode Moon down the driveway, Barney said to Szabo, who had just pulled up, "By the time you get the sling off, I'll have your horse safe for you to ride." From the window of his car, Szabo said, resisting the impulse to raise his voice, "As I recall, he's been safe for me to ride since he was a three-year-old colt." Barney just looked down and smiled.

When Barney restacked the woodpile, Szabo decided to treat it as an absolute surprise. He stood before the remarkable lattice of firewood and, while his mind wandered, praised it lavishly. He was reluctant to admit to himself that he was trying to get on Barney's good side. "It's one of a kind," he said.

Szabo's mother lived in a ground-floor apartment across the street from a pleasant assisted-living facility. She had stayed in her own apartment because she smoked cigarettes, which was also what seemed to have preserved her vitality over her many years. Further, she didn't want to risk the family silver in an institution, or her real treasure: a painting that had come down through her family for nearly a century, a night stampede by the cowboy artist Charlie Russell, one of very few Russell night pictures in existence, which would likely fetch a couple of million dollars at auction. The old people across the street would just take it down and spill food on it, she said. When Szabo was growing up as an only child, his mother's strong opinions, her decisive nature, had made him feel oppressed; now those qualities were what he most liked, even loved, about her. He recognized that when he was irresolute it was in response to his upbringing, but caution, in general, paid off for him.

Barney enjoyed tobacco, too, smoke and smokeless. One afternoon Szabo sent a shoebox of pictures and two much-annotated family cookbooks to his mother by way of Barney, who was heading into town to pick up a fuel filter for the tractor. Later Szabo cried out more than once, "I have only myself to blame!"

In a matter of weeks, Szabo was able to discard the sling and to exercise his shoulder with light weights and elastic strips that he held with one foot while feebly pulling and releasing, sweat pouring down his face. The next morning, three bird watchers entered the property without stopping at the house for permission and were all but assaulted by Barney, who chased them to their car, hurling vulgar epithets until they disappeared down the road with their life lists and binoculars.

"But Barney, I don't mind them coming around," Szabo said.

"Did they have permission, yes or no?"

There was no time for Szabo to explain that this didn't matter to him, as Barney had gone back to work. At what, Szabo was unsure, but he seemed busy.

Szabo had to be in Denver by the afternoon. He took an overnight bag and drove to town, past Barney, lurching from side to side on Moon, who bore, Szabo thought, a fresh look of resignation. He stopped on the way to the airport to see his mother, who sat in her living room doing Sudoku in front of a muted television, a cigarette hanging out of the corner of her mouth. On a stand next to her chair, her cockatiel, Toni, hunched in the drifting smoke.

"I'm off to Denver till tomorrow, Ma. I'll have my cell if you need anything." She looked up, put down her stub of pencil, and moved the cigarette from her mouth to the ashtray.

"Nothing to worry about here. I've got a million things to do."

"Well, in case you think of something while I'm—"

"Lunch with Barney, maybe drive around."

"Okay!" Luckily his mother couldn't see his face.

Melinda had things well in hand, had even reduced some of the piles on his desk by thoughtful intervention where his specific attention was less than necessary. She was a vigorous mother of four, barely forty years old, happily married to a highway patrolman she'd grown up with. They were unironic enthusiasts for all the mass pleasures the culture offered: television, NASCAR, cruises, Disney World, sports, celebrity gossip, and local politics. Szabo often wished that he could be as well adjusted as Melinda's family, but he would have had to be medicated to pursue her list of pleasures. And yet she was not just an employee but a cherished friend.

It was a tested friendship with a peculiar intimacy: Szabo's former wife, Karen, an accomplished ironist, had made several stays at the Rimrock Foundation for what ended up as a successful treatment for alcoholism—successful in that she had given up alcohol altogether. Unfortunately, she had replaced it with other compulsions, including an online-trading habit that had bankrupted Szabo for a time. Once it was clear that Szabo was broke, she had divorced him, sold the house, remarried, and moved to San Diego, where she was, by the reports of their grown son, David, happy and not at all compulsive. *What does this say about me?* Szabo wondered obsessively. Maybe she was now on a short leash. Szabo had met her husband, Cliff: stocky, bald, and authoritarian—a forensic accountant, busy and prosperous in the SoCal free-for-all. His dour affect seemed to subdue Karen. In any case, Szabo had loved her, hadn't wanted a divorce, and had felt disgraced at undergoing bankruptcy in a town of this size. He'd sunk into depression and discovered that there was no other illness so brutal, so profound, so inescapable, that made an enemy of consciousness itself. Nevertheless, he had plodded to the office, day after day, an alarming, ashen figure, and there he had fallen into the hands of Melinda, who dragged him to family picnics and to the dentist, forged his signature whenever necessary, placed him between her and her husband at high school basketball games, as though he might otherwise tip over, taught him to cheer for her children, and occasionally fed him at her house in the uproar of family life. When, once, as she stood by his desk in the office, he raised a hand to her breast, she amiably removed it and redirected his attention to his work. By inches, she had restored his old self, and solvency seemed to follow. He began to see himself as someone who had returned

from the brink. He liked making money. He liked visiting his little
group of suppliers in faraway places. He liked having Melinda as a
friend, and her husband, Mike, the highway patrolman, too. Mike
was the same straight-ahead type as his wife: he once gave Szabo a
well-deserved speeding ticket. Now Szabo's only argument with his
ex-wife's contentment in San Diego was that it seemed to prove to
David that it had been Szabo who drove her crazy.

As Szabo headed away from the Denver airport, he could see its
marvelous shape at the edge of the prairie, like a great nomads'
camp—a gathering of the tents of chieftains, more expressive of
a world on the move than anything Szabo had ever seen. You flew
into one of these tents, got food, a car, something to read, then
headed out on your own smaller journey to the rapture of traffic,
a rented room with a TV and a "continental" breakfast. It was an
ectoplasmic world of circulating souls.

On a sunny day, with satellite radio and an efficient midsized
Korean sedan, the two-hour drive to the prison that had held his
son for the past couple of years flew by. Szabo was able to think
about his projects for the ranch—a new snow fence for the driveway, a mouse-proof tin liner for Moon's grain bin, a rain gauge
that wouldn't freeze and crack, a bird feeder that excluded grack-
les and jays—nearly the whole trip. But toward the end of the
drive his head filled with the disquieting static of remorse, self-
blame, and sadness, and a short-lived defiant absolution. In the
years that had turned out to be critical for David, all he had given
him was a failing marriage and a bankrupt home. *I should have just
shot Karen and done the time,* Szabo thought with a shameful laugh.
The comic relief was brief. Mom in California, Dad in Montana,
David in prison in Colorado: could they have foreseen this disper-
sion?

Razor wire guaranteed the sobriety of any visitor. The vehicles
in the visitors' parking lot said plenty about the socioeconomics of
the families of the imprisoned: Szabo's shiny Korean rental stuck
out like a sore thumb. The prison was a tidy fortress of unambigu-
ous shapes that argued less with the prairie surrounding them than
with the chipper homes of the nearby subdivision. It had none of
the lighthearted mundane details of the latter—laundry hanging
out in the sun, adolescents gazing under the hood of an old car,

a girl sitting on the sidewalk with a handful of colored chalk. The place for your car, the place for your feet, the door that complied at the sight of you, were all profoundly devoid of grace—at least, to anyone whose child was confined there.

David came into the visiting room with a promising, small smile and gave Szabo a hug. He had been a slight, quick-moving boy, but prison had given him muscle, thick, useless muscle that seemed to impair his agility and felt strange to the father who embraced him. They sat in plastic chairs. Szabo noticed that the room, which was painted an incongruous robin's-egg blue, had a drain in the middle of its floor, a disquieting fact.

"Are you getting along all right, David?"

"Given that I don't belong here, sure."

"I was hoping to hear from you—" Szabo caught himself, determined not to suggest any sort of grievance. David smiled.

"I got your letters."

"Good." Szabo nodded agreeably. There was nothing to look at in the room except the person you were speaking to.

"How's Grandma?" David asked.

"I think she's doing as well as can be expected. You might drop her a note."

"Oh, right. 'Dear Grandma, you're sure lucky to be growing old at home instead of in a federal prison.'"

Szabo had had enough.

"Good, David, tell her that. Old as she is, she never got locked up."

David looked at his father, surprised, and softened his own voice. "You said in your letter you'd had some health problem."

"My shoulder. I had surgery."

Szabo knew that the David before him was not David on drugs, but now that the drugs were gone, he still hadn't gone back to being the boy he'd been before. Maybe it would happen gradually. Or perhaps Szabo was harboring yet another fruitless hope.

"Melinda still working for you?"

"I couldn't do without her. She stayed with me even when I couldn't pay her."

"Melinda's hot."

"She's attractive."

"No, Dad, Melinda's hot."

Szabo didn't know what David meant by this, if anything, and he didn't want to know. Maybe David just wanted him to realize that he noticed such things.

"David, you've got less than a year to go. Concentrate on avoiding even the appearance of anything that could set you back. You'll be home soon."

"Home?"

"Absolutely. Where your friends are, where you grew up. Home is where your mistakes can be seen in context. You go anywhere else — David, you go anywhere else and you're an ex-con. You'll have to spend all your time overcoming that, when everyone at home already knows you're a great kid."

"When I get out of here," David said in measured tones, "I'm going to live with Mom and Cliff."

"In California?"

"Last time I checked."

Szabo was determined not to react to this. He let the moment subside, and David now seemed to want to warm up. He smiled faintly at the blue ceiling.

"And yes, I'll write Grandma back."

"So you heard from her?"

David laughed. "About her boyfriend, Barney. I think that's so sweet. A relationship! Is Barney her age?"

"Actually, he's quite a bit younger."

As Szabo drove back to the airport, he tried to concentrate on the outlandish news of Barney's role in his mother's life, but he didn't get anywhere. He couldn't stop thinking about David, and thought of him in terms of a proverb he had once heard from a Mexican man who had worked for him: "You have only one mother. Your father could be any son of a bitch in the world." *That's me! I'm any son of a bitch in the world.*

He did have a mother, however, there in God's waiting room with a new companion. His late father, a hard-working tradesman, would have given Barney a wood shampoo with a rake handle. *But my standing, thanks to my modest prosperity and education, means that I shall have to humor Barney, and no doubt my most earnest cautions about the forty-year age gap between Barney and my mother will be flung back in my face,* Szabo thought. Suddenly tears burned in his eyes: he was back to David.

Drugs had swept through their small town one year. They'd always been around, but that year they were everywhere, and they had destroyed David's generation. The most ordinary children had become violent, larcenous, pregnant, sick, lost, or dead. And then the plague had subsided. David, an excellent student, had injected the drugs between his toes, and his parents had suspected only that he suddenly disliked them. Instead of going to college, he had apprenticed with a chef for nearly a year, before heading to prison. David didn't think that he would go back to drugs when he was released, and neither did his father. But his bitterness seemed to be here to stay, fed, likely, by his memory of the things that he had done in his days of using. Perhaps he blamed himself for the failure of his parents' marriage. The body he had acquired in the weight room seemed to suit his current burdened personality. The way he looked, he could hardly go back to what he had been.

The tractor was wet and gleaming in the bright sunlight. Barney was gathering stray bits of baler twine and rolling them up into a neat ball. He hardly seemed to notice Szabo's arrival, so Szabo carried his suitcase into the house without a word. Once inside, he glanced furtively through the hall window at Barney, then went back out.

"Good morning, Barney."

"Hi."

"This shoulder thing is behind me now. I think I'm ready to go back to work here." Barney looked more quizzical than the situation called for. "So let's square up and call it a day."

"Meaning what?" Barney asked with an extravagantly inquisitive look.

"Meaning the job is over. Thank you very much. You've been a great help when I needed it most."

"Oh?"

"Yes, I think so. I'm quite sure of it."

"It's your call, Szabo. But there's something about me you don't know."

"I'm sure that's the case. That's nearly always the case, isn't it, Barney?" Some ghastly revelation was at hand, and Szabo knew that there would be no stopping it. "But I'd be happy to know what it is, in your instance."

Barney gazed at him a long time before he spoke. He said, "I am a respectable person."

Szabo found this unsettling. Clearly it was time to have a word with his mother. He asked her out to lunch, but she begged off, citing the new smoking rules that, she said disdainfully, were "sweeping the nation." So he took her to the park near the river. Her size had been reduced by tobacco and her deplorable eating habits. She scurried along briskly, and any pause on Szabo's part found her well ahead, poking into garden beds and uprooting the occasional weed to set an example. They found a bench and sat. Mrs. Szabo shook out a cigarette by tapping the pack against the back of her opposing hand, then raising the whole pack, with its skillfully protruded single butt, to her lips. There the cigarette hung, unlit, while she made several comments about the weather and dropped the pack back into her purse. Finally she lit it, and the first puff seemed to satisfy her profoundly.

"How did you find David?"

"Fine, I think. The way I get to see him down there . . . it's uncomfortable. Just a big empty room."

"Is he still angry?"

"Not that I could see."

"He was such an angry little boy."

"Well, he's not little anymore, Mom. He's got big muscles."

"Let's hope he doesn't misuse them. He got that attitude from your wife. The nicest thing I can say about her is that she kept on going."

"She married a decent, successful guy."

"What else could she do? She didn't have the guts to rob a bank."

"You forget what David was like before his problems. He didn't have an attitude. He was a nice boy."

He could see she wasn't listening.

"Barney said you told him he was no longer needed."

"He knew it was temporary from the start."

"Well, he's certainly got my place pulled together. My God, what a neatnik! And he made me insure the Russell, which I should have done a long time ago. He thinks that David's in this pickle because he got away with murder while he was growing up."

"What? He's never met David!"

"Barney's a very bright individual. He doesn't have to know every last thing firsthand."

"I think his views on how Karen and I raised David would be enhanced by actually meeting David."

"Why?"

"Jesus Christ, Mom."

"Of course you're grumpy. Barney does so much for me and you want me all to yourself. Can't you just relax?"

Telling people to relax is not as aggressive as shooting them, but it's up there. The first time Barney had driven the tractor, he'd nearly put it in the irrigation ditch. Szabo had cautioned him, and Barney had responded, "Is the tractor in the ditch?" Szabo had allowed that it was not. "Then relax," Barney had said.

There was nothing like it: leaning on his shovel next to the racing water, the last sun falling on gentle hills crowned with bluestem and golden buffalo grass, cool air rising from the river bottom. Moon grazed and followed Szabo as he placed his dams and sent a thin sheet of alpine water across the hay crop. The first cutting had been baled and put neatly in the stack yard by Barney. The second cutting grew slowly, was denser in protein and more sought after by owners trying to make their horses run faster. All the way down through this minor economic chain, people lost money, their marvelous dreams disconnected from hopes of success.

Once winter was in the air, Szabo spent less time on his property and made an effort to do the things for his business that he was most reluctant to do. In November he flew to Düsseldorf and stayed at the Excelsior, eating Düsseldorfer Senfrostbraten with Herr Schlegel while pricing robotic plasma welding on the small titanium objects that he was buying from him. The apparent murkiness of Germany was doubtless no more than a symptom of Szabo's ignorance of the language. He wondered if all the elders he saw window-shopping on the boulevards were ex-Nazis. And the skinheads at the Düsseldorf railroad station gave him a sense of historical alarm. After a long evening in the Altstadt, Szabo found himself quite drunk at the bar of the Lindenhof Hotel, where he took a room with a beautiful Afro-Czech girl called Amai, who used him as a comic, inebriated English instructor, her usual services being unnecessary, given his incapacity. Since Szabo appeared unable to navigate his way back to the Excelsior, Amai drove him there in return for the promise of a late breakfast in the Excelsior's beautiful dining room. Afterward, she asked for his address so that they could stay in touch once he was home.

From Germany, Szabo flew directly to Denver. He slept most of the way and awoke to anxiety at the idea that this was probably the last visit he would have before David was released. In the chaotic year that preceded his son's confinement, he had never known what David was doing or to what extent he was in danger; in the last weeks of his marriage, he and Karen had admitted to feeling some relief, now that David was in jail, simply at knowing where he was. Perhaps it was that relief that had allowed them to separate. Yet Cliff's prompt appearance had aroused Szabo's suspicion: he sensed that California had beckoned while his marriage was still seemingly intact.

David was warmer toward his father this time, but more fretful than he had been on the previous visit. Szabo understood that David was probably as afraid of his impending freedom as Szabo was on his behalf. He seemed, despite the muscles, small and frightened, his previous sarcasm no more than a wishful perimeter of defense. And the glow of anger was missing. Szabo wondered if jet lag was contributing to his heartache. He hardly knew what to say to his son.

"In two weeks, you'll be in California," Szabo said.

"That was the plan."

"Is it not anymore?"

"Mom and Cliff said they didn't want me. I've got to go to Plan B."

"I'm sorry, David. What's Plan B?"

"Plan B is I don't know what Plan B is."

"What made your mom and Cliff change their minds?"

David smiled slightly. He said, "I'm trying to remember how Mom put it. She said that a new relationship requires so many adjustments that introducing a new element could be destabilizing. It was sort of abstract. She left it to me to figure out that I was the destabilizing new element. Then Cliff got on the phone and said that unfortunately closure called for the patience of all parties."

"Did you say anything?"

"Yes, Dad, I did. I told Cliff to blow it out his ass."

Szabo could have taken this as evidence of David's unresolved anger. Instead, he enjoyed the feeling that they were in cahoots. "How did Cliff take that?"

"He said he was sorry I felt that way. I told him not to be. I told him I didn't feel anything at all."

They were quiet for long enough to suggest the inkling of comfort. Finally David said, "Tell me about Barney."

"Barney! What about him?"

"Why did you send him here to see me?"

Startling as this was, Szabo did not react at first. He was quiet for a long and awkward moment. Then he asked quite levelly, "When did Barney show up?"

"While you were still in wherever. He said you sent him."

"Not exactly. Perhaps, based on our conversations, Barney thought it might be something I wanted him to do." Szabo had no idea why he was dissembling like this, unless it was to buy time. He suddenly recalled, from David's childhood, the purple dinosaur toy called Barney that was guaranteed to empower the child, a multimillion-dollar brainstorm for cashing in on stupid parents. "Did he explain what he was doing here? How did he get here?"

"He came in your car."

"Of course. Well, that was cheaper than flying. What was the purpose of his trip?"

"Are you asking me?"

"David, cut me some slack. I've been halfway around the world."

"Did you sleep in those clothes, Dad?"

Now Szabo was on the defensive, still in the clothes of his Düsseldorf night with Amai, whom, in this moment of bewilderment, he was certain he should have married. Escape was not so easy. If he hadn't fallen off a tractor and injured himself, this squirrel Barney wouldn't be in the middle of his life. What would he be doing? Living in Germany with Amai, siring octoroons and trying to keep her out of the bars? "I'm afraid I underpacked, David. I wore this suit at meetings and slept in it on the plane. So, Barney was here . . . for what?"

"I guess for counseling of some kind, to prepare me for the outside world." David winced at these last two words.

"Why would Barney think he was in a position to counsel you?"

"If you don't know, Dad, I'm sure I don't, either. At least he has a PhD."

"Is that what he told you?"

"Dad, I'm not following this! I didn't send him here—you did!"

"I know, I know, and I'm sure it's all to the good. Was Barney helpful?"

"You tell me. He said I should go home and take over the ranch."

"It's hardly a ranch, David. It's just some property. What made him think you should do that?"

"Nothing you need to hear."

"What do you mean by that? I want to hear what some jackass with a PhD had to say."

"You won't like it."

"David, I'm a big boy. Tell me."

"He said that you were incompetent and that it was only a matter of time before you broke your neck doing something you had no business doing."

Furious, Szabo took this in with a false thoughtful air. Karen had said almost exactly the same thing. But her words had been motivated by a wish to replace the property with a winter home in San Luis Obispo, a town that had ranked number one in a *Times* survey of residential contentment.

"I trust you told Dr. Barney Q. Shitheel that you were not interested."

"I didn't tell him that, Dad."

"What did you tell him?"

David smiled at his father. "I told him I wasn't welcome there."

"You could have come there anytime you wanted."

"Right."

"What's this? Dave, why are you crying?"

David wiped his eyes with the back of his hand and spoke with odd detachment.

"I knew I would never understand business, but I worked on a lot of ranches in high school. I was good at that."

Not all the fight was gone out of Szabo. Nor had he given up on the story he'd been telling himself. But even as he asked his derisive question he was reminding himself how he might have been absent for his own child. "Did you think selling drugs was a way of learning business?"

David looked weary. He didn't want to play anymore. "You're right, Dad. What was I thinking?"

"I'm not saying I'm right."

"No, Dad, you're one hundred percent right."

"Well," he said, "I'm right some of the time."

This exchange, more than anything, troubled Szabo. Here was David, broken down, imprisoned, soon to be released with his stigma. And Szabo was only adding to his insecurity, instead of trying to make the situation better.

There was plenty to do when he got home. And there was something to learn when he visited his mother: Barney had absconded with the Charlie Russell painting. The next morning Szabo met the detective who was interviewing his mother while fanning away the smoke with his clipboard. She only glanced at Szabo, crestfallen, defeated. From the detective, a handsome fellow in a short-sleeved shirt, too young for his mustache, Szabo learned that his ranch hand's name wasn't Barney; it was Ronny—Ronny Something. Ronny's gift was for slipping into a community with one of his many small talents: the sculptural woodpile had taken him far. The painting would go to a private collector, not likely to be seen again. "This isn't Ronny's first rodeo," the detective said. "The only thread we've got is the PhD. There is no actual PhD, but it's the one thing Ronny drops every time. There's been a string of thefts and they all lead into the same black hole. I don't know why everyone is so sure that Ronny wants to help them."

When Szabo repeated this to Melinda and saw her wide eyes, he just shrugged and shook his head. Maybe to change the subject, she asked after David, and Szabo told her that he would soon be coming home.

NATHAN OATES

Looking for Service

FROM *The Antioch Review*

AS SOON AS they called the first-class passengers I stepped to the head of the line, hurried down to my seat, and braced myself for the crowd that came slumping past minutes later with their loose, swollen bags. Any of them could stop, pretend to cough or adjust a strap, and a runty hand could pull out a cobbled-together shank which he'd stick into my chest, my neck, my cheek, where it would clatter against my teeth, again and again, sinking through the soft meat of my eye. I left my seatbelt unbuckled, ready to fly up and fight my way back to American soil. When the stewardesses began their pantomime of safety, I was able to relax a little, probably only because by that time I'd finished two vodka tonics. I was hoping to drink myself to sleep, but as we reached cruising altitude and the ice in my drink tumbled under the collar of my shirt, I knew I wouldn't be so lucky this time.

When I was first told they were sending me to this country to do an accounting of the Canadian mining firm's books, I told them I couldn't. I said, "My wife is sick."

There was silence on the other end of the line, and I was suddenly unsure if I'd ever met the man to whom I was speaking. I'd assumed he was the same Steve we'd had over for dinner a few years earlier. My wife had made enchiladas with mole sauce. Steve had picked around the plate, ate half his salad and a few scoops of refried beans, leaving two perfectly formed enchiladas like a big old fuck-you to his hostess, who'd spent hours in the kitchen, lifting the skin off broiled peppers.

The man on the phone eventually said, "I'm sorry to hear about that." Another pause, as though this made what came next accept-able. "Your flight's tomorrow, at seven."

"Seven?"

"A.M.," he explained.

As turbulence wobbled the plane, I leaned my head into the oily leather seat and breathed deep, but this made the pressure in my chest expand into a lead weight.

Halfway through the flight the woman beside me turned and grinned until I stopped pretending to be asleep. She was an American, a Mississippian, she clarified, and was going down to visit her daughter, who was about to marry a young man from the country's elite. She wore a beige suit like an ill-fitting exoskeleton. Every inch of exposed skin—face, neck, hands—was layered with foun-dation and powder, so a smell of petroleum oozed out from be-neath gusts of perfume. Her eyes were small and a beautiful blue, startling to find rooted in that puffy, twitching face.

"They're very nice people," she said, then admitted that in fact she'd never met them. "But they own three coffee plantations. The wedding is going to be at one of them."

Despite her grin, she was clearly horrified that her daughter was about to be swallowed up by a family of brown people, no matter how rich they might be, no matter how comforting the word *plan-tation*.

"You know, they're not actually Hispanic, they're Spanish. I mean, they have no Indian blood at all."

Eventually she left me alone and began searching through her cavernous plaid handbag, setting off an incessant clinking of lip-stick cases against her cell phone, wallet, makeup case, the tinny rattle of loose change. At one point she pulled out a photograph in a gaudy metal frame. In it a beautiful young woman in a tight-fitting white dress leaned against a stone wall. The woman stared for a few minutes then, with an elaborate sigh, dropped the frame back into the purse.

I'm sure I looked like a compatriot, an overweight, middle-aged man with thinning hair gone white except for a few strands of black that looked permanently wet. The starched collar of my button-down shirt, the faint pinstripe on my suit pants, and the shine of my black shoes all suggested not only that we were both Americans, but that back home we might even have been friends, would've invited each other over for dinner parties where we'd drink too much, flirt clumsily at the fridge, then turn our energies to moaning about our ingrate children, the awfulness of youth in general, and the folly of anyone who disagreed with us about anything. And, I knew, we *were* compatriots of a sort, but I was too tired, too angry at being on that plane when I should've been home with Joyce.

I'd promised no more trips after she got sick. I told her I'd work from home, or at least from the American headquarters of the firms I audited. But it turned out this wasn't possible, and so every few months I was off again—Zimbabwe, Peru, Bolivia, South Africa—in each place working to make sense of the tangle of fraud that constituted the local office's financial records. I had a particular talent for this, an ability to see through bureaucratic madness and to articulate a legally defensible financial record. Typically I went down to the capitals of these godforsaken places and took a limo to my hotel—the nicest in the country, holdovers from colonial days—and the next morning another limo would ferry me to the offices that were always staffed half with gringos who looked like they'd had too much local rum and half by locals who hadn't quite learned how to smother their bitter scent. I was given my own office, usually that of some recently fired executive, and I would make sense of the confusion they'd all bred in their frenzy to pull minerals from the earth.

We descended through a scrim of clouds. The city clung to a tangle of ravines at the foot of sheer black mountains, the lower slopes of which were smothered with shantytowns. The downtown was marked by dull gray buildings and a few half-finished concrete towers. Our plane touched down with a jolt, the seatbelt cut into my gut, then we seemed to be rising again before slamming down a second time, the engines whirring, the smell of burning rubber filling the cabin. Then we were there, trembling on the runway.

None of the three men holding name signs were waiting for me when I came through customs. The glass doors weren't tinted and the near-equatorial sun set off a pulsing headache behind my eyes. When I checked my cell phone, set up with worldwide access, it said, *Looking for Service*.

Maybe it was my exhaustion, my hangover, or the soldier who stepped away from the wall, eyeing my bag, but I felt suddenly weightless and lost, as though waking from one dream into another when I should've been back in the real world, not caught in this greasy airport with the high, rising scream of a woman at the customs point as soldiers tossed her underwear, her socks, her shirts to the floor, then held up a pair of blue jeans and scythed them in half with a knife. Whatever the reason, I panicked and joined a clump of passengers heading for the glass doors.

"Excuse me?" an American voice said. There beside me were two young hippie travelers, a boy and a girl, both grinning like idiots. They wore loose, dirty clothes that might've been hemp and stank of patchouli and sweat. Loose leather sandals showed off filthy feet, toenails blackened with grime, feet they surely planned to tan before going back home with dysentery and a few snapshots of indigenous kids atop a trash heap.

"Do you know which way the train is?" the girl asked.

"There's no train," I said, hurrying after the crowd.

As we rushed along, the tall, thin boy held up a travel guide and said, "No, it says there's one that goes into the city center." He said this with a kind of desperation, which was understandable. Stretching out around the airport was a dead zone of warehouses with metal shutters pulled over the doors. Power lines sagged from leaning poles. All this made it look as if there had once been a city here, but it had long ago been abandoned.

"No," I said, "the book's wrong. There's no train." I quickened my pace, hoping in their confusion they'd fall away.

"So how do we get to the city?" the girl asked, scurrying to keep up.

"Take the bus," I said, pointing at the crowd ahead of us, which bulged around the doors before squeezing out, like a clot of blood from a narrow wound. "Or a taxi."

"Dude, isn't that expensive?" the boy said.

"Depends on what you think of as expensive," I said.

The girl was still smiling, bobbing her head as though we were listening to a good, thick reggae beat. Then we were outside in the too-bright light. Sitting at the otherwise empty curb was a black SUV and in it were two men wearing sunglasses. They leaned forward, and though it was possible they were just trying to get a better glimpse of the American girl's thin white shirt, I felt sure they were waiting for me and so I started walking faster, pushing through the crowd. Behind me the American kids were shouting. I hunched down and jogged to the orange bus. In that SUV a rifle could be sliding up between the men, scope swirling out of focus before sharpening in on the white hairs at the back of my head.

The bus driver was leaning in the open door, and for a moment my Spanish abandoned me. I gestured at the door and nodded. I glanced back at the SUV. One of the men was standing in the street, pointing. Finally I found the word, *"Abierto."*

"Lo siento," the driver said, stepping aside. I sank into a narrow green seat, my legs pinched up against my gut, suitcase and brief-case piled to my chin.

At that moment, I finally paused to wonder what in the hell I was doing. My limo driver was probably inside right now, he'd probably just gone to the bathroom, but here I was, in the open, jammed into this bus, which was already filling up with peasants hauling bags of all shapes and sizes they'd managed to smuggle past the driver, who screamed at everyone to toss their luggage onto the roof.

"Is this taken?" The American girl was smiling at me, pointing at the empty six inches of seat.

Once settled, her leg pressing against mine, she held out a hand. "I'm Allie."

"Robert," I said. Her hand was slim and cool, and in the midst of my confusion I held on too long, until she was forced to pull back with a pitying smile.

Soon every seat was full and the aisle was packed. The American boy, Billy, was pinned between two fat ladies, his spiky blond hair brushing the ceiling as the bus lurched away.

"Is this your first time here?" Allie said, leaning across me to look out the window so her breast rested on my arm. I tried to see the road behind us, to see if the SUV was there, but the angle was wrong.

"No," I lied, because it was easier.

"It's mine. But I was in Mexico last year for a couple months. In the Yucatán."

I tried to smile, though my mouth was so dry my lips stuck against my teeth.

We passed a few dozen warehouses and pulled up onto a truck-clogged highway. Men bent beneath enormous piles of sticks, or stones, walked along the road, their faces gray with the diesel and dust kicked up. We passed a line of auto-body shops where cars sat stripped and piles of tires leaned toward the street. Mangy dogs and naked children scampered in and out of the open garages while shirtless men hefted greasy tools and wiped their sweating faces with handkerchiefs.

"Dude," Billy shouted, leaning toward our seat. "Have you ever been to Tonterrico? I hear the waves are awesome."

I didn't answer, all my energy focused on ignoring the puddle of what was possibly piss sticking my shoes to the floor.

At the bus station, I paid for my ticket and those of the kids, who patted their pockets as though they'd lost their wallets. I'd hoped this generosity would be enough to get rid of them, but they followed me to the hotel shuttle. There was no sign of the SUV, and as I was ushered to a plush red seat by a man in a tuxedo shirt and bow tie, I felt a measure of calm returning. While the driver stood in the door to see if there were other passengers—there weren't—I noticed that neither of the kids had backpacks or, for that matter, bags of any kind. They looked tired and unwashed, though that, I knew, might be an affectation.

"Are you staying at the Palacio?" I said. These kids were pretending to be vagabonds, and so I knew they'd never put up the cost of the room, which was, considering the general destitution of this entire region, extravagant. But now that my confusion had receded, I felt sorry for them. They were scared and lost and I could help them out, a little.

Allie said, "We don't have a reservation, but maybe. Is it nice?"

I said it was unquestionably the best.

"Well, so maybe we will," Billy said, plastering his face against the window.

As the shuttle pulled away, Allie started telling a story about the time she'd traveled to St. Petersburg and ended up getting in a cab whose driver promised to take her to a club.

"He said it was the hip new place. Then we got off the road and were driving through these warehouses and I got pretty nervous. I mean, I thought he was going to rape me or something, but then we turned a corner and there was this one warehouse, with lights and techno music. I guess I was just relieved, so I didn't think it was so weird when the driver got out of the car. The music was so loud it was like shaking your head apart, and he opened the door for me. I didn't step inside. I could see that the place was empty, I mean, almost empty, except this huge speaker stack and these towers of strobe lights and then I noticed like four or five guys, all holding baseball bats, and on the ground in front of them was this guy, all beaten up. The guy on the floor looked up and shouted, 'Help!' He was American. I started running. If I'd been wearing sandals, I'd be dead. I ran and ran and that fat fuck of a cabbie couldn't keep up and eventually I hid in this empty warehouse. I could hear the men go by, looking for me, and they came by again later. I was hiding behind this stack of metal barrels, but if they came into the warehouse they totally would've seen me. It was the middle of the night, you know, but I ran out and went to another warehouse, in case they decided to search that first one, and I heard them shouting, a ways off. When it was light I snuck out and walked back to the city along the train tracks. It was pretty goddamn scary, though."

In all likelihood this was a myth she'd heard while traveling, or one she'd read on the Internet. That it wasn't true didn't matter; what mattered was telling the story and the practice this gave her. In a few months she'd come down from the remote mountains to get drunk in gringo bars on the coast and talk about all the crazy stuff she'd seen. It wouldn't matter if anything she said was true, because facts weren't important; what was important was the idea of herself that traveling confirmed: she was brave and adventurous and open-minded and now she could go home thirty pounds lighter and filthy, which would frighten her parents enough to allow her to live off their money for a few more years.

"That's totally fucked up, man," Billy said, his face up against the window as we pulled past the gray government buildings. "Hey, isn't that the Department of Interior?"

"So are you traveling or what?" Allie said, picking at the dirt ground under her nails.

"No, I'm here for work."

"Where do you work?"

"I'm a consultant."

"For what, the government?" From the hardening of her consonants it was clear she had me figured out: I was a bad guy and she was more than eager to judge, not all that different from my daughters, both of whom fancied themselves world savers. They had the security to use their educations and opportunities however they saw fit—one was an assistant DA in New Jersey and the other was a schoolteacher in Brooklyn—all because I'd worked my entire life to make enough money so they could attend Columbia and Brown.

"Not the government," I said. "Independent companies."

"What kind of companies?"

"A mining company. I'm auditing their operations here." I said this in a rush as though I was flustered, which I guess I was. That's how I got any time my daughters started in on universal health care, or how awful American foreign policy was. Susan, our oldest, the teacher, was home helping Joyce while I was away, and for her I'd pounded a sign into the front lawn: THANK YOU, GEORGE BUSH.

Allie just stared, as though waiting for horns to sprout from my forehead. Billy was still muttering about this building and that building and the civil war.

"Aqui, El Palacio," the driver said, easing to a stop.

I left the American kids frowning at the glimmering facade of the hotel and hurried into the revolving door. The lobby, with its slick stone floors and dribbling fountain, was empty except for a cluster of boys in bright red jackets and black pants who looked desperate to snatch my bag away.

In my reserved room I went to the drawer of the bedside table and found the promised handgun and shoulder holster. I splashed cold water on my face, dried it on a plush towel, lay down on the slightly lumpy mattress, and watched the jerking ceiling fan.

I woke to the knocking at the door and groped for the gun, nearly falling out of bed, shouting, "Hold on. Just hold on."

Through the peephole I saw a bellboy. He was barely five feet tall and so thin his arms and hands looked withered, his fingers long and spindly. He rattled away in Spanish, spraying spit.

"What?" I said. "English. Speak English."

"Guests, down." He pointed at the floor. "Wait. You. Guests."

"Who? Who is it?"

He shook his misshapen head and pulled his lips up into what he must've imagined was a smile.

"Why didn't you call?"

"No phone work," he said, pointing into my room. "Guests. Down. Bar." Then, probably sensing I wasn't going to tip, he shuffled away.

I checked the phone. There was no dial tone, just a blank space. I checked my cell, hoping to call Joyce and make sure Susan had arrived. The phone said, *Looking for Service.* Before leaving the room I grabbed my briefcase. You could never be sure with these companies. They were often frantic and might want to see something to comfort them right away.

The bar was off the lobby, through a frosted glass door. I let my eyes adjust to the darkness, taking in the sour smell of bleach, half-full ashtrays, and rum. An oily sunset was smeared across the one window.

From a booth near the window a woman waved. It was Allie, and beside her was Billy. They were drinking tall, fruit-adorned cocktails.

"We were waiting," she said, pointing at their drinks, in which quivered flecks of poisonous ice. "Someone's got to pay for these drinks, after all."

Still in something of a daze, I joined them, settling the briefcase on my lap. The waiter appeared and soon we were sipping a round of beers.

"Are you staying here?" I asked, not quite able to pull myself fully into the waking world.

"Dude, are you crazy?" Billy said. "This place costs a fortune."

"We found a hostel," Allie said. "Not too far away."

"Well, that's great," I said, tipping my bottle at them, then taking a sip and trying not to gag.

"But we thought we'd come and meet you for dinner." She reached across the table to pat my hand, as though they felt sorry for me. At that moment her smile reminded me of Susan, with that smug twist to her mouth. I'd assumed these kids were in their early twenties, but now I thought they might be the same age as my daughters, late twenties, on the cusp of realizing that life wasn't a game, that it was hard and ruthless and that the main thing was to keep from getting completely and totally screwed over by others.

"Sure," I said. "We can get some dinner. I bet the food's okay here."

"Don't be silly," Allie said, leaning forward to slap my shoulder. "Not here. We know a great place nearby."

"Is that a good idea? The food can be pretty dodgy down here." I touched the gun under my arm.

"Come on," Billy said, biffing me on the shoulder. "We'll be fine, man. It'll be an adventure." He stared at the briefcase on my lap, seemed about to say something, then just grinned dopily.

I should've gone to my room and back to sleep. Maybe it was exhaustion, or maybe, like that idiot Billy said, I just wanted to do something different, something that might help me slip for a moment out of my life.

"Just don't order salad. You'll be fine," Allie said. "And you better get the check, big guy," she said, then threw back her head and chugged the rest of her beer, clinking the bottle down on the table. Gasping for breath, she said, "Ready?"

They refused my offer of a taxi and so we walked, gathering attention on every street—three gringos ripe for a mugging or, if the locals were feeling more industrious, a kidnapping. The chances of this increased the farther we walked, out of the governmental area, through what counted here as a "middle-class" neighborhood, and past a hostel with a few gringos hanging around out front. I asked if that's where they were staying and they smiled dimly.

We walked on, into a slum. The narrow passageways between crumbling concrete walls were littered with garbage and an open sewer trickled down the middle. All the children were barefoot and ravenous, dark eyes glittering as they displayed their stumpy teeth. A clutch of them gathered around us, tugging at our pockets and sleeves and smearing swarms of bacteria over my fingers and the brass lock on my briefcase, so eventually I cradled it against my chest. *What the hell am I doing here?* I kept thinking, but I didn't turn back. I began to wonder if I'd picked up some tropical bug and was in the early stages of delirium. Sweat soaked my back. I touched the handle of the gun again and again for comfort.

This was probably just the sort of thing Susan had done during her recent trip across India. She'd come back with a new wardrobe of saris, a streak of red dye in her light brown hair, and stories about the noble poor and our responsibility to them. Like Allie and Billy, Susan had played at destitution, renting rooms from families in remote villages where she could've easily been raped or killed. During her recent visit she'd worn me out with her stories and self-righteousness. One night, after listening to awful, jangling music for an hour, I'd helped Joyce to bed, hooked up the tubes, and said, "Well, that was quite a performance."

"Performance?" she said, in the raspy near-whisper that was all she'd been able to manage for the past year. The brittle strands of her hair clung to the crisp pillowcase.

"Susan," I said, kissing her papery cheek. "That music."

Joyce closed her eyes and said softly, "I thought it was beautiful."

"Beautiful?" I said. She opened her eyes, and at that moment she looked frightened of me. I tried to calm myself. "Don't be silly, Joyce. It was awful."

"No," she said, closing her eyes again. "No, Robert." And then she was asleep. Music leaked up from below for hours and I ground my teeth until my jaw throbbed.

I told myself that Allie and Billy weren't much different from my daughters, which is obviously part of the reason I went with them: I wanted to protect them, and in so doing I thought maybe I could teach them something useful. The longer I was around them, the more ragged they looked. Both were severely underweight, especially Allie, whose jaw was drawn so tight it looked painful, and she had the wild look of hunger, the kind of fear that could get her into real trouble. There was something black and feral in her eyes, as though they didn't quite see you, only what she could get from you. She'd carried her Central American adventure too far and soon, if she wasn't careful, would end up truly lost.

At the door of the restaurant the urchins fell away. At first my relief they were gone was so great I didn't notice that the restaurant doubled as a brothel, but by the time we were seated at a rickety plastic table, I'd noticed the sickly girls, none older than sixteen, lined up against the far wall, shifting their legs apart so their tiny dresses rode higher. The barstools were full of heavy men wearing cowboy hats which they tipped back on their heads to peer at us through the smoke haze.

"Apparently," Allie said, scooting up to the table, "the tacos here are killer."

A tiny Indian woman with wildly unkempt hair took our order. I lied and said I'd eaten but that dinner was on me, of course. A few urchins approached the door warily, eager for us to emerge, drunk, easy targets.

When the food came, the American kids bent over the paper plates and crammed everything into their mouths, even the lettuce, sauce dripping over their dirty hands, which they licked clean like dogs. I signaled to the waitress for another round of tacos, and they tore into them, letting out little groans of pleasure. Wiping their mouths on their sleeves, without a word of thanks, they pushed their plates away and grinned at me.

"Hey," Allie said, sitting up straighter. She pointed at me. "Do you have any money?"

"What?" I said. "Of course."

"So, like, do you think we could borrow some?" She cocked her head and grinned, and when she did I noticed she was missing several teeth, as though they'd been pried from her raw red gums.

"For what?"

"To buy stuff," she said, so brightly, so stupidly, that I pulled out my wallet.

"How much?" I said, peering at the lump of nearly useless local money and the crisp American bills behind.

"I mean, whatever you can spare." She was still smiling, but it had a harder edge now. This wasn't the first time she'd asked someone for money.

I pulled out two American twenties and handed them across the table. She squinted at them as though not quite believing I was so cheap, then slipped them beneath the table.

"That's great. Thanks," she said.

"Hold on." I pulled out another two twenties.

"Thank you," she said softly, folding the bills carefully and tucking them away. "I'll pay you back."

"Don't worry about it."

Done with me now, the American kids started yakking about something, music, I thought, though the arcane names of bands, or brands, or TV shows proved impenetrable. I fell into the role of observer, watching men slip in from the street, skirt the far wall until they reached the line of girls, one of whom would peel off and lead the man through a curtained doorway. One of the girls had noticed me watching and kept catching my eye, smiling, maybe thinking I'd be good for a big tip.

"So are you, like, actually going up to the mine?" Allie said, cutting Billy off in the middle of one of his stories.

"Excuse me?"

"The mine, are you going there?" She was squinting, as though I were far away.

"No. There's plenty of work to do at the headquarters."

"Yeah, I bet," she said, propping her knobby elbows on the table.

Like my daughters, this girl clearly had some fantasy about a world made up of good guys and bad guys. This was a liberal dream, one that sensible people eventually realized was a limited and immature way of seeing the world.

"I've heard about that mine," Allie said.

I knew she meant in *Harper's*. Susan had mailed me a copy of the issue. The article focused on the displacement of the local population and the tensions this generated within the community and the possibility that it might reignite the civil war. In truth, I'd only skimmed the pages, bloated as they were with nonsense.

"I guess that makes you an expert, doesn't it?" I said.

"I think it's pretty fucked up," she said. "I mean, how can you work for that company? They're stealing those people's lands."

"Those people don't own the land. That's the point."

"That's such bullshit!" she shouted, slapping the table.

The men at the bar turned on their stools.

"Don't be ridiculous," I said, just above a whisper. "The opportunities that mine presents for this country outweigh the concerns of a few subsistence farmers." I hated myself for getting sucked in, but I'd never been able to stop myself. Thanksgiving dinners always ended in acrimony in our house.

"Of course it does!" Allie was shouting now. Everyone was watching us. "Opportunities for the rich who've raped this country for hundreds of years, and for North American corporations. Which I guess is what your job is, right? Grease the fucking gears."

There was something in her tone that made me think she wasn't just someone who'd stumbled across an article, which had mentioned, now that I thought about it, the presence of international human rights organizations, serving as observers and even human shields for the local communities when the mining company sent in men to burn the villages. Seeing her indignation, I began to wonder if maybe she was one of these. Even brainless Billy could've been an activist.

"I think you're simplifying things. The world isn't that easy," I said.

"It's not?" she shouted. "What's so complicated? Thieves come down and steal land, property, goods, and call themselves a company. That's how it's always been." Her face was red and the cords of her neck stood out. A little vein pulsed along her forehead. Billy watched all this with a bemused smile, as though we were speaking a foreign language.

"That's how a child thinks," I said. "Just because you read something in a magazine doesn't mean you understand anything."

"What the fuck are you talking about? What fucking magazine? I guess you" — she lunged forward, trying to poke me in the chest, but the table caught her in the stomach — "are just naturally full of fucking wisdom, aren't you?"

Before I could say anything she stood and stomped to the bar, squeezing in between two men. Billy fussed with the label on his bottle, then followed. They whispered together furiously while I finished my beer and gestured for another. Little peaks of their bitching rose into audibility every now and then. When I'd nearly finished my new beer, they went and sat at another table, back near the prostitutes.

Maybe at that point I should've left. But I'd seen the way the men in the bar were looking at the American kids, and though they were strangers, I felt responsible for them. I ordered another beer, told the waitress I was paying for everything the Americans had, and sneaked a look at my cell phone, which was still getting no service. Though the lopsided clock on the wall said it was only six o'clock, dark had fallen. Back home, Joyce would be exhausted, barely able to shuffle to the bathroom, where she'd strain to urinate and then brush her gray teeth. Susan would have to help lift her mother into bed, hook up the tubes, and set the level of the oxygen. These are things I'd done every day for the past year when I was home, and I'd come to think of them as rites no one but me knew how to enact. I hated when reality imposed on this feeling, as it continually did when we had to hire nurses to help while I was abroad. This time Joyce said she didn't want a stranger. She couldn't stand another bored, tired nurse changing her bedpan, lifting her frail shoulders from the sheets to slip her nightgown off before sponging her down, massaging her legs, and slipping a clean gown over her head. I'd written out how to do all this in explicit detail for Susan, but I was worried something would go wrong. Joyce might die, and even though I knew this was inevitable, knew that soon enough she'd be gone, I wasn't ready for it and couldn't accept it. And now I was here, thousands of miles away and out of touch. I wanted to be there, to take care of her, to sit up in bed when I heard her sighing in pain, or just shifting her hips. I was alert in a way I haven't been since Susan was born and for the first few weeks had been able to sleep only nestled between us. All that time I slept thinly, always aware of her delicate body on the mattress. Instead of thrashing around in the sheets as I usually did, I was suddenly calm and careful, and it was how I felt taking care of Joyce, the slight weight of her body as I cradled her in my arms, lifted her up easily, and set her down in the soft seat of her wheelchair. But what was I supposed to do when the man who might've been Steve called? If I'd refused to come down here, they'd have fired me, had nearly already done so because of my "personal conflicts" that were "hindering my accountability," and if that happened we'd be left without health insurance.

Distracted by these thoughts, I didn't notice the two men join Billy and Allie. The men looked about the same age as the Americans but were of a whole other world. Both men had cowboy hats tipped down over their narrow faces. I'd seen men like this all over the world, charming enough on the surface, but an inch down they were criminals. I could tell from the way they sat in their chairs that beneath their shirts were knives, or guns. The two men laughed, stood up, and gestured to the Americans. Allie and Billy complied. They knocked at a door on the back wall, which opened a crack, then let them in.

By the time I fumbled up out of my seat and across the room, the door was closed. The nearest prostitute grinned at me, tugging down the neck of her blouse.

I knocked and waited. While I did, I reached into my jacket and lifted the gun half an inch out of the holster, let it fall back. In my other hand I gripped my briefcase, full of financial papers and spreadsheets and my laptop computer. When no one answered my knocks, I turned to the bartender, who avoided looking at me. *"Abierto la puerta,"* I said. The bartender smiled at me, then nodded and stepped around the bar and unlocked the door.

"Dancing," he said, speaking Spanish slowly, as if I were a child. "Good dancing."

A steep flight of stairs led down into a room that pulsed with blue light and a dense, throbbing music. The stairwell was smothered with water-sodden posters—political ads, deodorant advertisements, and what looked like rock bands, men and women studded with piercings, sticking their tongues out and flicking off the camera as they danced atop blood-red letters that had blistered and burst apart. The door above was slammed, a lock thrown.

The music was too loud to hear voices in the room, the walls of which seemed to be shaking with the violent strobe light, and it took me a moment to recognize Allie and Billy at a table near a low wooden platform out of which rose a greasy metal pole. The Americans were laughing, bent doubled over as if in pain, and the two men they'd been talking with were smiling and smoking, holding out what must have been joints as the kids straightened up. There were half a dozen other tables, only one of which was occupied, by a single man in a long trench coat, a baseball cap pulled low over his face. I sat at the table nearest the stairs, turning my chair so I could see if someone came down behind me. A tiny, shriveled woman stepped from the shadows, her old body grotesquely squeezed into a leather bra and panties, her loose, cellulite thighs quivering as she stepped beside me and glared until I ordered a beer. Watching her slink back to the bar in the corner, I noticed a wall covered with leather straps, whips, and a long, thin machete.

I jumped when the music suddenly went silent, just long enough to hear Allie say, "Exactly. That's exactly what I'm—" and then the music erupted again, a crashing heavy metal that felt as if it were scraping the inside of my eyes. A silvery cloud drifted along the low ceiling, filling the room with the overripe stink of marijuana.

At the far end of the wooden stage a heavy black curtain was pushed aside and a young woman came out unsteadily on high silver stilettos and nothing else, her small, high breasts not moving even when she tottered into the bright puddle of a spotlight. She stopped in the middle of the stage and stood smiling shyly, her skin shining blue with sweat, or oil. She stared straight ahead, blinking heavily in the spotlight, smiling. One of the men at Allie and Billy's table stood up, stretching his arms over his head, leaning down to whisper something to Allie, who laughed and nodded. Slowly, as if everyone weren't watching, the man walked to the wall beside the bar and took down a short-handled black leather whip with three strands that sagged at the ends. Hefting it to test the weight, he walked back to his table, made another joke, and then, as the music rose to an even more frantic pitch, stepped onto the stage beside the woman.

I stared at my beer, but I could hear the wet, heavy snap of the whip and once I heard, through the din of the music, a single cry of pain. Only when the music shifted between songs and I heard a woman's voice—"No, I'm serious"—did I look up.

Allie was being pushed toward the stage by one of the other men, his mouth open, teeth flashing with laughter. Allie tried to turn, but the man grabbed her arms and spun her around to face the stage on which the naked girl was bent over, her face hidden by a fall of hair. Allie shook her head, but the man on the stage leaned down, grabbed her wrist, and jerked her onto the stage. Billy, I noticed, was staring at his hands in his lap, as if about to go to sleep. The man on the stage held the whip out toward Allie. She turned to step down, but the man grabbed her arm and pulled her back and thrust the whip into her hand. I couldn't tell, with the flashing light, with the blue haze, with the pounding music, but I thought she might be crying as she looked down at the whip in her hand, but I know that as she stepped up beside the kneeling girl she looked up, back at me, as if she'd known all along I was there. I put my hand on my gun, out of fear I guess, but also because I felt sure at that moment that I was in danger, that after she was done with the girl, she'd come for me. Then the fear left her face and Allie twirled the whip around her head and gyrated her hips. Beneath the music I could hear the men cheering as I scrambled out of my seat, knocking over the untouched beer on my table, and ran up the stairs, slipping so I hit my knee painfully, so that I limped through the door after knocking wildly until it was opened.

Outside the bar I got lost immediately but kept hobbling until I found a larger street, lined with auto-body shops, against the fences of which snarling black dogs hurled themselves. I walked along the side of the road, tucking the gun back into the holster, my briefcase in the other hand, glancing back until I spotted a cab and flagged it down.

Now it's nearly morning. Allie and Billy are surely dead, raped and tortured and robbed, all because they thought life was a game. In a few hours the men from the mining company will come for me. We're having breakfast here before heading to the office. It's all there on my itinerary. The phone in my room is still dead. My cell phone still has no service and of course there's no Internet, so I can't check on Joyce, can't make sure Susan arrived, that they're all still safe.

There's nothing more to write. But I can't stop thinking about what must've happened to Allie. I can't stop thinking there must have been something I could have done to save her, to keep her safe.

In a few weeks her mother will start to worry. In a month she'll call the embassy and her daughter's degenerate friends to see if they've heard anything. She'll sit up for hours, staring into the brittle, suburban dark, unable to even begin to imagine what might have happened, or what the world that swallowed her daughter was like. With no answers, there'll be nothing she can do but wait and hope for some final word, for anything other than the silence.

GINA PAOLI

Dog on a Cow

FROM *Ellery Queen's Mystery Magazine*

OUTSIDE, THE DOWNPOUR continued unabated, each raindrop intensifying the stale, humid dreariness of the confining motel room. Trussed in the corner with a piece of cord from the cheap Venetian blinds, Dan rubbed the throbbing side of his head against the wall in the corner farthest from the door of the tiny room. It was sometime past two in the morning. The little one, Brucie, had just slugged him with his ring-encrusted fist: Dan's wedding ring was on that fist now; his money and credit card were in Brucie's pocket. Brucie reclined in the dingy stuffed chair beside the bed, digging at his fingernails with a flat, blunt carpenter's pencil.

The big one, Jane, rested on the sagging bed, back against the water-stained wooden headboard, her tremendous arms crossed over her equally massive chest. Her hair, red streaked with black, had been fashioned into an improbable pageboy cut, an unfortunate choice that further accentuated the fleshy features on her round face. Part of a tattoo on her right bicep peeked out below the sleeve of her faded yellow T-shirt. It looked like the forepaw of a dog, and for some reason Dan imagined the dog was a frisky, bright-eyed poodle. Tiny bottles of nail polish, cylinders of mascara and eye shadow, tubes of lipstick, and several compacts of face powder lay scattered on the bed before her. She slowly bent forward and wagged a stubby finger at the gaudy containers as if selecting the right one would solve an important problem.

Dan's courage had weakened a little after that last punch from Brucie, but he still managed to convince himself that he could wait them out. He'd probably already suffered the worst of it. Hell, if he just got a chance, he could talk his way out of this. They only wanted a little traveling money, and since he had given them all he had, they'd soon grow bored with their little game and let him go. Still, he should try to do something. Maybe the story, maybe he could reduce the tension by telling them the story.

The story, which had come to him just a few hours before, had been forming in his mind even as he'd been sitting there tied up. It had an urgency of its own, and despite the discomfort and pain from his numb hands and the scuffs on his face, its tenuous threads began to knit themselves into a ragged tapestry and suddenly he could see the outline of it and knew enough to begin the telling. He had nothing to lose, and maybe it would help somehow. So he worked up a few drops of saliva and prepared his swollen tongue to make words.

They'd been sitting in silence since Brucie pounded on the TV to remove some static from the sound, resulting in a blank screen and no sound at all. That had been an hour or more ago. He'd been told to be quiet and he knew that Brucie had a short fuse, but Dan had faith in his own skills as a storyteller.

"It's raining like hell out there, like it's never going to stop," he said tentatively. There was no reaction to these first few words, so he continued. "It reminds me of a story I heard about a flood. It happened about twenty years ago, right here in eastern Colorado, though I'm not sure if it was up north on the South Platte or down on the Arkansas. Both rivers flood sometimes in the late spring when the snowmelt has already filled the river and a rainy spell sets in.

"So the rains came and swelled the river over its banks and into the pasture of this farm that was usually a half-mile from the river. The farmer had his cows penned up by his barn, but the river was rising steadily, so he let them out and herded them up onto the prairie sandhills above his farm. He struggled through the mucky soil, but he and his dog got them out and up into the hills with only one of the cows running off. When he was sure the others were safe, he and the dog took off to find the lone cow, a young milker who had always been a little skittish.

"Let me tell you about this dog. It wasn't the kind of dog the farmer would have picked for a work dog. It had come wandering into the farmyard a couple of years earlier, and after a week of tossing rocks and shouting at it, the dog was still skulking around. Against his better judgment, the farmer began to leave food scraps in an old Ford hubcap behind the barn, and soon the dog began to follow him around as he did his chores. He soon found that the dog had a touchy and unpredictable nature. The farmer sometimes caught a gleam in the dog's eye that seemed like a challenge, as if it would as soon go for you as listen to what you had to say. But the dog learned to handle the cows, so the farmer put up with it and let it live in the barn.

"The dog's mongrel collie coat hid the splashes of mud that stained it as he roamed about, searching for the cow. They worked well together, covering a lot of ground. The signs they found pointed to the brainless cow heading right down into the flooded cottonwoods that bordered the swollen river.

"When they came to the edge of the flood, the farmer waded into the slow-moving, muddy water. He looked back and saw that the dog had hesitated. He cursed it and commanded it to come, but it only paced at the water's edge. Finally he went back and picked up the unwilling animal and carried it with him. When he was fifty yards from the edge and still only up to his ankles, he dropped the dog. It looked back anxiously to the muddy land but moved on as the farmer did, staying by his side.

"It was too close to dark for the farmer to search for very long, as he didn't know when the flood crest would hit the area. For all he knew, it would reach clear to his farmhouse, but he was stubborn and single-minded, and as the gray sky turned to black he kept up his search, slogging along in his rubber work boots, already fighting his way through waves of uprooted plants and small trees and drowned varmints. He had no luck spotting the cow, and only turned back when it was dark enough that he needed the yard lights up by the house to guide him home.

"He didn't notice the loss of the dog until he waded onto the bog that had been his alfalfa field. The animal had been alternately swimming and scrambling onto branches and raised clumps of grass as they wended their way through the flooded cottonwood forest. The farmer remembered the dog being near him only ten or fifteen minutes before, as he heard its whine when it traversed a long log and didn't want to jump into the water again, and he had cussed it and chided it along. He looked back at the huge dark expanse of the murmuring flood and whistled a couple of times and then trudged up to his house. What a mess the day had turned into. He told himself that if the cow and the dog survived until morning, he'd find them then."

"What the hell does this have to do with anything? Who gives a damn about a lost dog or cow?" Brucie said. He stood up and put the carpenter's pencil behind his left ear. He was small and thin, maybe five-four and 140 pounds, and he wore dirty jeans with holes in the knees and a red flannel shirt over a black T-shirt. His hair was black and thick and he needed a shave. He had a mean kick and hard, fast fists.

"I think it's a good story," said the big woman, Jane. Dan had heard Brucie call her Jane several times, usually with a nasty descriptor in front of Jane, like Lard-Ass or Two-Ton. "You know I love dogs. I don't think I ever been closer to a cow than a hamburger or a glass of milk, though." She laughed heartily, shaking the whole bed so that the headboard banged against the wall.

"How do you know it's a good story? You ain't even heard the whole thing."

"Well, let him finish it, then."

"Nah. I'm tired of hearing him talk. Besides, if he has something to say, I want it to be that he remembers the number for the cash machine so we don't have to wait for the goddamn bank to open."

"He said he didn't remember. Even when you hit him," she said. Then she lowered her voice. "When are you going to learn that hitting never helps?"

Brucie didn't say anything for a minute, just cocked his ear toward her like he was waiting for another stupid remark. Then he slowly turned his head and looked across at her, his blue eyes turning to slits so all that showed was a venomous, milky gray. She tried to evade his stare but wasn't able to: the smile behind that hearty laugh disappeared and her heavy shoulders descended lower and lower until she sagged into a sad, rounded lump.

Brucie had her intimidated all right. Dan had noticed how quiet she was in the car, but it hadn't meant much to him then. He generally never picked up hitchhikers, especially when he had a full slate of appointments and an order book with too many blank pages, but today he'd been bored and *out there*. *Out there*, where the wind and the rain put him. He could go for weeks without doing a stupid, crazy thing, and then along would come a blow and suddenly he would decide to take a 200-mile detour to find some ribs cooked just the way he liked them, or that he needed a rest and he would end up spending three days in a motel room, drinking whiskey all night, crying to every sad song on the radio.

He knew something was going to happen when he realized he had driven for two hours with his radio off, racing out of western Kansas and into Colorado in an eerie trance. He had his eyes hard to the road, following the flashes of lightning like the dazzle from a hypnotist's watch. The wind carried the rain across the road, billowing it in waves that nearly flooded the highway before they gusted away. It was like driving along a stormy California beach.

Then he saw them, in a lightning flash, the little one huddled against the big one on a stretch of nowhere 60 miles into Colorado. So he pulled over and picked them up, thinking he was just being humane, but knowing it was really the wind and the rain and being *out there*. They didn't say much, only making small talk, revealing themselves in little ways, and after a hundred miles he thought that he was going to be all right, that just having the company was pulling him back, was calming him down. Then the seed of a story began to sprout, something about a flood, about a lost cow and a dog, lost to the storm and the flood.

The motel squatted in the far corner of a lonely crossroads on the two-lane, 10 miles away from a stagnant and dying farm town of a few thousand people and 20 miles from the interstate, where cars rocketed along oblivious to its existence. There was just the one motel and the filling station with the lunch counter across the highway. The café wouldn't even open until 6 a.m., when the farmers and truckers and other traveling souls might stop in for breakfast. He abruptly decided to pull in, because the story was coming too fast and he wanted to let it grow at its own pace. He would spend the night at the motel, and in the morning go across to the diner and tell the story to the locals, judging its success by smiles and nodding heads and a coffee cup that was always full; or become embarrassed by turned backs and snickers and the loud clanking of silverware against thick ceramic plates.

The occasional praise from these small audiences made his long trips on the road bearable. He spent his days driving hundreds of mind-numbing miles back and forth across the prairie and fields of eastern Colorado, western Kansas, and Nebraska, pestering service-station owners into buying the latest equipment to service the latest, increasingly complicated cars. Or failing to convince them, as had been the recent trend. No, he didn't mind, because he still had adventures in his head, and he loved the chance to meet and entertain new people with his stories.

There was an overhanging awning and a bench in front of the diner, and the big woman said they would be all right there until it opened, that they were dry now, thanks very much for the ride. He felt a little bad leaving them there, but at least he'd gotten them out of the rain.

Across the road, he had to wake up the motel clerk, who groggily fumbled with his pen when Dan checked in, and it seemed to take forever, but he was a nice enough fellow and Dan thought he might share the story with him tomorrow when it was polished and ready to tell. He had the trunk of his Toyota open and he was fumbling around with his bag when the dim light from the buzzing motel sign suddenly became even dimmer. A shadow flashed across his hand on the bag and when he looked over his shoulder, the woman hovered over him. For a moment he imagined she might have a question to ask, or have come to ask for a little food money, but then he felt the jab in his back and he flexed upright, banging his head against the lid of the trunk. A blow behind the ear quickly followed.

"Don't move like that again, buddy," said the voice behind him, "or you'll get more than a slap upside the head." This time the jab was stronger and sharper, and he realized it was a knife at his back. He should have been surprised, but wasn't, chastising himself that he hadn't noticed that they were the kind of grungy hitchhikers who showed you a smile as you passed and then cursed you and gave you the finger if you passed them by. He hadn't noticed, he'd been *out there,* and then the story had come and he'd become distracted and careless.

Now Jane got up from cowering on the bed and went to the window. She pulled aside the curtain and looked out into the darkness. The side of her face, he could see, was illuminated by the pink neon from the motel sign, and there were shiny trails of tears running down from her eyes.

Brucie came over and squatted down on his haunches. He crossed his arms and looked at Dan. Dan guessed he was about twenty-five, but he could have been some perpetually adolescent forty-year-old. He smiled at Dan until Dan found himself smiling, too, unable to say why, nodding at the silliness of it all, how it seemed more like some prank than a robbery. No one robbed you this way.

Brucie uncrossed his arms and his left shot out, the closed fist catching Dan on the side of the head. He had been turning away as he nodded and the blow glanced off, but was still hard enough to stun him. There was another fist to his face and he felt the tearing of the inside of his cheek between the bony knuckles and his teeth, leaving the sudden, grim taste of blood. Dan thought about the angelic look on Brucie's face, the mask that hid the nasty workings of a small, mean man who never had anything but small, mean thoughts. He took two or three more blows, not really able to keep track of the damage, they came so fast.

"You made this too hard, man," he heard Brucie say. Dan's ears rang and the man's voice sounded hollow and far away. "What kind of salesman don't carry his money in cash? Plastic ain't the way for a man to carry his money. It ought to be cash."

Dan fell onto his side. Brucie was still squatting beside him. Dan had his eyes closed. He felt a hand on his hair as he was dragged up, back into a sitting position.

"I think you're lying about that damn number. I think you're wasting my time because you think you're going to get away with something. Let me tell you what," he said. Dan opened his eyes, squinting now through the pain. Brucie's face was only inches away. His breath reminded Dan of the wind from the beef packing plant back home, the odor of rotting meat so intense it weighed down the breeze that carried it.

"I don't want the number anymore. When that branch bank or whatever it is in that little town up the road opens, you're going to clean out your account, and if you're lucky, we'll let you live. If you'd given us the number for that card, we'd already be gone. You just had to make it hard. Well, I can make it hard, too."

Then he stood, giving Dan's hair a hard yank and throwing his head back against the wall. He glanced at the woman, jangling the keys he had taken from Dan earlier. "I'm going out to check out that car again; I know he's got some more cash stashed somewhere. Make sure he don't move. And don't be talking to him." He slammed the door as he left.

Dan's head ached as the booming of the door shook the thin walls of the motel room. He sucked away the blood from the numerous cuts inside his mouth, wanting to spit it out but feeling weak and impulsively swallowing. The echoing pain in his head started to subside as the flow of blood decreased and what he swallowed began to taste less salty.

Jane continued to look out the window. He hadn't seen how she reacted to Brucie's blows. She had said she didn't like hitting. But she did not seem disturbed now; maybe she only meant she didn't like being hit herself. Dan was sure that it happened, that the little man beat up on the big woman. There were no bruises on her that he could see, but he knew that it happened.

She turned away from the window and walked back to the bed, sitting down to a groaning screech from the box springs. A sigh came out of her that seemed to go on and on.

"I liked that story you were telling," she said. "I wish he'd let me talk to you so's I could hear how it ended. He doesn't like it when I have fun over something he hasn't made up."

"I could tell you the rest of that story," he said slowly, trying to keep the edges of his teeth away from the cuts inside his mouth.

"Don't talk. He's mad enough already. He don't have good control when he gets this mad."

"I think you'd like the rest of the story," Dan said. "I can speak quietly."

She turned her head toward the door. He saw her chewing her lower lip. Then she sighed another windy sigh. "Talk real low," she said. "I mean real low."

The pain from his jaw kept his mouth from opening more than an inch or so. A loose flap of skin on the inside of his cheek caught on his back teeth when he spoke, but he had to finish the story. He could see that his only chance was the woman. He took a deep breath and tried to let the story come back. Of course, the story had changed now, and it came to him so fast he could barely keep the words from stumbling over each other as they came out of his mouth.

"The farmer lived alone and had a cold supper of bologna and pickled peppers, listening to the far-off crashing and grinding together of trees as they fell against each other and were lost to the current of the rising flood. He didn't think the waters would reach the farmhouse or the barn, but if they did, he didn't know what he'd do with those thirty head of cows when they needed to be milked in the morning.

"After he finished eating he lit his pipe and went out onto the front porch and looked out into the hazy night, the sky somehow lightened by the lowering rain clouds. It wasn't long before he heard it, the piercing cry of a panicked animal, sharp against the roar and murmur of the flood. He turned his head, using his good ear to focus on the point and gauge its location, several hundred yards downstream of the house.

"'Serve the damn thing right if it drowned,' he said, and then put out his pipe and went back out to the barn and put on the chest waders he used when he went fishing for brook trout up in the mountains. He grabbed a halter for the cow and a flashlight and trudged away from the house and the barn, too quickly reaching the edge of the waters. He hesitated a moment, giving himself one last chance to turn back, and then began high-stepping his way through the flooded alfalfa field.

"Feeling the fool, he waded deeper and deeper, playing his flashlight over the dark water, which had become surprisingly smooth now except for the occasional wake of some branch or dead critter and the accompanying foamy mustache. 'That damn cow is probably gone, and what do I care about the dog?' he said aloud, but continued on.

"The sound of barking led him farther out into the flood than he had thought he could reach, out through the cottonwoods and closer to the deep channel of the river within this new river. He moved gingerly now, as the water had reached his thighs, telling himself, *Ten more steps, only ten more,* and then he would go ten more after that.

"When he first saw the dog, it was balanced on a log pressed against a tree by the current. It had stopped its barking and held its dark, shiny eyes against the flashlight. Relieved in a way he didn't want to admit, he saw that he only had to take a few more steps and he would reach the dog and then he could carry it back to shallow water and begin to focus his worry on the real problems this flood had brought to him.

"But he didn't make even that next step, as his foot caught on some submerged branch or root and he fell forward, the cold water flooding over the front of the waders, drenching his shirt and the top of his pants. He quickly regained his stance, cussing himself and cussing the dog. He tried to stand fully upright, but some instinct or maybe the thick, low clouds, heavy on his shoulders, kept him hunched over.

"He flashed the light toward the dog again and realized that it wasn't standing on a log at all. The dog held its precarious perch on the cow, where it had become lodged against the cottonwood tree, the cow bowed in the middle, its head low in surrender to the current. Instead of feeling relief at finding both of the animals, the farmer sighed in resignation at the effort it would require to free them and get them back on dry land.

"Looking closer, he saw that the cow had a wound on its neck, a loose flap of skin that showed red even as the lapping waters tried to wash away the blood. He checked the dog again and saw its lolling tongue and bloodstained muzzle, shocked but somehow not surprised.

"'You,' he shouted at the dog, never having given it a name, only 'dog,' only 'you.' He shouted the word, the name, in a stern voice, an accusing voice, that failed to stir the dog as it lowered its head and bared its teeth.

"The cow suddenly reared its head out of the water and appeared to recognize the farmer with wide, mad eyes. Abruptly closing those eyes, it tried to lunge toward the farmer, suddenly breaking loose from the grasp of the current and sliding away from the tree, the dog struggling to keep its balance.

"The farmer pulled out the halter, thanking his good luck that he didn't have to pull the cow out from behind the tree himself, and as he held the halter out toward the head of the cow, the dog moved forward on the cow, balancing on the cow's neck, and tore savagely at his hand. The teeth caught him in the web between his thumb and forefinger, leaving a deep gash and intense pain.

"Enraged, the farmer looked about him for a floating branch, anything that might be floating by with which he could beat the dog, beat it loose from the cow and let it fend for itself. It had gone crazy and was worthless to him now, or at least for the time being.

"Finding nothing for a weapon, he swung at the dog with that painful, closed fist and caught it in the head. It didn't fall, but backed up enough that the farmer thought he could slide the halter over the cow's head.

"'Come on, you young heifer,' he said, holding out the halter, waiting for the cow to recognize it, to settle its head into the familiar nylon headgear. The snout of the dog came out of nowhere again, the sharp teeth catching the outside of his already injured hand. He swiped at it but missed again.

"'Damn it, you bitch, get your head in here,' he shouted at the cow, leaning back a little, thinking the dog might not be able to reach him.

"At last the cow did come forward, with a sudden bawl and a violent lifting of its head, catching the halter with its nose, but not square on enough for him to get it over the cow's ears. So he grabbed those ears and held on and tried to slide it up over one ear at a time.

"He'd forgotten the dog in that instant when he sensed success, when he thought the hardest part would be done. So when it came leaping out at him, grabbing hold of his own ear and tearing it as it shot by, the farmer screamed in such rage and pain that he dropped the halter and started splashing about, swinging his arms, wanting only one solid punch, one painful crack on the dog's head. He had to get rid of the dog or it would kill him.

"The struggle had preoccupied him to the point where he'd lost any sense of his location. He had probably been slipping down the slope of the hole for a few seconds before he noticed that the water was pouring over the top of his waders, sloshing down all the way to the rubber boots, quickly filling them. He still had hold of the cow's ears, and he quickly realized that that cow had become his lifeline, his only hope. He needed to use the cow's buoyancy to keep him from going down and not coming up.

"The dog nipped at his ear again, but he didn't care. He had the cow's ears and thought that he should try to slide up and put his arms around its neck. He still had hope, a slim hope, that he would get out of this mess, and the cow seemed to cooperate, staying still and floating along with the current until maybe they would settle into a shallow place.

"It became an intense struggle, as he tried to keep his head above water while his waders ballooned and became heavier and heavier, pulling harder and harder. He heard the dog splashing behind him, staying with them, but no longer attacking him. The dog, that damn dog, would kill him one way or another.

"So when the cow suddenly rolled away from him and he lost

his hold on the ears, and then rolled back and over him, forcing him down, he knew that he had only himself to blame. Not the cow, not even the dog. When he knew he wouldn't come up again, when his last breath bubbled away and the cold water filled his lungs like it had filled his waders, his last thought was that the damn dog would survive him and probably the cow as well."

The room was silent for a moment as Dan's voice died out. He had begun to talk quietly, as he promised, but the volume of his voice had risen as the story reached its conclusion. He wondered what Jane thought about the story.

The woman sat on the edge of the bed with her knees drawn up, somehow looking smaller. Without saying anything about the story, she reached for her purse on the table beside the bed and got out a pack of cigarettes. She lit one with a tiny disposable lighter, inhaled deeply, and slowly blew out the smoke through her nostrils. She continued to smoke without saying anything, finishing half of the cigarette. Then the doorknob rattled.

Brucie burst into the room, holding a magazine in one hand and a pint bottle in the other. He slammed the door behind him, looked around the room as he unscrewed the cap on the bottle, tilted it back, and finished it in one long swig. Then he tossed the magazine toward Jane, who tried to move but still got the flapping leaves of the magazine across her face. Brucie laughed and flipped the empty bottle toward Dan. Dan turned his head, the bottle glancing off the wall and hitting him in the shoulder.

It was a bottle of Old Grand-Dad that Dan always kept in the car in the event that he became stranded in a blizzard on the plains. It was in the emergency kit that had the space blanket, the little Sterno stove, the coffee, and the chocolate. He had never opened the bottle, so Brucie had to be drunk.

"At least I know you're a man now," Brucie said. "You got a girlie magazine and whiskey in your car."

"It's just a *Playboy*," Dan said, foolishly embarrassed for some reason.

"Yeah, and I bet you don't look at the pitchers." Brucie started giggling as he said this, confirming his drunkenness. As soon as he stopped, he looked thoughtfully at Dan and smiled. His eyes had become dulled, but Dan knew this was deceptive. The fury inside the man was hotter than ever.

"I'm feeling like I don't want to wait another couple of hours for that bank to open. I'm feeling like I want to get on the road right now. This fifty dollars will put gas in that car of yours and get us a meal. Maybe I should just call it good and move on. Maybe that's what I should do. What do you think, pardner?"

He had walked over beside Dan. Tired and hungry and sore as he was, Dan knew what was going to happen next. Fear flushed up from deep inside and for a moment he felt himself swelling with adrenaline, wanting to break the ropes and rise up and at least defend himself. But it lasted only that moment and he felt himself slumping, felt despair replace the adrenaline. He looked down at the man's boots, pointy cowboy boots, and wondered if he was going to use them to kick him to death.

Dan looked over at the woman sitting on the bed. She had moved to the edge of the bed. She had the magazine, the *Playboy*, in her lap. She looked down at the magazine, and Dan had the idea that she was trying not to say anything. She knew what was going to happen. Dan knew she had seen it before.

"Don't, Brucie," she finally said in a tired voice. "Let's just go, like you said. Let's just go somewhere else."

"Oh, we'll go, all right. Just let me say goodbye to our buddy Dan here. He's been so damned helpful." His eyes had brightened; the hateful heat inside was fueling his rage.

"Don't, Brucie. Please," she said. "I'll leave you if you do. I'll go, and you'll be on your own." She stood up and looked around and grabbed her purse from the nightstand by the bed. She glanced at the door and then back at Brucie.

Dan should have been watching the boots instead of the woman. One of them slashed at him and caught him in the side. He thought he heard a crack as the air whooshed out of him. He toppled over onto his side. He lay there, struggling to breathe, seeing the boots just inches from his eyes. When he was able to take a shallow breath, a sharp point of pain in his side blew all of the air out again.

"If you leave, I'll come find you. I'll find you and I'll talk to you just like I'm talking to Dan here. You'll come back."

Dan had his eyes on the boot this time and was able to turn to the side and absorb the kick with his shoulder. It hurt, but at least he could breathe. He wanted to ask for help from the woman, but he knew he was lost, and even in his fear and pain, he knew that the woman should probably leave while she had the chance. Maybe Brucie wouldn't find her. Maybe she would call the police in time. He heard her heavy footsteps and hoped that she would escape. All he could do was look at the boots and wonder how long he would last.

"Don't be stupid," he suddenly heard Brucie say.

The boots suddenly rotated, facing the other way now, and then slowly floated off the floor. Dan looked up and saw Brucie dangling in Jane's arms. She held him in a bear hug as he squirmed and kicked his legs, trying to escape.

Dan gritted his teeth through the pain, managing to right himself, leaning back against the wall. Jane's big arms completely encircled the little man, her hands clasped on opposite elbows. She turned with him as she squeezed, spinning around slowly like they were dancing. Brucie was kicking slower now, his pointy boots searching for the floor. His pale face had turned a bright red, his lips a strange pastel blue. Then the kicking stopped and she held him like some limp, life-sized doll. After he had been completely limp for several minutes, she laid him on the bed.

She stood over Brucie's body, her face stony and unreadable. She watched him sprawled there on the bed and even leaned a little closer, turning her head as if searching for the whisper of his breathing. She might even have been waiting for him to wake up so she could apologize and do something nice for him, or ask what they could do for fun. Any fun thing he wanted to do. But Dan could tell with certainty that Brucie would never wake up. Finally she sighed, her broad shoulders rising like the final swell of a volcano before it collapsed in on itself.

She turned and took heavy steps across the room and stood over Dan. He pushed himself away from the wall, trying to turn, thinking she would untie the ropes on his wrists. He could do the ones on his ankles on his own.

He felt her touch, but instead of loosening the ropes, her arms slid around him and then his feet were off the ground and their eyes were level. Dan was bigger than Bruce, but she held him with ease. Her brown eyes gleamed from the tears that filtered through her mascara and ran in dark trails down her cheeks.

"I ain't no cow. And Brucie wasn't no dog," she said, her breath soft with spearmint gum. "He was just a sad and angry little man. He used to be good to me, but lately he forgot how to do it. I kept thinking he would remember those good days when he wasn't so mean, but some things you can't change."

She squeezed him harder. "You got that straight? The next time you go talking about dogs and cows there won't be no mention of me or Brucie."

The incredible pain in his ribs made him suck at his lips, suck for air like it was in the spit and drool, and then he felt like he was swallowing his tongue, he was so desperate for breath. He nodded his head feebly to show that he understood. Then she carried him over beside the bed.

"I want you to tell me that number. I didn't mind that you lied to Brucie, but don't try it with me." She sniffed and blinked at the tears in her mascara-laden lashes as she spoke.

Dan nodded his head again to show that he would do that very thing and anything else she wanted if she would only give him some room for a breath. She stared at him grimly, her puffy face only inches from his, finally putting him down on the bed beside Brucie. When he got some fraction of his breath back, he told her the number, repeated it three times to make sure.

She stooped over Brucie and got the credit card and cash he'd stolen from Dan out of Brucie's shirt pocket. Then she touched her fingers to her lips and touched Brucie's cheek. "He weren't a dog," she said softly, "and I ain't a cow." Then she put the cards and cash into her little purse and went to the door. She paused to pull a small handkerchief from her purse and dab her eyes. "Tell the police what you want, but I expect I'm pretty easy to forget. I'll leave your car someplace further down the road." And then she slid out the door.

Dan lay for a long time on the bed, snatching teeth-gritting breaths, more afraid of the woman now than he had been of Brucie. He waited until the pain had subsided, until daylight shone through the window, and then he called 911. The local sheriff's deputies were skeptical about his story and questioned him for hours about Brucie's body. In the end, they let Dan go after confirming his identity, assuring him that they would be talking with him again. Dan refused to go to a hospital, which didn't seem to bother the deputies.

He found a rental car in the nearby town and drove the 200 miles to his home in Fort Collins. His wife nursed his wounds and taped his chest when he again refused to go to a doctor. He gave vague answers to her questions about what had happened, but she didn't press him. He would tell her all about it later, when he found the words. Or when the words found him.

Vic Primeval

FROM *San Diego Noir*

"YOU KNOW HOW these things get started, Robbie. You see her for the first time. Your heart skips and your fingers buzz. Can't take your eyes off her. And when you look at her she knows. No way to hide it. So you don't look. Use all your strength to not look. But she still knows. And anybody else around does, too."

"I've had that feeling, Vic," I said.

We walked down the Embarcadero where the cruise ships come and go. It was what passes for winter here in San Diego, cool and crisp, and there was a hard clarity to the sunlight. Once a week I met Vic at Higher Grounds coffee and we'd get expensive drinks and walk around the city. He was a huge guy, a former professional wrestler. Vic Primeval was his show name until they took his WWF license away for getting too physical in his matches. He hurt some people. I spend a few minutes a week with Vic because he thinks he owes me his life. And because he's alone in the world and possibly insane.

"Anyway," said Vic, "her name is Farrel White and I want you to meet her."

"Why?"

"Because I'm proud to have you as a friend. You're pretty much all I got in that department."

"Are you showing us off, Vic? Our freak-show past?"

He blushed. "No. But you do make me look good."

Vic was bouncing at Skin, an exotic dance club—strippers, weak drinks, no cover with military ID. "I don't love that place," I said.

"Robbie, what don't you like about pretty women dancing almost naked?"

"The creeps who go there."

"Maybe you'll get lucky. You're lucky with the ladies."

"What do you know about my luck with ladies, Vic?"

"Come on, man. You've got luck. Whole world knows that."

More luck than I deserve, but is it good or bad? For instance, seven years ago Vic threw me out the window of the sixth floor of a hotel he'd set on fire—the Las Palmas in downtown San Diego. I was trying to save some lives and Vic was distraught at having had his World Wrestling Federation license revoked. This incident could be reasonably called bad luck.

You might have seen the video of me falling to what should have been my death. But I crashed through an awning before I hit the sidewalk and it saved my life. This luck was clearly good. I became briefly semifamous—the Falling Detective. The incident scrambled my brains a little but actually helped my career with the San Diego Police Department. In the video I look almost graceful as I fall. The world needs heroes, even if it's only a guy who blacks out in what he thinks are the last few seconds of his life.

"Just meet her, Robbie. Tonight she goes onstage at eight, so she'll get there around seven-thirty. I start at eight, too. So we can wait for her out back, where the performers go in and out. You won't even have to set foot in the club. But if you want to, I can get you a friends-and-family discount. What else you got better to do?"

We stood in the rear employees-only lot in the winter dark. I watched the cars rushing down Highway 163. The music thumped away inside the club, and when someone came through the employee door the music got louder and I saw colored shapes hovering in the air about midway between the door and me.

I've been seeing these colored objects since Vic threw me to that sidewalk. They're geometric, of varying colors, between one and four inches in length, width, depth. They float and bob. I can move them with a finger. Or with a strong exhalation, like blowing out birthday cake candles. They often accompany music, but sometimes they appear when someone is talking to me. The stronger the person's emotion, the larger and more vivid the objects are. They linger briefly, then vanish.

In the months after my fall I came to understand that these

shapes derived not so much from the words spoken but from the emotion behind them. Each shape and color denotes a different emotion. To me, the shapes are visual reminders of the fact that people don't always mean what they say. My condition is called synesthesia, from the Greek, and loosely translated it means "mixing of the senses." I belong to the San Diego Synesthesia Society and we meet once a month at the Seven Seas on Hotel Circle.

Farrel had a round, pretty face, dark eyes, and brown hair cut in bangs, and one dimple when she smiled. Her lips were small and red. Her handshake was soft. She was short even in high-heeled boots. She wore a long coat against the damp winter chill.

"Vic tells me you're a policeman. My daddy was a policeman. Center Springs, Arkansas. It's not on most maps."

"How long have you been here in San Diego?" I asked.

"Almost a year. I was waitressing, but now I'm doing this. Better pay."

"How old are you?"

"I'm twenty-four years old." She had a way of holding your eyes with her own, a direct but uncritical stare. "Vic told me all about what happened. It's good that you've become a friend of his. We all of us need at least one good friend . . . Well, guys, I should be going. I'd ask you in and buy you a drink, but it's supposed to work the other way around."

I glanced at Vic and saw the adoration in his eyes. It lit up his face, made it smarter and softer and better. Farrel smiled at him and put her hand on his sleeve.

"It's okay, Vic."

"Just so good to see you, Farrel."

"Vic walks me in and out, every night. And any other of the dancers who want him to. You're a cop, so you know there's always someone coming around places like this, making trouble for the girls. But not when Vic Primeval is in the barnyard."

"I don't really like that name," said Vic.

"I mean it in a good way."

"It means primitive."

"It's only a show name, Vic. Like, well, like for a dancer it would be Chastity or Desire."

I watched the inner conflict ruffle Vic's expression. Then his mind made some kind of override and the light came back to his eyes. He smiled and peered down at the ground.

A hard look came over Farrel's face as a black BMW 750i
bounced through the open exit gate and into the employees-only
lot. It rolled to a stop beside us. The driver's window went down.

"Yo. Sweetie. I been looking for you." He was thirty, maybe,
and tricked out in style—sharp haircut, pricey-looking shirt and
jacket. Slender face, a Jersey voice and delivery. He looked from
Farrel to Vic, then at me. "What's your problem, fuckface?"

I swung open my jacket to give him a look at my .45.

He held up his hands like I should cuff him. "Christ. Farrel? You
want I should run these meatballs off? They're nothing to do with
me and you, baby."

"I want them to run *you* off. I told you, Sal. There isn't a you and
me. No more. It's over. I'm gone."

"But you're not gone, baby. You're right here. So get in. Whatever you'll make in a month in there, I'll pay you that right out of
my pocket. Right here and now."

"Get off this property," said Vic. "Or I'll drag you out of your
cute little car and throw you over that fence."

Vic glanced at me and winced right after he said this. When he
gets mad at things, he throws them far. People, too.

Sal clucked his tongue like a hayseed, then smiled at Vic as if he
were an amusing moron.

"No more us, Sal," said Farrel. "We're over."

"You still owe me eight thousand dollars, girl. Nothing's over till
I get that back."

I saw black rhombuses wobbling in the air between us. Black
rhombuses mean anger.

"I'll pay you back as soon as I can. You think I'm dancing in a
place like this just for the fun of it all?"

"Move out of here," I said. "Do it now."

"Or you'll arrest me."

"Quickly. It'll cost you forty-eight long cheap hours or two expensive short ones. Your pick."

"I want what's mine," Sal said to Farrel. "I want what I paid for."

"Them's two different things."

"Maybe it is in that redneck slop hole you come from."

The window went up and the car swung around and out of
the lot, the big tires leaving a rubbery low-speed squeal on the
asphalt.

"I'm coming in for a while," I said.

I had a beer and watched Farrel and the other dancers do their shows. They were uninhibited and rhythmic, to say the least. Some were pretty and some were plain. Some acted flirtatious and others lustful and others aloof. Farrel seemed almost shy, and she never once looked at either me or Vic from what I could tell. She had a small attractive body. Vic stood in the back of the room, lost in the lush plum-colored curtains, his feet spread wide and arms crossed, stone still.

After an hour passed and Sal had not come back, I nodded a goodnight to Vic and went home.

Two days later Vic left a message for me and I met him outside the Convention Center. There was a reptile show in progress, and many of the people were entering and leaving the building with constrictors around their necks and leashed iguanas in their arms and stacks of clear plastic food containers filled with brightly colored juvenile snakes.

"Look at this thing," he said. He reached into the pocket of his aloha shirt and pulled out a huge black scorpion. "They don't sting."

Vic Malic had enormous hands, but that scorpion stretched from his thumb tip to the nail on his little finger. It looked like it could drill that stinger a half-inch into you anytime it wanted. In his other hand was a clear plastic bag filled with crickets. They were white with dust of some kind. They hopped around, as crickets do.

"Scorpion food?" I asked.

"Yeah. And they dust them with vitamins for thirty cents."

He looked down at the creature, then slid it back into his shirt pocket. "That son of a bitch Sal is stalking Farrel. That was the third time I've seen him. He shows up everywhere she goes."

"Tell her to come fill out a report. We can't do anything until she does that."

"Doesn't trust cops."

"She seemed proud of her dad."

"I'm only telling you what she told me. Sal loaned her ten grand because she totaled her car with no insurance, and her baby had to have chemotherapy. Darling little baby. I saw it. Just darling but with cancer."

"That is a shame."

"Yeah, and he was all charm at first, Sal was. She kind of liked him. Started paying with favors, you know, but the way he had it figured was he'd get anything he wanted for two years and she'd still owe him half. Plus he likes it rough and he hit her. Then he said he's got friends. He can introduce her to them, you know—they'd really like her. He's a Jersey wise guy, all connected up. Says he is. You heard him. He said he wants what's his and what he paid for."

I know who the mobbed-up locals are here in America's Finest City. Sal wasn't one of them. We've had our wise guys for decades, mostly connected to the L.A. outfits. There's a restaurant they go to. You get to know who they are. I wondered if Sal was just a visiting relative, getting some R&R in Southern California. Or maybe a new guy they brought in. Or if he was a made guy trying to muscle into new territory. If that was true there would be some kind of trouble.

I watched the scorpion wriggle around in the shirt pocket. The pocket had a hula girl and it looked like the pincers were growing out of her head.

"I'm gonna get that eight grand for her," said Vic.

"Where?"

"I got a start with the book sales."

Vic has been hand-selling copies of *Fall to Your Life!*, which he wrote and published himself. It's about how "the Robbie Brownlaw event" seven years ago at the Las Palmas Hotel changed his life for the better. He does pretty well with it, mostly to tourists. I see him sometimes, down by the Star of India, or Horton Plaza, or there at the Amtrak station, looming over his little table with copies of the book and a change box. He wears his old Vic Primeval wrestling costume of faux animal skins—not fur, but the skins sewed together into a kind of bodysuit. It's terrifically ugly, but the customers are drawn to it. To attract buyers, he also sets up an aging poster of me falling through the sky. He used to charge five bucks a copy for the book, but a year ago it went up to ten. Once a month he still gives me a cut from each sale, which is 25 percent. I accept the money because it makes Vic feel virtuous, then turn it over to the downtown food pantry and ASPCA and various charities.

I did some quick calcs based on what Vic paid me in royalties for July—traditionally his best month due to tourists. My take was

$500, which meant that Vic pocketed $1500 plus change for himself.

"It'll take you at least six months to get eight grand," I said. "Plus winter is coming on and you've got your own expenses to pay."

Vic brooded.

"Do you have any money saved up, Vic?"

"I can get the money."

"So she can give it to him? Don't give her anything. Have her file a complaint with us if he's such a badass. She can get a restraining order. You don't know her and you don't know him. Stay away, Vic. That's the best advice you'll get on this."

"What do you mean?"

"What about this doesn't scream setup?"

"A setup? Why set up a guy who doesn't have any money? She hasn't asked me for one nickel. She's the real thing, Robbie. That little baby. I don't have a world-class brain, but my heart always sees true. Farrel passes the Vic Malic heart test."

"The best thing you can do is have her file a complaint."

"She won't. I already told her to. She said the cops can't do anything until they catch him doing something. What she's afraid is, it's gonna be too late when that happens."

Which is often true.

"But Robbie, what if you tell her? Coming from you, it would mean a lot more than from me."

The San Diego mob guys own and frequent a downtown restaurant called Napoli. It's an unflashy two-story brick affair not far at all from police headquarters. They have controlling interests in a couple of much swankier eateries here, but they do their hanging out at Napoli.

"Hey, it's Robbie Brownlaw," said Dom, the owner.

"Dom, I need a word."

"Then you get a word, Robbie. Come on back. How's San Diego's famous detective?"

He's a round-faced, chipper fellow, early sixties, grandson of one of San Diego's more vivid mob figures, Leo the Lion Gagnas. Leo and his L.A. partners ran this city's gambling and loansharking. Back in 1950, two men out of Youngstown tried to get in on the Gagnas rackets, and they both washed up in Glorietta Bay one morning with bullets in their heads. Leo and company opened Napoli back in '53. He was tight with Bebe Rebozo, who was a big Nixon fundraiser. Beginning in 1966 Leo did two years for tax evasion and that was it. He never saw the inside of a prison before or after.

We sat in his dark little office. There were no windows and it smelled heavily of cigar smoke and cologne. The bookshelves were stuffed with well-read paperback crime novels—plenty of Whit Masterson and Erle Stanley Gardner and Mickey Spillane. A floor safe sat in one corner and the walls were covered with framed photographs of Dom's ancestors and the people they entertained at Napoli—Sinatra, Joey Bishop, John Wayne, Nixon, Ted Williams.

I looked at the pictures. "Where's the new celebrities, Dom?"

He looked at the pictures, too. "They don't come around here so much anymore. A time for everything, you know? It's good. Business is good. What do you need, Robbie?"

I told him about Sal—his alleged New Jersey outfit ties, his bad attitude and slick black Beamer, his fix on a young dancer at Skin named Farrel.

Dom nodded. "Yeah. I heard. My nephew, he's a manager at Skin. I got some friends checking this guy out."

"Ever had any trouble out of Jersey?"

"Never. Not any trouble at all, Robbie. Those days are long gone. You know that."

"What if he's what he says he is, trying to move in?"

"In on what?"

"On business, Dom."

"I don't know what you mean, *business*. But somebody blows into town and starts popping off about he's a made guy and he's mobbed up in Jersey and all that, well, there's fools and then there's fools, Robbie. Nobody I know talks like that. Know what I mean?"

"I wonder if he's got help."

"He better have help if he wants to shoot off his mouth. I'll let you know what I find out. And Robbie, you see this guy, tell him he's not making any friends around here. If he's what he says he is, then that's one thing. If he's not, then he's just pissing everybody off. Some doors you don't want to open. Tell him that. You might save him a little inconvenience. How's that pretty redhead wife of yours? Gina."

"We divorced seven years ago."

"I got divorced once. No, it was three times. You know why it's so expensive, don't you?"

"Because it's worth it."

"Yeah."

"You've told me that one before, Dom."

"And I was right, wasn't I?"

I met Farrel at Skin that night before she was set to perform. We sat at the bar and got good treatment from the bartenders. Dom's nephew, a spidery young man named Joey Morra, came by, said hello, told Farrel the customers were liking her. I took down Farrel's numbers and address and the name of her daughter and hometown and parents. And I also got everything she could tell me about Sal Tessola—where he lived and how they met, what he'd done for her and to her, the whole story. I told her she'd need all these things in order to write a good convincing complaint. We talked for a solid hour before she checked her watch.

"You going to stay and see me perform?"

"Not tonight."

"Didn't like it much, then?"

"You were good, Farrel."

She eyed me. "I don't want Vic trying to get me the money. I didn't ask him to. I asked him *not* to. He's not the brightest guy, Robbie. But he might be one of the most stubborn."

"You've got a point."

"How come you're not married? You must be about legal age."

"I was once."

"I'd a found a way to keep you."

"You're flattering me now."

"Why don't you flatter me back?"

"Center Springs took a loss when you packed it in."

She peered at me in that forthright and noncommittal way. "It sure did. And there's no power in heaven or earth strong enough to drag me back there."

I saw the black triangles of dread and the yellow triangles of fear hovering in the air between us.

*

I followed her from Skin. I'm not suspicious by nature, but it helps me do my job. The night was close and damp and I stayed well behind. She drove an early-'90s Dodge that was slow and slumped to starboard and easy to follow.

She drove to a small tract home out in La Mesa east of downtown. I slowed and watched her pull into the driveway. I went past, circled the block, then came back and parked across the street, one house down.

The house was vintage '50s, one of hundreds built in La Mesa not long after World War II. Many of those navy men and women who'd served and seen San Diego came back looking for a place to live in this sunny and unhurried city.

A living room light was on and the drapes were drawn casually, with a good gap in the middle and another at one end. Someone moved across the living room, then lamplight came from the back of the house through a bedroom window on the side I could see. A few minutes went by and I figured she was showering, so I got out and strolled down the sidewalk. Then I doubled back and cut across the little yard and stood under the canopy of a coral tree. I stepped up close to the living room window and looked through the middle gap.

The room was sparsely furnished in what looked like thrift-shop eclectic—a braided rug over the darkly stained wood floor, an American colonial coffee table, an orange-yellow-black plaid sofa with thin padding. There was a stack of black three-ring binders on the coffee table. Right in front of me was the back end of a TV, not a flat screen but one of the old ones with the big butts and masses of cords and coax cable sprouting everywhere.

I moved along the perimeter of the house and let myself through a creaking gate, but no dogs barked and I soon came to a dark side window. The blinds were drawn, but they were old and some were broken and several were bent. Through a hole I could make out a small bedroom. All it had was a chest of drawers and a stroller with a baby asleep in it, and I didn't have to look at that baby very long before I realized it was a doll.

Farrel walked past the room in what looked like a long white bathrobe and something on her head. I waited awhile, then backed out across the neighbor's yard and walked to my car. I settled in behind the wheel and used the binoculars and I could see Farrel on the plaid sofa, hair up in a towel, both hands on a sixteen-

ounce can of beer seated between her legs. She leaned forward
and picked up one of the black binders, looked at it like she'd
seen it a hundred times before, then set it down beside her. She
seemed tired but peaceful with the TV light playing off her face.

Twenty minutes later a battered Mustang roared up and parked
behind the Dodge and Sal got out. Gone were the sharp clothes
and in their place were jeans and a fleece-lined denim jacket and
a pair of shineless harness boots that clomped and slouched as he
keyed open the front door and went through.

I glassed the gap in the living room curtains and Farrel's face
rushed at me. She said something without looking at Sal. He stood
before her, his back to me, and shrugged. He snatched the beer
can from her and held it up for a long drink, then pushed it back
between her legs and whipped off his coat. He wore a blue shirt
with a local pizza parlor logo on it. This he pulled off as he walked
into the back rooms.

He came out a few minutes later wearing jeans and a singlet,
his hair wet and combed back. He was a lean young man, broad-
shouldered, tall. For the first time I realized he was handsome. He
walked past Farrel into the kitchen and came back with a can of
beer and sat down on the couch not too near and not too far from
her. He squeezed her robe once where her knee would be, then let
his hand fall to the sofa.

They talked without looking at each other, but I can't read lips.
It looked like a "and how was your day" kind of conversation, or
maybe something about the TV show that was on, which threw
blue light upon them like fish underwater.

After a while they stopped talking, and a few minutes later Farrel lifted the remote and the blue light was gone and she had
picked up one of the black binders from the pile at her end of the
couch.

She opened it and read out loud. There was no writing or label
or title on the cover.

She waved the binder at him and pointed at a page and read a
line to him.

He repeated it. I was pretty sure.

She read it again and he repeated it. I was pretty sure again.

They both laughed.

Then another line. They each said it, whatever it was. Sal stood
over her then and aimed a finger at her face and said the line

again. She stood and stripped the towel off her head and said something and they both laughed again.

He got up and brought two more big cans of beer from the kitchen, and he opened one for her and took her empty. He tossed the towel onto her lap and sat down close to her, put his bare feet up on the coffee table by the binders, and scrunched down so his head was level with hers. She clicked the TV back on.

I waited for an hour. Another beer each. Not much talk. They both fell asleep sitting up, heads back on the sofa.

It was almost three-thirty in the morning when Farrel stood, rubbed the back of her neck, then tightened the robe sash. She walked deeper into the house and out of my sight.

A few minutes later Sal rose and hit the lights. In the TV glow I could see him stretch out full length on the couch and set one arm over his eyes and take a deep breath and let it slowly out.

Two mornings later, at about the same dark hour, I was at headquarters writing a crime scene report. I'm an occasional insomniac and I choose to get paperwork done during those long, haunted times. Of course I listen to our dispatch radio, keeping half an ear on the hundreds of calls that come in every shift.

So when I heard the possible 187 at Skin nightclub I was out the door fast.

Two squad cars were already there and two more screamed into the parking lot as I got out of my car.

"The janitor called 911," said one of the uniforms. "I was first on scene and he let me in. There's a dead man back in the kitchen. I think it's one of the managers. I tried to check his pulse but couldn't reach that far. You'll see."

I asked the patrolmen to seal both the back and front entrances and start a sign-in log, always a good idea if you don't want your crime scene to spiral into chaos. You'd be surprised how many people will trample through and wreck evidence, many of them cops.

I walked in, past the bar and the tables and the stage, then into a small, poorly lit, grease-darkened kitchen. Another uniform stood near a walk-in freezer, talking with a young man wearing a light blue shirt with a name patch on it.

I saw the autoloader lying on the floor in front of me. Then the cop looked up and I followed his line of sight to the exposed ceiling. Overhead were big commercial blowers and vents and ducting and electrical conduit and hanging fluorescent tube light fixtures. A body hung jackknifed at the hips over a steel crossbeam. His arms dangled over one side and his legs over the other. If he'd landed just one inch higher or lower, he'd have simply slid off the beam to the floor. I walked around the gun and got directly under him and stared up into the face of Joey. It was an urgent shade of purple and his eyes were open.

"The safe in the office," said the uniform, pointing to the far back side of the kitchen.

The office door was open and I stepped in. There was a desk and a black leather couch and a small fridge and microwave, pictures of near-naked dancers on the walls, along with a Chargers calendar and Padres pennants.

There was also a big floor safe that was open but not empty. I squatted in front of it and saw the stacks of cash and some envelopes.

The officer and janitor stood in the office doorway.

"Why kill a man for his money, then not take it?" asked the uniform. His name plate said *Peabody*.

"Maybe he freaked and ran," said the janitor, whose name patch said *Carlos*.

"Okay," said Peabody. "Then tell me how Joey got ten feet up in the air and hung over a beam. And don't tell me he did it to himself."

Carlos looked up at the body and shrugged, but I had an opinion about that.

"What time do you start work?" I asked him.

"Two. That's when they close."

"Is Joey usually here?"

"One of the managers is always here. They count the money every third night. Then they take it to the bank."

"So tonight was bank night?"

"Was supposed to be."

I drove fast to Vic's hotel room downtown, but he didn't answer the door. Back downstairs the night manager, speaking from behind a mesh-reinforced window, told me that Vic had left around eight-thirty—seven hours ago—and had not returned.

I made Farrel's place eleven minutes later. There were no cars in the driveway but lights inside were on. I rang the bell and knocked, then tried the door, which was unlocked. So I opened it and stepped in.

The living room looked exactly as it had two nights ago, except that the beer cans were gone and the pile of black binders had been reduced to just one. In the small back bedroom the stroller was still in place and the plastic doll was snugged down under the blanket just as it had been. I went into the master bedroom. The mattress was bare and the chest of drawers stood open and nearly empty. It looked like Farrel had stripped the bed and packed her clothes in a hurry. The bathroom was stripped, too: no towels, nothing in the shower or the medicine chest or on the sink counter. The refrigerator had milk and pickles and that was all. The wastebasket under the sink had empty beer cans, an empty pretzel bag, various fast-food remnants swathed in ketchup, a receipt from a supermarket, and a wadded-up agreement from Rent-a-Dream car rentals down by the airport. Black Beamer 750i, of course.

Back in the living room I took the black binder from the coffee table and opened it to the first page:

THE SOPRANOS
Season Four/Episode Three

I flipped through the pages. Dialogue and brief descriptions. Four episodes in all.

Getting Sal's lines right, I thought.

Vic didn't show up for work for three straight nights. I stopped by Skin a couple of times a night, just in case he showed, and I knocked on his hotel room door twice a day or so. The manager hadn't seen him in four days. He told me Vic's rent was due on the first.

Of course Farrel had vanished, too. I cruised her place in La Mesa, but something about it just said she wasn't coming back, and she didn't.

On the fourth afternoon after the murder of Joey Morra, Vic called me on my cell phone. "Can you feed my scorpion? Give him six crickets. They're under the bathroom sink. The manager'll give you the key."

"Sure. But we need to talk, Vic—face-to-face."

"I didn't do it."

"Who else could throw Joey up there like that?"

Vic didn't answer.

"Dom and his people are looking for you, Vic. You won't get a trial with them. You'll just get your sentence, and it won't be lenient."

"I only took what she needed."

"And killed Joey."

"He pulled a gun, Robbie. I couldn't think a what else to do. I bear-hugged and shook him. Like a reflex. Like when I threw you."

"I'll see you outside Higher Grounds in ten minutes."

"She met me at Rainwater's, Robbie. I walked into Rainwater's and there she was—that beautiful young woman, waiting there for me. You should have seen her face light up when I gave her the money. Out in the parking lot, I mean."

"I'll bet," I said. "Meet me outside Higher Grounds in ten minutes."

"Naw. I got a good safe place here. I'm going to just enjoy myself for a couple more days, knowing I did a good thing for a good woman. My scorpion, I named him Rudy. Oh. Oh shit, Robbie."

Even coming from a satellite orbiting the earth in space, and through the miles of ether it took to travel to my ear, the sound of the shotgun blast was unmistakable. So was the second blast, and the third.

A few days later I flew to Little Rock and rented a car, then made the drive north and west to Center Springs. Farrel was right: it wasn't on the rental-car company driving map, but it made the navigation unit that came in the vehicle.

The Ozarks were steep and thickly forested and the Arkansas River looked unhurried. I could see thin wisps of wood-stove fires burning in cabins down in the hollows and there was a smoky cast to the sky.

The gas station clerk said I'd find Farrel White's dad's place down the road a mile, just before Persimmon Holler. He said there was a batch of trailers up on the hillside and I'd see them from the road if I didn't drive too fast. Billy White had the wooden one with all the satellite dishes on top.

The road leading in was dirt and heavily rutted from last season's rain. I drove past travel trailers set up on cinder blocks. They were slouched and sun-dulled and some had decks and others just had more cinder blocks as steps. Dogs eyed me without bothering to sit up. There were cats and litter and a pile of engine blocks outside, looked like they'd been cast there by some huge child.

Billy answered my knock with a sudden yank on the door, then studied me through the screen. He was midfifties and heavy, didn't look at all like his daughter. He wore a green-and-black plaid jacket buttoned all the way to the top.

"I'm a San Diego cop looking for your daughter. I thought she might have come home."

"Would you?"

"Would I what?"

"Come home to this from San Diego?"

"Well."

"She okay?"

"I think so."

"Come in."

The trailer was small and cramped and packed with old, over-stuffed furniture.

"She in trouble?"

"Farrel and her boyfriend hustled a guy out of some money. But he had to take the money from someone else."

Billy handed me a beer and plopped into a vinyl recliner across from me. He had a round, impish face and a twinkle in his eyes. "That ain't her boyfriend. It's her brother."

"That never crossed my mind."

"Don't look nothing alike. But they've always been close. Folks liked to think too close, but it wasn't ever that way. Just close. They understood each other. They're both good kids. Their whole point in life was to get outta Center Springs and they done did it. I'm proud of them."

"What's his name?"

"Preston."

"Did they grow up in this trailer?"

"Hell no. We had a home over to Persimmon but it got sold off in the divorce. Hazel went to Little Rock with a tobacco products salesman. The whole story is every bit as dreary as it sounds."

"When did Farrel and Preston leave?"

"Couple of months ago. The plan was San Diego, then Hollywood. Pretty people with culture and money to spend. They were going to study TV, maybe go start up a show. San Diego was to practice up."

"The scripts."

"Got them from the library up at Fayetteville. Made copies of the ones they wanted. Over and over again. Memorizing those scripts and all them words. They went to the Salvation Army stores and bought up lots of old-time kinda clothes. They both did some stage plays at the junior college, but they didn't much care for them. They liked the other kind of stories."

"What kind of stories?"

"Crime stories. Bad guys. Mafia. That was mainly Preston. Farrel, she can act like anything from the queen of England to a weather girl and you can't tell she's acting."

"Have they called lately?"

"Been over a week."

"Where do you think they are?"

"Well, Center Springs is the only place I know they ain't. I don't expect to ever see them out this way."

I did the simple math and the not-so-simple math. Eight grand for two months of work. Farrel dancing for tips. Preston delivering pizza and working his end of the Vic hustle. Vic caught between Farrel's good acting and his own eager heart. And of course betrayed, finally and fatally, by his own bad temper.

I finished the beer and stood. "Two men died because of them. Eight thousand bucks is what they died for. So the next time you talk to Farrel and Preston, you tell them there's real blood on their hands. It's not make-believe blood. You tell her Vic was murdered for taking that eight thousand."

"I'll do that."

"Thanks for your time."

"I can come up with a couple a hundred. It's not much, but . . ."

I saw the orange triangles bouncing in the air between us. I thought about those triangles as I drove away. Orange triangles denote pity and sometimes even empathy. All this for Vic Primeval, as offered by a man he'd never met, from his vinyl chair in his slouching home in the Ozarks. Sometimes you find a little speck of good where you least expect it. A rough diamond down deep. And you realize that the blackness can't own you for more than one night at a time.

THOMAS J. RICE

Hard Truths

FROM *The New Orphic Review*

THE TELEGRAM CAME in the late afternoon on a rainy Tuesday in late April 1958.

Jimmy Dunphy had been delivering mail to this remote farmhouse in the Wicklow mountain range for over thirty years, but he still felt a tingle of excitement each time that distinctive little green envelope showed up in his bundle. Hogan's of Rathdargan was the last stop on his route, and he always looked forward to a relaxed chat with Kitty Hogan, full-figured woman of the house. Sometimes—if she was in a good mood—she'd invite him in for a cup of tea and a scone to fuel the long, uphill bike ride home to his cottage on the other side of Sugarloaf Mountain.

Telegram presentation was one of Jimmy's specialties, one he'd polished to a performance art. Unlike regular mail, telegrams meant something was up—and Jimmy loved to watch the faces of people in the grip of suspense. Today he was bitterly disappointed to see that only young Myles, not his mother, was there to share the moment. Was he going to have to waste a performance on this fourteen-year-old upstart? This younger generation had no appreciation of true dramatic talent; most had never even heard of O'Casey, Behan, or Bernie (aka George Bernard) Shaw, born just over the mountain in Carlow. Too busy traipsing to American cowboy pictures and dance halls. Then again, how were they ever going to learn if their elders didn't show them?

Peering through the rain under his shiny postman's cap and black parka, Jimmy grinned and stepped boldly onto the stage—his own Abbey Theatre. First he held the prized envelope high for inspection—like a trophy ready for presentation. Rolling it over several times in his arthritic hands, puffing vainly on his unlit pipe, he held the telegram aloft one last time before the final moment of exchange.

Myles Hogan didn't hear the postman's whistle right away; he had his hands full dosing an ailing calf from a plastic bottle in the cowshed. But the brace of border collies sounded the alarm, nearly flattening him in their raucous scramble for the cowshed door. Myles liked Jimmy Dunphy and usually welcomed his theatrics, but not today. There was too much work to do; he was soaking wet and in no mood to humor the old man.

Finally, with great reluctance, Jimmy surrendered the telegram into Myles's impatient hand. Stung by the rude reception, he turned wearily to face the hilly, wet meadow he'd cut though to reach the farmhouse. No tea. No scones. Not even a glimpse of Kitty Hogan's brunette curls.

Turning abruptly to leave, noticing Jimmy's hangdog expression, Myles felt a pang of regret and tossed off a quick apology: "Thanks, Mr. Dunphy. Sorry to be in such hurry. Hungry calves, ya know . . ."

Jimmy seized the opening like a lifeline.

"Maybe I should wait till yer mammie has a chance to read it. Ya never know . . . She might want to send word back . . ."

It was a clumsy attempt at ferreting out what was in the telegram; Myles knew how the gossip mill worked and had no intention of feeding it.

"No, thanks, Mr. Dunphy. Mammie's busy right now, but I'll let her know your offer."

Jimmy was not so easily put off, especially by a young bucko getting too big for his breeches. "Maybe we should let the mammie decide. Ya never know . . ."

"That's all right, Mr. Dunphy. Thanks anyway." With that, Myles met the old man's eyes with an unsmiling dismissal, turned, and raced down the steps, tripping over the tangle of border collies stacked up below him before righting himself and sprinting for the kitchen, where his mother was baking bread over the open hearth.

"Mammie, Mammie, it's a telegram!" he yelled as he barged into the dimly lit kitchen, borders charging in tow. Kitty Hogan looked up from a deep reverie. She was cranking the handle of the bellows which fed a glowing turf fire. Over it, a covered iron skillet rested. She started, as if coming awake, brushed a wayward curl from her forehead, and nervously wiped her hands on her faded, striped blue apron. A shadow of dread crossed her lined though beautiful face.

In Kitty's forty-four years, telegrams meant only one thing: bad news. The last one had been two years before, announcing that her beloved Aunt Mary—a second mother to her—had died in New York. The one before that, in October of '55, had summoned her to Dublin, where Maura, her youngest daughter, had been run over at a crosswalk near O'Connell Street Bridge. She'd died two days later at the St. Vincent's Hospital, without regaining consciousness. Maura was a bright, good-natured girl, just eighteen, the last of the five sisters at Temple Hill Nursing School, all on meager scholarships. She'd only been in the city a week.

Meeting his mother's hazel eyes, Myles handed her the telegram with trembling fingers. Kitty hesitated before reaching for it, took a deep breath, and walked to the dresser at the back of the kitchen. Hours seemed to pass before she eventually opened the drawer, pulled out a paring knife, and slit the green envelope in one swift flick. Even the borders sensed the tension and sat on their haunches, as at feeding time, their gazes riveted on Kitty's every move. She stepped toward the light of the front window, took another deep breath, and plucked out the folded, official note, which she read silently to herself, several times; then, finally, aloud:

Coming home Friday (May 1). 6pm bus to Enniskerry. Jack.

Tears streamed down Kitty's pale cheeks, dripping on her apron. She swatted them away as a smile erased the shadow, spreading from her lips to her streaming eyes, then to her whole body. She let out a scream of pure ecstasy. "Oh, Jesus, Mary, and Joseph! Jack is coming home. Your father is coming home. Oh, my God! Oh, my God! I knew he would come someday. I knew God would answer my prayers . . . I just knew it . . ."

She whirled about the concrete floor in a wild dance of joy Myles had never seen before, almost knocking him over as she swung her arms wide. Inspired by her exuberance, the borders started to bark, joining the circular dance. Suddenly Kitty pulled up, self-conscious and blushing, almost childlike. She smoothed the faded apron, brushed back the curls from her forehead, and regained her normal no-nonsense comportment.

"Now listen, Myles, we have a ton of work to do to get ready. We have only two days, mind you. We'll have to paint the road gate, clip the hedges, and cut all those thistles in the cow field. Oh, and Myles, you'll have to go up to Billy Roach and get a haircut. What would your father say if he saw you looking like that? He'd think I was raising a teddy boy . . ." She rattled on in this vein, extending the list in her assertive fashion, but Myles had already tuned her out and was walking toward the cowshed to finish his feeding chores.

This was the moment he'd dreaded for two years, ever since he'd quit Enniskerry National School in the middle of the fifth grade to help his mother on the farm.

Myles was the only one in the family who seemed to accept the fact that his father was never coming home. He'd heard the story so many times, with so many variations and subplots, that he felt it was just another fairy tale. Kitty had tried to make excuses for Jack and present him as a heroic figure, but Myles never bought the fiction, sensing an unspoken truth: the real hero was the woman who stuck with him and his older sisters instead of farming them out to relatives, or worse: Killane orphanage, the workhouse in Gorey.

Kitty Hogan was a maddening bundle of contradictions Myles could never figure out. She could be gentle and nurturing, treating Myles as an equal, a partner. Ever since he could talk, she had sought his views on all sorts of grown-up matters, large and small: Should she sell the bonhams or fatten them? Should she plant Furlong's Field with oats or lease it to John McDonald? Should she let the girls go to the dance in Bray Sunday night? And she wasn't just humoring a child; she really listened to what he had to say and encouraged him to tell her the truth, especially when it was hard.

Like two years ago when he left the turkeys' run open and a fox killed the whole flock; it was their only Christmas cash crop. "Mammie, I have a confession to make." He found her in the middle of baking a cake for supper. "Well, this sounds serious. You look like you've seen a ghost." Myles sat down, fought back tears, and spilled the story. "It's all my fault. You told me to lock the gate every time I came out, but I didn't. I just forgot it, like an eejet. And that's when the fox must've slipped in. I never saw him. Just heard the racket and ran in there. It was too late. He'd killed them all and was gone. There wasn't even any blood. Just broken necks. Like I said, it's all my fault and I don't mind if you whip me with the belt. I deserve it . . . I'd do anything if it'd make 'em come back . . . anything."

Instead of a whipping, she gave him her brightest smile, wrapped her arms around him, and said, "You're a good man, Myles Hogan. Any fool can tell the truth when it wraps him in glory. It's the hard truth that separates the men from the boys. Now, let's have some tea and scones before we have to break the news to your sisters that we have to cancel Christmas this year." As she said this, her voice broke and she turned away to hide the tears.

This was in sharp contrast to the way she treated the girls, whom she dismissed as a bunch of "gillagoolies." His sisters resented this, of course, and took it out on Myles with fiendish creativity. Knowing his fear of the dark, they seldom missed an opportunity for nightly terror games. Once, when he was about seven, they put a small goat in his bedroom, complete with horns; the devil come to claim his prey. Myles promptly went into screaming convulsions, to gales of triumphant giggling from under the bed.

The harsh punishments meted out by his mother only made Myles feel more guilty. He tried to make it up to his sisters by currying favor, but to no avail. It was their mother's approval they craved, not his. But for them, that approval would always be in short supply.

Myles had always been puzzled by the deference people showed his mother. All sorts of people—men, women, prosperous, and poor—seemed to speak of her with a kind of reverence, like they might speak of the bishop or prime minister. It had a magical power that seemed to cast a protective shield around him and his sisters as soon as people knew their names. Being Kitty Hogan's son was special in Enniskerry; everyone seemed to understand that, for reasons Myles could only guess at. "Can I give ya a lift? Ain't you Kitty Hogan's boy?" "Sure it's all right. Ya can have it for five bob. Aren't you one of the Hogans of Rathdargan?" "Yer mother's a great woman. She done a lot for this country. You must be very proud to be her son." Once he asked her what people meant by this, but she brushed it off with, "Oh, son, we all did a lot for our country in the old days. It's not worth talking about. Now, run down to the lower meadow and bring in the cows!"

But he knew there was more to it. He had seen some of it first-hand.

He recalled the fate of the schoolteacher, Brigid Breen, after she slapped his oldest sister, Nora, for misbehaving in school. For other children, beatings in the National School were expected and accepted. Except the Hogans. Myles remembered the terrible spectacle of Miss Breen falling on her ample knees on the gravel road, pleading for mercy, as Kitty stood leaning against the stone wall, cool as a lioness ready to pounce.

Miss Breen's plea was in vain. With one backhand swipe, the hefty schoolmarm practically flew across the road, landing in a pile of nettles, nose gushing like a crimson fountain. "Now, Miss Breen, let that be a lesson to you. That's how it feels to be slapped by someone stronger than you are. Never lay a hand on one of my children again. Do you understand me?"

"Yes, Mrs. Hogan. Oh, for the love of God, please . . . It was just a misunderstanding. It'll never happen again. You have lovely girls. All so bright . . ."

"Thank you, Miss Breen. I'm glad you approve of them. If they give you any trouble, just let me know. I'll deal with them myself. I discipline my children, not you. Your job is to educate them. Don't you agree?"

"Yes, yes . . . of course. We all have a job to do. Thank you, Kitty . . . I mean, Mrs. Hogan."

"You're most welcome, Brigid. Safe home, now."

The other episode that puzzled and frightened Myles was the exchange he'd overheard between his mother and the Hannigan twins two years before. Billy and Bobby Hannigan were neighbors. They worked the big family farm and general store in Newtown, just off the Dublin Road, near Sally Gap. They were tall, burly red-heads, popular with the girls and well liked by one and all. Both were gifted football players, dominating defenders for the senior Wicklow team. They came from a well-respected family. Their father (Sean the Gap, as he was affectionately known) was a feared and famous IRA guerrilla fighter. The twins seldom visited Rath-dargan, so it was a surprise to hear their voices downstairs speaking in hushed tones with his mother early one Friday morning as Myles was waking.

Billy Hannigan, in his distinctive tenor voice, was speaking softly as Myles came fully awake.

"With all due respect, Mrs. Hogan, what we do or don't do with girls at the dances, that's our own business. I don't see where ya get off summoning us here to lecture us about Molly Redmond or what happened at the dance in Kilkenny Sunday night. If she has a complaint about anyt'ing, she should call the Garda."

Kitty's voice, calm and deadly, came back—the same tone Myles had heard her use with Miss Breen. He felt a tightening in his stomach and fought back a wave of nausea. Suddenly he felt sorry for the Hannigan twins and had to resist an impulse to.

His mother's voice continued the deadly inquisition.

"That's a good speech, Billy. It shows courage, which is admirable, given your situation. Now, Bobby, what do you have to say for yourself?"

"Not a t'ing, Mrs. Hogan, except that I'm sorry it had to come to this. Tell ya the God's honest truth, we didn't mean no harm. We had a few pints an' t'ings got a bit out of hand, I s'pose. An' the reason we're here is 'cuz me father has great respect for you 'n what ya did for the cause. We all have. We meant no harm, as God is my witness, Mrs. Hogan."

"Very good, Bobby. God is your witness, always has been and always will be, but we won't need to call on him just yet. Your brother should take a page from your book, since contrition is the gateway to redemption. But you're both whistling past the graveyard if you think this is just about making nice.

"No. That won't do at all. Here's why: I've known Molly Redmond since she was a little baby. Her mother and I were in the movement together long before you lads were even a gleam in your daddy's eye. She's a lovely girl and it so happens I'm her godmother—not that you should know that.

"But after the dance last Sunday night, she came by for our little chat, as usual. Only this time she was hysterical. She told me everything. Everything. About what you blackguards did to her in Kelly's hay shed—or tried to do, I should say. I'm glad you have a few scruples left. Since her mother died in that ferry accident, I'm the one she turns to for advice. Thank God she did. And that's your bad luck . . ."

The long, ominous silence that followed was finally broken by Billy Hannigan's blustery voice.

"Look here, Mrs. Hogan, like I said, we came over here 'cuz Da respects you—we do, too, don't get me wrong—but what do ya want from us? Molly is no saint; she's a bit of a tayser—if you ask me. So I don't know what you want from us. What's done is done. It won't happen again, I can assure you of that. Is that the sort of t'ing ya want us to say?"

Upstairs, Myles had moved a little closer to hear his mother's reply. He could see her pacing back and forth through the cracks in the floorboards.

"Oh, I know it won't happen again. That's not what I'm worried about. No, not a whit. But as I said, it's not going to be as simple as assuring me of your noble intentions. The road to hell is paved with those, as the fella says. Your amends will be much more tangible than mere words. As a show of good faith, I want three hundred pounds in twenty-pound notes for Molly's education, with a written explanation to her that this is your way of apologizing to her and her family for the emotional distress you caused. Be sure you both sign your names with Sean, your da, signing as witness. I also want you to donate one of your best Jersey cows to Pete Redmond to make up for the one that got killed on Dundrum Road last month. It was the only one they had. It's only a neighborly thing to do anyway; I'm sure your da won't mind.

"Oh, and while you're at it, it would be grand if you cut out five Cheviot ewe lambs and donated them, too. The Redmonds have had a couple of bad years and need a bit of sun to shine their way. You'll never even notice, but it'll make a world of difference to them."

Whatever had happened downstairs, the Hannigan twins went mute. Not a word of protest was spoken, as Myles heard their hobnailed boots scrape the concrete kitchen floor.

"Right so, I see you boys understand me. Much better than calling the Garda, wouldn't ya say? I'll see you at eight sharp tomorrow. Oh, if for any reason you don't make it, I'll be up by noon for a little conference with himself. Yer father and I go back a long ways, as you know."

Billy Hannigan was back the next morning at eight sharp, just as Kitty had ordained. He did not come in, but after a quiet conversation at the kitchen door, he walked slowly out of the farmyard. Myles watched him from the upstairs window, red curls flowing over his collar, as he closed the iron gate and walked slowly up the laneway. Even now, Myles remembered his mother's last words, in that menacing "Miss Breen" voice:

"Don't thank me. Always knew the Hannigans would rise to the occasion. Say hello to your parents for me and tell them there are no hard feelings here. I'm sure the Redmonds won't be pressing charges. That's the kind of thing that can ruin a young man's life. None of us would want that to happen, especially to a Hannigan. Safe home, now, Billy."

Myles recalled his visceral relief at what he saw as a reprieve for the Hannigans. He'd feared the worst for them, like Miss Breen. But they were men, of course. It was different. He couldn't imagine what they'd done to Molly Redmond to make his mother so mad—maybe pulled her hair or tried to kiss her—but he was glad it was over and done with. It still rankled him that this whole village seemed to know something about his mother that he did not. One thing was sure—it struck the fear of God in them. That part was a comfort to Myles; some people deserved to be afraid. Fear was the only thing they understood, like some of the brutal mountain boys at school. But it also scared him, for reasons he could not explain. And he was sick of being called "Young Hogan of Rathdargan." He longed for an identity that he, Myles, could call his own.

He was also weary of hearing the depressing details of his father's neglect of his family dredged up and embellished, year after year. It was a story the whole community seemed to delight in telling and retelling, with each recitation a little less credible, a little more vicious.

How Jack missed his birth—as he did for all but one of his eight children born in their two-room farmhouse—and came home just in time to find his only son a cadaverous cluster of skin and bones, slumped in a coma. This rare visit had come in October 1943, as the winter winds were returning to their ghostly antics, herding leaves from the giant oaks into every corner and crevice of the desolate farmyard.

A robust infant, Myles had lost half his body weight to a twin epidemic of whooping cough and German measles that had ravaged thousands of children across Europe. Myles's blond three-year-old sister, Sheila, had suffocated in Kitty's arms. The local doctor—an alcoholic who practiced without a license—had prescribed baking soda.

Kitty just had to pray and wait "for God to take her," as she told Myles one chilly afternoon years later by the turf fire, where Kitty often surprised him with her reflections. Father Cavanagh, the parish priest in Enniskerry, was two days late coming to offer last rites and condolences. Uncle Patrick, Kitty's alcoholic brother, had been charged with the job of fetching the priest, but went to Dalton's Pub and forgot.

People never seemed to tire of telling how his penny-pinching Uncle Mike—Kitty's grand-uncle—had insisted that the undertaker delay closing Sheila's tiny white coffin until Myles should expire and join her in it. (After three days, when Myles seemed to be hanging on, they went ahead with the burial.) True to form, Uncle Mike was calculating the cost of another coffin and Jack missed Sheila's funeral.

But he arrived in time to save Myles's life. Or so the legend went. He'd heard of Kitty's predicament through the grapevine in Birmingham, where he worked on the line at Austin Motor Works. There was talk of a special type of paraffin lamp that worked magic in bringing relief to children stricken by the epidemic. Jack claimed he'd bought one for the family as soon as he got word. It was too late for Sheila, but for Myles, it worked; he got immediate relief and came out of his coma within hours of his father's homecoming.

As far as Myles was concerned, he never believed the heroic rescue story. It just didn't fit the man he'd come to believe his father to be. It seemed just another example of Jack Hogan getting off the hook. If it had been true, why did he leave them the next morning, without a word of goodbye, without leaving Kitty a single penny, or even a boarding-house address? He simply walked out and left her to cope with her grief, to face the bleak winter with a house full of children and an empty cupboard.

Myles knew the real story, much less noble; he'd pieced it together from snippets of gossip he wasn't supposed to hear. Jack had lost his shirt gambling on "the nags" and had abandoned his family when Jim Dalton and Pete Coady, the local publicans, began to deny him credit for his belligerent binges, tolerated as long as he sang and paid for every round.

Jack's comings and goings were never quite clear to Myles. As far as he could tell, Jack first abandoned Kitty and their six daughters in February 1937, five years before Myles was born. That time he stayed away for two years and then came home only to dodge the WWII draft. He stayed for three years, then vanished again in February 1942, two months before Myles was born.

After that fleeting visit for Sheila's funeral in the fall of 1943, Jack went missing again, this time for keeps, it seemed. Other fathers who had to work in England came home every Christmas, Easter, and for the summer holidays. But not Jack Hogan. While his friends proudly displayed their visiting da at midnight mass, Myles meekly followed his mother as she marched to the front of Enniskerry Chapel with her brood of six to claim the family pew. No husband. No word. No hope.

Until now.

As word of Jack's heralded homecoming spread, the story of his departure gained new life. The neighbors warmed to the gossip, trumping Kitty's romantic renditions of Jack's adventures with details of their own.

"Now, when was it that Jack left again . . . ?"

"Did he sell the bay mare to Father O'Meara—or was that the black stallion he'd won with at Gowran?"

They recited and embellished every painful detail of the deception. How he'd lied about taking the mare to Foley's blacksmith's shop. Joe Foley told Kitty the shoes had never been fitted. They relived the story of how he'd sold the last brood mare, Dolly, before jumping the ferry to Holyhead, then on to Birmingham.

That Jack Hogan. What a character! Never a dull moment when he was around. It hasn't been the same since . . .

Myles heard from others how his mother had first got news of Jack—over a year later—and then only because he was accidentally spotted by a cousin singing at a concert in Shrewsbury, England, on a Saturday night.

"Ah, what a wonderful tenor voice he had . . . Myles, sure some a dat talent musta rubbed off from yer father. Can you sing 'Slievenamon'? It was one of his favorites . . ."

There were times when Myles really hated him, with a burning, vengeful, damn-you-to-hell hatred. He was baffled by his mother's loyalty to her elusive husband. He hated how the locals kept reminding him of what a great hero his father was in the IRA as captain of the fabled "flying columns" and their daring assaults on the British occupation forces. Myles particularly resented the constant, invidious comparisons—whether in sports, singing, dancing, or work. "Sure yer all right, but you'll never be as good as yer father. He was a great man for the football. Do you play . . . ?"

More complicated was Myles's constant awareness of missing,

not the flesh-and-blood man who was Jack Hogan, but the *idea* of a father and what he saw his friends enjoying with their das—hurling, boxing, football, prideful glances, tender touches to soothe the bumps and bruises. At such times, Myles longed for his da to be around, but it was a fleeting emotion, like dreams of winning the Irish Sweepstakes or owning his own team of Arabian horses.

After twelve years without so much as a single visit—Jack was a mere ferry ride away—Myles had given up, hardening his heart to the notion. The only sign of life he saw from his father over the years was the annual abusive letter pressuring Kitty to sell the farm. No money, not even a pound note; just a rant about how she'd always held him back with her lack of trust. Sneaking a peek at those missives, Myles could scarcely believe his eyes.

She'd once confided, in one of her fireside reflections, that the letters began in the aftermath of Jack's concerted efforts, against Irish law, to sell Rathdargan farm "out from under her"—without her permission, which he knew she would never give.

After getting one of these letters, Kitty cried for days, trying to hide her heartbreak behind red, swollen eyes. "I have such a problem with the pollen this year," she'd offer, fooling no one.

For all of that, there were still times when Myles tried to will the father of his dreams into existence. One specific incident stood out in his memory. He was about nine at the time. It was fox-hunting season. The local hunters found him indispensable for one reason: the Hogans had a terrific little fox terrier, named Nell, a white-and-tan spark plug with classic markings.

Nell was famous for her ferocity and skill at flushing foxes from their dens—or dragging them out, if they were so foolish as to take her on. During the hunting season, there was a hunt every Sunday, and Nell was Myles's front-row ticket to the action. He was proud to be able to tag along, though it was dangerous—loaded shotguns in every hand. He was not even allowed to hold, let alone shoot, the old single-barreled shotgun that hung from its rack at the head of the stairs.

Myles knew it was Nell the hunters wanted; he was along as baggage, resented by some of the hunters for slowing them down. On this particular Sunday afternoon the hunting party was in hot pursuit when they encountered a fast-running brook, three feet deep and four wide. The fox and dogs cleared the brook with no effort.

Impatient fathers boosted their own sons over the stream but in their haste forgot about Myles.

He remembered standing on the bank, crying, praying to Saint Anthony, patron saint of lost things, for his father to appear. When he didn't, Myles cursed Saint Anthony for letting him down. "The curse a God on you, Saint Anthony. Ya never come through when I need ya. An I'm never going to ask you for another favor as long as I live. Ya can go to hell." He recalled his other grievances against Saint Anthony when the stakes were high, like the time he'd lost his only hurling ball in the thick brambles behind the barn.

Eventually Myles found a low spot downstream and waded across. But by the time he caught up with the hunt, he was soaked, bleeding from thornbushes, and sobbing. No one even noticed that he'd been missing. Nell had the fox cornered and her distinctive growls were punctuated by sharp yelps, meaning she was in trouble. It was only when Myles called her off that the hunters paid attention.

Saving Nell from the likely carnage of a cornered vixen meant spoiling their fun. "Sure we were getting along fine until ya came along and ruined it. Maybe next time we'll just bring the dog . . ."

Jack Hogan came home to Rathdargan on May Day 1958. It was a perfect spring day, rare in the moody western Atlantic. It dawned sunny and cloudless, and for once never broke. May, Ireland's greenest month, had once again delivered its bounty.

The upper fields, next to Carrigoona Commons, were ablaze with daisies, their tiny white-and-yellow flowers forming the magic carpet dreamed of all winter. Daffodils, lilies, and forget-me-nots danced in the gentle breeze, blending their fragrance with the massive lilac hedge that formed a purple canopy over the hand-crafted iron gateway to the farmhouse.

Birdsong echoed across the valley. The swallows were back—a welcome sign of spring—to reclaim their nests in the eaves of the cowshed. It was an idyllic setting to celebrate a family reunion.

Myles was like a jack-in-the-box at school that day, and was chastised repeatedly by Miss Breen, who found his conduct out of character. Having skipped two grades, he was one of her favorites, and she expressed her disappointment in no uncertain terms. Others, for the same transgression, would have been dealt six lashes of the dreaded "rod"—a mountain ash plant about two feet long. A standard teaching tool, used more than the atlas or textbook.

In Myles's case, Miss Breen had her reasons to show restraint. Besides, she genuinely liked and approved of Myles; just not today. "I must say that I find your conduct most unbecoming. Whatever has gotten into you, Myles Hogan? Very disappointing. I'm going to think twice about further privileges for you to go fetch you-know-what." This was her reference to Myles's perk of fetching her cache of jelly-filled doughnuts from Coady's grocery. She gave Myles one for his labor; it was their secret. But everyone knew of Miss Breen's weakness for doughnuts; it was hard to hide with her sixteen-stone waddle. And Myles's pals at school razzed him mercilessly for being "teacher's piggy pet."

Myles bolted from school at the clang of the bell, taking the shortcut across Carrigoona Commons. Normally he dawdled, taking at least two hours to cover the two miles. Pickup hurling games, a fistfight to kill the boredom, skinny-dipping at Powerscourt Waterfalls, all offered distractions on the journey. This day he was home in no time, determined to finish weeding his patch of the vegetable garden. He wanted to leave no room for Jack's famous fault-finding, which Kitty inadvertently taught him to dread. "Wait till your father comes home. He won't put up with that . . ."

The mere thought of these encounters infuriated Myles. *Who the hell is he to tell me about my duties? Hasn't he neglected his for twelve years running? And haven't I done fine without him all these years? And what about Mammie? Sure she'll just become sad again, as she always has whenever his name is mentioned? And he'll just leave us again, anyway? Maybe I can just wait him out.*

In the midst of elaborate preparations, Kitty had been on the lookout all afternoon. As Myles did when his sisters came home from nursing school, he watched for Ned Delaney's Vauxhall—the only taxi in Enniskerry—to appear on the Carrigoona Road, which he could see for miles from his perch on the Rathdargan ridge.

Kitty wore a bright yellow dress with a brown belt—an outfit Myles had never seen before—and her dark, curly hair blew in the breeze. He'd never seen her look so beautiful, or so happy, smiling and laughing at things that weren't even funny. He guessed she was practicing her new routine.

Five-eight in her bare feet and a strong, athletic figure, Kitty knew how to make the most of her elegant good looks. This day she wore nylons and high heels that invited disaster on the farm-yard cobblestones. The four surviving girls were away at nursing school, so the welcoming party was down to Myles and his mother.

Hour after hour he watched the Dundrum Road. Most of the cars just kept going, not making that right-hand turn at the cross-roads for Rathdargan. Finally, after hours of lookout duty, he spotted Delaney's Vauxhall. It turned right. Knowing it had to be Jack, he sounded the alarm: "Here he comes! They just turned at Doyle's Cross."

With the alert, Kitty went charging toward the lilac canopy, run-ning the full 200 yards of winding sycamore laneway, uphill in her high heels. In that moment of euphoria, of hope against hope, all was forgiven: the abandonment; the drunken abuse; the decep-tions and neglect. Once again Jack Hogan was being given a hero's welcome; Kitty's faithful heart greeted him as any loving husband coming home from a normal, essential breadwinning trip.

Myles couldn't stand it; he refused to join the parade. He ex-pected to be coaxed, as usual, but Kitty hadn't even noticed his absence. He sat on the front steps, brooding, while Kitty and the border collies rushed to greet the prodigal father. By the time they emerged jubilantly through the gateway next to the farmhouse, 30 yards away, Myles had arrived at a plan of action.

His parents strode forward as in a wedding parade. Kitty had both of her arms locked around Jack's trim waist. Myles saw his matter-of-fact mother clinging to this stranger with a distant, dreamy look he'd never seen before. It was as if Jack had never left, as if the cover story had been true all along, and this loyal provider had just gone to the forge to have the mare shod.

Jack's white cotton shirt billowed in the wind and he carried a battered tan suitcase. He was tall and handsome, just as people had been telling Myles all his life. What if he'd been wrong? What if the stories were all true? Jack was laughing, full of life and bask-ing in the glow of Kitty's adoration. They looked like a couple right out of *Failte* magazine, out for a stroll in the lush Wicklow countryside.

Kitty was cheerfully explaining why Myles hadn't been with the welcoming party at the road gate. Apparently he was shy. Finally, with a sharp change of tone, she turned toward Myles and issued one of her sharp commands: "Myles, come meet your father, right now!"

Myles stood up and walked slowly toward the stranger, working hard not to betray the terror he felt at what he was about to do. He felt his big, bold plan dissolve with each step, like a slow leak in his bike tire. They met about halfway to the farmhouse, just above the open spring well. The trickling of the running spout in the yard suddenly grew noisy. Myles had to stifle an urge to turn and run.

Their eyes met for the first time, father and son, searching, like boxers in an opening round. No trust; animal suspicion. Myles noticed his father had the same deep blue eyes and dimpled cheeks as himself. Now those older eyes twinkled with mischief, as if Jack were about to tell a hilarious joke.

He smiled at Myles conspiratorially, then reached in his pocket with crowd-pleasing deliberation, saying to no one in particular, "So this is my great big son. I brought you something I think you're gonna like . . ." With great flourish, he pulled out a gorgeous silver watch, a fashionable Timex. It had a chain about a foot long, with a silver T-buckle on the end. He held it high for all to admire, then lowered it to Myles's outstretched palm.

Without a word, Myles took the watch, gazed at it for a long few seconds, then threw it with all the force he could muster straight at his father's head, yelling, "I don't want yer watch! I don't want anythin' from ya! I wish ya'd just stay away from us . . ."

He didn't wait to see where the watch landed—just tore down the laneway toward his refuge, the garden, vaguely registering over his shoulder the flurry of apologies from his mother. "He's not like this at all. I don't know what got into him. Oh, Jack, please don't be upset. I'll talk with him . . . He'll apologize . . . I'm so sorry . . . I had no idea . . ."

Myles had learned from watching Kitty over the years that the best balm for upset is hard work. Now he threw himself into weeding the lettuce ridges, head down, back to the house, where he could hear the subdued voices of his parents. Then he heard footsteps on the garden path. Kitty was coming to reprimand him, to order him to apologize. He didn't turn around, just kept working, bracing for the verbal assault.

It never came. To his surprise, it was his father's voice that broke the silence: "This is a beautiful garden you've grown here, son. So clean. I used to plant lettuce and onions in this very same spot when I was your age. It's the sunniest place in the whole orchard.

Did you know we used to call this 'the orchard'? The field over the house used to be filled with apple trees—people would come from all over to pick them. The trees would be in full bloom right about now, all shades of pink and white. We had such great yield, we just gave them away for free. The cattle and pigs ate the rest."

He kept up the monologue, squatting down in the row beside Myles in his polished shoes and white shirt, moving with him up the row. This went on for at least a half-hour, during which time Myles kept working but never looked at his father or said a word. The speaker might as well have been invisible. Finally Jack stood up, dusted off his pants, and mumbled something about needing to wash up for dinner before vanishing behind the orchard wall.

Myles waited till he heard the wooden gate close behind him, then broke into tears of confused rage that watered the fledgling lettuce plants, lasting till he finished the row, exhausted and afraid of facing his mother.

At last Kitty emerged, under the guise of picking scallions and lettuce for supper. To his surprised relief, she assured him that she was not upset, that she understood it would take time for him to get used "to having a man around the house."

It was the last thing he needed to hear. His anger returned, surprising both of them: "I'm never gonna get used to it. We were doin' fine without 'im. And I'm not goin' to call 'im Da either, an' there's no use trying ta make me."

"All right, a Cushla, I know this is hard for you. But I still expect you to show your manners and to be polite. There's no excuse for rudeness. Promise me that you won't let us down. Do this for me, please!"

Myles dug at his tear-stained face with two muddy fists, promised her without conviction, and went in to wash up for dinner. He was used to being without a father, but now it was beginning to look like he was about to lose his mother, too—at least the one he'd known up to now. Fine, maybe he'd just run away to England; that would show her about a "man in the house." He could find work on the buildings; four of his cousins had already gone to Sheffield and they were only three years older.

Jack Hogan proved hard to resist; he had a magic about him that Myles felt drawn to. Even mundane tasks like shearing sheep or clipping the pony became occasions of performance and celebration. Everyone—men, women, and children, even the animals—seemed to vie for his attention. He was charming, entertaining, and loved to make people laugh.

Myles knew his father had won several singing competitions, both in Ireland and in England, but he had no idea what that meant. Then, on his second night home, Myles came to understand why Jack Hogan was known as "The Voice."

With plenty of Guinness being passed around, conversations buzzing in the kitchen, the usual suspects had arrived to perform their party pieces. No one was paying much attention—everyone talking at once—until someone shouted, "Hush up! Jack is goin' ta sing."

As if someone had hit a master switch, the house instantly falls silent. Jack stands up, steps confidently to the middle of the room, takes a deep breath, and launches.

His selection is Thomas Moore's classic, "She Is Far from the Land," a song familiar to all.

From the first line, all Myles's resentments and plots for escape dissolve. His father's voice is unlike anything he's ever heard—sweet, enchanting, and almost like a musical instrument in its perfection. Like the rest of the audience, Myles finds himself swept up in the emotion of the moment, crushed by the grief, still embracing it with both ecstasy and anguish that he has never experienced with other singers. By the end of the first verse, several people, women and men, are openly weeping. Some are actually sobbing, shoulders heaving. Handkerchiefs are out, arms clasping shoulders in comfort, and Myles finds himself crying openly with the others, without self-consciousness.

The words, poetry sung from the heart, etched themselves in Myles's memory, words he would recite and sing in faraway places decades later:

> She is far from the land where her young hero sleeps,
> And lovers are round her, sighing:
> But coldly she turns from their gaze, and weeps,
> For her heart in his grave is lying!

In full performance persona, Jack swings toward the kitchen audience he'd had his back to for the first verse. His hands form a moving circle in front of him as he sings, making deliberate and lingering eye contact with each person as he delivers the next lines:

> She sings the wild song of her dear native plains,
> Every note which he loved awaking;
> Ah! little they think who delight in her strains,
> How the heart of the Minstrel is breaking!
>
> He had lived for his love, for his country he died,
> They were all that to life had entwined him,
> Nor soon shall the tears of his country be dried,
> Nor long will his love stay behind him.

For the finale, he comes full circle, pauses for several seconds, then turns toward the finish. The silence is perfect as he hits the pièce de resistance.

> Oh! Make her a grave, where the sunbeams rest,
> When they promise a glorious morrow;
> They'll shine o'er her sleep, like a smile from the West,
> From her own loved Island of sorrow!

As Jack finishes on a caressing inflection of *sorrow*, his audience sits stock-still, mesmerized. Then come the tears, mingled with self-conscious giggles. The applause is long and loud, everyone on their feet, even Mick Murphy, who never rises unless to relieve himself or to go home. They are uniformly awestricken. Shouts of "No trouble taya, Jack! More! More! Give us 'The Foggy Dew'" can be heard in the adjoining townsland.

Jack obliges, without coaxing, leading off with "The Foggy Dew," then "Dawning of the Day," "If I Were a Blackbird," closing with a nationalist favorite, "The Croppy Boy." He delivers his medley of ballads with the same fluid energy, the beautiful voice, the engaging presence. Long before the final song, Myles has been captured by his father's magnetic field, holding on to his jacket, proud to claim him as his very own da.

The ramblers notice the gesture and applaud that, too, long and loud. In the background Myles can see Kitty, beaming her approval as she busies herself with the tea.

The spring and summer flew by in a blur of manly activity. Myles spent hours with his da, just the two of them, working on blocked drains, collapsed fences, and overgrown hedges. Sometimes they just wandered around the farm, like two pals, taking stock of the dilapidation, while Jack displayed the same comedic skills as their aging neighbor, Andy Murphy—mimicry, jokes, foibles, legends—all in a day's work.

Jack seemed to have lots of money, spent it freely, and was in no hurry to find work outside the farm or new ways to provide for the family. No one questioned the source of his largesse. Irishmen often came home from England feeling flush and spending lavishly, even if they couldn't afford it. After all, Jack had been gone for over a decade and might have changed his ways. Rumor had it that he'd won the lottery in Birmingham. Another had it that he had a recording contract with Decca Records and had been given a big advance. Sure, wasn't he "a finer tenor than John McCormick"?

More remarkable still, he never touched a drop of drink all summer. Given the man's reputation, that was nothing short of a miracle. Jack brushed it off with a simple comment that drink "doesn't agree with me anymore" when pressed with "Sure one bottle of stout won't kill ya."

Some days, instead of farm projects, they went hunting down in the lower meadows. At last Myles had his chance to do what he'd been dreaming about for years: show off Nell's skills and his own knowledge of game and fox habitat to his da. In turn, Jack taught him how to shoot the ancient single-barreled shotgun that had hung unused in the upstairs rafters. Kitty had warned Myles against the dire consequences of even touching the gun, though he sometimes sneaked in and played war games, pretending he was an IRA marksman, killing scores of British soldiers as they came swarming across Sugarloaf Mountain.

That was before Jack came home. Now he was allowed to take target practice openly in the orchard, using a thick wedge of oak nailed to an apple tree as a bull's-eye. Once he got used to the violent kick of the butt against his jaw—which knocked him flat the first time he pulled the trigger—he showed a lightning speed and accuracy that drew praise from all quarters. Soon Myles was bagging pheasant and rabbits weekly, beating his father to the mark when the dogs flushed the game from the furze.

It was on one of those hunting expeditions that Myles came to know another side of his father. He also learned a well-kept secret about his mother that cast her in whole new light. The conversation began after Myles had downed a pheasant with a brilliant shot and Jack, sensing his son morphing to a man, opened a delicate subject: his years in the IRA.

"You know, son, the crack of a gun always reminds me of when I led the flying column down in Bunclody back in '19. We'd been tracking the Black 'n' Tans for a week after they burned out the whole village of Kiltealy. Well, we hit 'em at three in the mornin' . . . blew up the barracks where they were billeted, out toward Vinegar Hill. Never knew what hit 'em. Bastard foreign riffraff . . . Criminal element turned loose from British prisons and armed on condition they come over an' massacre us. Five of 'em escaped the first blast, but we blew their balls off as they came charging out of the back."

"What happened after that, Da?"

"They caught us in Enniscorthy four months later, but not before we'd done several more jobs like that."

"How come they didn't kill you like they did when they caught Padraig Pearse and the others in the Easter Rising?"

"Did yer mother never tell ya the story? Sure I'm not surprised; it's not like her to dwell on the past. Or to brag."

Myles was now listening to an entirely different man than he'd known before. Gone was the funny raconteur. In his place was a soldier, focused and gleaming at the memory of battle. This was the real IRA hero, the one he'd never believed existed. Yet here he was listening to the firsthand account, like a dream come to life. Myles sank down on the stone wall, ready to drink it all in, watching his father's glistening blue eyes harden as he warmed to the story.

"Well, see, we were arrested and taken to the local jail in Enniscorthy. The whole county knew what happened: someone had informed on us, one of our own. We were to face the Tan's firing squad the following Wednesday. So here's what happens. We were allowed one last visit from family and friends to say our goodbyes. No men, only women. I was dating your mother at the time, sort of—she was Kitty Cusack then, a gorgeous slip of a girl, but secretly a commander in the local Cumann na mBan.

"I thought only the men could be commanders?"

"Oh, no, son. The women were commissioned, too. Kitty had a reputation—well deserved, may I say—as a fierce Republican. Absolutely fearless. And deadly. She shows up on Tuesday night, acting the green, gawky country girl—'Sorry to bother ya, sir'—with freshly baked brown bread, four packs of Sweet Afton fags, and guess what else?"

"A hacksaw blade?"

"Ha, you've been reading too many comics. No—a sawed-off shotgun, stowed under her big winter coat."

Jack smiled at the memory and lit his pipe, puffing to fill the silence. Myles felt his pulse race. His mother with a shotgun? Was this the same woman who forbade him to even handle the old shotgun gathering dust upstairs before his da came home? He watched Jack's face for a few more seconds before asking, "So did she manage to hide the shotgun from the guards?"

Jack laughed and rolled on. "No, that was not the plan. She had a different idea. The guard, a Tanner, never knew what hit 'im; she fired at point-blank range . . . right through the coat . . . blew a hole in him the size of yer fist."

Myles tried to swallow, but felt his mouth go dry and his chest tighten. Then he heard himself say in a faint voice that sounded high-pitched and distant, "You mean ta tell me that Mammie killed the guard . . . I mean, the Tanner?"

Jack smiled indulgently at the boy's amazement, continuing calmly, as though telling a bedtime story. He moved in closer to Myles, holding his gaze, warming to the subject, enjoying both the memory and the discomfiture of his audience.

"Oh, absolutely. Dead as a doornail. He made one fatal mistake—didn't think a country lass would have the nerve to pull the trigger. Stupid ejeet dared her: 'Go ahead,' he sez, 'ya Feinian bitch. I dare ya. Ye don't got the fucken nerve.' Sure we all heard 'em yell it from up an' down the cell block. We knew they'd be the last words the Tanner ever spoke. Didn't know Kitty Cusack like the rest of us . . . That woman had nerves of steel; tougher than most of the lads in the movement. Kitty always took care of business. Always got the job done."

With that, Jack looked off in the distance and paused to relight the pipe. A long silence followed before Myles broke in, choking back tears.

"I never knew any of that, Da. Mammie never told me . . . How could she? So how did you escape?"

Another long pause, puffs on the pipe, and a resigned sigh. "Well, after Kitty sprung us—all twelve of us . . . Oh, listen, 'tis a long story, son. We split up. Packie Hayden, Denny Brennan, an' me stayed together an' got out to Canada; ended up in Montreal. We had contacts and a lot of help up the chain of command. But that's why yer mother and I had to meet up in New York after it had all settled down years later.

"I'll tell ya the rest some other time. Sure Mick Collins and I were best buddies; started out as handpicked lieutenants in the IRB — Irish Republican Brotherhood — before De Valera and the treaty tore us all asunder. I can't bear to even think about the betrayals and treachery; all those fine young men and women, tortured and martyred for . . . for what? Look what it got us."

The memory seemed to wilt him. Gone was the aloof storyteller, spinning a yarn. His soft tenor voice broke and tears welled up in the blue eyes, turning gray in anguish. Embarrassed, he turned away, trying to regain his composure. "I'm sorry, son. I shouldn't have told you all this. Promise me ya won't tell yer mother I told you about Enniscorthy. I shoulda let sleeping dogs lie . . ."

"I promise, Da. I won't say a word."

With that, Jack stood up, stuffed the pipe in his pocket, and started up the hill toward the red-tiled farmhouse. They walked the distance in silence, deep in their own thoughts, Myles a few steps behind his father. His mind raced with questions and the dawning realization that his world had just been turned upside down.

Suddenly the mysteries of deference to his mother made sense.

After each incident, Myles had assumed his mother, a naturally dominant personality, intimidated her targets with sheer force of will. Now he understood the pitiful pleading, the sudden show of compassion, the ready admission of guilt. They all had one thing in common: terror. They weren't facing his mother; they were facing Kitty Cusack, legendary commander in the Cumann na mBan and secret enforcer for the IRA.

But did they know the whole truth? That she'd shot a Black 'n' Tan prison guard, and the only living witness was Jack Hogan? Maybe the whole truth was worse. Perhaps she'd shot others? If so, how many? And who besides Jack knew?

Myles was left to ponder these questions alone. He would have to bide his time before he could even broach the subject with his da, and Kitty was completely off-limits; on that front, he was sworn to secrecy.

After that one extraordinary tale of his jailbreak, Jack returned to his other persona: an endless fountain of hilarious mimicry, ancient wisdom, songs, and poetry. Myles, in turn, decided to focus on the bright side of this newly revealed heritage. He was the only son of Kitty Cusack and Jack Hogan, Cumann na mBan and IRA insurgents who'd trounced the Black 'n' Tans, hooligans and murderers all. This was nothing to be ashamed of. In fact, he was proud of his pedigree. After all, Kitty and Jack had put it all on the line for Irish freedom when it mattered most. He didn't know anyone else who could say that about *both* their parents.

So resolved, he got up each day now intent on making the most of being alone with his da. He never raised the topic of the IRA again, and Jack avoided all references to his days "on the run." Instead they seemed to have reached a tacit agreement that Kildargan farm would be their new cause.

Jack taught Myles the verses to all his favorite songs—"Slievenamon," "The Croppy Boy," "Dawning of the Day," and Myles's favorite, "Kevin Barry." They cleaned out the old car shed, built a workbench, and cut down several hardwood trees—ashes and oaks—for the new paddock they'd planned behind the stable.

At night Hogan's farmhouse turned into a lively "rambling house," the center of community fellowship and entertainment. Gone were the days of isolation when Myles and Kitty wouldn't see a soul from one Sunday to the next. The Voice had raised the ante; singers never heard from before emerged to perform and match their talent against himself. The same with the music—and all the other performances, including the storytelling, poetry, and occasional tug of war on the long summer evenings. It was the best summer of Myles's life, far and away. He finally had a father of his own, and one who was supremely talented, great fun, and a genuine IRA hero to boot.

Then, one balmy August evening, their idyllic summer ended.

The ramblers had assembled for another night of music and storytelling, but Jack was still down in Enniskerry on some errand. Myles heard the border collies first, their barking chorus unusually shrill—with Parnell, the big black alpha, dropping into an ominous crouch, hackles up, slamming against the kitchen door with increasing urgency, as if engaged in some mortal combat with an invisible foe. This was a sound Myles had never heard the borders make before, and he felt a shiver invade his whole body.

Kitty finally tuned in to the banging against the kitchen door and turned to Myles without noticing that he'd turned pale. "Myles, will you go out and call off those dogs! They're giving me a headache with all that randy-boo." When she saw his hesitation, she picked up the Tilly lamp and, without further comment, stormed into the dark farmyard to see what all the fuss was about. "Parnell! Shep! Rover! Come to heel! I said, HEEL!"

With that the dogs went mute; but not quite. They stopped barking, but Parnell kept baring his fangs in an ugly snarl, while the others growled and refused to lie down as they normally would when Kitty took charge. As one, they paced back and forth, glaring toward the outer gate with baleful suspicion.

Standing just beyond the gate, frozen in fear, was a homely little woman dressed in black, with a large hat on top of a wizened little head. As she stepped into the farmyard, Myles could see her large pair of glasses reflect the light as she introduced herself as Fanny Wilcox, explaining that Ned Delaney had driven her up from Enniskerry but had to go for another fare, leaving her to carry her large suitcase down the long driveway by herself. She looked exhausted, leaning on a cane, and Kitty immediately felt sorry for her. "Well, come on in and have a cup of tea and some refreshments, Fanny. You look famished and sure who wouldn't be after lugging that suitcase down the lane all by yourself. I'm surprised at Ned to leave a woman in such a lurch. Shame on him."

Fanny waved this aside with "No, no—Ned seemed like a nice chap, really. Very polite and friendly, 'e was. I don't want to put you to any trouble, but I'm looking for Paddy Hogan, and I understand 'e lives 'ere." Here was an accent Myles had never heard, and he could barely make out a word.

"I'm afraid you may have the wrong farm, Fanny. This is Jack Hogan's house, and he's away at the moment, but we don't know any Paddy Hogan."

Fanny sipped her tea, glanced through her horn-rimmed glasses at the assembled ramblers, and Myles, before speaking. Then, with a condescending cackle and an air of conspiracy, she leaned toward Kitty and whispered, "You may want to 'ear the rest of wot I 'ave to say privately. Can we go into another room, then?" Caught off-guard, Kitty blushed and said, "Of course, of course . . . sure let's go up to the parlor so that we can talk. Myles will join us." Myles moved past the ramblers toward the parlor, but as he walked by Fanny, he felt her cold, clawlike hand grasp his wrist and whisper, so that all could hear, "I don't think we want our knuck here listening to wot I 'ave to say." Kitty recognized the British taunt: knuck—dimwit, eejit—but hadn't heard it since her days as a nursemaid in London, when it was used to ridicule Irish country girls fresh off the boat on the "downstairs" staff of her upper-crust employer.

Ignoring Fanny, she guided Myles in front of her as the three of them withdrew to the parlor, the formal room reserved for company, to the gawking silence of the ramblers. Kitty poured more tea and invited Fanny to proceed, which she did with an air of being in a deep conversation with a long-lost friend. Her story, which took over an hour to tell in her halting, Yorkshire style, erased all doubt of its credibility.

"Paddy came to live at Windgate House about five years ago. I'd been running the boarding house ever since me 'usband died in WWII, rest his soul. He was a career military man, you see, Captain Wilcox. A good man; a good provider. Paddy and I grew very fond of each other, and got engaged a year ago. He told me all about 'is life—about Rathdargan farm, about 'aving a sister wi' six children, five daughters and a boy, who'd lost her 'usband in the war, just like me. He told me how he was helping her out, letting 'er stay 'ere, though 'e was legal owner of the farm. But 'e was allowing his sister—ye—to live 'ere out of kindness, not cuz 'e had to, mind you. And 'e always did say how 'e intended to come back to Ireland to run the farm when the time was right.

"Being 'is fiancée, I trusted 'im with my life's savings, five hundred pounds, which 'e said 'e needed to fix up Kildargan, till 'e could send for me. I was planning on selling Windgate House as a going concern—I'm tired of all the 'eadaches that go with running a boarding 'ouse. You 'ave no idea wot goes on."

Myles looked at Kitty as the story ended. The only sound in the parlor was the loud ticking of the grandfather clock by the heavy mantelpiece, over which stern portraits of Hogan ancestors across the generations hung. Outside, the border collies were still barking in their high-pitched chorus, and Parnell, the alpha, was pacing back and forth, still growling, disturbed by something unseen in the summer night.

From Fanny's account, there was no doubt that "Paddy" was Jack, up to his old tricks. As always, they'd caught up to him, only this time with his wife and son as stricken witnesses and a gallery of ramblers to spread the gossip as fast as their legs could carry it.

Myles knew trouble when he saw it and this had all the makings. He looked at the intruder with unvarnished hostility. Fanny Wilcox had not been granted her fair share of nature's bounty. In fact, she was one of the ugliest people Myles had ever laid eyes on; more detached observers would readily agree. Under five feet and somewhat obese, she walked with a bowlegged limp and had one glass eye that looked dead, almost amphibian. To cap it off, she spoke in a high-pitched Yorkshire dialect, "Gur blimey, a rum lot, eh wot?"—as enervating to the Celtic ear as fingernails on a blackboard.

To Myles's amazement, Kitty finished her tea and, with elaborate politeness, then invited Mrs. Wilcox to stay: "Just for the night." But Myles was having none of it. "Mammie, I don't believe a word of what she's saying. How do we know she's telling the truth? And why can't we wait till Da comes home? Besides, where is she going to sleep? We don't have any room for visitors, unless she wants to sleep in the hay shed." He said all this while glaring at Mrs. Wilcox and before Kitty had time to issue a reprimand. Embarrassed by his outburst, she now took control. "Myles Hogan, you will not talk to a guest like that. Apologize at once!" But Myles was in no mood to back down in front of this creature he sensed was up to no good. "I will not apologize. I haven't done anything to apologize for. But I'm going to see what Da has to say before I listen to one more word from either a yez." With that he bounded out of the parlor and made an elaborate display of stomping up the creaky wooden stairs.

Jack came home after all the ramblers had departed. It was quiet in the kitchen when he walked in to the unlovely presence of Fanny, sitting by the fire, teacup in hand. Caught red-handed, "Paddy" came clean and acknowledged that yes, he and Fanny had "grown fond of each other." Myles, listening from the upstairs loft, couldn't believe his ears. He'd been wrong and now his worst fears were being realized. This creature was going to stay here, which meant he would have to give up his room and sleep in the dark, dingy parlor on the lumpy old horsehair sofa.

There was one thing Myles didn't understand: his father's lack of taste. Surely, Myles thought, if his father was going to find another woman to "date," he could have picked someone who was at least presentable. Myles just couldn't imagine his handsome father being seen with Fanny Wilcox in public, or whatever else "being fond of" meant. When he mentioned this to his mother, she simply said, "Men will do strange things for drink, son. I hope you never know what that's like."

The comment made no sense to Myles, but, watching his mother's mouth tighten, he let it go. But he vowed then and there that this ugly and evil creature had to go. He had no idea of how, but he knew he hated her and would stop at nothing to protect his family from this cackling menace.

Whatever was worked out by the adults, Mrs. Wilcox seemed in no hurry to leave. Whenever she went for one of her solitary walks around the farm, Myles could hear his parents fighting. First his mother's voice raised in consternation; then his father's usually soft tenor voice taking on a hoarse, frightening harshness. Sometimes, too depressed to work, Myles would idle in the hay shed, leafing through a comic book, pretending to be busy. Terrified of losing his da again, he began to conjure up schemes to rid Kildargan of Mrs. Wilcox.

This took little effort, for Fanny Wilcox—having always been childless—made no bones about her dislike for children, especially boys and Myles in particular. She kept on referring to him as "our knuck"—a phase he, fortunately, never understood—in her grating, screechy dialect. No one told her to knock off the obvious taunting. Later she tried charming him, but soon gave up in the face of his silent disdain. Myles went out of his way to be rude, refusing to even be in the same room when she was present.

After a month of brooding hatred, he decided to kill Mrs. Wilcox. It soon became an obsession. At first he felt guilty, pacing his room at night and imagining his confession to Father Cavanagh. After all, this would be murder, clearly a mortal sin. Fires of hell for eternity—no priest could even offer him absolution.

On the other hand, Mrs. Wilcox wasn't even a Catholic. She was barely human—some kind of Protestant. She was going to burn in hell anyway. Surely it was no sin to rid his family of this parasite; it'd be like killing a rat or shooting a cuckoo to keep it from preying on an innocent robin's nest. God would understand this and so would Father Cavanagh.

Seizing on this line of thought, Myles felt relieved, free to focus on concrete plans.

His first idea was to follow Fanny on one of the walks, push her into one of the sinkholes near the far field, where no one would ever find her. Myles had seen one of those quagmires swallow a two-thousand-pound cow; even eight strong farmers pulling on the end of a rope couldn't save her. He discarded the notion only when he remembered how slowly the cow sank; it took at least eight hours. He could imagine Fanny Wilcox, stuck and screaming in her shrill Yorkshire gibberish that the whole valley would be summoned to witness her accusations.

He finally settled on a concrete plan. It was as simple as it was vicious. He would invite Mrs. Wilcox to go hunting with him in the lower meadow, there would be an accident, and she wouldn't come back. He rehearsed his lines for the aftermath.

"I don't know, Mammie. It all happened so fast. Mrs. Wilcox wanted to learn to shoot and I let her give it a go. The borders were barking, which startled her, then the gun backfired and then she was laying there, the dogs surrounding her barking like they'd gone mad . . . I'm really sorry. I shouldn't have let her use the gun. It's all my fault."

He imagined his mother and the neighbors trying to console him.

"Now, Myles, you shouldn't blame yourself. Mrs. Wilcox was a grown woman, capable of making a decision. I'm sure you were just trying to be nice to her. But I know this must be very hard for you."

It was now only a matter of how to get his quarry in the lower meadow on a different kind of hunting expedition. Never an athletic person, Mrs. Wilcox was not likely to jump at the chance to go hunting; but Myles was determined to convince her.

"Mrs. Wilcox, would you be interested in seeing where the pheasants lay their eggs in the far field?"

"Wot is this? A wildlife outin' being offered by our knuck? Well, well, well . . . Wonders never cease. An' I thought ye didn't like me very much. We'll see. Maybe when I'm feeling a little bettah. Not today, luv. Run along now."

"All right, Mrs. Wilcox. I could even teach you how to shoot rabbits and foxes. Might come in handy sometime if you're going to be around Kildargan."

"Well, it might, at that. I nevah thought a' that. Me, shootin'. Blimey! You 'ave some imagination for a young lad. I may have misjudged ye. I do believe I'll take ye up on it, soon as I'm feelin' a bit more chipper."

Myles smiled and shivered at the ease of his conquest. Now the question: did he have the nerve to pull this off? He'd killed and seen killing before: Billy Flood butchering a hog; Packie Ryan shooting his old sheepdog, Ben; Peter Doyle putting down the bay colt with the broken leg. No one liked it; they just did what had to be done in the situation. This was no different; just something that had to be done. Another hard truth.

He carefully rehearsed each step until he had it down by heart. First have her handle the gun to get her fingerprints on it—all the detective comics made this point. Then teach her to aim it. Next, take the gun away in mock anger at her awkwardness, start to walk away, turn around, aim, and fire at point-blank range. Easy. Like shooting a jackdaw on a fencepost.

For several weeks, as the days grew shorter, Myles began to panic, badgering Mrs. Wilcox about her promise to go hunting. She kept putting him off; it never seemed to be quite the right time. Maybe she was on to him, evil mind reading evil mind. He seldom slept for more than a couple of hours, and when he did, his dreams turned to nightmares of blood and gore from which he'd awake screaming. Even daylight brought no relief, his mind a chamber of horrors: Father Cavanagh's voice condemning him to hell; Mrs. Wilcox's mangled ghost at the window; Myles hanging from a scaffold at Mountjoy Jail, body twisting in the wind.

He was cleaning out the cowshed when Jimmy Dunphy's high-pitched whistle sent the borders into their frenzied greeting. They knew Jimmy but never ceased to greet him with full-throated barking, delighted at the chance to show off their guarding prowess. This time Jimmy was lucky: Kitty was there to greet him with her steady smile, which faded when she saw the little green telegram in his arthritic fingers.

He went into his ritual delivery, which infuriated Kitty and destroyed any chance Jimmy had of being invited in for a tea and scones. Myles came up from the shed at the sound of the borders, just in time to hear Jimmy plead, "Maybe I should wait in case you want to send word back." This time Myles didn't say anything; he just gave Jimmy a hard stare as Kitty abruptly turned her back on Jimmy and trotted down the stairs, tripping over the borders as they swarmed with the excitement of the moment.

Halfway to the kitchen, Kitty pulled up and said, "Oh, my God, the telegram is for Fanny. Do you know where she is?" Myles had seen her go for her regular walk about an hour earlier, and he instinctively grabbed the telegram and ran in the direction he'd seen Mrs. Wilcox go.

He met her at the hazel corral, walking slowly toward the farmhouse, taking in the warmth of the sun as it rose from behind the Sugarloaf. She looked small and vulnerable, and for a moment Myles felt sorry for her and guilty of his wicked design on her life. Seeing him sprinting toward her, she immediately erased his guilt with, "Well, well . . . if it isn't our knuck, snooping around, are we?" Myles just stared at her in his practiced nonchalance, held up the telegram, and said, "Mammie said this is for you. The postman just delivered it."

Fanny snatched the telegram from Myles's outstretched hand and slit the little green envelope with one sharp flick of her talonlike fingernail. Myles watched her as she read the brief message. After several seconds, she looked past him with her glass eye and muttered, "Oh, dear. I must go back at once. There's been a dreadful death at Windgate. Poor Peter Boyle, one of my boarders, has hanged hisself in the upstairs bathroom." With that she turned and trotted toward the farmhouse in her bandy-legged gait, puffing and panting, with Myles walking behind her at a fast clip to keep up.

Mrs. Wilcox quickly related her story to Kitty. Jack was out in the fields, fixing fences, and Myles ran down to tell him the news. He said nothing, just came back to the house, briefly spoke with Fanny, then grabbed Myles's bike and rode off to Enniskerry to fetch Ned Delaney for Fanny's departure in the morning.

Next morning, as the sun's first rays edged across the Sugarloaf range, Myles staggered downstairs to find Mrs. Wilcox packed, with Ned Delaney's green Vauxhall idling at the road gate. She begged Myles for a hug, and without hesitation he clung to her and sobbed as though his heart were breaking.

"Wot's a mattah? Don't take on so. I didn't even think ya liked me . . . Blimey! Our knuck has a 'art after all."

"Bye, Mrs. Wilcox. Sorry we didn't have a chance to go hunting. Maybe some other time—if you ever come back."

"Aye, son. Maybe then. Between you 'n' me, that may be a while. I doubt I'll be back. But you can come stay wi' me in Birmingham.

I know a lot a young ladies that'd like the cut a yer jib, if ya know wot I mean. Take care, lad. Yer not such a bad knuck, after all . . ."

The Hogan family—all three of them—waved goodbye as Delaney's taxi disappeared around the bend down the Wexford Road. They walked back to the house in silence, like a funeral procession, each in a private turmoil they dared not speak.

Something had died during Fanny's stay; intuitively, they all knew that the innocent laughter and family joy they'd known just a few weeks ago was gone forever. The only question for Myles was how he would get through the next few days without letting his relief, grief, and anger spill out all over the kitchen floor. What was he going to say to his da? To Mammie? To his pals in school? To the snooping neighbors?

Predictably, Jack took the line of least resistance: as soon as the green taxi was out of sight, he promptly changed his clothes, pumped up the bike tires, and muttered something about going to Borris to talk to Jimmy Doran about a horse. From the look on Kitty's face, Myles knew she didn't believe a word of it. They had no reason to trust him or believe a word he said. Myles could see some combination of worry and alarm on his mother's face. It was a new look, one that he had never seen before.

No longer able to stand the furtive look on his father's face, Myles hastily dodged out to the hay shed to pursue his chores. From there he could overhear his parents' voices, raised in anger. Kitty spoke first: "How do I know you're going to Doran's? You always make up some cock-'n'-bull story when all you're doing is goin' to the Joyce's pub. Or are you just going back with Fanny to Windgate? Why don't you just be man enough to tell me this time, not sneaking off, as usual?" Jack, his soft tenor now hoarse with anger: "I'll do whatever I feckin' well please, and no woman is going to tell me where I can come or go. I was goin' to Jimmy Doran's, but now I think I'll go straight to Joyce's. Why the hell not? Might as well be hung for a sheep as a lamb. It's all the same to the high-and-mighty Kitty Cusack. You can go straight to hell, woman, for all I care." Myles heard his mother mutter something unintelligible before they broke off with his da slamming the kitchen door behind him and storming into the farmyard with his hat and coat on.

As Jack angrily wheeled the bike toward the road gate, the borders suddenly became excited and barked menacingly at his back, the way they did at departing strangers. Irritated at the ruckus, Jack wheeled on the closest border collie, Rover, and kicked him viciously in the rib cage. The young dog whined and ran toward Myles for comfort, as Jack slammed the gate behind him with a few muttered curses at the dogs.

That night—the first without their odd guest—the ramblers arrived at dusk, as usual, their expectations high. The borders kicked up their usual racket but quickly settled down to enjoy the routine camaraderie. Mrs. Wilcox's presence had not dampened the ramblers' spirits or concentration one bit. It would take more than her awkward attempts at participation to do that. In fact, they'd been more than gracious to her, Myles noted with some resentment.

He'd hoped for a show of support; instead he'd become the target of edgy lectures on the virtues of being polite and "not letting his family down." *That's a good one,* he thought bitterly. *I'm the one who's disgracing the family by not cozying up to this bowlegged creature from Birmingham.*

When Jack was not home as the ramblers ambled in, the disappointment and curiosity was palpable. From the forced humor and the knowing looks, it was clear what they were thinking: the worst, the obvious, why not? Had that not been borne out since Fanny's arrival in August? Surely there was no reason to assume things were going to be suddenly hunky-dory. They could barely restrain the winks when Kitty told them that himself had only gone to Borris to see Jimmy Doran. They knew better. The more Kitty reassured them, the more pity Myles could detect in their ruddy faces.

They knew all along the arrangement couldn't last, and while they felt sorry for Kitty and Myles, they felt even sorrier for themselves. Myles could see it in their sad faces, looking at the door as people filed in, staring past each familiar face to see if Jack might be among them. Then the shattered look when it was "only" Packie Breen, Jim Gallagher, Danny Doyle—the regulars.

By eleven o'clock the neighbors had disbanded and Jack had not come home. With mumbled words of comfort—"Sure, he probably just got held up at Dalton's"—each little group wandered off into the inky night.

About 2 a.m. the borders started up, waking Myles from a deep sleep. He peeked out the window and could see them in the moonlight, swarming around the road gate. It seemed as if someone was trying to come in the gate, someone they didn't know. Who could be coming at this time of night? This went on for some time, about a half-hour, then they fell back, growling and seemingly cowed. Then all fell silent and Myles fell back to a fitful sleep.

Around 3 a.m. Myles came suddenly awake with an urgent hand on his shoulder. His mother was shaking him, a strange tension in her voice: "Myles, wake up! Wake up! Will you please come into the other bedroom with me? Your father's been drinking and I'm afraid." Like he'd been stuck with a hot poker, Myles sprang out of bed. His fearless mother, afraid? He'd never known her to be afraid of anything or anybody in his whole life. What could she be afraid of? What was his da going to do to her?

As he came in the inner bedroom, Myles could hear the borders, back in their high-pitched barking, some joining Parnell in his deep-chested growl. Why were they growling at Da? Would they remember that he'd kicked Rover? Were dogs capable of revenge for one of the pack?

That's when all hell broke loose. As Myles shuffled toward the damp outside bedroom, he heard his father crashing through the front gate. He could hear the distinctive voice over the din of the borders, shouting in a hoarse, drunken diatribe. Myles fought back his fear, thought he might be having a nightmare, an illusion soon erased by the menacing voice descending on the house. Abruptly the dogs went silent, a silence that was almost deafening in contrast to the howling chorus of a moment ago.

Then came the hoarse, bullying voice: "Get up, Kitty! Get up and make me my tay! Goddamn you, woman. You bitch . . . you whore. Why don't you have the door open for me when I come home? I'll teach you to show some respect when I get my hands on you. How dare you humiliate me in front of Fanny Wilcox—a woman who never done you no harm. I'm gonna show the whole cockeyed world who's gaffer around here for once and for all . . ."

Kitty started to cry, first slowly, in a stifled sobbing, then in an anguished, high-pitched confession, in terror of what was about to unfold. The wailing, desolate sound was unnerving for Myles to hear, all by itself.

"Oh, a Cushla, this is a side of your father I'd prayed to the Blessed Virgin you'd never see. He can be so cruel when he has drink taken. I'm not worried so much for myself, but if he does anything to hurt you, I don't know what I'll do . . . I just don't trust myself to . . ."

As the sentence trailed off in a wail, an ear-splitting thud from downstairs told Myles that Jack had just kicked down the kitchen door, which was never locked. The splintering timber could be heard for miles. Cowering under the blanket, shivering in fear, Kitty and Myles waited for their fate to unfold. Cursing at Kitty, yelling for her to "come down, bitch . . . I'll teach you to . . ." Myles could hear his father staggering toward the dark stairwell.

Fighting back panic, gasping for breath, Myles's own cowardice struck him, like a sharp kick to the pit of his stomach. What kind of man would be hiding like this? What kind of man would be putting up with this abuse? Had his mammie not just asked him for help? Well, she was going to get it.

A towering rage rose up through Myles's body at his mother's tormentor. No longer was this beastly intruder his charming, fun-loving da; this was just a nasty, foul-mouthed animal invading their home. All fear and compassion gone, Myles made a decision then and there: this brute was not going to make it up these creaky stairs even if he, Myles Hogan, had to die stopping him.

In one smooth motion, Myles sprang out of bed, grabbed the old single-gauge shotgun from its rack on the wall, and yelled, "She's not comin' down. If ya want the tay, make it yerself." The words flew from his mouth, like he was channeling a grown man, someone older and braver. He cracked the shotgun, checked the live cartridge—just as he'd seen hunters do before sending out the bird dogs—and stepped toward the stairwell, ready for battle.

Hearing his son's trembling voice for the first time, Jack's whiskey-fueled anger exploded anew. "Ah, the little bastard is going to challenge his da, is he? Well, I'm going to put some manners on you while I'm at it. You've been asking for a good whippin', and now you're goin' to get it."

With that, he lunged for the stairs.

Myles pulled the heavy shotgun up to his shoulder, hands shaking as he fumbled for the trigger. He aimed the long barrel at the empty stairwell, yelling at the top of his lungs, "Come on! Ya bastard ! I swear ta God, I'll blow yer fecken' head off if ya take one more step."

From behind him, Myles heard his mother's voice, calm and steady now—a complete contrast to the wailing victim of a few moments ago. "Give me the shotgun, Myles, right now, and step back from the stairs." Myles was used to obeying his mother when she adopted that tone; despite his resolve, he reflexively handed over the gun. She motioned him to back up behind her with a quick snap of her head.

A wintry blast shook the rafters, chilling the dimly lit bedroom. Myles recognized that voice, conjuring frightful images: Miss Breen's bloody nose; the cowering Hannigan twins; the dead Tanner. In a flash, Myles's rage turned to fear—fear for his da and the danger he was in. His mind raced. What should he do—beg her to stop? Jump in front of the gun? Start screaming to distract her?

In the end he just stood there, frozen at the terrible spectacle before him as Jack kept stumbling closer to the top step. Too drunk to navigate the steep steps, he kept falling down, then dragging himself back up to continue the ascent. He was only one step from the top when he saw Kitty and the shotgun's shadow in the flickering candlelight. Up until that moment, he'd kept up the drunken rant. Seeing the gun, he hesitated briefly, then charged ahead with renewed ferocity.

"Well, well, well . . . if it isn't the fucken warrior queen herself. Kitty Commandant Cusack, the pride of Cumann na mBan. The vicious bitch who never quite got what she had coming . . . I've punched yer silly eyes shut before and will again, just for pointing that fucken gun at me. Who do you think yer dealin' with here? The Tans? Do you take me for one of them eejits you can scare the shite out of with yer fierce fucken stare and general's bearing? Fuck you! I'm gonna teach you who's gaffer around here . . ."

Kitty's voice cut off the diatribe in that low, calm voice Myles had learned to dread: "No, Jack, that's over. You're never goin' to lay a hand on me again. Not tonight; not tomorrow; not ever!" She said this without emotion, the shotgun steady as a rock, and without taking her eyes off her husband, who stood swaying in the stairwell, still wearing his faded overcoat and rain-soaked felt hat.

For a moment Jack hesitated, cocking his head to one side, as if considering her words. Undaunted, he lurched over the final step, yelling, "Why, you miserable bitch, I'm gonna take that fucken shotgun 'n' shove it—"

That's when Myles heard the thud of the hammer and saw his father's white shirt explode in crimson across his chest, his body jerking backward into the dark stairwell. Everything went into slow motion. He had lots of time to observe the details of Jack's surprised expression, the wordless calm of his mother's profile, and the seemingly endless racket of the creaky staircase as it absorbed the crash of the tumbling body.

The borders started up again. This time the sound had gone from the high-pitched bark to keening—all of them in unison, as if on some invisible signal. They were answered across the valley by other borders, keening back, their eerie chorus reverberating around the Sugarloaf range.

Myles stared in horror as Kitty's right hand slowly and steadily set the shotgun against the bedroom wall. She betrayed not the slightest tremor as she picked up the flickering candle and followed her husband's tumbling corpse down into the kitchen. The turf fire was still smoldering in the grate and a moaning wind swept down from the Sugarloaf, rattling the ancient doors and windowpanes. The borders continued to keen as Myles absorbed the horror of the scene on the kitchen floor, the same concrete floor where it all began a thousand years ago, on that first magical evening in May.

An hour later, a somber, rain-soaked dawn was breaking over Enniskerry as Myles pedaled his Raleigh across the Dargal bridge, just a mile from the parish priest's house. Still in a daze, head down against the driving mist, he relived the scene in the kitchen: his father's blood-soaked corpse stretched by the fireplace; his mother calmly blowing the bellows, as if nothing had changed.

"Mammie, what are we going to do?"

"Go straight to Enniskerry and fetch Father Cavanagh!"

"Right now, in the dark?"

"Right now. It'll be light by the time you get there."

"What should I tell him?"

Kitty slows the bellows, then stops, glancing around the kitchen. The borders have gone silent, creeping into the kitchen, subdued, licking Myles's fingers and lying down in a circle around Kitty, by the bellows. The ticking of the grandfather clock amplifies the heavy silence; hazel eyes meet blue, holding them in a longed-for caress through the miasma of the smoking turf; then comes the calm, dispassionate response:

"The truth. Tell him the hard truth, like the good man you are."

Local Knowledge

FROM *Ellery Queen's Mystery Magazine*

THE CALL CAME IN at 11:54 a.m., December 15, 1995. Body found at Tups Tavern, 35 East 35th Street. Webb thought the call routine until he arrived.

Tups, frequented by sailors and longshoremen, was on the lake-front. Superior glistened, never freezing over, never covered with snow. But not pretty either, not in this part of town. In this part of town, the massive lake was dark and dirty, not sky blue like it was everywhere else.

Drug deals went down nearby and the local hookers worked dockside. Knifings were common. But this victim hadn't been knifed.

He'd been shot.

Patrols had followed procedure. Two squads, parked at an angle on the broken concrete parking lot, colored the tavern's gray walls red, blue, red, blue. Barflies stood near the open gunmetal doors, drinks in hand, coats draped over their shoulders to protect them against the cold.

They watched Webb as if he were one of them.

Which, in a way, he was.

He slipped between the dented bumpers, thankful he still fit into small places. Fifty crunches, one-armed pushups, a half-hour run around the football field, all required before he allowed himself to hug a barstool and drink until his tongue was numb. He always said the exercise let his body perform his job and the booze kept his mind from dwelling on it.

But he wondered sometimes, especially when he saw himself

reflected in those shabby tattered people whose drinks were more important to them than the life drained on the concrete.

He didn't acknowledge them. Instead he stopped beside the squads and memorized the scene.

Body belonged to a tall middle-aged man, lamb's wool coat—too rich for this part of town—exit wound a bloody mess in his back. Shoes shiny Italian leather, almost no scuff marks on the soles, dirt caking the right toe and the left heel. Right hand outstretched, slightly sun-wrinkled, white, with a gold ring, large ruby in the center. Salt-and-pepper hair, neatly trimmed, no strands out of place. Face pressed against the ice- and sand-covered concrete, features not visible from above.

Daylight was thin under a thick layer of clouds. Coroner would have to work in artificial light. Webb slipped on a pair of surgical gloves, crouched, and touched the back of the outstretched wrist.

Still warm. Webb glanced up, saw bloodstained holes in the pile of ice-covered snow plowed to the edge of the parking lot.

"Anyone know him?" he asked, as he crouched lower and peered at the man's face. Then he realized he didn't need to ask.

He knew the man. Tom Johanssen, returning home after thirty-three years.

Tom Johanssen. The first time Webb had seen him, they'd been in high school. Webb was the gangly new kid from Louisiana—a whole country and half a culture away from northern Wisconsin. Tom was all black hair and smiles, broad shoulders, chiseled features, and smarter than anyone else. Only he didn't flaunt it, just like he didn't flaunt the girls. Boys liked him, too, wanted to be in his shadow, and that was the first time, maybe the only time, Webb had ever experienced—had ever fallen under the spell of—true charisma.

Then Tom shattered it all, the entire brilliant future, the golden dreams, by getting Jenna Hastings pregnant. Two days after graduation, they married, and Webb saw Tom only occasionally: buying groceries at the Red Owl, or riding home from work in the big yellow electric-company truck. Webb went to college and Tom stayed behind, and it wasn't until five years later that Tom surfaced again, playing lead in a local country band.

Webb had gone to see the band just after he graduated from Mankato State and just before he entered the police academy.

Tom stood center stage, black hair curling over his forehead, gui-tar slung across his shoulder. Girls crowded him as if he were Elvis, and Jenna was nowhere to be seen. Webb had watched mesmer-ized, and had wondered then if Tom was divorced.

But the divorce came after the scandal, leaving Jenna with four boys and Tom with another mistake on his record. He joined the service and went to Germany. Married again, became successful, and sent his folks piles of money. Year after year he promised to come home, the prodigal son, now back in favor.

He never did come home. Not for his grandmother's funeral or his grandfather's. His sister's wedding or his son's.

He never came home.

Until now.

"I'm taking you off the case." Bernard was hunched over his desk, beefy arms covering two separate piles of papers. He was staring at the file in front of him as if his next words were written on it.

Webb leaned against the door, arms crossed. Despite the stuffy heat of Bernard's office, Webb still felt a chill, as if the cold from the death scene had got deep into his bones. "I can be objective."

"Like hell." Bernard caught a thin strand of hair and twirled it over his bald spot. "You went to high school with him. Flor-ence—"

"I went to high school with him, Ethan went to high school with him, and Mike Conner is Jenna's brother-in-law. Stanton's kid mar-ried Tom's kids' half-sister—and Pete flew Tom out of town in '62. Everybody in this town is connected to Tom somehow. You lived next door to him for six years." Webb's hands, hidden beneath his arms, were clenched into fists. He didn't know why he was fighting for this one so hard.

"I know," Bernard said. "That's why I want to give this one to Darcy."

"Darcy?" Webb tilted his head back so his crown hit the wood. Bernard was watching him, tiny blue eyes lost in his florid face.

Webb had trouble arguing this one. He'd fought for Darcy Dan-vers. No one had wanted to hire a woman cop, let alone a woman cop from out of town. She'd come in with more ribbons than any-one, more experience with real crime. She was athletic and tough, smartest woman he'd ever met—hell, smartest anyone he'd ever met—and a real street fighter.

"She doesn't know this town," he said, trying not to wince. That had been Bernard's argument against hiring her, the city's argument against keeping her, and the basis of Webb's defense of her five years back.

"She knows it good enough," Bernard said. "She'll follow through where the rest of us won't."

"I'd follow through," Webb said.

"Even on Flo?"

Webb closed his eyes, his sister's face rising before him, not as it was now, but as it had been that night long ago, puffy, tear-streaked, miserable.

"Even on Flo," he said.

But he didn't get a chance. Bernard took him off the case anyway. Webb staggered out of the office, short of breath and dizzy. Too many emotional shocks. First Johanssen, dead, then losing the case. It should have been his. It had to be his, to make up for thirty-three years.

Darcy was standing at her desk, a file of ancient clippings open in her hands. At forty, she was teenager-skinny, her arms long corded muscle, her breasts nearly flat against a trim torso. Her brown hair was cut short, above her ears, and the lines on her face were only visible up close. From a distance, she looked like a fifteen-year-old boy.

"I want to help you," he said.

"No dice." Her voice was cigarette-gravel. Two packs a day, filterless. Cigarettes for her, booze for him. Somehow they made it through the long, cold winters. "Bernard took you off this case."

"You'll need a local guide."

"I can find one."

"Maybe," he said. "You don't know what Johanssen did."

She closed the file. "Dumped his wife and four kids for a sixteen-year-old groupie who claimed she was nineteen. Took her to Germany, married her without getting a divorce. Second marriage still might not be legal."

"Surface stuff." He took the file from her, glanced down. It was from another case, a knifing at the same bar, in '62. He tossed the file on the desk.

"There's always knifings at Tups," he said.

"When Tom Johanssen's band was playing?"

"Nobody plays at Tups. Tom Johanssen's band was drinking. Johanssen and Cindy Waters were already on an airplane for Minneapolis."

"How'd you know?"

"Local knowledge," he said. "Still think you don't need me?"

Darcy studied him. Her left eye was gray, her right eye green, a fact that had always intrigued him.

"So," she said slowly. "Where were you when Johanssen got shot?"

"Got a TOD yet?"

"About ten-thirty, give or take. Coroner's not in yet."

Webb shrugged. "In my car. Listening to the scanner and thinking about lunch."

"Alone?"

"In this town, detectives don't have to partner."

She frowned at him. He once told her she was the only partner he wanted. "Can anyone give you an alibi?"

"Does anyone need to?"

The room had gone silent around them. Maybe he'd raised his voice. He didn't know.

"It might help," she said, picking up the file he'd tossed. "Word has it Johanssen screwed your sister."

"Got that wrong," Webb said. "He didn't screw my sister. He destroyed her."

Webb's sister, Florence, wasn't pretty. She'd never been pretty, not even as a little girl, but she'd been close. The wrong kind of close. Her features, taken separately, were perfect: oval eyes, long narrow nose with just a hint of an upturn, high cheekbones, and bow-shaped lips. Put together, they looked like she'd been colored by a child with a crayon too fat for the child's hand.

But what made it worse was that she wanted to be pretty. More than she wanted anything else.

She almost achieved it with Johanssen. She'd been twenty-one then, trim, with hair so black it shone blue in the sunlight. Her smiles had come from her heart and she walked with a lightness she would never have again.

Webb used to think she had finally grown into her body until he stumbled on Johanssen, shoe- and shirtless in Flo's bedroom in the middle of a Thursday afternoon. Flo had been in the bathroom. Webb could hear the water running.

Johanssen had grinned, hair tousled, cheeks still flushed, the sheets smelling of sex. *Your sister's one hell of a woman,* he'd said.

Webb had squeezed his fists tight, held them against his sides, not sure he wanted to fight in his parents' home. *You've got one hell of a woman at your place.*

Not for much longer, Johanssen'd said as he slipped on his shirt.

That what you're telling Flo?

Yep.

It'd better be true, Webb had said, *or I'll be coming after you.*

I'm sure you will. Then Johanssen had grabbed his shoes and slipped out the window, as if he'd done it a thousand times before. And he probably had.

The conversation had echoed in Webb's mind for years afterward. The beauty of it was that Johanssen had never lied. He'd never promised that he'd take Flo with him when he left. At least not to Webb. And probably not to Flo.

But Johanssen's strange honesty couldn't excuse what he finally did do. He'd chosen Flo because she was needy, and she'd fallen for him so deep that she'd never love anyone again. That would have been enough for Webb, but there was more.

Johanssen'd chosen Flo because of her college money. She'd won two science prizes her last year of high school, the only girl in the state to do so at that time, and she'd gotten three grand in awards. That, plus a thousand-dollar inheritance from a dead aunt and savings from four years of full-time work while living at home, brought Flo's savings account to well over $5000.

In 1962, with that much money, a man could buy a house.

Or go a long way toward disappearing forever.

On the afternoon he left, Johanssen slept with Flo for the last time. Then he'd convinced her to go to the bank, take out all her money, and give it to him. He'd buy plane tickets with it, he said, start a new life far away from here, with a new wife. He just never said who that new wife would be. And while Johanssen's band was getting drunk at Tups Tavern, Flo had sat in her parents' living room, in her very best dress, looking as pretty as she would ever get, waiting for a knock that never came.

She'd refused to press charges, said it was her fault, and didn't change her mind no matter how much her family pushed. She kept her job, never tried college, never moved out of the house, and never fell in love again. And whatever chance she had at pretty died that night, along with her heart.

Sometimes Webb thought it was all his fault. He should have beaten up Johanssen in Flo's bedroom and chased the bastard out of her life.

But he hadn't. And that was something thirty years of police work could never change.

One missed moment, one bad call, had ruined his sister's life.

Forever.

Flo still lived in their parents' house. It was a three-bedroom starter home, built postwar, and had a little over a thousand square feet counting the basement. Their parents had been dead ten years and Flo had yet to buy her own furniture. She still slept in the same room she'd had all her life.

Webb walked in without knocking. He shut off the television, like he always did, and crossed the empty living room into the kitchen. His sister sat at the wobbly metal table, slapping cards on the faded yellow surface, a cup of cold coffee at her side.

"You've heard," he said.

"Every asshole in town's called me," she said, without looking up. "Thinking I'd be pleased."

"Are you?"

"I don't know yet." Her hands were shaking. He didn't know if that was from the caffeine, the news, or both. He always suspected that she'd harbored a hope about Tom Johanssen, a hope that Johanssen would come back for her, that he'd made a mistake.

Webb went to the counter, grabbed the pot off her Mr. Coffee, and poured the remaining coffee into the sink. Then he tossed out the grounds. The garbage below the sink was overflowing. He'd have to take it out before he left.

He made a new pot of coffee, grabbed a chocolate from the basket on the sideboard, and took his normal seat at the table. Behind him, the Mr. Coffee wheezed. It was at least fifteen years old.

Flo set her cards down and studied her hands. They were so thin he could see the bones. Her skin was a sallow yellow—she never got any sun—and he doubted that she ate more than enough to keep herself alive.

"What was he doing here?" she asked.

"I don't know."

"How long had he been here?"

"I don't know that either."

"Don't know or won't say, Webster?" Her voice cracked as she spoke, taking some of the force from it. The force, but not the pain.

"Don't know." He ran a hand through his thinning hair. He'd been so worried about her that he hadn't learned the basic facts. A mistake he had never made before. Maybe Bernard had been right.

Maybe Webb didn't belong on the case.

"You always know." She got up, poured the coffee out of her cup, and then stuck her cup between the dripping coffee and the pot.

"They don't want me on this case." His voice was low.

She spilled, cursed, and ripped off a paper towel. Then she paused, leaning over the sink. "Because of me?"

He debated not telling her, but that wasn't fair. Then she'd think he was lying about what he knew.

"Yeah," he said, staring at her cards. Frayed edges, chocolate stains on the back. She played solitaire a lot. "Because of you."

She didn't move. "It shouldn't make a difference, should it, Webster? Thirty-three years ago? That shouldn't affect now, should it?"

"I don't know," he said, pushing away from his mother's kitchen table. "You tell me."

Options. Choices. The facts Webb knew about Tom Johanssen ended about 1970. He'd left a half-second before the scandal broke, joined the army, flew Cindy Waters to West Germany, and married her there. After he got out of the military, he'd moved to some wide-open western state, Montana, Idaho, Wyoming, or Utah, and worked for some computer firm. There were rumors of continued scandalous behavior, from affairs to drug abuse to corporate raiding. He made a fortune. Enough for two houses of his own. He paid off his parents' and his grandparents' mortgages, had two more children, flew his older children to Montana-Idaho-Wyoming-Utah once every few years for skiing and the obligatory parental visit.

And not once did he return.

Not once.

Until now.

That was where Webb's investigation had to start. At Johanssen's decision to return to the land of his sins. Never mind that Webb was off the case. Darcy'd still be digging up graves by the time he had answers to the most pressing question.

The secret wasn't in who Johanssen had hurt. Webb suspected that the list probably extended well beyond midwesterners. The secret lay in what had made him change enough to come home.

If Webb found that, he'd find the killer.

He knew that as well as he knew his own sister's name.

He had to work fast. Once Bernard caught him, he was out of time, probably with a suspension, badge and gun turned in for good measure. So he laid the attack like a well-planned military maneuver. People first, machines second.

Johanssen's parents still lived on the corner of Maple and Pine in a red-and-white clapboard house that had seemed bigger when Webb was a kid. He had only been to the house a few times, the most memorable a class picnic at the end of his junior year. The house had seemed wrong, even then. Johanssen was too glamorous, too intelligent to come from a house that had no books on the walls, and which had yellow and brown slipcovers all over the furniture. His parents, Gladys and Phil, were so firmly working-class that Webb had trouble associating them with their son. As the picnic wore on that bright sunny afternoon, it soon became clear that Johanssen had done the planning, the cooking, and the cleaning to make it all happen. Webb had felt a stab of pity. His own parents would have helped even if they didn't believe in a project, but it was obvious that Johanssen's wouldn't.

Webb grabbed his badge before he got out of the car. He didn't like rooting this deep into his own past. He didn't like the memories and the way they made him feel, as if he were smaller than he really was. In life Johanssen had made him feel that way; he seemed to do the same in death.

The sidewalk leading to the front door was cracked and broken. The concrete steps showed the signs of harsh winter. A fake grass welcome mat that dated from the sixties sat soggily near the stoop. Webb was careful not to step on it as he knocked.

The yellow curtain covering the window nearest the door moved slightly. Then voices echoed, and finally the door opened. The hunched old man staring through the screen was barely recognizable as Phil Johanssen.

"Mr. Johanssen," Webb said, holding up his badge. "I'm Detective Webster Coninck. I've come to talk to you about your son."

"No need to be formal, Webb," Phil Johanssen said, as he pushed open the screen. "I remember you just fine. Sorry about your losing your folks. Gladys sent a card both times."

"I know," Webb said. "Flo and I appreciated it."

Flo had gasped each time she saw the word *Johanssen* on the envelope. She had hoped that the card inside came from Tom.

Webb slipped inside. The house smelled of mothballs, liniment, and fried foods. Phil Johanssen still wore his slippers. His blue pants hung on him, and his red-and-black plaid shirt looked like it dated from the seventies.

Gladys stood in the door to the kitchen. She looked much the same, only faded, as if she had been in the sun too long and it had leached the color from her. Her hair, once the exact same shade as Tom's, was now gray, and the wrinkles on her face had the effect of dulling it.

"Webster," she said, and her strong alto took him back to his teenage years quicker than anything else ever could. "I was hoping you'd come."

"Mrs. Johanssen," he said. "I'm so sorry about Tom."

She made a small snort and took his hand. Her grip was surprisingly firm. "Come into the kitchen. I haven't had a boy at my table in too long."

The kitchen had been remodeled. It had a window over the sink, and oak cabinets that still gave off a faintly new scent. The countertops were a shiny ceramic, and the stove, refrigerator, and dishwasher were matching white. The table, covered with a vinyl tablecloth, sat against a bay window opening into the backyard. Plants littered the large sill. On the walls around them, Gladys's spoon collection alternated with Phil's pipe collection.

That was the smell Webb missed, the faint odor of pipe smoke clinging to everything.

"He gave up smoking for his health," Gladys said, following Webb's gaze. "But he couldn't give up the pipes."

She sat down beneath the spoon collection. Phil sat in front of the bay window. Webb sat across from her. The chair was covered with a crocheted cushion that didn't fit his body.

"Has anyone else spoken to you?" he asked, careful to keep his voice gentle.

"Just the boys who came to tell us the news," Phil said.

"Like on the TV," Gladys added. Her hands rested on the vinyl cloth, fingers laced together. Her knuckles were white from the tightness of her grip.

So Darcy hadn't been there yet. She would arrive soon.

"So," Webb said, "when did Tom tell you he'd be coming home?"

"Didn't know until them cops showed up," Phil said. "You'd think the boy would call if he was coming home after all those years."

"So you had no idea he was coming?"

"I did." Gladys had her head down, her hands pressed so tight that they were turning red. "He called two days ago. Said he'd be here tonight. I didn't say nothing because I thought he wouldn't come. Like all them other times."

"Dammit, woman." Phil shoved his chair back. "You could have said something."

"The disappointment—"

"Wouldn'ta killed me." He got up, bowed in an odd, formal way to Webb, then left the room.

Gladys's lower lip trembled. She brought her head up. Webb was sorry for thinking that they hadn't cared about Tom's death. They had been trying to put a good face on it.

For company.

"It would have hurt him something awful, Webb. The last time Tom didn't show, Phil went to bed for a week. Didn't want to do that to him this time."

"You said there'd been other times when Tom said he'd be here and didn't show?"

She nodded, grabbed a tissue from her sleeve, and dabbed at her nose. "Every three years like clockwork. He never made it. Not once. And he always felt so bad after that he'd pay to take us out there. But it ain't the same as coming home."

"No, ma'am, it isn't."

"I don't know why he hated it so bad. It was like the town burned him and he couldn't face it again. I kept telling him that folks'd forgiven him, but he didn't seem to hear. He was a good boy, Webb. You know that."

"He made quite an impression on me," Webb said.

Gladys studied her hands. Her thumbs worked against each other as if she were rubbing pain out of them. "I'm sorry about Florence," she said, her voice a whisper.

He opened his mouth, closed it, unsure what to say. He almost said that it didn't matter, but it did matter. Tom had ruined his sister's life.

"You tell her that money's still here. I got it in an account for her. Remind her."

Webb went rigid. The room spun and he realized he hadn't taken a breath. Gladys looked up, the lines in her face deeper somehow, and he made himself breathe. He couldn't hide his surprise.

"You—?"

But Gladys didn't answer. She pushed her chair away from the table, stood, and walked to the sink. She grabbed a glass from the sideboard and filled it with water. Her reflection in the window was wavy and indistinct.

"He was a good boy, my Tom," she said. "He just forgot sometimes that things have consequences. Like never coming home. His kids would've liked him here, you know? At a game, maybe, or that play Donnie was in. It'd meant a lot." She took a sip. "Guess it don't matter now."

"Who killed him, Mrs. Johanssen?"

"That's the question, isn't it?" She set her glass down, but she didn't turn around. "Not sure I want to find out the answer."

Neither was he. But fear had wrapped itself around his heart, and he had learned long ago to face that fear, to stand it down as if it were a charging dog or rampaging drunk.

He was on this path. Nothing, not even his own fear, would make him leave.

The Johanssens had offered to repay Flo her $5000, and she had never taken them up on it. They had it in an account in her name, had since 1971. When Tom sent them the money to pay off their own mortgage.

Webb didn't want to think about how much money was there, what kind of life Flo could have had if she'd only tried.

He drove away from the Johanssens' sick and shaking and wishing for a drink.

Instead he turned onto Hill, drove past the high school, past the duplexes owned by John Johanssen, and stopped at a crudely constructed A-frame on what looked like a vacant lot bordering John Johanssen's property.

Three brothers. Tom, John, and Scott. Scott Johanssen was the youngest, Vietnam vet, five children and no job.

The yard was a mixture of snow and dirt. Toys, half buried in the muck, were colorful reflections in the glare of a powerful porch light. Webb got out of the car and trudged on the unshoveled path. It was icy and awkward, with tramped footprints. Voices echoed from inside the house. Sharp voices, male and female, that cut off abruptly when he knocked.

There was no screen. When the unpainted door eased open, the scents of dirty diapers and dryer lint floated to him on a bed of warm air. A woman stood behind the door, her body thick with the aftermath of a pregnancy, her blouse stained with milk. The toddler in her arms was kicking her in a vain attempt to get down.

"Scott Johanssen, please," Webb said.

"You a cop?" she asked.

He nodded, reaching for his badge. But she didn't wait. She stood aside and yelled, "Dad, another one!" as she let Webb inside.

He stepped into a kitchen filled with old dishes and an overflowing diaper pail. In the center of the room, a weather-scarred picnic table stood, covered with crumbs and an overturned child's juice glass.

"Through there," she said, waving a hand at the A-shaped doorway.

He followed the trail of baby clothes and toys until he reached shag carpeting that might have been brown and might have been orange. This room smelled no better than the other. The furniture was old and brown, the upholstery torn. A TV was crammed against the unfinished wall, a red mute across Dan Rather's face.

Scott Johanssen was crammed into a Barcalounger that sagged under his weight. The footrest tilted, obviously broken. Scott was balding but still baby-faced, his round features a fatter, younger version of Phil's.

"Webster Coninck. Why the hell they got you on the case?"

"Dad," the woman said from the doorway.

Scott shrugged, and slapped the remote on a cup-strewn metal table. "Fair question when you remember that Webster here vowed undying hate toward my brother thirty-some years ago."

"I came to offer condolences, Scott."

"Yeah, and monkeys'll fly out of my ass."

"Dad," the woman said. "The children . . ."

"It's my house, Cheri," Scott said. "You don't like how I talk, you and them kids can go back to that asshole husband of yours."

"I'm sorry," she said to Webb, and then disappeared into the kitchen.

Scott peered up at him. "Condolences my ass," he said. "You want to know if I killed him."

"Did you?"

"Should have, for all the times he left Mom and Dad hanging. And them kids. They worship him, you know, and he didn't even have the time of day for 'em. Not even when he flew 'em to Utah. He'd let that slut of his take 'em places, and then he'd show up maybe for supper, maybe for one day of skiing, and that's all they'd talk about. Me and John, we were always there for 'em, but we were never enough. I was a fat bum, and John was too slick. Their dad was perfect because he was mostly a figment of their imaginations. That's what Tom was good at. Making up lies about himself that other people'd believe."

"What kind of lies?" Webb asked, figuring he'd let Scott talk if that was what he wanted.

Scott snorted, slid one finger forward, and shut off the TV. A whine that Webb hadn't been aware of disappeared. "Lies? You mean like that corporate job that made so damn much money? I called him at work lotsa times, always got him direct. Then I lost the number, called information, and got the receptionist. She said she'd never heard of him. I got"—he grinned—"well, lessay I can be a mean s.o.b. when I wanna, and she put me through to personnel. Said they had a Tom Johanssen in their records. He'd been there and left years ago. That was in 1979, and when I'd ask him about it, Tom'd just laugh and say, 'Scott, there's business and then there's business.' As if I didn't know that. Every grunt ever lived knows that. Just didn't want to hear my brother saying it, you know?"

Webb wasn't sure he did know. He shifted. His feet had left a fresh snow-mud trail on the flattened carpet. "You ever see him on those trips back here?"

Scott narrowed his eyes. "How'd you know about them?"

Webb shrugged. "Amazing what you hear when you're listening."

Scott pushed back on the arms of the chair. The back of the Barcalounger hit the wall.

"I was still drinking," he said. "So it had to be eight-eight, eight-nine, down to Tups. I had just come from Ma's and she was in a fine fix because she thought Tom was coming home. But he never showed. He was good at that, too. So I wander into Tups and take my usual spot when who do I see through that stupid glass bead curtain Tup used to have but my brother in one of his fancy suits, talking to some fat asshole I've never seen before or since."

"What happened?" Webb asked.

"I was drinking." Scott picked up the remote, tapped its end against the metal table, making a sound like a brush on a snare drum. "So I wasn't thinking, you know? I shout his name and stumble back there and by then him and his buddies are gone."

"You sure it was Tom?"

"I was drinking," Scott said. "I wasn't drunk. Besides, he sent me cash money to apologize for being a jerk and asked me not to tell Ma. Told Dad, though. Big mistake. He tried to find Tom, and when he couldn't, he spent near a year in Tups, hoping he'd come back. He never did. Then Tom flew 'em all out on one of them Utah ski trips, and when Dad come home, he didn't want to talk about it anymore."

"You know what Tom was doing here?"

"Nope, and I'm sure Dad don't, either. Like I said, Tom was good at making you think one thing when he was doing another."

Webb knew that. He knew that very well. "So what do you think happened to Tom?"

"I think somebody finally got tired of all the lies and used a bullet to shut him up."

"Any idea who that somebody was?"

"Nope." Scott stopped tapping the remote and pushed a button. The TV flicked on, so loud that Webb jumped. "I'm sure you're not hurting for suspects, though."

The winter darkness that Webb hated had settled in by the time he left. The sky was black—no stars, only clouds—and the streetlights made the snow seem white. Black and white with no gray. Not even the world had room for nuance anymore.

John Johanssen lived out near Jenna Hastings Johanssen Conner. John's house was a 3500-square-foot mock Tudor. It stood on a hill with a view of the river valley, the rolling land, the copper water tracing its way through taconite country. John owned fifteen acres here, and half the town besides. His rents were sky-high and his reputation nasty. But his buildings were never empty, and if Tom hadn't become such a legend, John would have gotten credit for being the rich Johanssen brother.

John's wide, winding driveway had a square snow-blower-built wall on each side. The snow was still picture-perfect, icy pure and fresh-fallen white. The garage door was down. Webb parked on the far side, careful to leave room for a second car to park beside him. He got out, slammed his car door, and the sound echoed in the winter air. He followed the snow-blown trail to the immaculately shoveled front porch.

He grabbed the carved brass knocker with his bare right hand. The shock of cold ran through his skin and up his arm. He banged once, then waited, scouting for a doorbell.

He didn't need it. John's wife, Evvie, pulled the door open and braced the frame with her right hand. She was too-rich thin and wore fresh makeup despite the late hour. "He's not here, Webster," she said.

"I wanted to talk to both of you," Webb said.

Her smile was tired. "You know I can't do that without John."

John had never liked it, not from the day they got married. Any independence Evvie showed somehow reflected on him. Evvie couldn't talk to another man alone. Webb had been on some of the calls as a beat patrolman. John never hit his wife, but the yelling had terrified the neighbors more than once. Webb suspected that was one of the reasons the couple had moved so far out in the country.

Webb didn't argue. He could talk to them together if he needed to. "Where is he?"

"Funeral home. Someone has to make the arrangements." She brushed a strand of unnaturally dark hair from her face. "I've been trying to call the folks in Utah. The numbers don't work, except the home number, and Cindy won't pick up."

"Someone at the station probably notified her."

"Hope so. We shouldn't have to take care of him. He never did his part for this family." Then she shrugged. "Shouldn't have said that, should I? Speaking unkindly of the dead."

"It's not a sin," Webb said.

"At least, not in the world of Tom Johanssen." She sighed. "I'll have John call. I know he wants to talk. This has him shook."

"And you?"

"I'm surprised it didn't happen years ago." She took her hand off the doorframe. "Thanks for understanding, Webb."

"Always have," he said.

She nodded and eased the door closed. It snicked shut, and he stood for a moment, his hand still aching with cold. He'd always liked Evvie. She and John were high school sweethearts, and seemed to have an understanding. But Webb thought John had never treated her well enough, despite the house, despite the trips, despite the money. She had no life away from him, and she should have.

At least Webb thought so. But he wasn't sure if that thought came from his own desire to see Evvie alone and have a real conversation, just once, without the guilt.

He sighed, walked off the steps and back to his car. When he got inside, the porch light switched off.

The home Jenna Hastings made with her second husband, Steve Conner, was one mile and an entire income district away from John Johanssen's. Jenna lived in a small three-bedroom ranch at the base of one of the rolling hills. Her nearest neighbor on the left had a front yard littered with dead appliances and car parts. Her nearest neighbor on the right had lost his home in a winter fire fifteen years ago and replaced it with an Airstream because he hadn't been insured. Jenna had tried to make hers nice, with flower boxes outside the window and a fresh coat of paint every few years. But the little house still looked like what it was—a starter home for a family that had never moved on.

Webb used to drive out to Jenna's a lot when Steve was still on the force. They'd have barbecues and parties for the department, and Webb'd watch her four Johanssen boys take care of her two Conner girls. Handsome children all, with the same restless intelligence he'd once seen in Jenna's eyes.

He turned onto the highway leading to the Conner place and was startled to see the road filled with cars. Black-and-whites parked haphazardly, their blue and red lights bright splashes against the snow. His mouth was dry, his stomach suddenly queasy. He had purposely had his scanner off, and now he flicked it on, the buzz and crackle of voices uncomfortably loud.

Steve Conner was standing under the outdoor light, coatless, arms wrapped around his torso. He was yelling at one of the patrolmen who stood, head bowed, blocking Steve from the house. Other officers were walking in and out of the open front door. Even from this distance, Webb could see the damp footprints on Jenna's red-and-black rug.

He got out of his car slowly, like a man in a nightmare. The air, frosty cold, didn't touch him. His feet squeaked on the snow, and some of it fell over the edge of his shoe and instantly melted on top of his sock. He scanned each squad until he saw what he was looking for, Jenna's too-white face pressed against the rolled-up window, watching as her husband continued to argue with the officer in charge.

All beat officers, no detectives. That made him shaky. He grabbed one of the patrolmen—a woman, actually, Kelly Endicott, who had gone to school with one of Jenna's kids.

"Who ordered this?" he said.

"Headquarters." She shook his arm off.

"Who?"

She shrugged. "No one wanted a name attached."

"What's the charge?" he asked, hoping that he'd stumbled on something else, that this was a mistake that had gotten out of hand.

"Murder, Webb." Endicott's voice was soft. "They found the gun."

He put a hand to his head. It didn't make sense. They had to do firing tests and match-ups and hours of lab work, and even then they couldn't be certain that the gun they had was the one used in the murder. The idea of ballistics as used on TV detective shows was as much a fiction as the locked-room mystery.

"What'd they find?" he asked.

"Conner's old service revolver, under one of the cars at Tups. It'd been fired. Conner says the gun was stolen one night when he was at Tups."

Webb nodded. "He reported it years ago."

Conner, a gun nut, had made a special petition to keep his weapons. Webb had kidded Conner about losing his revolver. *Hated the force so much you've gone and lost the one thing to remind you of it.*

Webb rubbed his hand over his face. His skin was getting chapped from all the exposure to the frosty air. "How come Jenna and not him?"

"No motive," Endicott said. "He'd never met Johanssen. She had cause, so they say."

"She's had cause for thirty-three years," Webb said. "Doesn't mean she'd do it now."

"I don't like it any more than you do, Webb. Seems to me someone just decided how this would fall, and didn't do the backup work." She tugged on her cap. "But what do I know? I'm still considered a rookie."

She walked away from him, back to Conner and the officer he was yelling at. Webb glanced at Jenna. She had gained weight since high school. She had a matronly fullness, the kind of motherly warmth once drawn in ads for Campbell's chicken noodle soup. When she saw Webb, she shook her head, and held up her hand as if he shouldn't come near. He shrugged, and she shrugged in return. Then he retraced his steps to the car, got in, and went back to the station to see who had caused this travesty.

During the winter, after five, the station had a different feel, a dark, gloomy feel, as if no hope could return to the world. Most of the desks were empty, but cops milled around, finishing business, leaning on counters, talking on the phone. Webb hated night activity. In this town, night activity was always sad activity: drug arrests, drinking violations, domestic violence disputes. Later, after midnight, the bar fights and the knifings would happen, but now the station's business was usually about kids in trouble with nowhere to turn.

The cops couldn't help them, either. The best the kids could hope for was to return to the parents who had neglected them in the first place. The worst was juvie, the petty-criminal training ground.

Webb slipped inside. The station smelled of chalk dust and

old coffee grounds. The concrete walls muted voices, made them sound as distant as and less important than the voices on the police scanner.

Darcy sat behind her desk, hands in her short cropped hair, a cigarette burning to ashes in a tray below the bright glare of the desk lamp. She was staring at the notes in her phone log, cheeks red with a stain Webb had learned to identify as anger.

"What's the idea not showing up at your own collar?" he asked.

She didn't look up. "Wasn't mine. It was Bernard's."

"The gun's not going to hold up."

"You're telling me." She kicked her chair back. Her eyes were full of red. "Serial numbers were scratched off years ago. Bernard claims the notches in the handle make it Steve's. His brother confirms it. But the gun's wiped clean, no prints, and only one shot fired. Johanssen was killed point-blank, so the killer has to have powder burns. I'll betcha Jenna Conner doesn't."

"Why her? Why not Steve?"

"Former cop with a brother still on the force?" Darcy snorted. "You tell me, smart-ass."

"Shouldn't have arrested her at all, then."

"No, they shouldn't have, but they want it wrapped." She pulled a file from beneath her log. "Makes this all worthless."

Webb pulled up a chair. "What is it?"

"Johanssen's arrest record. Longer than my arm, some drug-related, all smuggling. No convictions, not even any overnight stays in jail. Big lawyers, big money."

"And you think they bought someone here?"

She shook her head. "I think this town's too wrapped up in its past to know what's going on in its present."

Webb nodded. The analysis made sense. Tom Johanssen betrayed his wife, so she murdered him, first chance she got. What did it matter that she had to wait thirty-three years to do so?

The problem was, the same logic applied to Flo.

He swallowed, not liking the options. "You know about the trips, then."

"Every three years like clockwork," she said. "Supervising international barges with some 'special' loads. A real hands-on kinda guy."

"Drugs?"

She shook her head. "At first, I think. Then contraband. Going in and out. The Utah company was a front for chip smuggling. Disbanded last year just before the feds caught up to it."

"So you think this was a related hit?"

"I'm sure of it," she said. "He screwed up, let some investigator get too close. That's why the Utah office closed. His friends didn't like it, and they killed him."

"That's not evidence, Darce."

"Evidence." She waved a hand. "Look at the evidence. The hit's professional. There're no prints, no witnesses, no gun ID, and a weapon left at the scene. Someone wanted him, and they knew if they got him here there'd be plenty of other suspects."

"And a police department unused to these kind of cases."

Her smile was tired. She picked up the cigarette, flicked the long trail of ash into the tray, and took a drag. "I didn't say that."

He smiled back. "But you could have."

"I could have."

He sat down in the metal chair beside her desk. The green upholstery had a rip in it that whistled under his weight. "Let me see the file."

She tossed it at him. "This bothers you?"

"The whole thing bothers me. Tom was a bright guy. Why come here to meet a shipment if he knew his people blamed him for the raid last year?"

"Money?"

Webb frowned, remembering Flo's face on the last beautiful day of her life. "He had other ways of getting that."

He opened the file. Many of the sheets inside were old. Arrest records originally done on typewriters and recopied so many times that the dirt dots outnumbered the keystrokes. As usual on the old ones, the photos were missing, removed to put in a mug book or on another, more successful arrest sheet. The fingerprints were dark whorls of unreadable lines.

He flipped. The later arrest records were on a computer print-out. Information, but no original arrest sheets. There was reference to an FBI file, and notes from Darcy's conversation with the head of the FBI's case. A reference sheet in the very back also had a DEA file number.

"There's a lot of stuff here, but not a lot of paper," he said.

She nodded. "They've been trying for him for a long time. He knew computers. He could make details disappear."

Webb closed the file and handed it back to her. Just like Tom. Slippery to the end. Never appearing to be the person he actually was.

Webb pulled his gloves out of his coat—and paused, not liking the hunch that had just grabbed him and wouldn't let him go. "Who did the autopsy?"

"Cerino. There wasn't a lot to do, since it was an obvious gunshot wound, so she did a prelim to establish time of death. She'll do the rest tomorrow."

"DNA, fluids, fingerprints?"

Darcy was frowning at him. "Why? We have a positive ID."

"Mine?" Webb asked.

"Yours, and his brother's."

"Scott's?"

"John's."

Webb felt oddly lightheaded. "Get someone to fingerprint the corpse and check it against the federal database."

"I doubt he's in the base. I said he disappeared things—God." She stamped out the cigarette. "You don't think he disappeared himself, do you?"

"Why not?" Webb asked. "He did it before. He's the only one who would have known there would be other suspects here. I don't care how good a professional hit man is, he doesn't research those kinds of details."

"But the ID—you ID'ed him."

"I haven't seen him since 1962."

"But his brother—" Darcy started.

Webb held up a finger, then picked up the phone. He listened to the dial tone as he thumbed through Darcy's battered phone book until he found the number he was looking for. He wedged the phone between his shoulder and ear, and dialed.

"Evvie," he said when she picked up the phone. "Webb again. Sorry to bother you. Is John there?"

"No." She sounded small, hesitant. "He's at his folks'. You can reach him there."

"I will," Webb said, "but tell me one thing. When was the last time John saw Tom? Did he go on any of those Utah trips?"

"Heavens, no," she said. "John's too proud to let anyone pay his way anywhere. The last time we saw Tom had to be the last time we went west, which was in—I don't know—'79? '80? At least fifteen years ago."

"Fifteen years," Webb said. "Thanks."

He set the receiver down. Darcy was staring at him. "No one's that devious," she said.

"You don't know Tom."

"But his parents could have identified him."

"He knew they wouldn't," Webb said.

Darcy shook her head. "He couldn't have relied on that."

"Sure he could," Webb said. "He knew how it worked around here. He knew the department. He knew we would call John for the ID. John takes care of the family. And the entire town bends over backward to protect Tom's parents."

"But his other brother—"

"Hates his guts. Everyone knows that. You want a reliable identification, you call John."

Darcy was frowning. "So how did Tom get the gun?"

"It was stolen from Tups, right? If you look, you'll probably find that Tom was in town at the same time the gun went missing."

"You think he'd been planning this that long?"

Webb gave her a bitter smile. "Tom always has a backup plan."

She shook her head once, as if it were all too much for her. "I'll get right on it," she said.

FBI and DEA involvement somehow circumvented the usual state-to-state rigmarole. Darcy had impressed on them the need for immediate action. The fingerprint ID was fast, made even faster because the dead man was from California, a state that finger-prints all its citizens who get driver's licenses. The body belonged to Anthony McGregor, a computer consultant who had left home three days ago. He had told his wife that he was on a buying trip to the Midwest with a new client, a man with a lot of cash and a lot of connections, a man whom McGregor met through a mutual friend, a friend who had once commented on McGregor's strong resemblance to the client. McGregor had hoped the trip would provide an upward shift in the family's fortunes.

Three hours after his death, Anthony McGregor tried to get a direct flight from Minneapolis to Miami. Since he didn't book in advance, he wasn't able to fly direct. He had a layover in New York City, a layover that extended from one hour to four because of ice problems at Kennedy. Two FBI agents and two DEA agents met Anthony McGregor when he disembarked at Dade County Airport. Strangely, Anthony McGregor was two inches taller and fifty pounds heavier than noted on his driver's license. He'd also lost his need for corrective lenses.

"We get him when the FBI's through with him," Darcy said. "The murder's in our jurisdiction."

Webb rubbed his eyes and took a sip of his cold coffee. He'd been up all night. "You get him, Darce."

"He's ours, Webb."

Webb shook his head. "I'm not going to taint this one. You got a clean case."

"You don't taint it," she said. "You solved it."

He smiled at her, liking that loyalty, knowing that sometimes this was where friendship hid — in the purposeful forgetting of important details. "I added local knowledge."

"Crucial local knowledge."

"Nothing more than some interviews would have provided."

"But not within the right amount of time. We solved this while he was still in transit—"

Webb held up his hand, stopped her. "Darce, he screwed my sister, remember?"

"Oh," Darcy sighed. "A jury'd love that."

"Wouldn't they, though?"

She took out a pack of cigarettes, tamped it, then reached inside. It was empty. She crumpled it and threw it at the wastebasket, missing, as usual. "How bad do you want him?"

"Bad enough," Webb said, "to get out of the way."

"He sure ruined a lot of lives."

"He did that," Webb said. "And some of the lives ruined themselves."

Thirty years of police work. Thirty years, and he finally caught the man he'd wanted to catch all along. Webb stepped outside the station into a pale peach and orange dawn. The snow reflected the sun, making the whole city and the lake beyond look rosy.

But he couldn't claim credit, and he wasn't sure he wanted to. He wasn't sure he'd be a hero in his sister's eyes.

He sighed, ran his hand through his hair, and felt the stress of the last twenty-four hours in the oily strands. A shower, breakfast at a diner, and then he'd see Flo. He'd have to work on her now. She couldn't live in silent hope anymore. She couldn't play the victim any longer. If he were prosecuting, he'd call her as a character witness, and he'd make sure to have her talk about the double-cross, the first double-cross on Tom Johanssen's record.

She'd have to do it with Johanssen sitting across from her, older now, but still handsome, and rich enough to have real smart attorneys at his side. She'd finally have to stop taking responsibility for Tom Johanssen's actions. She'd have to see him as he was.

Just as Webb had had to do.

He'd felt that little stab of betrayal in the police station, when his hunch rose to the forefront of his mind. He'd identified the body. He'd put himself on the line for Tom Johanssen once again. Believing the hype, believing the image, and almost letting the bastard go.

Again.

Webb had lied to Darcy. It wasn't because of the future court case that he'd stepped aside. That was a good superficial reason, but not the true one.

The true one was that he didn't want to see the fallout from Tom Johanssen's latest double-cross. Before, the victims had been his wife and kids, and Flo. This time Johanssen'd set up his whole family, his folks, his brothers, his ex-wife's new husband, and an entire town. He'd used the animus he'd created thirty-three years ago as a smokescreen to cover his flight to a new life.

At the expense of his ex-wife, his children, and one reasonably successful California computer consultant who had the misfortune to resemble Tom Johanssen enough to fool people who hadn't seen him in years.

Local knowledge.

It worked both ways.

Webb got into his car. He felt as if a burden had lifted, as if the dark cloud he'd been living under had finally passed by. He could move on now, maybe even escape the black-and-white winters, find a place with a bit of nuance, a bit of gray.

He turned the car around and headed east, into the light.

Into the warmth.

LONES SEIBER

Icarus

FROM *Indiana Review*

LATE THAT AFTERNOON, they were ordered from the crippled field. Sweat streaked sunburned faces and soaked their prison blues. To the west, the sun had grown huge and crimson as it nipped the horizon; broken strings of pink clouds, the tops darkening to purple and black, drifted above its crest. Ramsey hadn't seen it from such a perspective, not segmented by chainlink or razor wire, in years. Although shadows had grown long and distended, it would be midnight before the heat would abate. The monotonous drone of insects, awakened by twilight, sounded like rapid, wireless static.

He and the others who had searched were shackled from hand to foot and then chained together. As they shuffled toward the Bluebird, prodded in the back with shotgun barrels if they stumbled, the links rattled like tempered wind chimes. After climbing aboard, they were herded to the rear into a steel mesh cage from which the seats had been removed and the windows blackened and barred. Since the bus had remained at the field all afternoon, the bare metal sides could sear flesh, so they sat on the floor, in the center of the cage, huddled back to back, arms resting on folded legs. Webster's body had not been loaded. Ramsey assumed he lay where he had been killed, submerged in the sea of oats.

After they were counted, a guard, wearing a dun-colored uniform, slammed and locked the narrow sheet-steel door. He stepped to the side, peering through the mesh, and flashed a whiskered, yellow grin as he rattled the keys, like ringing a bell. He was just one of many, all seeming emotionally cloned, governing Ramsey's life, shamelessly flaunting their authority and license to abuse. Most, it comforted him to hope, probably despised their plight as much as he did his. He imagined them living in dented trailers, strewn like discarded cans along unnamed dirt roads, some alone, drinking themselves to sleep while watching reality TV; others with bitchy, pregnant wives and burdensome children running wild.

While Ramsey and the others waited, sweltering, body odor thick, the guards opened a cooler. They popped tops and guzzled beer. With his free hand, the driver twisted the key. The starter growled, slowing with each rotation, until just when it seemed it might expire, the engine coughed and backfired to idle. He shoved the floor shift forward several times, stomping the clutch and scraping gears until the transmission engaged, the bus lurching ahead, the driver struggling to steady the steering wheel with one hand. Cans, some trailing foam, sailed out the open door. The interior began filling with a thin blue haze and the stench of burned oil and spent gasoline. The bus wobbled along the rutted dirt road, the chassis grating like a rusted hinge.

Although residents had named the squalid settlement Carson Springs, as the town grew, the artesian sources and natural springs, which once fed twisting, unmolested streams churning over stones abraded smooth by time, had been harnessed and diverted through hand-hewn canals leading to the town. The clay banks of the depleted streams became etched with gaping cracks, the waterless depths littered with skeletal remains, the bordering forests withered and broken.

Before the townspeople arrived to civilize the town by building the first church and banning the sale of liquor, ancient, nihilistic pioneers, with a penchant for women who were not delicate, had subsisted for decades on the same land, distilling, fishing, hunting, and enduring hardships they felt earned them an endowed immunity from newly imposed limits. But when one of the original settlers lethally avenged a "squatter's" intrusion, he was tried and sentenced to death. Most of the residents, including children, attended the execution, which had become a social event. The condemned, his expression defiant, his hands tied behind, sat backward on a mule. A crudely fashioned noose, the attached rope dangling loose from a live oak limb, was strung around his neck. A minister read the Twenty-Third Psalm. After he sanctimoniously proclaimed "Amen" and slapped the Bible closed, the sheriff re-read the jury's verdict and then nodded to the animal's owner, who cracked a whip across the animal's flank. It bolted, leaving the man dangling. The drop had not broken his neck, so for several minutes his legs stroked the air, as if he were trying to run.

No one claimed the body, because those who had first settled the land with him had already packed up and moved, rather than conform to flags and the Word, northwest to distant mountains where they hoped to find a less troubled land.

Years later, after the town had grown and graveled streets had been named, the state paved SR 92 which ran straight 30 miles from the state line, north past Carson Springs, to connect with highways leading eventually to the Canadian border and both coasts. Sheltered by ridges dense with hardwood and pine, the town grew in the center of a copiously fertile valley bordering the prairie, the western landscape featureless and barren and worn, the horizon, wavering with the sun, stretching between blue mountain ranges so distant they looked like fallen clouds.

George Smiley built Carson Springs' first store, a sagging building, which looked as if it had been constructed of driftwood, sitting skewed on a rock foundation. George sold anything one might need, merchandise in disarray, pots and pans, yokes and bridles, hanging, in no particular order, from rafters and unadorned walls. For a while he sold the only gasoline in Carson Springs, dispensed from a single ethyl pump in the middle of the furrowed dirt parking lot, the Sinclair dinosaur standing on its pedestal out by SR 92. Even after Fred's Market, a spotty, regional chain, moved in with lower prices, wire buggies, clean-shaven clerks in white aprons, and two grades of Esso, most folks still, out of loyalty, shopped with George, a generous man who would gladly run a tab for anyone who walked through the door.

Why his wife left and moved in with her sister back in St. Louis, no one ever knew, not even his boy, Dewey. Some gossiped of another man, others of a divine irrationality unique to the frontier, compelling some to flee, others to wander wide-eyed, speaking in tongues, into the desert mists where nothing can survive except sooty gray rats that evolution has taught to place only two feet at a time against the blistering sand. Within a year George came down with cancer, and he succumbed six months after the diagnosis. Most folks felt one thing led to the other.

"Doctors said he was eat up," the story went, "but he never was the same after she took off. I think that's what brought it on. His body and spirit just give up. It happens, you know?"

Dewey tried running the store for a while after his father's death, but everyone knew he was a braggart and a drunk, usually opening late, if at all. The old loyalties soon faded after George's death, and Fred's became the place to shop. One Saturday, when he woke with a hangover and no money, Dewey held a sale, everything for whatever folks felt like paying. People filled toe sacks and cardboard boxes, while Dewey berated their treachery and rattled change into a metal pail beside the door. By noon the shelves and racks were bare. The building wasn't worth much, and you couldn't give the land away, since so much of it went unclaimed, so Dewey walked away without bothering to lock the door.

Once inside the double electric gates, they stumbled from the bus. The guards who had transported them removed the shackles; two guards responsible for the entrance counted them again. One stood on the threshold of the control booth, hands plunged in his back pockets, his lower lip packed with tobacco. The other called out names listed on a clipboard, holding it at arm's length and squinting. Each inmate responded with eyes submissively averted. When he came to Webster's name, he nodded before calling it louder than the others, his voice slick with contempt, and then, after making a show of the intervening pause, marked through it with a flourish.

The shuffle of voices, colliding, indistinguishable, filling Ramsey's days on the crowded compound had by that time been confined behind locked dormitory doors, the grounds empty except for prowling guards, the only sounds a distant whippoorwill, its plaintive cry unanswered, and an annoyingly nasal female voice barking coded numbers and names from portable radios clipped to the guards' belts. Night had silenced the insects inspired by the gloaming.

Since the other inmates had been fed, the guards led them into the empty chow hall and handed each a standard sack meal: a stale bologna sandwich, the bread soggy with mayonnaise, an apple, and a glass of lemonade, which most never drank. A black working the kitchen had been caught pissing in the vat. They ate at burled pine picnic tables. Although posted regulations forbade speaking in the chow hall, during scheduled meals, with hundreds of inmates shuttling in and out by dorm assignments, each allowed fifteen minutes to eat, the scraping of feet along with the clanging of metal plates and utensils being tossed onto a conveyor created a cacophony indigenous with captivity. However, with so few in the cavernous room, a fork dropped inadvertently, keys rattling, a sneeze, a murmuring between guards, whispers, almost, became amplified in the spaciousness, echoing, as if one wall were answering another, like spirits conversing. The relative silence tempted Ramsey to shout his name, just to hear it repeated, softer each time until it dissolved to silence, like dying, he thought, without the attendant trauma, the most he could hope for, but there would be sanctions if he dared, a period of solitary confinement, like living in a shadowy cave, or worse: the loss of his windows.

After Fred's came to Carson Springs, Sonic followed a couple of years later, the Desert Inn Motel soon after that, and then, given its logistical advantages and undemanding labor pool, Chrysler built a small factory at the end of a new, quarry rock road to manufacture radiator thermostats. At times it employed as many as thirty people. With approval from Fred's corporate management, the city council began planning to expand the local store into a truck stop to service the eighteen-wheelers speeding by each day in increasing numbers. Excavation had begun for the additional underground diesel tanks, but then, as part of a flood control project, the Army Corps of Engineers dammed the Tamaha River where it sliced deep between precipitous slopes in the neighboring state, which heartily endorsed the endeavor because of the recreational areas for boating along with a market for lakeside lots it would create. Within two years, however, a tongue of warm, murky water began filling low-lying areas several miles north of Carson Springs. Lacking political influence, their protests were harmlessly absorbed by a bureaucracy designed to quell dissent. SR 92 soon disappeared beneath 10 feet of brackish water. Eventually the Corps began regulating the spillways and the advance that had become a languorous but methodical flood abated, but Carson Springs had become the end of the road. SR 92 emerged many miles to the north across the great, stagnant lake at a town named Vale, but it couldn't be seen even on the clearest day.

*

Ramsey lived with almost two hundred inmates, mostly blacks, far fewer whites, and one Ukrainian who didn't speak English, but after having his head pummeled like a punching bag a few times, translation became unnecessary. Housed in one of eight dormitories, each a dusty, concrete block building with galvanized roofs and epoxied slabs, iron-framed, double bunk beds filled the interiors, three rows down the center and two, parallel to the others, lining the longer walls, the beds about eighteen inches apart. For his first two years, Ramsey was assigned a lower bunk, the head against the wall. And then his longevity and lack of disobedience merited an upper bunk, but still with nothing behind but reinforced concrete block. Two years later, he was moved to an upper bunk with a window behind, and then, on the anniversary of his eighth year, an upper bunk in a corner with a view out two windows, one of four coveted locations.

With access to their factory no longer profitable, Chrysler moved the operation to Mexico, leaving the workers staring in dismay at the plant's shuttered doors and despising more each day the unassuming migrants laboring in the fields. Someone artlessly sprayed *FUCK YOU* across the front wall in red. Then the bank foreclosed on the Desert Inn, with its ten rooms and pink flamingos standing crooked on wire legs. One morning the dark-skinned woman with a red spot on her forehead who ran it loaded her station wagon and headed south, leaving the beds made with clean sheets and the green neon sign on SR 92 blinking VACANCY. And then the Sonic, whose presence had been overly ambitious, dismissed its employees with two days' notice and $100 severance. Fred's remained in business, but half its employees lost their jobs. The pits that had been excavated for the proposed diesel tanks filled with muddy water and became breeding ponds for mosquitoes during the summers. The population of Carson Springs began aging and declining, so when the state proposed building a prison nearby, no one objected, the citizenry fearing poverty more than the threat of escaped convicts.

After they had eaten, lines were assembled outside and then began moving in different directions toward their respective dorms. Cameras mounted high on building corners swiveled to track each group. Ramsey had never been on the compound at night, the grounds so fully lighted that no shadows were cast; no trees, no leaves to mottle the ground; the stars, whose humbling canopy he missed, blinded.

The noise inside the dorm, without rhythm or tone, seemed more aggravating than usual after the relative quiet of the day. Some played cards or Scrabble while others lay in bunks staring emptily with hands laced on their stomachs; a few, who knew how, were reading. Showers were over, but since Ramsey and the others who had searched were late through no fault of their own, the guard magnanimously turned the water on for three minutes, reminding them that he was not required to, and handed each a clean towel. Ramsey always tried to shower immediately after supper, before the tiled floors became slick from inmates masturbating with impunity in the large, open stall.

Once in his bunk, he tried to block the noise, broken words mostly and mirthless laughter, by remembering its absence outside, as if by concentrating, everything around him could be locked in a cell of its own. Solitude, besides freedom, was the thing he missed most. Squinting against blinding fluorescents dangling just out of reach, he woke each morning groggy-eyed to screaming bells, which marked the sequence of relentless rituals dictating his life. During the day, if the din became unbearable, he'd retreat to the remotest corner of the recreation field to try and escape the sounds, but even there the air was stained by cop-killer rap drifting from ghetto blasters inside the open shed where the blacks, their dreadlocks dangling like willow bangs, worked with weights to further enhance arms so bloated they looked like wings. While many whites withered as captives, laboriously shuffling their feet, as if somehow gravity had been heightened, most blacks seemed to thrive, strutting the compound, reveling in the social reversal.

Someone asked about Webster. Ramsey told them what he knew. Although he tried to push it from his mind, the image of Webster lying among the crushed oats, the top of his head scalloped away, burned with a sunken anger. Ramsey doubted the body would be claimed, most outside allegiances, including his own, surviving no more than a year. To him, it seemed inevitable. How many weekends could they sit with families and ask about a sister or a brother, a father or mother, a son or daughter, and speak hopefully of a future that might never come? On Sundays, some stood as close as permitted to the front gate, plaintively watching the visitors enter, waiting for someone they knew, or perhaps, expecting no one, trying to remember what it was like to be free and have someone care.

Webster would be buried without ceremony or marker in an overgrown field that bordered the dump; no one would mourn his loss.

As they had boarded the Bluebird at the field that afternoon, emergency vehicles began arriving, their red and blue lights turning the twilight into a violence of slashing red and blue. And then the business of assigning responsibility, if possible, for the girl began; cameras flashed; men, slipping white coveralls over their street clothes and snapping on latex gloves, crawled on hands and knees, sifting through the maze of stems, dropping minute pieces of this and that into clear plastic bags, a wooden stake with a Day-Glo ribbon stapled to the top, marking the location.

After Dewey ran through the money from the sale at his father's store, he took a job loading feed at Slater's Mill for six dollars an hour. On that Tuesday he called in sick, as he often did, and drove out to the abandoned factory in his pickup, an oxidized blue Dodge with rusted rocker panels and a primered front fender. He emptied what remained in a bottle he'd stashed under the seat and napped until it wore off. He woke with a boner and a parched throat. He checked himself in the rearview mirror. His eyes were bloodshot, and he hadn't shaved in days. He raked a hand through his hair, reset the mirror, and headed into town, empty cans and broken tools rattling around the truck bed. After passing the old trailer sitting on a red clay lot scooped out of a loblolly pine thicket that ran from the factory to the edge of town, he saw the girl, walking toward him, her hair braided to the waist, a book bag dangling from her shoulder; he thought nothing of it at first, but then he slowed and stopped beside her, his elbow crooked out the window.

"Hey," he said, and smiled. "What's your name?"

"Melissa Gayle," she said, squinting against the sun and shading her eyes. She wore a starched white blouse and a plaid skirt, the hem several inches above her white socks and black patent leather shoes.

"Going home?"

"Yeah."

He opened the door by reaching through the window and stepped out, looking both ways along the road.

"You know me. You and your momma used to shop at my store."

"I remember."

"Come on, I'll give you a ride home."

She pointed in the direction of the trailer.

"It ain't that far."

He took her arm.

"Come on, I wanted to talk to your momma anyway."

He lifted her into the cab and shoved her to the passenger's side. He tossed the book bag into the bed, started the truck, and turned around.

"That's where I live," she said as he sped past the trailer toward the abandoned factory.

An old singlewide sat down the factory road from what townspeople called "the junction to nowhere," beneath a large willow, its twisted mane reaching the ground and bunching atop the sloppily tarred roof. Although within walking distance of town, no other dwellings were built close enough to be called neighboring. The trailer had been placed there fifteen years before by the town's only realtor, who also sold and serviced farm implements. He posted a rental sign in the front window. People had moved in and out, none staying more than a year. Most were drifters and drunks who had to be forcibly evicted. It had been empty for several months when the woman showed up one day in a fully packed, humpbacked Oldsmobile station wagon and rented the place, just her and the little girl. No one ever saw her with a man or any strangers entering or leaving the trailer. At first she drove to town, but something happened to the Oldsmobile. The tires eventually dry-rotted flat.

The woman was bone thin, birdlike, even, pale-skinned, with a long face and large eyes, her hair, the color of stone, tied behind in a bun. Like her mother, the girl was all knees and elbows but with red hair and freckles. Each month the woman deposited a railroad pension check in the bank, paying cash for food, always counting her change carefully. If someone spoke, she would respond politely with a shy smile.

The woman enrolled the girl in Rosewater Elementary and Middle School, the only one in the county.

"She was never a problem," said one of the teachers.

"Smart as a whip," said another.

The woman had even invited the visitation ladies inside the first Thursday night they came to call, fixing coffee, chatting civilly, promising to attend Sunday school, which she did the following weekend. The women gave *Jesus and His Disciples* coloring books and a box of crayons to the girl before they left, holding a brief prayer meeting at the opened door.

Around dusk on the day Dewey had picked the girl up, he drove back from the factory alone, both arms itching from weed rash and insect bites. His hands trembled. He passed through town, honking and waving at the sheriff, who sat outside the office, elbows draped over the back of a wooden bench. Dewey drove north on SR 92 toward the water, the lights in his rearview mirror having vanished, and turned off onto a grassy path matted down by truck tires that few people knew about, and those who did held their tongues. Sumac and low, broad-leafed trees obscured the entrance. Despite idling the truck in gear, it still bottomed a couple of times, limbs clawing the windshield and scraping the sides, cottontails scampering out of the beams. An old bootlegger named Mel lived at the end in a two-room log cabin with hubcaps nailed along the front wall. Several rusted cars sat on concrete blocks, hoods yawning open, an engine dangling by chain from a thick sycamore limb. A reflection of the moon rippled in the lake behind his cabin.

Dewey took a quick step back when a German shepherd, snarling and baring its teeth, lunged at him as Mel cracked the door.

"I'm tapped out," the old man growled in a smoker's voice, holding the dog's collar with both hands. "Come back in a day or two."

"I need something now," Dewey said, opening his hands submissively.

The old man kicked the door shut.

Dewey drove back to town. A dually pulling a carrier full of bawling cattle passed in the opposite direction, the radio blaring music. He stopped across from the courthouse, under a streetlight, and counted his money. He had enough for the 30-mile trip down SR 92 to an all-night liquor store just across the state line.

*

Searchers found no trace of the girl at the dump or around the abandoned factory. Fishermen launched jon boats into the murky lake, probing shadowed marshes along the shore, but soon abandoned the effort. Some in hip boots waded the drainage ditches surrounding a large field banded by barbed wire and choked with oats ready for harvest, looking for evidence of damaged and broken stalks, suspicious trails, all the obvious places where someone might have thoughtlessly discarded a child. No such evidence was found.

Vultures were a common sight, floating in imprecise circles on thermal pillows, constantly trolling, so few people paid them any mind, but when they began drifting above the field in greater numbers, the implication became clear.

Since the field was so large, over a square mile, and the crop so dense, the sheriff asked the prison for help. Ramsey and other inmates, all with records free of disciplinary infractions, were caged in the Bluebird and driven to the field. Flanked by guards armed with shotguns, they stepped unshackled from the bus.

Determined to complete the search before dark, the sheriff assembled two lines at opposite ends of the field, each to proceed methodically toward the center. Due to the size of the field and the waist-high crop, one line could not see the other. Except for the vultures and strings of manmade clouds dispersing as soon as they formed, nothing occluded the sun, inclined toward afternoon and punishing without quarter, shirts sweat-plastered to itching backs, the air thick with heat that Ramsey felt through the soles of his brogans. A shuffle of birdcalls, along with the croaking of frogs and the ratcheting sound of summer insects, formed an unscripted, ubiquitous chorus. Dragonflies rested their twin sets of veined, translucent wings by lighting atop the swaying pods for a moment, their bodies swathed in twisted rainbows. Mosquitoes began swarming and feasting upon exposed skin. No-see-'ems clogged nostrils and ears.

They waited for what seemed an unnecessarily long time as a deputy communicated with someone on the other end by portable radio. Finally he blew a whistle for them to proceed. That the crop would be damaged could not be helped. Men and women stretched across the field, each a few yards from another, moving deliberately, arms extended, hands brushing the ripened pods aside, scanning the ground. Even the owner, his wife and sons, and their migrant workers, chattering in their own private language, joined the search. As Ramsey pushed ahead, his pants brushing the stalks aside made a sibilant sound with each step, like breath being expelled, as if he were treading upon a living being.

Although it would last less than a day, Ramsey relished the freedom, not freedom with the sense of being unfettered, but the quiet and the vast prospect above, which seemed unlike the one visible from the compound.

At first he wasn't sure. The shimmering horizon distorted what appeared to be figures spread across the field, but then heads and torsos began to form, as if rising out of the earth.

As the two lines came within sight of each other, those with Ramsey glanced at one another, expressions bemused, catching the faintest odor carried by shifting breezes, at first dismissing it as an aberration of the heat, until it grew stronger and could no longer be ignored. His line tightened and closed on itself, approaching the fence, hands covering noses and mouths as the stench became nauseous. They stomped the oats flat, trying to find the source. The one who found her, an older man wearing overalls and a straw hat, shouted and raised his hand. He tied a red bandanna across his face. Dozens crowded around the body. For a careless moment, guards, their weapons lowered, forgot about the inmates. The girl lay naked, her arms and legs splayed, as if she had been tossed over the barbed wire from the access road just a few yards away. Decomposition and the feeding of scavengers led to speculation that she had been killed soon after she went missing. Beetles and maggots swarmed the frail body, a haze of green-backed flies hovering with a low, malevolent hum. Her face was unrecognizable, the skin covering her body drawn tight to the point of splitting and darkened as if sheathed in teal. The time elapsed since she'd disappeared had allowed the oats to right and repair themselves, concealing the body. A thickset woman, in a long, flowered dress with puffed sleeves and wearing a denim bonnet, dropped to her knees, and with hands clasped under her chin began to pray aloud, but no one else made a sound. A female cardinal, its color robbed by gender, squatted on the top strand of the nearby fence, bobbing its tail for balance.

Neither Ramsey nor anyone else had noticed the black named Webster back away until he was several yards from the group and someone shouted. It was as if they all had been awakened from a trance, requiring a moment to orient themselves. That's when he began running, his arms and legs flailing like a string puppet, as if he were frolicking rather than trying to escape, which, with the thickness of oats, would have been impossible. Without being ordered to, he stopped and turned, facing his captors. He ripped his prison-blue shirt free and tossed it aside. Bathed by the sun, his sweat-drenched body seemed to glow. He held his arms straight to the sides, smiled, and dropped his head back. For a moment, with only an unblemished sky behind and his upper body seeming to emerge from a blur of gold, he appeared suspended. Then a shotgun exploded. Webster dropped from sight, the moment embedded in Ramsey's memory. He thought of the Zapruder film, as Kennedy clutched his throat, a crimson spray blooming behind, marking the moment of his death, and of his uncle, who raised him and thankfully had passed on before Ramsey was disgraced, setting a watermelon on a stump for target practice, the pulp and seeds scattering like brain tissue and bits of skull. Everyone rushed to where Webster lay, everyone except Ramsey. He remained beside the girl's body. It didn't sicken him to stare at her remains; neither did it fill him with sorrow nor a sense of outrage. Could he remember a time when it might? Or had he evolved antithetically? After so many years, he couldn't be sure.

While the others huddled, staring at Webster with train-wreck fascination, Ramsey could have dropped to his knees and crawled away, obscured by the oats. In the confusion he might not have been missed for at least half an hour; by that time he could have been well on his way, and with night coming on, an effective search could not have been launched before morning, but then what? He had nowhere to go, no plan, a short-lived escape for which the consequences would have been severe.

After leaving the liquor store, Dewey felt like celebrating, one hand resting atop the steering wheel, the other wrapped around the neck of a bottle of low-grade alcohol. He sang along tunelessly to a cassette playing "You're the Reason God Made Oklahoma," his voice switching from normal to an annoying falsetto as Shelly West alternated verses with David Frizzell. But then, another sound. He flicked the volume down. A rod knocking, like a morning-after headache. He pumped the brakes up and pulled into a 7-Eleven. He got out and lifted the hood. He uncapped a gallon jug of recy-

cled forty-weight and filled a dented tin can that he then carried to
the front. Acrid smoke spewed into his face when he spilled some
on the exhaust manifold. He lowered the hood but then raised it
again when it failed to latch and slammed it shut with both hands.
A jagged chunk of Bondo fell off.

After crossing back into the state, a colonnade of grain eleva-
tors, which had stood empty for years, flashed momentarily in
the sweep of passing light, but then no other structures, no lights
ahead, behind, or to the sides, nothing but 30 miles of untamed
forests between him and Carson Springs. A foraging possum wad-
dling across the road turned to face the truck, its eyes glowing red
when caught in the beams.

"Roadkill!" Dewey laughed and swerved to crush it beneath the
left front tire, but as he did, the right side dropped onto the shoulder. He jerked the wheel to the left, tipping the truck. It rolled
down an embankment, jettisoning metal and glass, until it came
to rest on its roof in a muddy swale, steam hissing from under
the hood. Dewey lay broken and bloodied on the shoulder where
he died, but not quickly. Sometime later, after the lights of the
crumpled truck had gone dead and the radiator expelled itself,
an eighteen-wheeler, its cab glowing yellow, sped past. The driver
glanced at the road, not realizing he was lost, and then at a swindle
sheet spread across the steering wheel. The book bag had tumbled
from the bed of Dewey's truck and come to rest beside the road's
segmented center. The tractor's front tandems ripped it apart,
shredded paper swirling upward in their wake like confused but-
terflies.

Robert Earl had seen it in others, tradition dictating their lives,
growing old in family albums that would someday be put aside and
forgotten; at times, when alone, their gaze fixed at some middle
distance, wondering if there might have been more. And he had
tried it himself, a marriage that led to divorce, his wife married to
another. Two boys he'd never wanted, calling another man father.
But he thought of it, the way destiny had wound its way through
his life, as just the way things were, random, one event following
another capriciously, without pattern. The secret, he concluded,
was to expect nothing and accept the inevitable. He paid what the
court had deemed fair, and for that he got to spend two weekends

a month with his boys. He'd rather have not seen them at all, just in passing, maybe, but it would have been unseemly and injurious to his image. Although they were grown and gone, for years he tolerated the four days by watching them fight and buying whatever they wanted. He thought of it as penance.

By the time the cruiser, its lights off, pulled in between the willow and the disabled Oldsmobile, it was almost dark; the trailer windows glowed. He had been elected to eight two-year terms as sheriff, so it was something he'd done many times: telling parents that their son or daughter had been crushed beyond recognition in a grinding head-on collision, or a wife that her husband had dropped dead of a coronary while counting his change at Fred's, or apportioning anguish and relief in an emergency room, reading from a list following a fatal school bus crash. It had nothing to do with him, and he ordered his life so it wouldn't.

Two deputies accompanied him, one driving, the other in the back seat, not for support for what some might consider a trying moment of responsibility, but more a demonstration of authority. Once, after leaving the washroom at Sonic and zipping his pants as he walked along the hallway leading to the serving line, he heard someone yell, "All your fuckin' cash, man." He stopped and pulled his .357 Magnum from its holster to shoulder level, the barrel pointed at the ceiling. He could see the robber's back reflected in the front window. He then stepped clear of the dividing wall and leveled the pistol, which was only inches from the temple of the robber, who held a Glock on the frightened cashier.

"Drop it," Robert Earl said, but pulled the trigger before the man had time to respond.

They closed the restaurant for half a day to clean shards of skull and bloody tissue from the fry baskets, the condiment bins, and the walls.

He and two deputies attended the funeral, standing to the side, shoulder to shoulder, hats in place, as the dead man's brothers comforted their mother. He and his men were not there as a matter of respect, or to express regret for having done what had to be done, or to solicit some expression of forgiveness or at least understanding, but as a warning, much as he and his men in the 1st Cavalry had done in Vietnam by tucking death cards in the mouths of fallen Vietcong.

The door to the trailer opened as they climbed from the cruiser and placed ten-gallon hats atop their heads, leveling the brims. The woman stood, hands on hips, as a silhouette, the light behind seeming to bend away and around her so that she appeared as a stick figure, slight in stature but intimidating and anonymous.

"You found her," the woman said in a flat, hollow voice. It was not a question.

"Yes, ma'am," Robert Earl said just as dispassionately. "I'm afraid so."

She stepped back into the light and, by casually opening her hand away from her side, invited them in. On a coffee table with a glass insert, an open coloring book with crayons scattered across the top.

After they sat, backs rigid, on the end of their bunks nearest the aisle for the eleven o'clock count, and the lights were turned off, the snoring and the stench of near-naked bodies sweating in the still, humid air began. Ramsey lay on his stomach, chin resting on his laced fingers. He would not fall asleep easily, and when he did, he was still vigilant, with an edgy awareness, like some exposed animal, in peril, always seeking but never finding shelter. He watched the field, a gentle cross breeze caressing his face. Although he could not see the men still searching for clues, flashing lights sweeping in ocher waves across a shelf of fog sliding unevenly like silt low above the field said that some remained. He thought of Webster, not of the moment when his head exploded, but of the moment, the timelessness of it, between the decision to leave and the end, which had not really been an ending at all. Most would say it had been an act of desperation, which if reflected upon rationally would never have been attempted, and, after a cursory investigation, which would exonerate the guard who had fired, that was how it would most likely be reported, as an aborted escape, but Ramsey alone knew he had succeeded, that, like a translucent cicada husk clinging to a winter-stripped limb, Webster had left nothing behind to kill.

Ramsey had seen him on the compound but noticed nothing to distinguish him from hundreds of others, most, like Ramsey, with little hope of ever being released, and if they were, of use to no one, danglers, feeding along the edges. But Webster had not been just another jailhouse punk. He had had vision and, when he had smiled and offered himself sacrificially, had imparted to Ramsey the gift of clarity.

Without reference he had no sense of time, but it must have been close to midnight before the flashing lights surrendered the night; a razor-thin sliver of grinning moon hovered, its edges feathered by mist, as the great, silent field began repairing itself.

CHARLES TODD

Trafalgar

FROM *The Mammoth Book of Historical Crime Fiction*

Mumford, Cambridgeshire, 1920

The old dog died at two o'clock, thrown unceremoniously out of his warm bed by the fire and onto the cold January ground.

And it was this fact that troubled Rutledge as he delved deeper into the mystery of Sir John Middleton's death.

It was the housekeeper-cum-cook, gone to the village for onions for Sir John's dinner, who found the old dog lying by the wall under the study window. Mrs. Gravely, stooping to touch the graying head, said, "Oh, my dear!" aloud—for the old dog had been company in the house for her as well—and went inside to deliver the sad news.

Opening the door into the study as she was pulling her wool scarf from her head, she said anxiously, "Sir John, as I was coming in, I found—"

Breaking off, she cried out in horror, ran to the body on the floor at the side of the Georgian desk, and bent to take one hand in her own as she knelt stiffly to stare into the bloody mask that was her employer's face.

Her first thought was that he'd fallen and struck the edge of the desk, she told Rutledge afterward. "I feared he'd got up from his chair to look for Simba, and took a dizzy turn. He had them sometimes, you know."

The doctor had already confirmed this, and Rutledge nodded encouragingly, because he trusted Mrs. Gravely's honesty. He hadn't been particularly impressed by the doctor's manner.

Rutledge had been in Cambridge on Yard business, to identify a man brought in by the local constabulary. McDaniel was one of the finest forgers in the country, and it had appeared that the drunken Irishman, taken up after a brawl in a pub on the outskirts of town, was the man the police had been searching for since before the Great War. He fitted the meager description sent round to every police station in the country. In the event, he was not their man — red hair and ugly scar on the side of the face notwithstanding. But Rutledge had a feeling that the McDaniel they wanted had slipped away in the aftermath of the brawl. The incarcerated man had rambled on about the cousin who would sort out the police quick enough, if he were there. When the police arrived at the lodgings that their man in custody had shared with his cousin, there was no one else there — and no sign that anyone else had ever been there. The case had gone cold, and Rutledge was preparing to return to the Yard when the chief constable came looking for him.

"Sir John Middleton was murdered in his own home," Rutledge was told. "I want his killer, and I've asked the Yard to take over the inquiry. You're to go there now, and I'll put it right with the chief superintendent. The sooner someone takes charge, the better."

And it was clear enough that the chief constable knew what he was about. For the local constable, a man named Forrest, was nervously pacing the kitchen when Rutledge got there, and the inspector who had been sent for from Cambridge had already been recalled. The body still lay where it had been found, pending Rutledge's arrival, and according to Forrest, no one had been interviewed.

Thanking him, Rutledge went into the study to look at the scene.

Middleton lay by the corner of his desk, one arm outstretched as if pleading for help.

"He was struck twice," a voice said behind him, and Rutledge turned to find a thin, bespectacled man standing in the doorway. "Dr. Taylor," he went on. "I was told to wait in the parlor until you got here. The first blow was from behind, to the back of the head, knocking Sir John down but not killing him. A second blow to the face at the bridge of his nose finished him. I don't know that he saw the first coming. He most certainly saw the second."

"The weapon?"

Taylor shrugged. "Hard to say until I can examine him more closely. Nothing obvious, at any rate."

"Has anything been taken?" Rutledge asked, turning to look at the room. It had not been ransacked. But a thief, knowing what he was after, would not have needed to search. There were framed photographs on the walls, an assortment of weapons—from an Australian boomerang to a Zulu cowhide shield—were arrayed between them, and every available surface seemed to hold souvenirs from Sir John's long career in the army. A Kaiser Wilhelm helmet stood on the little table under the windows, the wooden propeller from a German aircraft was displayed across the tops of the bookshelves, and a half-dozen brass shell casings, most of them examples of trench art, were lined up on a cabinet that held more books.

"You must ask Mrs. Gravely that question. The housekeeper. She's been with him for a good many years. I went through the house, a cursory look after examining the body, to be certain there was no one hiding in another room. I saw nothing to indicate robbery."

"Any idea when he was killed?"

"We can pinpoint the time fairly well from other evidence. When Mrs. Gravely left to go into Mumford, he was alive and well, because she went to the study to ask if there were any letters she could take to the post for him. She was gone by her own account no more than three quarters of an hour, and found him lying as you see him when she returned. At a guess, I'd say he died between two and two-thirty."

Rutledge nodded. "Thank you, Doctor. I'll speak to her in a moment."

It was dismissal, and the doctor clearly wished to remain. But Rutledge stood where he was, waiting, and finally the man turned on his heel and left the room. He didn't precisely slam the door in his wake, but it closed with a decidedly loud snap.

Rutledge went to the window and looked out. It was then that he saw the dog lying against the wall, only its feet and tail visible from that angle. Opening the window and bringing in the cold, damp winter air, he leaned out. There was no doubt the animal was dead.

He left the study and went out to kneel by the dog, which did not appear to have been harmed in the attack on Sir John. Death seemed to be due to natural causes and old age, judging from the graying muzzle.

Hamish said, "There's been no one to bury him."

An interesting point. He touched the body, but it was cold, already stiffening.

Back inside, he asked the constable where he could find Mrs. Gravely, and he was told she was in her room at the top of the house.

He knocked, and a husky voice called, "Come in."

It was a small room, but backed up to the kitchen chimney and was warm enough. Castoffs from the main part of the house furnished it: a brass bed, an oak bedside table, two comfortable wing chairs on either side of a square of blue carpet, and a maple table under the half-moon window in the eaves. A narrow bookcase held several novels and at least four cookbooks.

The woman seated in the far wing chair rose as he crossed the threshold. She had been crying, but she seemed to be over the worst of her shock. He noted the teacup and saucer on the table and thought the constable must have brought it to her, not the doctor.

"I'm Inspector Rutledge from Scotland Yard. The chief constable has asked me to take over the inquiry into Sir John's death. Do you feel up to speaking to me?"

"Yes, sir. But I wasn't here, you see. If I had been—"

"If you had been," he said, cutting across her guilt-ridden anguish, "you might have died with him."

She stared at him. "I hadn't thought about that."

He began by asking her about Sir John.

By her account, Sir John Middleton was a retired military man, having served in the Great War. Rutledge could, of his own knowledge, add that Sir John had served with distinction in an HQ not noted for its brilliance. He at least had been a voice of sanity there and was much admired for it, even though it had not aided his army career. Had he made enemies, then?

Hamish said, "Aye, it's possible. He didna fear his killer. Or put up a struggle."

And that was a good point.

"Was he alive when you reached him?"

"Yes, I could see that he was still breathing, ragged though it was. He cried out, just the one word, when I bent to touch him, as if he knew I was there. As if, looking back on it now, he'd held on, waiting for me. Because he seemed to let go then, but I could tell he wasn't dead. I was that torn — leaving him to go for the doctor or staying with him. "

"What did he say? Could you understand him?"

"Oh, yes, sir. *Trafalgar,* he said. Clear as could be. I ran out then, shouting for help, and I met Sam on the road. He was willing to take a message to Dr. Taylor, and so I came back to sit beside Sir John, but I doubt he knew I was there. Still, it wasn't until Dr. Taylor was bending over him that I heard the death rattle. I think he tried to speak again, just before."

The doctor had said nothing about that.

"Are you certain Sir John spoke to Dr. Taylor?"

But Mrs. Gravely was not to be dissuaded. "I was in the doorway, facing Sir John's desk. He had his back to me, the doctor did, but I could just see Sir John's mouth, and his lips moved. I'd swear to that."

"Did he know that it was the doctor who was with him? Was he aware, do you think, of where he was?"

"I can't speak to that, sir. I only know he spoke. And the doctor answered him. "

"Could you hear what was said?"

"No, sir. But I thought he was trying to say the old dog's name. Simba. It means lion, I was told. I can't say whether he was trying to call to him or was asking where he'd got to."

"How did Dr. Taylor respond?"

"I don't know, sir. I could see the doctor rock back on his heels, and then came the death rattle. I knew he was gone. Sir John. There was nothing to be done, was there? The doctor said so, afterward."

Rutledge could hear the echo of the doctor's voice in her words, "I couldn't do anything for him."

"And then?"

"Dr. Taylor turned and saw me in the doorway. He told me to find my coat and go outside to wait for the ambulance. But it wasn't five minutes before he was at the door calling to me and telling me there was no need for the ambulance now. It might as well be the hearse. Well, I could have told him as much, but then he's the one to give evidence at the inquest, isn't he? He had to be certain sure."

Rutledge went back to something Mrs. Gravely had said earlier. "Trafalgar. What does that mean to you?"

The housekeeper frowned. "I don't know, sir. As I remember from school, it was a battle. At sea. When Lord Nelson was killed."

"That's true," Rutledge told her. "It was fought off the coast of Spain in 1805. But Sir John was an army man. And his father and grandfather before him." He had seen the photographs in the study. At least two generations of officers, staring without expression into the lens of the camera. And a watercolor sketch of another officer, wearing a Guards uniform from before the Crimean War.

"Will you come down with me to the study? There are some photographs I'd like to ask you to identify."

"Please, sir," she answered anxiously. "Not if he's still there. I couldn't bear it. But I'll know the pictures, I've dusted them since they were put up there."

"Fair enough. The woman, then, with the braid of her hair encircling the frame."

"That's Lady Middleton, sir, his second wife. Elizabeth, she was. She died in childbirth, and the boy with her. I don't think he ever got over her death. "

"Second wife?"

"He was married before that. To Althea Barnes. She died as well, out in India. He'd tried to persuade her that it was no place for a woman, but she insisted on going with him. Two years later she was dead of the cholera."

"The young man in the uniform of the Buffs?"

"His brother Martin. He died in the first gas attack at Ypres."

"And the old dog, outside the study window. That, I take it, is Simba? When did he die?"

"It was the strangest thing!" Mrs. Gravely told him. "He was lying by the fire, as he always did, when I left for the village. And I come home to find him outside there in the cold. He was still warm, he couldn't have been there very long. I can't think what happened. I come into the study to tell Sir John that, and there *he* was, dying. I couldn't quite take it all in."

He thanked her for her help, and left her there mourning the man she'd served so long and no doubt wondering now what was to become of her.

Sam Hubbard, the farm worker who had gone for Dr. Taylor, had had the foresight to summon the rector as well. Rutledge found him standing in the kitchen talking to Constable Forrest and warming his hands at the cooker, mud on his boots and his face red from the cold.

He turned and gave Rutledge his name, adding, "I've buried the old dog under the apple tree, as Sir John would have wished. They planted that tree together. A pity Sir John can't be buried there as well."

"Did you find anything wrong with the dog? Any signs that he'd been harmed?"

Sam shook his head. "It was old age, and the cold as well, I expect. He was having trouble with his breathing, Simba was."

"Did you work for Sir John?"

"He sent for me when there was heavy work to be done. Mr. Laurence, who lives just down the road, doesn't have enough to keep me busy these days. And in my free time, I did what I could for Sir John. He was a good man. There weren't many like him at HQ. More's the pity."

"In the war, were you?"

"I was. And I have a splinter of shrapnel in my shoulder to prove it."

Rutledge considered him. He'd been coming up the road when Mrs. Gravely had hailed him, but he could just as easily have been going the other way, turning when he heard her and pretending to know nothing about what had happened here in the house. And he'd taken it upon himself to bury the old dog.

"Where were you this afternoon? Before Mrs. Gravely asked your help?"

Sam Hubbard's eyebrows flew up. "Do you think I could have killed Sir John? I'd have died for him, for speaking up during the war and trying to keep as many of us poor bastards alive as he could. They were bloody butchers, save for him. Caring nothing for the men who had to die each time there was a push or a plan. If it was one of the likes of *them* lying dead in the study, you'd have to wonder if I had had a hand in it. But not Sir John."

The passionate denial rang true—but Hubbard had had time to consider the questions the police would be asking. Tell one's self something often enough, and it soon became easier to believe it. Like the rehearsals of an actor learning his part.

Mr. Harris, the rector, was in the parlor. He had seen the body before the constable had got there, and he seemed shaken, standing by the parlor windows with a drink in his hand.

"Dutch courage," he said ruefully, lifting the glass as Rutledge opened the door. "I don't see many murder victims in my patch. And I thank God for that. How is Mrs. Gravely faring?"

"She's a little better, I think. What can you tell me about Sir John? Have you known him very long?"

"I'd describe him as a lonely man," Harris told Rutledge pensively. "I encouraged him to take an interest in village affairs, to see the need for someone of his caliber to serve on the vestry. But he was loath to involve himself here. It's not his home, you know. He was from Hereford, I believe, but sold up and moved here after the war. He said the house was not the same without his wife, and he couldn't bear the *emptiness*—his word. Elizabeth was much younger, you see. Sir John was married twice. Once early on in his career, and then again some months before the fighting began in 1914."

"Did he bring Mrs. Gravely with him from Hereford?" He'd noted her accent was not local.

"Yes, she was taken on by Elizabeth Middleton just before their marriage, and she agreed to stay with him after her mistress died."

"I understand his first wife died in India. Of cholera. Is there any proof of that, do you think? Or do we just have Sir John's word for what happened to her?"

"That's rather suspicious of you!"

"In a murder case, there are few certainties."

"Well, I can only tell you that it's written down in the Middleton family Bible. It's on the bookshelf behind the desk. I've seen the entry."

But what was inscribed in the family Bible was not necessarily witnessed by God, whatever the rector wished to believe.

"Did they get on well?"

"I have no idea. Except that he described Althea Middleton once as headstrong. Apparently she'd insisted on having her way in all things, including going to India."

"Did she also live in Herefordshire?"

"I believe she came from somewhere along the coast. Near Torquay. I went there once on holiday, and knew the area a little. Sir John mentioned her home in connection with my travels. The second Lady Middleton—he called her Eliza—was a love match, certainly on his part. He wore a black armband throughout the war and told me if it hadn't been for his duty, he'd not have been able to go on without her."

"No children of either marriage?"

"None that I ever heard of. Which reminds me, speaking of family. You might include poor Simba in that category. I saw his body there under the window." Harris shook his head. "The dog was devoted to Sir John. I'd see the two of them walking across the fields of an afternoon, when I was on my rounds. I wonder who put him out. It isn't—wasn't—like Sir John. Odd, that, I must say."

"Odd?"

"Yes, he would never have shown Simba the door, not at his advanced age. The dog had belonged to Elizabeth, you see. Sir John had been worried about him since before Christmas, when his breathing seemed to worsen. It got better, but it was a warning, you might say, that his end was near. Sir John would have gone outside with him, and brought him in again as soon as he'd done his business."

"But they walked the fields together?"

"Yes. I meant over the years, you know. Not recently, of course."

Which, Hamish was pointing out, could explain why the killer came to the house rather than accost Sir John on an outing.

But the dog had been with him today, Rutledge replied. *And the dog was put outside. Had the visitor arrived at the door just as his victim was preparing to walk the dog?*

Hamish said, "He was killed in the study, no' in the entry."

"Does Trafalgar mean anything to you?" Rutledge asked Harris.

"It was a great sea battle. And of course it's a cape along the southern Spanish coast. The battle was named for it, I believe."

"That's no' likely to figure largely in a military man's death in Cambridgehire," Hamish commented.

Rutledge thanked the rector, and Harris went in search of Mrs. Gravely, to offer what comfort he could.

There was a tap at the door, and Rutledge went to open it himself.

Dr. Taylor had returned, and nodding over his shoulder to

the hearse from Cambridge, he said, "If you've finished, I'll take charge of the body."

"Yes, go ahead. When will you have your report?"

"By tomorrow morning, I should think. It ought to be fairly straightforward. We have a clear idea of when Mrs. Gravely left for market, and when she returned. And the wounds more or less speak for themselves. I don't expect any surprises."

Nor did Rutledge. But he said, "Have a care, all the same."

Taylor said sharply, "I always do."

Rutledge stepped aside, watching as the men collected Sir John's body from the study and carried it out the door.

As he walked with them to the hearse, one of them said to him, "I was in the war. I'll see he's taken care of." Rutledge nodded, standing in the cold wind until the hearse had turned and made its way back onto the road into Mumford.

As he swung around to go back inside, he saw Mrs. Gravely at an upstairs window, a handkerchief to her mouth, tears running down her cheeks. Behind her stood the rector, a hand on her shoulder for comfort.

Rutledge was glad to shut the door against the wind, and rubbed his palms smartly together as he stood there thinking. Had the killer knocked, he wondered, and waited until Sir John had answered the summons, or had he come in through the unlocked door and made his way to the study?

Hamish said, "He knocked."

"Why are you so certain?" Rutledge answered the voice in his head. It was always there—had been since July of 1916, when Corporal Hamish MacLeod was executed for refusing to carry out a direct order from a superior officer. The price, Rutledge knew, of MacLeod's care of his men, shifting the burden of guilt from his own shoulders to Rutledge's. It had not been easy that day to send weary, sleep-deprived soldiers over the top again and again and again, knowing they would not survive. But orders were orders, and although numbed to the cost, as the battle of the Somme raged on, Rutledge had done what he could to shield them. It hadn't been enough, he knew that, and Hamish knew it. And Hamish had broken first, willing to die himself rather than watch more men sacrificed. The machine-gun nest was impregnable, and every soldier in the line was all too aware of it. No amount of persuasion had shifted Hamish MacLeod from his determination not to lead another attack, and in the end, an example had had to be made.

And Rutledge, well aware that the young Scots corporal would not see England again, had delivered the coup de grâce to the dying man. But Hamish MacLeod did come back—in Rutledge's battered mind: an angry and vengeful voice at first, and then, with time, a relentless companion who yielded no quarter, sharing the days and nights and silent only when Rutledge slept, although dreams often brought him awake again, into Hamish's grip once more.

"Because the man was struck from behind. He wouldna have let a stranger get behind him."

It was a very good point, and Rutledge agreed. A knock, then, and Sir John opened the door to someone he knew. They walked back into the study, and at some point the old dog was put out. Before or after Sir John had been attacked? There was no way of knowing. Yet.

He went into the study and began his search.

He saw the Bible at once, on the shelf just as the rector had told him. Opening it to the parchment pages between the Old and New Testament, Rutledge scanned the record of family marriages, then turned the page to look through the listing of deaths.

There was the entry for Middleton's first marriage, and, in darker ink but the same hand years later, his second. Entries also of his wives' deaths.

Althea Margaret Barnes Middleton, of cholera, he read, with the date and *Calcutta, India* after it.

And then, in a hand that was shaking with grief, *Elizabeth Alice Mowbray Middleton, in childbirth.* Under that, *John Francis Mowbray Middleton, stillborn.*

Putting the Bible back where he found it, Rutledge began to go through the desk drawers. Two of them held sheets of foolscap. He realized that Sir John had been writing his memoirs of the Great War. Glancing through the sheaf of pages, he saw that Middleton had just reached the Somme, in 1916. The next chapter was headed *Bloodbath.* He quickly returned the stack to the drawers, then paused to consider the possibility that Sir John had been killed to stop him from finishing the manuscript. But if that was the case, why leave the pages here, to be found—and possibly completed—by someone else?

Hamish said, "Was it unfinished, or is part missing?"

"I can't be sure." He made a mental note to speak to Harris about the manuscript.

The rest of the desk held nothing of interest, and the bookshelves appeared to be just that—shelves of books the dead man had collected over a lifetime, with no apparent secrets among them.

He saw the small box on a reading table next to the bookshelves, and picked it up. It was very old, he thought, and inlaid with what appeared to be ivory and mother of pearl. Opening it, he looked inside. It was lined with worn silk, but otherwise empty.

As he was putting it back in place, a title in gilt lettering on the shelf by the table caught his eye, and he frowned. *A History of the Barnes Family.*

That was the maiden name of Sir John's first wife. He pulled the volume from the shelf and looked at the title page. There was an inscription on the opposite page: *To Althea, with much love, Papa.* The frontispiece was a painting of a house standing at the edge of what appeared to be a lake, Georgian and foursquare, with a terrace overlooking a narrow garden that ran down to a small boat landing, jutting out into the water. Rutledge turned the book on its side to read the caption.

Trafalgar. Dartmouth, Devon.

He turned to the index and looked for the name there. There were several references to the house as well as the battle. The house, he discovered on page 75, was built in Dartmouth in 1800, on the site of an earlier dwelling, and rechristened Trafalgar after the head of the family had served on HMS *Victory*, Nelson's flagship on that fateful day. The water in front of the house was Dartmouth Harbour.

Going in search of the rector, Rutledge found him having tea with Mrs. Gravely. Harris stood as Rutledge came into the kitchen, saying, "What is it?"

"Just a few more questions," Rutledge said easily. "What do you know about Althea Middleton?"

"Very little," Harris admitted. "Only what Sir John told me over the years."

"Her family is from Dartmouth."

"Yes, as a matter of fact, I told you she had lived near Torquay. Not surprising. Her father was a navy man, like his father before

him, apparently—and probably his father's father as well, for all I
know." He smiled wryly. "Sir John told me once that her father was
appalled that she had fallen in love with an army officer. He had
felt that nothing less than a naval captain would suit."

"One of her ancestors served aboard *Victory*."

"Did he indeed! I don't think Sir John ever mentioned that fact.
Just that hers was a naval family and he'd enjoyed more than a few
arguments with her father about sea power and the course of the
empire."

"Sir John also appears to have been writing a history of the
Great War."

"He always said he was tempted to write about his experiences.
I didn't know he'd actually begun. It would have been worth reading, his view of the war."

Mrs. Gravely said, "A history? He liked to work of an evening,
after his dinner. I wasn't to disturb him then, he said. He was a
great reader. I never gave it another thought on mornings when I
found the study floor littered with his atlases and notes."

Rutledge turned back to Harris. "Who lives in the Barnes house
in Dartmouth now?"

"There's a house? I had no idea. Let me see, there was something said once about Althea Middleton having had a brother.
But as I remember, he was disinherited. And Barnes himself died
whilst his daughter was in India."

"Then it must have been his daughter who inherited the property, and it passed to Sir John at her death." He would ask Sergeant
Gibson at the Yard to look into the matter.

"His solicitor is the same as mine," Harris told him, and gave
Rutledge directions to the firm in Mumford.

"Would you care for a cup of tea, Mr. Rutledge?" Mrs. Gravely
asked. "I was just about to make a fresh pot."

"Thank you, no," he said. "Has anyone come to call on Sir John
in the past few weeks?"

"Not since before Christmas," she answered him. "And then it
was a man who'd lost his foot in the war and had been given a
wooden one in its place. I heard him come up the walk, because
it made an odd sound. A thump it was, and then a lighter sound,
as he put his cane down with the good foot. The old dog growled
something fierce, and I had to hold on to his collar when I went to
the door."

A cane. The murder weapon hadn't been found, the likelihood being that the killer had taken it away with him. A cane could have done the damage to Middleton's head and face, if wielded with enough force.

"Do you remember his name?"

"He didn't give it, sir. He said, 'Tell Sir John it's an old comrade in arms.' And I did as he asked. Sir John went to see for himself, while I took the old dog into the kitchen with me."

Was that why the dog had been put outside? Because he knew —and disliked—the killer?

Rutledge thanked her and went back to his search of the house. There was money in a wallet in the bedside table, but it had not been touched. Nor had the gold cuff links in a box on the tall chest by the bedroom door. What had the killer been after, if not robbery?

Trafalgar? A property in Dartmouth?

The deed.

Rutledge left to find a telephone, and had to drive into Cambridge before he was successful. He put in a call to Sergeant Gibson at the Yard and gave him a list of what he needed.

"I'm driving to Dartmouth," he said. "I'll find a telephone there as soon as I arrive."

"To Dartmouth?" Gibson repeated doubtfully. "You know your own business best."

"Let's hope I do," Rutledge replied. He left a message with the Cambridge police and set out to skirt London to the southwest.

It was early on the third day that he arrived in Dartmouth, having spent two nights on the road after running short of petrol near Slough. Colorful houses spilled down the sides of the high ridge that overlooked the town and the water. Most of them were still dark at this hour. Across the harbor was the town of Kingswear, just as dark. He found a hotel on a quiet side street, a narrow building with three floors, its facade black and white half-timbering. The sleepy clerk, yawning prodigiously, gave him a room at the front of the hotel with a view of the harbor. He stood by the window for some time, looking down toward the quay and the dark water, dotted with boats silently riding the current.

The Dart River opened up here to form the harbor, and castles—ruins now—had once guarded the entrance to this safe haven. It was deep enough for ships, and wide enough for a ferry to convey passengers from one side to the other. Just whereabouts the house called Trafalgar was situated, he didn't know. He hoped the hotel clerk might.

In the event, the man did not. "Before my time, I daresay. You could ask at the bookshop on the next corner," he suggested later that morning. "Arthur Hillier is the person you want. Oldest man hereabouts. If there was a house by that name, he'll know of it. But I doubt there is. You've come on a wild goose chase to my way of thinking."

Rutledge found the bookstore just past the shoemaker's shop. It possessed a broad front, the tall windows displaying books on every subject, but mostly about the sea and Dartmouth itself, including works on the wine trade with France and fishing the cod banks. A bell jingled as he opened the door, and an elderly man looked up, brushing a strand of white hair out of still-sharp blue eyes.

"Good morning, sir," he said cheerfully. "Here to browse, or is there something in particular you're looking for?"

"Information, if you please," Rutledge replied. "I'm trying to locate a dwelling that was here some years ago." He had brought with him the volume on the Barnes family history and opened it to the frontispiece. "This house, in fact."

Hillier pulled a pair of eyeglasses from his sweater pocket and put them on. "Ah. Trafalgar. It isn't called that anymore. For a time it was a home for indigent naval officers, and after that, it was a clinic during the war. Now it's more or less derelict. Sad, really."

"Do you know anything about the former owners?"

"Well, you do have the Barnes history, don't you? But I knew the last of the family to live there. Not well, you understand. Fanciful name for the house. It was called that after an ancestor was wounded the same day Lord Nelson was killed. Quite the fashion to commemorate the battle with monuments and the like. Trafalgar Square in London was one of the last to do so; I expect they didn't know what else to do with that great patch of emptiness. At any rate, the house was River's End before that—just where the Dart opens into the harbor, you see." He gestured to the door. "Come with me, and I'll show you. "

Rutledge followed him out of the shop, toward the harbor. "There's a boat," Hillier was saying, "that will convey you to the mouth of the River Dart. Where it broadens into the harbor, you can just see the rooftops of Trafalgar over that stand of trees. They weren't there in my day, those trees. You could see the gardens then. Quite a sight in the spring, I remember."

He could see where Hillier was pointing, but the morning sun hadn't yet reached that part of the harbor, and he had to take the man's word for it that the house was behind the trees. But then he looked a little farther along. There, just visible over the treetops, was the line of a roof.

"The boatman is just there, at the foot of the water stairs. Jesse is his name. He'll see you there and back without any trouble."

"You said you knew the last of the family to live there. What do you remember about him?"

"He was troubled with gout and often ill-tempered," the bookseller answered. "But catch him in good spirits, and he could tell sea stories that were marvelous to hear."

Rutledge thanked Hillier and walked on toward the harbor. He found the water stairs and the small boat tied up just under them. Jesse was nowhere to be seen. Rutledge turned to look back at the town just as a man popped out of the pub on the corner, rolling down in his direction, a wide grin on his unshaven face.

"Morning," he said. "Going sommers?"

"I'd like to hire your boat for an hour or so. Are you willing?"

"I come with the boat," he said, close enough now for Rutledge to smell the gin on his breath. He began to cast off, gestured to Rutledge to step aboard, and sat down to pick up the heavy oak oars.

"Where to?"

"The house you can hardly see behind the trees over there."

"The clinic that was? Why do you want to go there? Not much to see, now."

"Nevertheless . . ."

Nodding, Jesse moved out of the shelter of the water stairs, pulled into the current, turned smartly, and headed upstream. "We're against the tide," he said. "It will cost you more to go up than to come down."

"I understand."

It was cold down here on the water, wind sweeping down the chute between the high ridge on which Dartmouth sprawled and the lower one on the opposite bank. In the distance he could hear a train whistle, and soon after, the white plumes of a steam engine could be seen coming into Kingswear. As they reached midharbor, Rutledge buttoned his coat up to his collar against the bite of the January air. But Jesse, in shirtsleeves, seemed not to feel the cold, plying his oars and glancing over his shoulder from time to time to take stock of any other river traffic that morning. A quarter of an hour later, Jesse drew up by what had once been a fine private landing, rotting now and slippery with moss.

"Going to explore, are you? Watch where you step or I'll be fishing you out of the river."

As he clambered out on what was left of the private landing, he saw that it would be precarious at best to make his way across the broken boards. Moving gingerly, he finally gained the tree line and stepped ashore. The trees had grown unhindered for fifteen years or more, he thought. He needed an ax, really, to fight his way through the undergrowth that blocked any semblance of a path.

Eventually he'd made it to the garden beyond—itself a thicket of dead plants, weeds, and vines. Above it was a terrace, and he climbed the broad steps to the long French doors that let into the house. To his surprise, one of them was unlocked, and after the briefest hesitation, he went inside.

It was out of the wind, but the house was cold in a different way: unused, unheated, winter seeping into the very bricks. The room in which he found himself had once been beautiful, with a pale green paper on the walls, a pattern of Chinese figures in blues and reds and deep gold sitting in a formal garden. But it was stained now, and torn in places. A temporary wall, still there, divided the spacious room in half. If there had been any of the original furniture here, it had certainly now gone.

He made his way to the door, found himself in a passage, and began to explore. The stairs had been battered and bruised by the comings and goings of staff and patients, and the only furniture he saw was the remnants of cots in a few rooms, mostly with legs missing or springs broken. Not worth removing, he thought, when the clinic was closed. He wondered if Sir John had been aware of the state of the house, or didn't care. He walked through the rooms, noting how they had been used, and how they had been left. A broken window on the ground floor had allowed leaves and rain to ruin the floorboards, and a desk in what must have been Matron's office lay on its side, a nest of mice or squirrels in one half-opened drawer.

He found nothing of interest—except for signs that someone had been here before him, footprints in the dust, a bed of worn blankets and quilts by the coal stove in the kitchen, and indications that someone had also cooked there—a dented teapot still on the cast-iron top, and a saucepan on the floor.

Who had been in this house? A vagrant, looking for shelter against the winter cold and happening on it quite by accident, or someone who had come to this house because he knew it was there? A former patient? Or someone else?

Hamish said, "Look at the dust."

And he lit a match, studying the pattern of footprints hardly visible in the pale light coming through the dirty windowpanes.

The person who had been here had left his mark. Two shoes, one dragging a little as if the ankle didn't bend properly. And the small round ferrule of a walking stick. Or a lame man's cane.

Rutledge knelt there considering the prints, hearing again Mrs. Gravely's description of how Sir John's December caller had sounded coming up the walk to the door. These prints were not recent. He would swear to that. Fresh dust had settled over them, almost obliterating them in places.

He went back through the house looking for something, anything, that might be a clue to the interloper.

All he found was a crushed packet that once held cigarettes. It had been tossed into the coal stove and forgotten. He smoothed it out as best he could and saw that it was an Australian brand.

Giving it up, he went back to the door onto the terrace and stepped out, shutting it behind him.

Jesse was still sitting in his boat, smoking a cigarette of his own.

"Where can I buy Australian cigarettes?" Rutledge asked the man.

"Portsmouth, at a guess. London. Not here. No call for them here. Why? Develop a taste for them in the war, did you?"

"No. I found an empty box in the house. Someone had been living there."

Jesse seemed not to be too surprised. "Men out of work in this weather take what shelter they can find. I came on one asleep in my boat a year back. Wrapped in a London newspaper for warmth, he was. I bought him a breakfast and sent him on his way."

"Any Australians in Dartmouth?"

"Up at the Royal Navy College on the hill, there might be," Jesse told him, maneuvering the boat expertly into the stream again. "But they'd be officers, wouldn't they? Not likely to be breaking into a house." The ornate red-brick college, more like a palace than a school and completed in 1905, had seen the present king, George V, attend as a cadet. Jesse bent his back to the oars, grinning. "What do you want with a derelict old house?"

"It's not what *I* want," Rutledge said pensively, "but what someone else could very easily wish for." He turned slightly to look up the reaches of the River Dart, already a broad stream here as it fed into the harbor. "It wasn't always in disrepair."

But to kill for it? Hamish wanted to know.

That, Rutledge answered silently, would depend on what Sergeant Gibson discovered in London.

He found a telephone after Jesse had delivered him back to the old quay in Dartmouth. Watching through the window as the ferry plied the waters between the two towns, he asked for the sergeant, and after a ten-minute wait, Gibson came to the telephone.

"The old man, Barnes," the sergeant began. "He died in a freak accident. Slipped in his tub and cracked open his head. Foot was swollen with gout at the time. There was some talk because the staff was not in the house when it happened. They'd gone to a wedding in Kingswear. The constable come to investigate thought there was too much water splashed about the bathroom. But the servants were all accounted for; the son predeceased his father, and the daughter was in India. The inquest brought in accidental death."

"The son was dead?"

"As far as anyone knew. He'd got himself drunk and wandered onto Dartmoor. They never found his body, but his cap was hanging on a ledge, halfway down an abandoned mine shaft. A shoe was found at the edge. When the father was told, he cursed himself for disinheriting the boy. He was certain it was suicide."

But was it?

That was years ago, and should have no bearing on a murder in Cambridge in 1920.

"Sometimes memories are long," Hamish reminded him.

And Hamish should know, Rutledge thought grimly, for the Scots were nothing if not fanatical about revenge and blood feuds.

"Who owns the property at present?" he asked Gibson.

"It came to Sir John when his wife died."

Just as he'd thought.

He left Dartmouth for the long drive back to Mumford. Once there he located the offices of Molton, Briggs, and Harman, who were, according to the rector, Mr. Harris, solicitors to Sir John Middleton.

Mr. Briggs, elderly and peering over the thick lenses of his glasses, said, "The police informed us of Sir John's death. Very sad. Very sad."

"Since he had no children, I need to know who stands to inherit his property."

"Now that's very interesting," Briggs said, clearing his throat. "He has left the cottage in Mumford to Mrs. Gravely, for long years of devoted service." Taking off his glasses he stared at them as if expecting them to speak. "I doubt he expected to see her inherit so soon." Putting them back on his nose, he said, "There is a bequest to the church, as you'd expect, and certain other charges."

"And the property in Dartmouth? How is that left?"

"The one formerly known as Trafalgar? It was to go to a cousin of his first wife, but she died of her appendix. He made no decision after that. Until last December, that is, when he came in to tell me that the house was to go to the son of his late wife's brother."

"The brother died on Dartmoor. Years ago. After being disinherited."

"The brother fled to Australia from charges of theft. The death on Dartmoor was staged to save the family the disgrace."

"The brother was a convict?" Rutledge asked, surprised. Even Sergeant Gibson had failed to uncover that information.

"Yes. He gave the police a false name. His father went to Dartmoor and staged his son's death. To spare the then Lady Middleton. So Sir John told us in December."

"Then the son couldn't have returned to kill the father."

"The fall in the bathroom? He was drunk. He stayed drunk much of the time."

"Was Sir John quite certain this was his brother-in-law's son?"

"Yes, he had the proper credentials. It's quite in order."

And the son had gone to Dartmouth and slept in the house that would be his. Had he then decided to hasten that day? Or had he been given permission to begin repairs on the house?

Mr. Briggs didn't know. "I was told to make the necessary changes to Sir John's will. I was not privy to any other arrangements between the two."

The house would require hundreds—thousands—of pounds to make it habitable again, let alone to restore it. The young Barnes, with his wooden foot, had been there and seen what was needed.

Had he come back, when he realized that the bequest was an empty promise and that the house would fall down around his ears long before Sir John died a natural death?

"Where can I find this young Barnes?"

"I was given an address in London. I was told that he could be reached through it."

Briggs fiddled with the papers in front of him, found the one he wanted, and told Rutledge what he needed to know. "I expect it is a residence rather than a hotel," he added.

But Rutledge recognized the address. It was a small hospital where the mentally disturbed from the war were committed when there was no other course open to a doctor.

Rutledge thanked Briggs and turned the bonnet of his motorcar toward London.

The street where the hospital stood was not far from St. Paul's Cathedral. Two adjoining houses had been combined to form a single dwelling, and the main door was guarded by an orderly with great mustaches. Rutledge showed his identification and was admitted. Reception was a narrow room with a long desk against one wall. Another orderly sat there with a book in front of him. He looked up as Rutledge entered.

"Sir?" he said, rising to stop Rutledge's advance. "Are you looking for someone?"

"Yes. A man by the name of Barnes. He was in the war, has a wooden foot. I expect he's a patient here."

"Barnes?" The orderly frowned. "We don't have a patient named Barnes. There's a Dr. Barnes. Surgeon. He lost his foot in the Near East."

Surprised, Rutledge said, "Is he Australian?"

"He is indeed."

"I'd like to speak to him, if I may."

The orderly consulted his book. "He's just finished surgery, I believe. He should be in his office shortly."

Rutledge was shown to a door where a middle-aged nursing sister escorted him the rest of the way, to an office behind a barred door.

"We must be careful with our patients," she said. "Some of them are very confused about where they are and why they are here. It's sad, really," she went on. "They're so young, most of them."

"What sort of surgery does Dr. Barnes do?" he asked as she showed him into the drab little room.

"Today he was removing a bullet pressing on the brain of one of the men in our charge. Very delicate. But it had to be done, if he's to have any hope of living a normal life. The question is, will he ever live a normal life, given his confusion?"

She sounded tired and dispirited. He thanked her and sat down in the chair in front of the desk, prepared to wait.

When Dr. Barnes finally entered the office, he wasn't what Rutledge had anticipated. Young, fair, intense, he seemed to fill the room with his presence.

Rutledge rose.

"What brings Scotland Yard to Mercy Hospital?" he asked, going around the desk and taking the chair behind it.

"I'm afraid I've come to give you bad news. Your uncle is dead."

The tired face changed. "Sir John? What happened? He was healthy enough when I saw him last."

"Someone came into the house when Mrs. Gravely was in Mumford and killed him."

The shock was real. "Dear God!"

"It appears you'll be inheriting Trafalgar sooner than you expected."

Dr. Barnes made an impatient gesture. "He was kind enough to leave it to me. I don't think he wanted it, come to that. But he could have said no. Still, I have no time now to restore it. Or even think of restoring it." He made a face. "Nor the money, for that matter. I'm needed here, anyway. For the time being. Well, to be honest, for some time to come."

"You went to call on Sir John in December. And you were in the house in Dartmouth then—or soon after that. You broke in."

The smile was genuine, amused. "Hardly breaking in. But I had no key. And it was to be mine. I decided it would do no harm. How on earth did you know? Did someone see me? Or the smoke from the fire in the kitchen?"

"Marks in the dust," Rutledge said. "Of a foot that dragged, and a cane."

"Ah. Have you found who killed Sir John? I hope you have. He was a good man."

"We have no leads at present," Rutledge said with regret. He hesitated, then added, "The last thing your uncle said, as far as anyone knows, was one word. *Trafalgar.* It seemed likely that he was referring to the house. Why should that have been on his mind as he lay dying?"

Dr. Barnes got to his feet and turned, looking out the high window. There was nothing to be seen from it, except for the wall of the house next door, some four feet away. "You think I must have killed the old man, don't you?" He turned. "I can probably supply witnesses to swear I was here — nearly round the clock for the past month or more. But that isn't what matters. I didn't harm him. I told you, it would do me no good if I had killed him twice over. There isn't time to do anything about the house or the land."

"If he'd changed his mind and left it to you, one might wonder if he'd have been equally as easily persuaded to leave it to someone else."

"But to whom?" Barnes asked. "Who did I have to fear?"

"I don't know," Rutledge said. "But that one word, *Trafalgar,* is damning."

Barnes sat down again. "There must be some other meaning."

"Yes. But what?"

Barnes shrugged. "My family wasn't the only one with a connection to the battle. Surely."

"Sir John had no connection to it. There was only the house in Dartmouth."

"There was the war. He made enemies there, very likely. I heard tales of what he did at HQ. He tried to bring reason to the decisions being made."

And Sir John had been writing his memoirs. It was possible.

Hamish said, "The blows. He couldna ha' been thinking clearly."

"Yet," Rutledge replied silently, "yet he remembered the old dog."

Thanking Barnes for his time, he rose, saying, "I must have my men question the staff here. There will be statements to sign."

"Yes, to be sure. I have nothing to hide." As Rutledge reached the door, Barnes said, "I'd like to come to the services. Will you see that someone lets me know when the arrangements are made?"

"Mr. Briggs will see that you're kept informed."

As he was leaving, the heavy door to the stairs swung open and a sister came out, carrying a tray of medicines. For an instant he heard the screams of someone in a ward above, and he knew what that meant. A living nightmare, the curse of shell shock.

The screams were cut off as the door swung shut. Shuddering, he went through the other door and was in Reception once more where he could breathe again.

Outside in the street, he walked for half an hour before returning to where he'd left his motorcar. It had been necessary to exorcise the memories those screams had reawakened.

"Do you believe yon doctor?" Hamish asked as Rutledge turned the crank.

"He'll have dozens of witnesses to prove that he was here at the hospital. So, yes, I believe he had nothing to do with killing Sir John." He got into the motorcar. "But that isn't to say that he didn't hire someone to do the deed for him." He considered the screams he'd heard. Was there a patient in the hospital whose fragile mental state might make him a perfect murderer? Who could be set in motion by a clever killer, chosen because he could be depended upon to do as he was told to do?

It was far fetched. But at the moment Rutledge was running out of options.

Hamish said, "It comes back to yon dog, ye ken. Why was he put out in the cold?"

Would a damaged mind think to rid himself of the dog? Why had it been necessary? Simba was too old to attack and do any real damage. Although, Rutledge thought as he pulled into traffic, anyone with a dog bite in Mumford, or even as far away as Cambridge, would need treatment. And that would lead to discovery and questions by the police. Even Dr. Barnes would find it hard to explain how one of his patients could have been bitten.

Turning the motorcar around, he drove toward Cambridge. It was late when he arrived, but Mrs. Gravely was still awake, a light on in the kitchen, and he lifted the knocker, letting it fall gently rather than imperatively. She opened the door tentatively, then smiled when she recognized him.

"I'm that glad of company," she said. "I don't quite know what to do with myself. There's no one to cook or clean for. The police tell me to leave everything be, and the doctor tells me poor Sir John's body hasn't been released, and until it is, I can't begin the baking for the funeral. No one knows when there'll be an inquest." She gestured to the furnishings as he stepped into the house. "I haven't been told what I'm supposed to do with all Sir John's things. No surprise I haven't been sleeping of nights."

He wondered how she would react when the will was read and she learned that the cottage was hers. Would she be pleased—or would the memory of Sir John's body lying in the study haunt her every time she walked into the room?

He let her make a cup of tea for him, and then said, "The man who came here in December, the one with the wooden foot, is actually the son of the first Lady Middleton's brother."

"My good Lord," she said fervently. "I'd have never guessed." She paused, measuring out the tea. "But why didn't he say so? Why tell me he was an old comrade in arms?"

"Perhaps he thought Sir John might refuse to receive him if he used his own name."

Frowning, she shook her head. "I expect that was so. Still . . ." She left the word hanging and busied herself taking down cups and saucers, retrieving the sugar bowl from the cupboard, then walking into the pantry for the jug of milk.

"You've cleaned for Sir John these many years. Did he have anything in this house worth stealing? I don't count money. Or gold cuff links. Something of great value. Something that would make killing him worthwhile?"

Because Dr. Barnes hadn't the money to restore Trafalgar, whatever he might claim about time.

"I can't think that there was. Some of his books? I don't know about such things, but someone else might."

"It didn't appear that there were books missing."

"That's true," she agreed. "I'm used to dusting them. They're all there save one."

Rutledge took the Barnes family history from his pocket. "My doing, that. I needed to show someone the photograph in the front."

"I'll see it's in its rightful place," she said, moving the book aside and setting down his cup of tea. "There's a bit of chocolate sponge cake, if you'd like that," she told Rutledge. "I made it for my dinner."

He thanked her but refused. After a moment she sat down across from him. "There are the weapons between the photographs, in the study. But none of them was taken."

Not even all of them would raise the sum needed to restore Trafalgar. "It doesn't matter," he said. "If it were robbery, it would be for something worth thousands of pounds. Not a few hundred."

She nodded. "I worry, sometimes," she said, looking away as if embarrassed. "If I'd been here that day—or come back from the greengrocers a little sooner—could I have prevented what happened? I know you told me I might well have become a victim, too. But it weighs on my mind, you see. I needn't have gone into Mumford that day. His dinner would have been all right without that onion."

"I doubt it," he told her bracingly. "Most killers would wait for their chance. If you hadn't left that day, you would have left on another."

Hamish said, "It's a kind lie."

He went through the study and the parlor again, looking for something missing—some explanation for why a man had to die—knowing very well that Mrs. Gravely would have noticed and brought it to his attention long ago.

It was all as he'd seen it the first time. The tidiness of the soldier, used to spartan conditions. The collector of books, most of them on warfare, Cambridge, even India. The husband, who loved his second wife and kept her portrait where he could see it, but who bore no grudge against his first wife, headstrong though she may have been. The fastidious man who was always freshly shaven and carefully dressed, judging by the body.

Rutledge went back to the bookshelves and ran his finger down the line of titles. Nothing out of the ordinary. Several volumes of biography: William the Conqueror, Henry II, Edwards I and III. Soldiers all, in the days when kings led their men into battle. The tactics of the American general Robert E. Lee. The strategies of Napoleon.

He stopped and pulled out one of the books at random. As he opened it, something fell out and drifted lightly to the floor.

Stooping to pick it up, he saw that it was an article cut from a newspaper, yellowed and thin.

It was about the destruction of the Great Mews of Whitehall Palace. The stables of Edward I and his predecessors. This had been done early in the eighteenth century, when the ramshackle mews was more of an eyesore than it was useful. Rutledge glanced at the spine of the book and saw it was a biography of Edward I. The cutting was well before Sir John's time, and turning to the end covers, he saw that the name inscribed there in an ornate bookplate was that of Sir Robert Middleton. Father? Grandfather? Uncle?

He set the book aside and picked up the Bible. Searching the list of births and deaths, he realized that Sir Robert was a great-grandfather of Sir John's. Not a contemporary of the destruction of the royal mews, but Sir Robert had been alive in the first part of the nineteenth century, when various architects, including the famous Nash, had taken on the task of creating a square that would fit into the overall view of a new and spacious London. The name given to the finished square came from the column bearing the statue of Admiral Nelson: Trafalgar Square. But as Hillier, the Dartmouth bookseller, had said, it had been among the last of the memorials to Lord Nelson.

Interesting, but it was, as Hamish was reminding him, decades in the past. Hardly pertinent to a murder in 1920.

Glancing at his watch, Rutledge saw that it was half past one o'clock in the morning. The house was quiet, and he thought perhaps Mrs. Gravely had gone up to her bed. Still, he sat down at a table in the parlor and read the faded cutting. It told him very little more. Picking up the book, he thumbed through the pages, looking for any reference to the royal mews. There was nothing of interest. He went back to the study, searched for other books on Edward I, and carried them into the parlor. Had it been only coincidence that the cutting was in that particular history?

It was close on five when Mrs. Gravely came in with sandwiches and a pot of tea. He ate absently, his mind on the hunt. When she came to take away his plate and cup, she said, looking over his shoulder, "He must have loved that book. I can't count the times I'd find it on his desk when I was dusting."

Rutledge turned to see what she was pointing to. A slim volume bound in worn leather, printed a hundred years ago.

It was written by a man called Baker, and it purported to offer an account of the crusade the then Prince Edward Longshanks made to the Holy Land. He had already turned homeward in

1272 when he learned of the death of his father, Henry III, and that he was now king. He was two years in reaching England to be crowned. Legend claimed that with him he brought a small gold reliquary, encrusted with precious stones and containing a piece of the True Cross. It remained with him through the early years of his reign, although it was more common to give such relics to a church in thanksgiving for his safe return. As he'd been sickly as a child, it was thought he kept the relic for his own protection. But when it failed to save his dying queen, Eleanor of Castile, in a ferocious fit of temper he ordered it buried in the largest dung pit in the stables.

According to Baker, it had been lost to history from that time forward, until a workman had discovered it during the demolition of the stables in the eighteenth century. The man had shown it to his brother-in-law, a yeoman farmer in Kent, who paid him handsomely for it, and the object had remained in the farmer's family, passing from father to elder son in each generation. It had become known, Baker went on, as the Middleton Host, although the family had denied any knowledge of it, and with time the Host and the family itself had been lost to history. The remodeling of the land once occupied by the stables had revived the tale, but Baker had been unable to prove whether it was true or not. He had contacted a number of families by the name of Middleton in Kent and elsewhere, but had failed to find any trace of the story.

Rutledge sat back, considering what he'd just read. Then he rose and went back to the study to look at the small wooden box by the bookshelves.

There was no way of knowing what it had contained. Even Mrs. Gravely, when questioned, had no idea what had been kept inside — if anything. She had dusted it but never opened it.

But suppose — just suppose — it had held the Middleton Host.

That would match with the message that the dying man had tried to pass on to his housekeeper.

Trafalgar. Not the name of his late wife's home, but the square in the heart of London. Would he have told the secret to Althea Barnes? A great joke, that, one she might have appreciated and passed on to her father and her brother.

What would such a reliquary be worth? Monetarily and intrinsically.

What would it be worth to Dr. Barnes, working daily with men whose minds were destroyed by war? Had he come, in December, to ask for the use of the Middleton Host? And instead been pawned off with promises of the house in Dartmouth? A house he had no use for and couldn't afford to keep up? An albatross, compared to the cure the reliquary might achieve in men who could be brought to believe in its power.

Rutledge went to the door, called to Mrs. Gravely that he would be back shortly, and hurried to his motorcar. Driving into Cambridge as dawn was breaking, he went to the telephone he'd used before and put in a call to the clinic where Barnes worked.

He was informed that Dr. Barnes was with a patient and couldn't be disturbed.

Swearing under his breath, he walked out to his motorcar and was on the point of driving to London when another thought occurred to him. Even tired as he was, it made sense.

The old dog.

Mrs. Gravely had claimed that Sir John had spoken to Dr. Taylor just before he died. She had nearly been sure that he'd asked about his dog. And the doctor had responded with a single word. *No.* She had thought that the doctor was telling Sir John that the dog was dead.

Turning the motorcar around, he drove back to Mumford. He searched the high street of the little town, then looked in the side streets. Shortly after nine, he found Dr. Taylor's surgery, next door but one to the house where the doctor lived, according to the nameplates on the small white gates to both properties.

Hamish said, "'Ware." And it was a warning well taken.

Knocking on the surgery door, Rutledge scanned the house down the street. He could just see a small woman wrapped in a coat and headscarf, standing in the back garden, staring at the bare fruit trees and withered beds as if her wishing could bring them into bloom again. The doctor's wife? That told him what he needed to know.

The nurse who admitted Rutledge was plump and motherly, calling him *dearie,* asking him to wait in the passage while she spoke with the doctor. "His first patients of the day are already in the front room. It's better if you come directly back to the office."

"It's about his report on the postmortem of Sir John."

"He has already mailed it to the Yard," she said. "I took it to the post myself."

Rutledge gave her his best smile. "Yes, I've been in Dartmouth. It hasn't caught up with me yet."

She nodded and bustled off to tell the doctor that Rutledge was waiting.

Dr. Taylor received him almost at once, saying, "Mrs. Dunne tells me you haven't seen the postmortem results." He sorted through some files on his desk and retrieved a sheet of paper. "My copy," he added, passing it across the desk to Rutledge. "You're welcome to read it."

Rutledge took the sheet, scanning it quickly. "Yes. Everything seems to be in order," he said, glancing up in time to see the tension around Dr. Taylor's eyes ease a little. "Two blows, one to the back of the head and the second to the face. Weapon possibly a cane." He handed the report to Taylor. "There's one minor detail to clear up before the inquest. Mrs. Gravely told me that Sir John spoke to her as she was coming into the study. Was that possible, do you think?"

"I doubt if he was coherent," Taylor said easily. "A grunt. A groan. But not words as such."

"She also reported that he spoke to you. And that you answered him, just before he died."

Taylor frowned. "I thought he was asking if the old dog was still alive. I told him it was dead. I wasn't sure, you understand. But I thought if that was what he was trying to say, I'd ease his mind."

He had just contradicted himself.

"I don't think that the dog's death was something that would comfort him."

Taylor shrugged. "I wasn't in a position to consider my answer. As I told you, he wasn't coherent. I did my best in the circumstances."

"Actually, I think he was probably asking if you'd use the Middleton Host to save the old dog. And you refused. You had to, because Mrs. Gravely was standing there in the doorway."

Taylor flushed. "What host?"

"He must have told you at one time or another. A medical man? That a king had found it useless and thrown it in a dung heap. But then Eleanor of Castile was probably beyond help by the time the reliquary reached her. She died anyway. King Edward loved his wife. Passionately. Everywhere her body rested the night on the long journey south to London, he built a shrine. The wonder was, he didn't smash the relic. But I expect he felt that the dung heap was a more fitting end for it. A fake, a sham."

"I have no idea what you're talking about, Inspector. And there are patients waiting."

"It was a story that must have touched Sir John. He hadn't been able to save either of his wives, had he? The host was, after all, no more than a pretty fraud."

The doctor's face changed. "That's an assumption that neither you nor I can make. Sir John was a soldier, a skeptic, hardly one to take seriously legends about relics and miracles. Where is this taking us?"

"I'm trying," Rutledge returned blandly, "to establish whether or not Sir John loved Elizabeth Middleton as deeply as—for instance—you must love your wife. Because it was for her you did what you did. Not the patients out there in the waiting room." It was a guess, but it struck home.

Taylor opened his mouth, then shut it again.

"Why did you put the dog out? Did it attack you? If I asked you to have another doctor look at your ankles or legs, would he find breaks in the skin to indicate you'd been bitten? Even if it has begun to heal, the marks must still be there. Would you agree to such an examination?"

Taylor rose from behind the desk. "Yes, all right, the dog was dying when I got there. Sir John was kneeling on the floor beside it when I opened the door and called to him. He told me he was in the study, and to come quickly. Still, the damned dog growled at me and got to its feet as I struck the first blow. I had to get rid of it, because Sir John was still alive and I needed to hit him again. The cold finished it off, I expect. Its breathing was shallow, labored." He moved to the hearth. "My wife has just been diagnosed with colon cancer. I'd already asked Sir John if I could borrow the reliquary. To give her a chance. He told me it had done nothing for his wife, dying of childbed fever. But I didn't care. I was ready to try anything. I just wanted to *try*. But he was afraid that if my wife recovered on her own, Mumford would be swamped with the desperate, the hopeless, believers in miracles. He said it would be wrong. Time was running out, and yet that afternoon he begged me to do something for his *dog*. It was obscene, I tell you."

He reached down, his fingers closing over the handle of the fire tongs. Lifting his voice, he shouted, "No, no—you're wrong! Put them down, for God's sake."

And before Rutledge could stop him, he raised the tongs and brought them down on his own head, the blow carefully calculated to break the skin but not knock him down. And as blood ran down his face, he dropped the tongs and cried out, "Oh, God, someone help me . . . *Mrs. Dunne . . . he's run mad.*"

And in a swift angry voice that reached only Rutledge's ears, Taylor said, "She's ill, I tell you. I won't be taken away when she needs me. Not by you, not by anyone."

He rushed at Rutledge, grappling with him.

The door burst open, Mrs. Dunne flying to the doctor's aid, pulling at Rutledge's shoulders, calling out for him to stop.

Rutledge had no choice. He swung her around, and she went down, tripping over the chair he'd been sitting in. He turned toward the hearth, to retrieve the fire tongs as Taylor reeled against the far wall, calling, "Stop him—"

Mrs. Dunne, scrambling to her feet, must have thought Rutledge was about to use the tongs again, and she threw herself at him, carrying him backward against the hearth, stumbling over the fire screen.

Her screams had brought patients from the waiting room, pushing their way through the door, faces anxious and frightened as they took in the carnage, drawing the same conclusions that Mrs. Dunne had leapt to. A woman in a dark green coat gasped and went to the doctor's aid, and he leaned heavily against her shoulder. Two men put themselves between Rutledge and his perceived victim, one of them quickly retrieving the fire tongs from where they'd fallen, as if afraid Rutledge could still reach them.

It was all Rutledge could do to catch Mrs. Dunne's pummeling fists and force her arms to her sides so that he could retrieve the situation before it got completely out of hand. Hamish in the back of his mind was warning him again, and there was no time to answer.

In a voice used to command on a battlefield, he said, "You—the one in the greatcoat—find Constable Forrest and bring him here at once."

Taylor said, stricken, "He's trying to arrest me . . . for murder . . . I've done nothing wrong, don't let him lie to you. For God's sake!"

They knew Taylor. Rutledge was a stranger. The man in the greatcoat hesitated.

The doctor swayed on his feet. "I think I'd better sit down." The woman helped him to a chair, and his knees nearly buckled under him.

She said, "I'll find your wife."

He gripped her arm. "No. I don't want to worry her." Taylor took out his handkerchief to mop the blood from his face. "Just get him out of my office, if you will."

Rutledge crossed the room, and the man with the tongs raised them without thinking, as if expecting Rutledge to attack him. But he went to the door and closed it.

"You'll listen to me, then. I'm Inspector Rutledge, Scotland Yard." He held up his card for all of them to see. "I've just charged Dr. Taylor with the murder of Sir John Middleton. As for those tongs, he himself wielded them. I never touched them, or him."

"I think you'd better leave," Mrs. Dunne snapped. "He's a good man, a doctor."

"Is he? I intend to order Sir John's dog exhumed. I expect to find shreds of cloth in his teeth." Hamish was reminding him that it was only a very slim possibility, but Rutledge ignored him. "What's more, I intend to ask a doctor from Cambridge to examine Dr. Taylor's limbs for healing bites. And the clothing he was wearing the day of the murder will be examined for mended tears."

He saw the expression on Mrs. Dunne's face. Shock first, and then uncertainty. "I mended a tear in his trousers just last week. He'd caught them on a nail, he said."

"Then you'll know which trousers they were. If the shreds match, he will be tried for murder. We can also look at those tongs, if you will set them carefully on the desk. The only prints on them will be Dr. Taylor's and yours, sir. Not mine."

"Can you do that?" the man holding the tongs asked, staring down at them.

"There are people who can."

He moved to the desk, putting them down quite gently. Dr. Taylor reached for them, saying, "He's bluffing—look, it's my blood that's on them."

Rutledge was across the room before Taylor's fingers could curl around the handle of the tongs, his grip hard on the doctor's wrist, stopping him just in time.

The man in the greatcoat said, "I think I ought to fetch Constable Forrest after all, if only to sort out this business."

He left the office, and they could hear the surgery door shut firmly after him.

The doctor said, "I tell you, it's not true, none of it is true." But even as he spoke the words, he could read the faces around him. Uncertainty, then doubt replacing belief.

The woman in the dark green coat said, "I really must go—" and started toward the door, unwilling to have any further involvement with the police. The other man, without looking at the doctor, followed her in uncomfortable silence.

Taylor called, "No, wait, please!"

Mrs. Dunne said, "I'll just put a sign up on the door, saying the surgery is closed," and hurried after them.

Rutledge turned to see tears in Taylor's eyes. "Damn you," he said hoarsely. "And damn the bloody dog. I love her. I wanted to save her. Do you know what it's like to realize that your skills aren't enough?" He turned from Rutledge to the window. "Do you know how it feels when God has deserted you?"

Rutledge knew. In France, when he held his revolver at Hamish's temple; he knew.

"And what would you have done if the reliquary failed you, too?" Rutledge asked.

"It won't. It can't. I'm counting on it," he said defiantly. "You won't find it, I've seen to that. By God, at least she'll have that!"

But in the end they would find it. Rutledge said only, "What did you use as the murder weapon?"

Dr. Taylor grimaced. "You're the policeman. Tell me."

Hamish said, "He did the postmortem. Any evidence would ha' been destroyed."

And there had been more than enough time for Taylor to have hidden whatever it was on his way back to Mumford before he was summoned by Sam Hubbard.

When Constable Forrest arrived, Rutledge turned Taylor over to him and warned him to have a care on their way to Cambridge. "He's killed once," he reminded the man.

He watched them leave, and Mrs. Dunne, who had come to the door as the doctor was being taken away, bit her lip to hold back tears.

Rutledge walked to the house next but one to speak to Taylor's wife, and it was a bitter duty. Her face drawn and pale from suffering, she said only, "It's my fault. My fault." And nothing would dissuade her. In the end, he had to tell her that her house would have to be searched. She nodded, too numb at the moment to care.

He left her with Mrs. Dunne and went to tell Mrs. Gravely that he had found Sir John's killer.

She frowned. "I'd never have believed the doctor could do such a thing. Not to murder Sir John for a heathen superstition. Poor Mrs. Taylor, I can't think how she'll manage now."

He left her, refusing her offer of a cup of tea. Then, just as he was cranking the motorcar, she called to him, and he came back to the steps where she was hugging her arms about her against the cold wind.

"It keeps slipping my mind, Mr. Rutledge, sir! And it's probably not important now. You asked me to keep an eye out for anything that was missing, and I wanted you to know I did."

"Is there anything? Besides the reliquary?" he asked, surprised.

"Oh, nothing so valuable as that." She smiled self-consciously, feeling a little foolish, but no less determined to do her duty. "Still, with the old dog dead, and Sir John gone as well, I never noticed it was missing until yesterday morning. It's the iron doorstop, the one shaped like a small dormouse. Sir John used it these past six months or so, whenever Simba needed to go out. To keep the door from slamming shut behind them, you see, while he walked a little way with Simba or stood here on the step waiting for him. He never cared for the sound of a slamming door. He said it reminded him too much of the war. The sound of the guns and all that."

Rutledge thanked her and drove to Cambridge to ask for men to search the sides of the road between Sir John's house and Mumford.

As they braved the cold to dig through ditches and push aside winter-dead growth, Rutledge could hear the doctor's voice again.

You're the policeman. Tell me.

Three hours later, he drove once more to Cambridge to do just that. A few black hairs still clung to the dormouse's ears, and on the base was what appeared to be a perfect print in Sir John's blood.

TIM L. WILLIAMS

Half-Lives

FROM *Ellery Queen's Mystery Magazine*

WHEN I TRACKED Terrell Cheatham's grandmother from her last known address to the subsidized apartment she'd moved into after her husband's death, she didn't do any of the things I expected. Instead of slamming the door in my face or denying that her grandson lived with her, she invited me in for a cup of coffee and then added a shot of bourbon to my mug, "just to keep the cold out of my bones." This was a long way from the reception a private investigator usually gets when running down bail jumps in southwest Memphis, where the average annual income is a few dollars higher than it is in Calcutta and even the most law-abiding residents see a white face as an intrusion from an alien and hostile world. I was so shocked I wanted to believe her when she insisted that her grandson was a "fine young man" who wouldn't cause me "an ounce of trouble."

Frances Cheatham seemed like a decent woman. She was in her late fifties or early sixties, still trim and attractive but with deep worry lines around her mouth and eyes, and I could tell she loved her grandson. From what I'd read in his jacket, Terrell Cheatham didn't seem like the kind of kid who belonged in jail. At twenty, he had a single blemish on his record. It had been two years since his arrest for breaking into the video-game store, and he'd kept clean since then. He'd completed a semester of college, earning a spot on the honor roll before he dropped out to take a full-time job in the kitchen at a Tops Barbecue on Elvis Presley Boulevard. If he'd shown up for his court appearance a week and a half ago — in

Memphis a trial two years after the offense is considered swift justice—Terrell would have faced no more than six months' probation.

"Terrell's momma left him when he was just a baby," she said now, blowing at the steam rising off a fresh cup of coffee and then shrugging. "Our son Marcus Junior gave Terrell to us to raise, but he came to visit Terrell every weekend up until the time he was killed in a car wreck outside of Jackson, Mississippi."

Her husband, Marcus Senior, had passed away less than a year ago. He was a good man, she said, one who'd worked for twenty-seven years as a night watchman at the West Parrish Industrial Park to put bread on the table and keep a roof over their heads.

"Bone cancer. He went fast, but don't let anyone tell you fast and easy are the same thing." Her smile was tired, maybe a little bitter. "I bet you hear your share of sad stories, don't you, Mr. Raines. Probably get sick of them."

I told her to call me Charlie and said how sorry I was about her loss. And she thanked me for that, even though we both knew words were little comfort.

There didn't seem to be anything else to say, so we sat in silence for a few minutes before Frances Cheatham forced a smile and said it looked like both of us needed a refill. While she was in the kitchen, I went to look out the front window. The last of the light was seeping from a January sky. When you say Memphis, people think blistering August heat, but there are days in January and February when the skies are mold gray, a slanting, almost-frozen drizzle falls from dawn to midnight, and a wind whips across the Mississippi that makes you wonder if you haven't been transported unaware from Beale Street to Boston. I was still standing at the window, dreading going back out into that cold, when a tall, scrawny kid dressed in a parka, sock cap, and sneakers crossed the street and headed into the parking lot.

"You see Terrell coming?" Frances Cheatham asked, handing me my coffee.

Before I could answer, a black Tahoe fishtailed into the lot, nearly slammed a row of parked cars, and then skidded to a stop. Peering over my shoulder, Frances Cheatham said, "Good Lord, they almost run right over Terrell."

Outside, the SUV's passenger door was slung open, and a man, fiftyish, white, not much bigger than an oak tree, got out. Terrell tried to run. *Tried* was the operative word. He didn't even get started before the guy in the overcoat raised a sawed-off shotgun and squeezed the trigger.

"Oh sweet Jesus!" Frances Cheatham screamed in my ear.

I pulled my .45 from beneath my jacket and ran for the door. I'd just opened it when the shotgun roared again. I knew it was too late for Terrell Cheatham, but I ran anyway, taking the stairs two at a time and nearly slipping and falling halfway down. His grandmother ran behind me, calling on the name of the Lord with each step she took.

Just as we reached the lot, the Tahoe screeched away. I caught a glimpse of the driver—white, older than the shooter, thick, curly gray hair and glasses—but then the Tahoe was gone, heading northeast toward the interstate. Cursing, I stuffed my .45 back into my holster without having fired a shot.

Frances Cheatham hunkered beside her grandson, screaming his name again and again. Now that the shooting was over, a few faces had emerged from the apartments, staring at the scene, some of them whispering their prayers.

"I've called an ambulance," a pretty girl about Terrell's age shouted.

An ambulance wasn't going to help. The first blast from the shotgun had caught him just below the kidneys; the second, fired point-blank, had taken off most of the back of his head.

"A PlayStation 3," Frances Cheatham said when I touched her shoulder. "That's why he robbed that store. That's all my baby wanted. And just look at what someone done gone and did."

Four days later, the homicide detective who'd caught Terrell Cheatham's case finally got tired of dodging my calls and ducking down the back stairs and agreed to meet me for a late lunch. Ray Pardue was a stoop-shouldered man with thinning, sand-colored hair and a nervous grin that never quite made it to a full-blown smile. Now he pushed aside a platter of Neely's barbecue spaghetti and gave me a pained expression.

"I feel as bad as you do for the kid's grandmother. But Jesus Christ, Raines, where have you been living the last ten years? Kids in South Memphis get murdered every day. The Chamber of Commerce don't advertise it in their See the River City brochures, but we both know the way it is."

He was right, of course, but Terrell Cheatham's murder was the only one I'd witnessed. "So you've got no leads." I said.

"You were a cop. You know how it goes. You're a day into one case when two or three more fall in your lap, so what do you do?"

"You focus on the easiest to solve."

"It's not that one victim's more important than another, but a bird in the hand . . ." He paused while the waitress set fresh beers on the table. "You take a gang-related murder like Cheatham's. Eventually someone will get pinched and want to make a deal. Until then, I got two other homicides to worry about."

Gang-related. Terrell Cheatham's murder hadn't rated a lot of coverage. The local news stations were too busy covering the latest scandal in the mayor's office and the groundbreaking for the Michael Montesi North Memphis Children's Health and Recreational Center, a multimillion-dollar complex that was being built by Vincent "Little Vinnie" Montesi, head of the Italian mob in southwest Tennessee, Arkansas, and Mississippi, in honor of his son. The news anchor talked a lot about the tragedy of nine-year-old Michael Montesi's death from leukemia and about the generosity of his grief-stricken father. They failed to mention all the kids who'd died from the drugs Montesi and his crew brought into the city, or the ones he'd orphaned during his reign at the head of the Montesi family. When you donate a few million dollars to a local charity, people tend to overlook the things you've done to make that money. The death of yet another black kid in a Memphis project didn't have the same appeal to the public imagination, but during the terse, thirty-second spot that the murder had been given, the news anchor had used the same phrase. Gang-related. Unless South Memphis street gangs had started recruiting late-middle-aged white men, someone was making a serious mistake.

"The shooter and the driver were white," I said. "I told that to the on-scene detective."

"She noted it in her report, but we got a half-dozen other witnesses who say the perps were young black men, late teens or early twenties." He stifled a belch with the back of his hand. "Acid reflux," he said. "I chew Tums by the dozens, take this prescription medicine that costs a fortune, sleep with my bed propped up on bricks so that I got a crick in my neck all the time. Doesn't do a damn bit of good."

"I saw them. They were white."

"And other people say they were young black men. What do you want me to tell you?" He pulled a five and a one from his wallet and dropped them on the table. "That should cover the tip."

"A kid whose only criminal record comes from stealing a couple of video games gets his face blown off and y'all decide it's gang-related, put it in a file, and forget it?"

He took a deep breath. "Look, Raines, I shouldn't be telling you this, because it's information that you got no right to have, but Terrell Cheatham was running with gang kids, two in particular. Demond Jones and Bop-Bop Drake. Drug dealers, pimps, suspects in a half-dozen robberies and a couple of murders. The way I figure it, either Cheatham got targeted by a rival gang or he had a falling-out with his good pals Bop-Bop and Demond."

"Your other witnesses tell you that?"

"Surveillance tape, witnesses, informants." He stood up, took his coat from the back of the chair. "And a guy who matched Cheatham's description is a suspect in an attempted murder."

"You're serious?"

"A forty-six-year-old truck driver for a company called Mid-South Transport. He was making a delivery in the neighborhood and had engine trouble. The guy was sitting behind the wheel, trying to get the ignition to fire, when three black kids, we're figuring Cheatham, Jones, and Drake, threw a Molotov cocktail at his truck." He wiped his mouth on the back of his hand, and his eyes were hard and angry. "I guess they figured blowing up a white guy was a fun way to spend a Friday night. Maybe you ought to drive down to Southaven, take a good look at the burn scars, and then ask Don Ellis what priority he thinks this Cheatham kid's murder ought to get."

"Don Ellis? From Southaven?" I said. "I think I know him."

"Well, you won't recognize him if you do."

I wasn't sure what to say to that, but it didn't matter. Pardue had already turned on his heel and was headed for the door.

Don Ellis's house was a small, two-bedroom ranch in a neighborhood that had probably been nice ten years ago. I sat on a beer-stained sofa in his living room, asking myself why in the hell I was here. No one had hired me; I hadn't been a cop in over ten years, and Terrell Cheatham's life and death were none of my business anyway. But for two days I'd been worrying it like a bad tooth. I couldn't get Frances Cheatham's raw, wounded voice out of my head, couldn't stop hearing her say, "A PlayStation 3, that's all my baby wanted," and couldn't get a handle on Terrell Cheatham himself. Who was he? An honor student, a hard worker, and a loving grandson or a gangbanger who'd tried to burn an innocent man alive? Finally I'd given in, looked up Don Ellis's address and number, made a call. Now I was waiting for him to identify Terrell Cheatham as one of his attackers so I could call the kid's murder karma or justice and get back to the serious business of repossessing cars.

But it didn't look as if it was going to be that easy. Don Ellis studied the photograph for a second, laid it back on the coffee table, and shook his head.

"He could have been one of them. But it was after midnight and the streetlights down there don't ever seem to work." He glanced at a picture of his ex-wife and his sons on the end table beside his wheelchair. "The truth is, the pain's been so bad and I been so doped up that I'm kind of hazy about that whole night."

I smiled and said sure, I understood. It was a lie, of course. Understand? I couldn't even imagine. The burns were less than six weeks old—he'd only been out of the hospital for three days—and his face resembled a rubber Halloween mask that someone had snagged from a bonfire. The skin was bubbled and shiny, bright pink in most places but splotched with patches of bleached-out white just below his cheeks. The damaged facial muscles made it seem as if his lips were twisted into a permanent sneer, and he spoke with the halting slur of a stroke victim. It didn't take a psychic to see his future: long hospital stays, multiple skin grafts, lots of pain.

"We should have kept in touch," he said. "After we graduated, I mean. You get so busy you don't realize you're losing touch with all your friends."

I said that's just the way it was, but we were never really friends, just classmates on friendly terms. I hadn't thought of him in years.

"So who is he?" Don finally asked.

He looked away from me when he asked the question, and I

had the feeling that he remembered a lot more about the night he had been attacked than he said. Call it intuition if you want. That sounds a lot nicer than cynicism or paranoia.

"A twenty-year-old kid who had his head blown off by a shotgun a few days ago," I said.

"The same age as my oldest boy." He picked up the photograph of his family from the table. "You got kids, Charlie?"

"No. Just didn't happen."

There was a lot more to it than that, but catching up on old times has its limits.

"When you have kids, you want to give them everything." He stared at the photograph and took a long breath that made him shudder. "What am I going to give them now? A truckload of debt? The thirty-three dollars I got left out of my SSI check?"

"Mid-South Transport isn't paying you? If you're in a union . . ."

"I'm not a truck driver. I'm a body man and painter, been doing it since the week I got out of school. The truck-driving thing was just on the side. After my divorce I had the free time, and with the boys starting college, I needed the extra money." He shrugged his narrow shoulders. "I try to send Cass a little something extra when I can. We had twenty-one and a half good years and you never know. People get back together the same as they split up, right?"

"You worked nights. Local deliveries?"

"The general area, yeah. Sal Junior, my boss at the shop, hooked me up with the gig. The pay was good and in cash and what was I doing anyway? Sitting around here by myself, drinking too much beer."

"Sal Junior." I made a connection I didn't want to make. "You work for the Arcados?"

His flinch was all the answer I needed. Arcado Automotive was the largest independent body shop in Memphis. Everyone knew that if you wanted a first-class paint job or if you needed a totaled '67 Mustang restored to cherry perfection, you went to Arcado Automotive. Everyone in law enforcement also knew that the garage had been a front for the Montesi crime family since JFK was in the White House. If Sal Junior was involved with Mid-South Transport, it meant something very profitable and most likely very illegal was going on.

"What were you hauling for them, Don? Electronics? Television sets? Hijacked cigarettes?"

"Nothing like that. Just garbage," he said. "And it didn't have nothing to do with my attack, anyway. I'd unloaded my truck at the industrial park. We were on our way out of the neighborhood when the engine broke down."

"I thought you were alone when it happened. You said *we*."

His eyes darted away from me. "The drugs," he said. "They make me fuzzy."

"I'm not trying to accuse you of anything."

"Look, Charlie. I'm tired, okay? I think I need to lie down."

"Don . . ."

"I'm going to lie down."

I got the message so I said sure, that was probably a good idea. Then he stopped me.

"Those kids who did this?"

"Yeah?"

He shivered a little, remembering. "I tell you the truth, Charlie. I think they just wanted to watch me burn."

Frances Cheatham looked as if she'd lost five pounds and added ten years since the day her grandson died. She sat in her shadowed living room, surrounded by flowers and condolence cards and her photo albums, sipping straight bourbon from a coffee cup.

"I don't see what my husband's job has to do with Terrell."

"I'm not sure that it does," I said.

But that was only partly true. Nate Randolph, my old partner in the homicide division, had surprised me by not only returning my call but actually doing me a favor. A decade ago I'd ended up in a situation where I had a choice between destroying evidence that could have put the former head of the Montesi family, Fat Tony, in prison for twenty years or saving the life of a woman who was very close to me. The internal affairs investigation that followed my decision led me to resign from the Memphis P.D. Guilt by association ended Nate's chance at making captain. Maybe his new wife had mellowed him.

Two years retired, Nate still had a lot of friends. It had taken him less than twenty minutes to find out that although they hadn't been arrested, Bop-Bop Drake and Demond Jones were considered the only suspects in Terrell Cheatham's murder and that four of the five witnesses who claimed the perps were young black men were employed at the West Parrish Industrial Park, the Depression-era sprawl of abandoned brick warehouses, corrugated tin shacks, rusted-out water and gasoline storage tanks, and collapsing docks on the banks of the Mississippi River just a few blocks from Frances Cheatham's apartment. The park had last operated at full capacity back during the Vietnam War but somehow seemed to employ everyone on the scene of the murder as well as Frances Cheatham's late husband.

"Terrell worked there, too, before he went to Tops," I said.

"It was temporary work, is all. About the time Marcus found out he had cancer, Terrell's job played out. Things always happen at the worst time." She glared at me from over the rim of her coffee cup. "At least, that's the way it works around here."

"Your husband worked the night shift," I said. "It's odd, don't you think? That the park would need twenty-four-hour security, I mean?"

"We were thankful to have a steady paycheck."

"Did your husband or Terrell ever mention Mid-South Transport?"

"Not that I remember," she said, but her eyes darted away from me.

"Mrs. Cheatham, you and I both know that Terrell was killed by two white men. Somehow five people claim the shooters were young and black. Four of the five work at the industrial park where your husband and grandson were employed. The fifth works for Mid-South Transport, a trucking company that makes regular deliveries to the park and one I'm fairly certain is a front for the Mafia. If your husband ever mentioned what goes on there . . ."

"He never said and I never asked." She met my eyes. "I've not hired you for anything, and you're not a cop, so I don't know what you think you can do."

It was a good question, and I didn't really have an answer. Part of it was pride, maybe. I didn't like being told that I hadn't seen what I knew I had. But it was more than that. The pain I'd seen in Frances Cheatham's face when she realized Terrell was dead and that impotent drowning feeling I'd had as I rushed into the parking lot a few minutes too late to do anything that mattered haunted my sleep. This was the only way I knew to put those memories to rest.

"If someone has threatened you or if you're . . ."

"Ain't no one done nothing," she said, her voice quavering and angry. "But what does it matter anyway? Nothing you or me do is going to bring my grandson back, is it?"

"No, ma'am," I admitted.

"Then what's it matter?" She shook her head and reached for her coffee mug. "It doesn't matter. Not now." Her eyes flashed at me. "This was our home. We told ourselves if we raised him right, things could be different for him, that if you was fair to people they'd be fair to you, that if you did the right thing it would *be* right. We was stupid, and I'm just a fool. My husband was a good man and Terrell was, too. At least he was going to be."

She stared into her empty coffee mug as if she could will whiskey to appear. After a minute she pulled herself from the couch, wobbling a little as she waited for me to stand.

"Sometimes you got to look after yourself. You can't always be worrying about what ought to be. Sometimes you just got to take care of your own."

I wasn't sure what she meant, but I agreed with her that sometimes you did. Then she reminded me that this was a dangerous neighborhood, especially for someone with my skin tone.

"What I'm saying," she said, in case I hadn't understood, "is that it would probably be best if you didn't come down here anymore."

Then she slammed the door. In the parking lot, a little boy, ten or eleven, maybe, stepped from between two cars. He was small, delicate-looking, with huge brown eyes that seemed to swallow his face, but he already had the walk, the aggressively slumped shoulders, the sneer of a gang kid. Ten years from now he'd have the jailhouse banter, the dead eyes, and the rap sheet to go with them—if he lived that long.

"You Raines, right? They some people want to see you."

"Oh yeah?" I said.

"I'm telling you," he said. "You pass that school up the block? See the courts in the back? Bop-Bop and Demond ballin' up there."

"Thanks for the message," I said, opening my car door.

"So you going?"

"Depends on what they want."

"Man, they don't tell me what they want. They just say go get that white guy, tell him we got something to talk about." He kicked at the pavement with the toe of a scuffed sneaker. "So?"

"You want a ride?"

He took an instinctive step backward and his large eyes got larger. "I don't get in cars with strangers."

"You tell me who you think had Terrell killed," Demond Jones said.

He was a rangy kid with a bushy Afro, a slow smile, and a shark's eyes. He sprawled on the icy metal bleachers near a fenced-in basketball court, his long legs stretched out in front of him, a Kool dangling from the corner of his mouth and a thirty-two-ounce can of Icehouse beer resting by his side. One row up, Bop-Bop Drake perched over his friend's shoulder like an overgrown parrot.

I wasn't sure what I thought about any of what they had said. I looked away, watched the four-on-four game on the court. Most of the players were good, but one was spectacular, quick and sure-footed with a smooth jump shot and a crossover dribble that could blow out a defender's ankle. I recognized him from sports reports on the local news. A sophomore in high school, he was being recruited by half the major universities in America and destined to be an NBA star, but none of the kids gathered around the courts were paying him any attention. Down here Demond and Bop-Bop were the stars, the heroes that all these thirteen- and fourteen-year-old kids wanted to be. It made sense. None of those kids had the talent of Kyrie Taylor, but they all knew they could learn to deal drugs or use a gun.

"You're telling me you guys firebombed that truck for political reasons." I finally said.

"We ain't saying we did anything illegal at all," Bop-Bop said. "I'm telling you that Terrell threw that Molotov because he was drunk and angry that they was killing us."

"Genocide is the word Bop-Bop's trying to think of," Demond said. "That's what Terrell kept saying when he was drunk. They're committing genocide, just like in Rwanda, but nobody knows it. T-Bone was smart. Educated, you know?"

"He was in your gang."

"What gang?" Bop-Bop asked. "There ain't no gangs around here."

"Terrell wasn't in nothing. He just came to us because he knew I'd listen to what he had to say."

"Why?" I asked. "Was there money involved?"

He gave me a slow grin. "You act like 'cause I do a little business I don't care about nothing else. Making money is the American way, ain't it?"

"He told you what was going on at the industrial park? Enlighten me."

"I'm not clear on the particulars, but I know something ain't right around here."

"He said they were dumping?"

"Chemicals and all kinds of shit like that. Illegal stuff from all over. T-Bone said it's why his granddad died of bone cancer." For the first time, Demond's eyes softened and I remembered that he wasn't just a gangbanger or a monster but also a nineteen-year-old kid. "He said it was the reason my baby sister got leukemia."

"There's all kind of people sick down here. The apartments where I stay? I know at least six families got kids with cancer. You just go down to the Med, you'll see," Bop-Bop said.

"T-Bone had all kinds of numbers and things he'd gathered," Demond said.

"He called it some foreign word," Bop-Bop said.

Demond gave him a look. "Dossier. It ain't foreign, man. It's American."

"Ain't no word I ever used."

"Damn, Bop-Bop, I know you went to school. Maybe you should have paid attention." Demond looked back at me. "Terrell had pictures he'd taken on his cell phone while he was working there, notes about things his granddad had told him, this research he'd done on the Internet. He showed us that stuff 'cause he knew I'd be interested, since I watched my baby sister die of cancer."

"What happened to it?"

"We ain't got it. That's for sure."

"Why did you firebomb the truck?"

"Let's just say Terrell might have put away a few too many and claimed he was going to take care of things his own damn self. A couple of his buddies might have gone with him, you know, maybe 'cause they thought he wasn't really going to do anything." He closed his eyes for a second. "Or maybe they went with him 'cause they were hurting pretty bad and wanted to strike out the same way he did because a little sister had died. Say this little sister was just six years old and crying for her brother to hold her hand but he was too scared because it hurt too damn much to see her that way."

"I'm sorry," I said.

"We all sorry, man." He took a long drag from his cigarette and then elbowed Bop-Bop's knee. "Tell him all of it."

Bop-Bop cleared his throat and fidgeted. He seemed as nervous as an actor on opening night.

"Well. It's like this." He halted, coughed into his fist, tried again. "Okay, say these two friends and Bone are . . ."

"Just tell him what happened," Demond said. "He ain't a cop no more. Besides, if he says anything, it's our word against his."

Bop-Bop thought it over a moment and then shrugged. "We were all wasted, you know, and T-Bone, that's what we called Terrell 'cause he was always talking about steaks, he kept saying they'd killed Paula, Demond's little sister, kept saying they poisoned her and wasn't no one going to do nothing but us. We were going to throw them bottles of gasoline through the front gates at the park, but on our way we saw the broken-down truck. T-Bone went crazy, yelling at them that they were child killers and as bad as the Nazis. Then he threw the Molotov and the truck caught on fire."

"You keep saying *them*," I said, remembering Don Ellis saying *we broke down*. "Were there two people in the truck?"

"That's where things get complicated," Demond said.

"Yeah, there was a guy in the passenger's seat. He jumped out of the truck with a gun."

"Maybe he had a gun," Demond said. "But it don't matter. He came out of the truck running toward us, and I put three bullets in his chest."

Bop-Bop glanced around and then leaned a little closer. "Guy's name was Giacomeli. We ran into him here and there in the kind of business we do."

"Sam Giacomeli?"

"Called himself Sammy the Saint," Demond said, snorting his disgust.

"You guys killed Paul Cardo's nephew," I said. "And Cardo is . . ."

"He's with the Montesis," Bop-Bop said.

"Not just with," I said.

"We know who he is," Demond said. "That's why we sent for you."

Bop-Bop nodded. "Word on the street is you're in tight with Montesi."

"That's not . . ."

Demond cut me off before I could finish. "Just name us a price, man. I ain't saying we'll pay it, but it'll give us a place to start negotiating."

"You want to hire me?"

"We don't care what you call it," Demond said. "We just want you to make it go away."

My first thought was that this was some kind of joke, but their eyes were desperately earnest. They kept watching me, waiting for me to say I could do something to help, the shaky smiles on their faces caught somewhere between hopeful and damned.

At eleven o'clock the next morning, I sat on a bench outside of the Physical Rehabilitation and Therapy building on the campus of Baptist Memorial Hospital and tried to make sense of it all. After I'd left Drake and Jones, I'd headed for the main branch of the Memphis library. Two hours later, I'd walked back out into the cold night with words like *benzene, dioxin,* and *dichloromethane* buzzing in my head. One sentence echoed: twenty-two billion pounds of toxic and hazardous chemicals released each year through illegal disposal. From New Jersey to Alabama, the mob had used its experience in late-night burial to make millions by handling sticky and usually toxic messes for corporate bosses who were more concerned with profit margins than questions. Whether they were in urban industrial wastelands or backwater burgs, the dump sites had at least two things in common: they were always located on the edge of poor, usually black neighborhoods and they continued to poison generations long after the dumping had been forgotten and both the mob's and the corporate shareholders' profits had been spent.

It was nearly eleven-thirty when a part-time home health aide parked Don Ellis's Dodge minivan in front of the building and scurried around to help him to the front door. When I walked into the second-floor cafeteria, Don was waiting at a table near a row of vending machines, sipping Dr Pepper through a straw. "I'm glad you called. Since you came to the house I ain't thought about nothing else. You left the picture of that kid at my house." He shrugged. "I'm a coward these days, Charlie. I lost what little nerve I had."

I felt sorry for him, but that didn't stop me from asking questions. I'm still enough of a cop that it rarely does.

"We hauled lots of stuff," he said. "Don't ask me what it was, because I don't know, other than there were vats and barrels of it, and it came in from everywhere. Even I could tell the logs and inspections were phony, but no one seemed to ask any questions."

"How long?"

"For me, five years off and on." He slurped his Dr Pepper, stared at a point somewhere past my head. "They've been dumping down there since the early seventies, I think, but that's just a guess."

"Why was Giacomeli with you?"

"It was just one of those things. He was at the industrial park on some kind of business. I don't ask questions. I just drive trucks. Anyways, his Mazda broke down. I offered to take a look, but it was late and he said forget it, he'd just catch a ride back with me. Then the truck started acting up. The last thing I remember him saying was 'Jesus Christ, two engines in one night, maybe I'm frigging cursed.' Then those kids came from nowhere and . . ." His voice trailed off, and he chased his straw around with the tip of his tongue, finally gave up and licked his lips instead. "After the fire started, someone must have made a phone call, because when I woke up everyone was saying I was alone. A guy visited me in the ICU, told me that's the way it happened and I didn't want to complicate matters by saying any different."

"Listen, Don," I said. "I still got a few friends on the force."

"Forget it," he said, his voice loud enough to turn heads in our direction. "I'm telling you this 'cause it's been on my mind a lot and you knew about it anyway, but I'm not talking to anyone else. Ever."

"Don, something needs to be done."

"Listen to me, Charlie. The thing I thought about while I was in the hospital was that maybe I had this coming, that maybe I deserved to die. But I got my boys and my ex-wife to think about." He licked his lips again. "I said what I got to say. And I'm never going to say it again."

I was furious. I wanted to tell him that he was right: he had become a coward. Maybe I even opened my mouth to do it, but the sight of him struggling to stand, his ruined face straining from the effort, left me wordless and ashamed.

Two hours later I lay on the asphalt outside my apartment building and stared up at the flushed and bloated face of the man who'd dented the back of my head with a pool cue and cracked a couple of my ribs with the toe of his snake-skinned cowboy boot. He looked familiar, but my mind was reeling from shock and pain, and I couldn't quite get a handle on his name or who he was or why he seemed intent on killing me.

"Look here, Charlie. Moan a lot, thrash around like you're really hurting, and this will go a lot quicker," he said in a voice that sounded as if he started each day by gargling broken glass. "I tried to beg off this one, but you know how it is." He stomped my left hand, ground the bones under his heel, grinned down at me. "You don't recognize me, do you?"

If I'd had the strength to do anything except whimper and cringe and try to remember the words of the Lord's Prayer, I would have told him that I didn't really give a damn who he was. He could have been Santa Claus, the Tooth Fairy, or the frigging Easter Bunny for all I cared. I just didn't want him to hurt me anymore.

"It's me, Frankie Giageos," he said. "I guess I put on a few pounds, huh?"

I blinked cold sweat from my eyes, squinted up at his face, and saw a guy I used to know buried beneath a fresh fifty pounds of fat. Frankie Gee. The last I'd heard, he was in federal prison for conspiracy to commit mail fraud.

"You got out," I said.

"Couple of months ago."

Then he kicked me again, left side this time, and I felt a rib crack. Say what you wanted about Frankie Gee, he was a professional. Another kick to the solar plexus and then he took a step back and stood looking down at me, breathing hard, the air whistling through his nose and rattling in his chest.

"I'm getting too old for this crap," he said, gasping for air.

"Me too," I said.

"That's pretty good, Charlie." He wiped his face on his coat sleeve and pulled a pack of Camels from his inside pocket. "I got a message for you."

I coughed hard, nearly passed out from the pain, but felt a little better when I saw that I'd spat out a mouthful of phlegm instead of blood. "Let me guess. Stay away from Parrish Industrial Park."

He lit a cigarette with a gold Zippo. "You know this stuff already, why am I here?"

He glanced over his shoulder at a silver Lexus parked in a hand-icapped space. A heavyset man with gray curly hair was sitting be-hind the wheel, sipping from a Styrofoam cup while he watched us. I recognized him as the man who'd been driving the SUV when Terrell Cheatham was murdered. Seeing him here with Frankie Gee brought his name back to me. Jackie Marconi, a bottom-feeder who'd been doing grunt work for the mob since he was sixteen. It looked as if he'd taken a giant leap up the ladder.

"Jackie Macaroni sits in the car while you're out . . ."

"'Jackie Macaroni.' That's good," Frankie said. "Since Tony re-tired and Vinnie's been so screwed up over his kid, God rest his little soul, things ain't the way they used to be. Between you and me, they ain't right at all."

"Cardo's calling the shots," I said.

"And Jackie there is the king turd in the toilet bowl." He flicked his cigarette away, grunted as he stooped to retrieve the sawed-off pool cue. "Cardo's serious about this one, Charlie. Next time I'll have to put a bullet in your head. Only reason you got a pass this time is because even though Tony ain't the boss no more, his opinion carries weight." He took another quick glance back at the Lexus. "If he were to make a direct request on your behalf, people would be inclined to listen. You hear what I'm saying?"

"I hear you, Frankie."

"You listening?"

"I hear you."

"Same old Charlie R," he said.

I wasn't expecting the kick in the crotch. It caught me off-guard, sent stars shooting behind my eyes and the bacon, egg, and cheese biscuit I'd gobbled for breakfast spewing onto the pave-ment. He hadn't pulled the kick or tried to soften the blow. Like I said, Frankie Gee was a professional.

"When you talk to Tony, give him my best wishes," he said.

I wiped the vomit from my mouth. "What makes you think I'm going to talk to Tony?"

"You're stubborn, Charlie. Not stupid."

When the Lexus pulled out of the lot, I curled up into a ball and lay on the asphalt, taking deep breaths of cold air until my stomach settled. A few curtains ruffled in the apartments across the way, but no one bothered to come out to help or took the trouble to call 911. Five minutes later, I crawled to my car and drove myself to the emergency room.

In a perfect world, his loyalty as an old friend and his commitment to justice, decency, and the American Way would have led Nate Randolph to use his influence to get the department to launch an investigation into illegal dumping and Terrell Cheatham's murder. But no one seemed particularly interested.

"Call the EPA," Nate said. "They got a hotline for things like this."

"That's all you got to say?"

"No," he said, nodding at the can of Tecate I'd set on his new coffee table. "Either keep that damn thing in your hand or use a coaster."

I reached for my beer, winced from the pain in my ribs. I'd gotten lucky. Only three were broken. The rest of me was so sore and swollen that I felt like I'd been locked into a barrel with a rabid wolverine and pitched over Niagara Falls.

"You've got nothing and you know it, Charlie," he said. "The word of a couple of street punks? The truck driver's going to deny everything."

"Frankie Gee didn't pay me a visit just to catch up on old times."

"Being right don't change anything." He finished his beer and set the empty back down on a coaster. "Call the EPA. They go in with a search warrant and find anything out of the ordinary, the feds will be on Cardo like stink on an outhouse."

"And by the time they get around to filing charges, all of the important witnesses will have disappeared and I'll end up in the Mississippi River."

He gave me a wicked grin. "Not my problem. I'm retired. Remember?"

*

I've seen movies and read books about ordinary people who are willing to disregard their own safety to testify against the mob or reveal the abuse of power by corrupt public officials or blow the whistle on corporate bosses who deny knowledge of the poisons they peddle. These people are real heroes, capable of putting the good of the whole in front of their own self-interest. I've always marveled at their courage and appreciated their sacrifice. But I'm not one of them. No one would describe my life as glamorous, and it's a long way from what I'd imagined it would be when I was a kid, but I was in no hurry to throw it away. Instead of calling the EPA, I called in a favor from an old friend.

The next afternoon I exited the 240 loop at Summer Avenue. At his Uncle Tony's request, Little Vinnie Montesi had agreed to spare me half an hour of his time. I'd expected him to choose one of the half-dozen Italian restaurants he frequented or, if I were lucky, the warehouse-sized gentleman's club he owned on Brooks Road. Instead I'd been summoned to a Waffle House that sat between a run-down motel where half the guests cooked meth in their rooms and a convenience store that seemed to specialize in prepaid cell phones and $3-a-bottle wine.

When I stepped into the restaurant, the hairs tingled on the back of my neck and my pulse roared in my ears. Three broad-shouldered men hunched over coffee cups at the counter. I didn't need to see their faces to know they were Montesi's men, but Vinnie himself was nowhere around. A setup? The thought made my mouth dry and my pulse throb in my neck. It struck me that I was putting a lot of faith in the respect Little Vinnie might have for his uncle. Before his health and his age had led him to a condo in Sarasota, Florida, Fat Tony ran the Mafia in Memphis for twenty-five years. He was greedy, power-hungry, ruthless when it came to competition, but he was also a rational man, capable of great loyalty and occasional generosity when it came to his friends.

His nephew wasn't just Tony's opposite in physical appearance. Around police stations in Memphis, Arkansas, Mississippi, and Alabama, the years since Tony retired and Vinnie took over were referred to as the Cokehead Reign of Terror. Vicious by nature and possessed by an addict's megalomania, Little Vinnie Montesi had set about renegotiating all of the old understandings. Black drug dealers, redneck meth cookers, and point men for the Mexican drug cartels had been turning up in vacant lots, abandoned warehouses, and torched cars for the last six years. Now, looking at those three broad backs and all those empty booths, I wondered if I hadn't made the worst mistake of a life that had been full of them.

Then one of the broad-shouldered men swiveled on his stool to face me, and my pulse and my nerves settled a little. Frankie Gee. I wondered what it said about my life and my chosen profession that seeing the guy who'd broken my ribs, stomped my hands, and nearly kicked my testicles into my sinus cavities was a comfort.

"Last booth," Frankie Gee said.

The seats were empty, but a waffle swimming in blueberry syrup, a half glass of chocolate milk, and a platter of bacon sat on the table. I slid into the side opposite the food and waited. A couple of minutes later, Vinnie Montesi came from the men's room, patting his face with a paper towel. In the movies people are always kissing the rings of Mafia bosses, but he didn't even offer to shake my hand. Instead he slid into the booth and gave me a curt nod. I knew he was younger than me by a good seven years, but today he seemed much older. He was ten, maybe fifteen pounds lighter than I remembered, with dark bruises beneath his eyes and fresh patches of gray in his dark brown hair. His movements were wooden and lifeless, a million miles from the jerky, earthquake-beneath-the-skin manner of a coke addict on a binge. He looked as if his grief for his son had scooped out his insides and left a hollow shell.

He picked up the glass of chocolate milk but instead of drinking it sniffed the rim and then set it back down. "You like milk?" he asked.

"Sure," I said, and then shrugged. "Not really. I pretty much stick with coffee and beer."

"I can't stand the stuff," he said. "Milk, I mean. Chocolate or white, either one. The taste makes me vomit, has since I was a kid." He picked up the glass again, and his smile was crooked and damned. "Before he got sick, Michael drank it by the gallon. He loved this place. Waffles, bacon, sausage, fried eggs. My wife, she's a health-food addict, always worrying about nitrates and sodium and on and on, but as long as Mikey was up to it, I'd bring him every Sunday." He shut his eyes for a second. "I thought I'd never want to step foot in this place again, but now . . . now it's where I come to feel peaceful. My wife, she goes to church. I come to this dump and order a bunch of food that makes me sick to my stomach."

"I'm sorry for your loss," I said, hating the hollow empty sound of the words as I spoke them.

He waved away my condolences. "My uncle likes you," he said. "The way he ran things . . . well, they aren't exactly my way, but that don't mean I don't appreciate him. Out of respect for him, I'll listen, but I'm not making promises."

When I finished telling him what I knew and what I suspected, he nodded to himself. Then he spent a couple of minutes staring at a point on the ceiling.

"I've heard what you got to say."

"And?"

"Paul Cardo's a businessman, so am I. The way we do things is, he deals with his problems and I deal with mine."

"You're saying you don't know what goes on at West Parrish Industrial Park?"

"Don't know and don't care."

"As long as you get your cut."

His tongue darted over his upper lip. "I have a piece of advice for you, Charlie, and I'm giving it because of your friendship with my uncle. This thing you told me today? You don't want to be telling it to anyone else, especially not anyone connected to the federal government. A thing like that . . ." He shrugged and gave me a rattlesnake's grin. "Well, my affection for my uncle only goes so far."

I took a deep breath, glanced at the untouched waffle and the half-empty glass of chocolate milk. "What did your son die of? It was cancer, right?"

"Leukemia," he said, his voice as cold as wind blowing over an iceberg. "Don't push me, Raines."

"I was in the Med the other day," I said. "The emergency room . . ."

"I heard about that, too."

"When they finished with the X-rays and the bandages, I had a little extra time, so I visited a few people, most of them from South Memphis."

"We're done here," he said.

I shook my head. "Take a ride with me."

"You're crazy."

"Take a ride with me."

He grimaced. "To the Med?"

"One hour. That's all I'm asking. Then I go away and keep my mouth shut. You don't have to worry about offending your Uncle Tony . . ."

"I'm not that worried."

"Then it'll save you the trouble of having me killed."

My heart hammered and a little voice in the back of my head shouted that the only thing I was going to accomplish here was to get myself murdered, but I held my gaze as steady as I could. Then he caught me off-guard.

"Tony says you lost a child."

Even though all that was over twenty years ago, I felt as if he'd sucker-punched me in the center of my chest. "A daughter. Still-born," I said. "It's not the same."

He nodded more to himself than me. "You ride with us and I'll give you an hour." Then he grabbed my wrist and leaned across the booth so that a passerby might have thought he was about to kiss me. "And if you ever try to use my son's memory to jerk me around again, I won't bother having someone kill you. I swear to God, I'll do it myself."

It didn't take an hour. After twenty minutes on the pediatrics wing of the Regional Medical Center, he grabbed my arm and stared at me with the wild, trapped eyes of a rabbit caught in a snare.

"I got to get out of here," he said. "I can't breathe. I just can't get any air."

Frankie Gee and another, younger soldier who'd come up with us turned to me as Vinnie bolted past them, his head down, his hand clamped over his mouth. When I tried to follow him to the elevator, Frankie blocked my path.

"Why'd you bring him here?" Frankie asked, his dark eyes glassy beads set in fat. "What the hell did you think you were doing?"

"Trying to save my life," I said.

Frankie's expression made it clear that he no longer thought of me as a friend. "Yeah, well, good luck with that," he said, but he stepped out of my way.

Vinnie Montesi sat on a brick wall just outside the entrance. A cigarette dangled from his lips, and he was frantically rummaging through his coat pockets.

"Lost my damn lighter again," he said. "Did I have it at the Waffle House?"

I shook my head and handed him my Zippo. "You all right?"

He fired the tip of his cigarette, took a drag, and exhaled toward the gray clouds that drifted from across the river. "I spent two eternities in these frigging places. Michael was in Baptist Memorial," he said. "But they're all the same. They feel the same. Like hopelessness and loss and bad memories. When Mikey died, he held my hand. He was too weak to squeeze it or anything, but he held on as long as he could."

"I didn't . . ."

He flicked his hand to tell me to shut up. Then when Frankie Gee and the other guy stomped toward us, ready to break the rest of my ribs, he flicked his hand again.

"Those kids up there. We gave them cancer, didn't we? The stuff we dumped at the park."

"Not all of them," I said.

"That's why God did it," he said. "Right? That's why Mikey got leukemia. We dumped that crap and made a lot of people sick, so Mikey got cancer."

"I'm not saying that."

"Never mind that Paul Cardo's been running this scam since the seventies or that my Uncle Tony raked in his share of the profits. I took my cut for six years so God killed my kid." He exhaled smoke at the sky. "But what are you going to do? He's God, right? The boss of bosses. You eat his crap and pretend you're thankful."

"I didn't bring you here to hurt you," I said, and wondered if my feeling sympathy for Vincent Montesi meant I'd gone crazy or the world had turned upside down.

"You know what I think? I don't think God waits until the afterlife to punish you. I think he does it right here." He flicked his cigarette away. "Way I see it? Screw eternity. Right here, right now is hell."

"Maybe not," I said, seizing what might have been the only opportunity I had to keep myself out of that cold, dark river. "Maybe every day is purgatory," I said, grabbing at the shadow of a rope. "Maybe it's your chance to put right what you did the day before."

It was pretty lame, I guess. Something I might have heard on a late-night drunk or read on a men's room wall. But it was all I had, and I was betting my life on it.

"Yeah?" he said, frowning, wanting to believe it. "Your chance to do what? Some kind of penance?"

I knew he'd taken the bait. "Maybe."

A smile flittered around his lips and then died. "So maybe you can set things right, get to heaven where you can see . . ." He let the thought fade and buried it alongside the smile. "Shutting down a business like that would cause problems. Paulie wouldn't be happy. I'd have to deal with it." He closed his eyes, nodded to himself. "But you know that, right?"

"Yeah."

"Three weeks," he said. "That's what I need to make sure there's nothing that could cause me or Tony any trouble. Three weeks. Then you can call the feds, let them start getting that garbage out of there. That's the only deal I'm going to offer."

The people in South Memphis had been poisoned for over thirty years, so I figured three weeks wouldn't matter that much one way or the other. If saving my life—and Demond and Bop-Bop and Don Ellis's, I told myself to feel a little better—meant that some of the guilty would go free? Well, they always do, don't they?

"All right," I said.

He stood then, motioned for Frankie and the other guy to head to the parking garage. There was no question about it. I wasn't invited.

"You really believe that?" he asked. "That every day is one more chance to do penance, settle old debts?"

"I want to," I said.

He turned away and left me alone. But that was okay. I knew what I'd just done and that people were going to die because of it, and alone seemed like the right place for me to be.

How would you want it to end? If it could turn out any way you wanted, what would be different? I wasted a lot of time asking my-self those questions. In the end, this is what happened.

Paulie Cardo and his mistress were found dead in her condo. According to Nate Randolph, the girl had been shot twice in the chest and hadn't suffered. They kept Paul Cardo alive for a while. After a couple of beers, I can tell myself that I'm not responsible, but I know better. When you suggest the idea of penance to a violent man, there's no reason to expect that his version of penance would be anything but violent.

In a perfect world, Demond and Bop-Bop would have realized the error of their ways. But of course that didn't happen. Six weeks ago Bop-Bop was arrested for slitting Demond's throat in a South Memphis pool hall. Most likely it was over an argument about the profits from their thriving drug business, but in perverse moments I wonder if Bop-Bop didn't finally get tired of Demond's vocabulary lessons and decide to silence him forever.

Vinnie Montesi has put on a few pounds and looks healthier, but I'd given him a balm for his conscience, not the key to a change of life. If you buy smack or coke or rent a prostitute anywhere from Dyersburg to Biloxi, odds are you're still lining Vinnie's pockets. Don Ellis committed suicide when the papers broke the story about chemical dumping in South Memphis. Maybe he did it because of the guilt or because he wanted to save his sons and his ex-wife from Vinnie Montesi's brand of penance. Whatever the reason, I like to think that in the end, Don Ellis found his courage.

For the next two weeks, people who were connected to the industrial park or Mid-South Transport turned up in the unlikeliest of places—burning wrecks on the interstate, sandbars in the Mississippi, abandoned warehouses downtown. It was an actuary's nightmare. I'd sentenced those people to death when I accepted Vinnie Montesi's offer to give him three weeks to tie up loose ends. To help myself sleep at night, I pretended that what happened to them was justice.

Eventually the FBI and the EPA gave up their investigations. The mob members who seemed to be involved ended up just as dead as the potential witnesses who might have testified against them. The corporate bosses and hospital administrators and paid-for politicians who made all this possible were never named in an indictment. Any chance that the people who profited from the dumping could have been found went away when I cut my deal with Vinnie Montesi.

I'm just like everyone else. I find it hard to live with the cowardly, self-serving parts of myself. I told myself that *if only* I'd had Terrell Cheatham's dossier, things would have been different, that I would have taken it to the papers or turned it over to the EPA and more of the guilty would have been identified. But thinking about the folder only brought more questions. What had happened to it? How had Cardo known where to find Terrell Cheatham but been clueless about Demond and Bop-Bop? That's when I started thinking about what Frances Cheatham had said.

When I paid my third visit to her apartment, spring had finally come to Memphis. Dogwoods were blooming. The sun was bright gold, and the entire world, even the toxic wasteland part of it, was cloaked with green. But inside Frances Cheatham's apartment, the shades were drawn and everything seemed to be coated with a layer of gray.

"He was a good boy," she said, tapping a photo album with her index finger. "Smart, too. I should have listened."

"He showed you his file. His dossier," I said.

"Just like he showed me the roses or the rainbows he drew in school when he was a little child." She picked up a glass and swallowed a mouthful of whiskey. "He loved his granddaddy, that's why he wanted to stop it. But he brought it to me. He told me what it was, what them men had done. He wanted to take it to somebody at the paper. I told him to take it to Mr. Lewinski instead. He was the white man who was head of security at the park. They were holding back on Marcus's pension."

"His pension?"

"Nine hundred and thirteen dollars a month. He had that coming, Marcus did. He worked hard and it killed him. So when Terrell showed me all that, I told him to take it to Mr. Lewinski, to tell him to give us the money my husband earned or we'd make it public. Terrell didn't want to. He kept saying it was wrong, that we had to do something, but I told him, 'Son, the only person that ever does something for you is yourself.' He loved me, so he let me talk him down. But you know that, don't you?"

"Yes, ma'am," I said.

"I told myself I was doing it for *him*, so he could have the money to go to college and get out of this neighborhood. But I was doing it for myself, too, because I was scared of ending up sleeping under an overpass and eating garbage. But I knew as soon as they sent him away and told me they'd call us that they meant to kill him. That's why I was so glad to see you. I figured he'd be safe in jail."

There was no point in telling her that half the cons and a third of the jailers were bought and paid for by men like Montesi and Cardo. Instead I said that she'd done the best she could. It didn't matter anyway. Lewinski was one of the corpses who'd turned up in the river.

"I'm sorry," I said, but the words just hung there.

On my way out the door, I stopped and looked back at her. She was tracing the photo album with the tip of her finger, cocooned in the guilt that would follow her to her grave. Then I thought about Vinnie Montesi drinking chocolate milk and staring at a syrup-covered waffle to hold on to the memory of his son and Demond Jones telling me that his little sister had begged him to make the pain go away. I thought about Don Ellis looking at his face in the mirror, wondering what had happened to the life he'd once known.

I closed the door behind me. Then I closed my eyes. For a moment I was back there in that hospital, smelling antiseptic and pine trees, listening to my wife weep and staring at the blue, lifeless lump that should have been my little girl.

A few blocks away, the cleanup at the industrial park was just beginning, but I knew it didn't matter. In the end, we don't dump the worst of our toxic waste in abandoned warehouses or slow-moving rivers. We carry it around in our memories until it's safely buried six feet underground.

DANIEL WOODRELL

Returning the River

FROM *The Outlaw Album*

MY BROTHER LEFT no footprints as he fled. There'd been three nights of freeze, and the mud had stiffened until the sloped field lay as hard as any slant road. Morning light met rime on the furrows and laid a shine between rows of cornstalks cut to winter spikes, and my brother, Harky, a mutinous man with a fog patch of gray hair drifting to the small of his back and black-booted feet, crushed the faded stalks aside as he came to them, and only these broken spikes marked his passing. His strides were long but curiosity curled his path, spun it about in small pondering circles as he glanced behind, followed by abrupt, total shifts in forward direction. The mud was unblemished but for the debris of cornstalks, and some of the pale dried shucks were spotted by kerosene drip pings. Harky still carried the fuming torch he'd made of a baseball bat and a wadded sheet, the torch he'd used to set the neighbor's house afire, to make amends, to show his love, and flammable droplets fell beside him partway across the field.

Our father chased my brother. He chased him down the road from the burning house, into the field, wearing a white bathrobe and loose slippers. With each step he fell farther behind as his old sick feet skittered over uneven furrows and tripped. The nosepiece from his oxygen tube was yet pinched to his face, and a length of tube waved about while the robe flapped open. He fell repeatedly and stalks stabbed his skin broken at the ankles and hips. He stood up from the field six times, or only five, then again tripped over a furrow, collapsed to the frost, and lay there, face to the mud, withered fingers clenching at stalks, robe flung wide.

Smoke and shouts drifted from the neighbor's house.

Father's breathing could be heard beyond the fence line, up the road, the hoarse snatching after breath, rattling inhalations. He was raw beneath the robe, his skin ashen and his blood thinned by medications. The broken spots on his ankles and hips quickly turned blue and leaky. He held on to the oxygen tube with one hand, holding it still and inhaling, as if there might be a trapped bubble of pure oxygen his lungs could burst and pull through in shreds. Fogged eyeglasses hung from a cord around his neck, and his glum white private hair and forlorn flopping parts were open to the cold. He lay there weak as a babe, but a babe who'd already snuck a drink this morning, scotch, and chased it with a forbidden cigarette.

Across the mud and downslope he spotted Harky and his fog of hair scuttling from the field at the far end, plunging over the wire fence and into the thicket. Six-foot-two of man, with a jostling cloud riding his back and a blackened baseball bat in one hand.

Father rose to his knees, gasping, then stood and wobbled his way back to the road, legs too limber for firm strides, blood from his broken spots making lazy trails down his skin. Our father, the joking drunk who was so bitter when sober, shuffled past the edge of the fallow field, toward the big hunkered old house of glowering white that had been the home of our mother's family for three generations before recent inheritance delivered it down to us Dewlins. Mother waited near the door, pacing between the four-sided pillars on the veranda where she'd played jacks as a girl, hopscotch, her eyes glistening and rounded with anger. Her hair was a carefully selected chestnut hue, girlishly long and casually brushed, and she wore a winter coat belted over her bedclothes. She watched our father limp to the house and did not reach out to help him until he climbed the steps. They both paused on the veranda and looked across the road, toward the flames dancing on the shiny new log cottage of the only close neighbor, a man named Gordon Mather Adams, a retired schoolteacher of some sort, a man I'd never spoken to, busy beside his eastern wall with a yellow garden hose and a panicked air, the excess water running from the flames down the slope of winter grass toward the river behind his house.

They stared for a few minutes, then she said, "I should've called in the fire, but . . ."

Father opened the door, crossed the threshold, and stepped onto the rug. He was bleeding from blue places, bleeding down his ankles, over that knob of bone, onto the large and intricate heirloom rug Mother's people had always spread just inside the door, drop after drop.

Harky had waited for the holidays to fashion a torch and commit his spectacular act of penance, waited for me to be in the house, on the scene, his witness. Over the fence he'd gone, that fog bouncing about his head, into the forest, and I did not chase hard, did not even hurry, but let him spend his energy fleeing for a while. The trees stood towering gray and numb over us both, shorn of green uplift, the bark bared to the heavy sky and chapping wind. I suspect some stark limbs attempted to point Harky toward escape, others to wag in admonishment, blaming him for palming his pills and drinking whisky again. He hopped onto rocks in the creek to cross the stream, missed only one, and pushed up the slope with his left boot splashed and a sock growing soggy, choosing not to realize how the near future would treat a wet sock on a freezing day. The limb he'd trust most gestured this way, onto the animal path that curled around the hill in a spiral rising to the crest. He knocked aside branches and winter brambles with the baseball bat, and his feet crunched across wastes of leaves and twigs.

Harky is running toward places that aren't there anymore. That limb aimed him in the direction of the vanished cabin our mother's family first squatted in after they'd followed game trails west from Kentucky to claim these acres. He knows the general whereabouts of the old hearthstone, but the four walls have fallen and become mulch, and the yard is grown over with woods, blended again with the forest. One tree, many trees, where did the cabin sit? The rocks of the chimney were taken down and carted to the next house the Humphrieses built—high, wide, and white, across the creek on richer ground. In spring warmth the original spot might be found by looking for brighter colors paraded amid the bland grasses: irises, daffodils, columbine. Great-great-great-grandma with the first name blown from her headstone and lost for good was quick to put down flowers near the house, dollops of cultivation in the yard that meant we live here now, inside this wilderness, and those common perennials are the only remains of a family place abandoned.

In his sick final years Grandpa Humphries sold the pasture, the cornfields, the wooded hillocks and ridges, sold every acre but the two that made a lawn for the house. He'd feared he might live closer to forever than predicted and need those dollars to find rest in his mind. Harky kneels to our old ground and rubs his hands through the sodden leaves, pushing them aside, making one tiny clearing after another, looking for nubs, withered blades of green. His breath puffs signals that don't last. Dead grasses fly to his clothes and cling. Dirt buries beneath his fingernails. He's in high spirits for a man who knows that his parole will be revoked in about an hour, maybe two. There's a pint bottle in his jacket and he stands up for a ruminative chug, but it is empty except for a few drops that are slow reaching his lips. He looks around the ground, studies trees he might know from years before, but doesn't spot any old acquaintances, and moves on farther behind the hill. He just can't find Granny-what's-her-name's flowers during this cold season.

The path is steep and vague in spots, barely there, with a few crashed trees to be crawled across or jumped. Running these woods, Harky is feeling redeemed in his bones, raised in his heart, a much better son now than he was before dawn. We'd of-ten hunted this land together when down from the city during holidays, boys afield in joyous pursuit of the small and wild, shar-ing our single-shot Sears twenty-two, avoiding the tensions in the house for hours at a stretch. I'd pop squirrels from limbs, since they have more taste, but Harky favored rabbits because they were easier to skin. When snow had fallen over the meadows, he'd de-light in tracking bunnies at dawn, stealthily following paw prints as they made circles easy to follow, then track the same paw prints around again, and again, never caring that if he just waited where he started, the rabbits would circle back within range and offer themselves to his aim: "But tracking is the fun part!" The air on the ridge is cold and smacks of fire, and when I make the turn at the crest, the pinnacle suddenly revealed, Harky is sitting calmly on a large slab rock watching the flames in the valley. That fog of hair drapes past where his ass meets the slab and dangles. The bat stood upright between his legs, black end down.

He said, "Think he'll be happy now?"

"You didn't get far."

"I knew they'd send you—bring any whisky?"

The seal hadn't been cracked on the bottle I handed to him.

He busted the whisky open and swallowed a big peaty breakfast, released a deep groan of appreciation, and dropped the cap into his pocket. I sat on the slab beside him. The mess of smoke below had grown. Deputies were standing in the road, and the volunteer fire department was arriving in pickups, little cars, dusty vans, and the one official fire truck they kept ready at Bing Plimmer's gas station.

"Is that house fully involved?"

Two men in waders dragged a hose toward the river, hunching away from the jumping heat. The deputies in the street seemed excited and were gathering around our mother, but she's an old hand at this and stands still, with her arms folded, and listens without argument. Harky's parole would be violated any minute now.

"I think that's what they call it."

"Then it might still burn down flat."

"The man'll only build it back again with insurance money. Maybe bigger."

"But not in time."

"He might live longer than you think."

"No. He'll die seein' the river where it's supposed to be again."

Those distant faces so tiny in the valley turned together and stared roughly in our direction. Harky laughed at them, pointed with his fist, and thumped the ball bat to ground. The fire seemed to be winning. Gordon Mather Adams looked to be weeping. Mother had been angry since the foundation was poured, the first nail driven, and clapped her hands with gusto as the hot ruin spread. A sheriff's car began to roll down the sloped road alongside the field. I swatted my brother on the knee and stood.

"Let's get deeper into the woods," I said. "Make it harder for them."

"You want to run with me?"

He passed the bottle, and I said, "You'll be gone a long time this time, Harky."

"Ahh, I have friends in the slams, baby brother, so don't worry." He raised from the slab and shuffled his feet, then sat again and pulled the boot and sock from his wet foot. The skin looked red. He wrung the sock until droplets fell, then pulled it on damp and laced up. He stood, happy with himself and smiling at the smoke in the sky, the voices all excited in the distance. "I could use a new little TV. With better color. And headphones."

Two walls were coming down. They folded inward and smashed across smoldering furniture and seared appliances, sparks bursting and riding the heat. The flames were renewed by the falling and frolicked. One more wall to fall and Father could die upstairs with the river back in his eyes.

I gave Harky the bottle, wiped my lips dry. "Today's got to be worth a party."

The sheriff's car had stopped on the road and the deputy stood in the opened door talking into the radio, calling for help. He was studying the woods, looking for paths he might follow to give chase, but we remembered them all from before we were born and walked on laughing, down the spiraled path to low ground and away through a rough patch of scrub, into a small stand of pine trees and the knowing shadow they laid over us, our history, our trespassing boots.

Contributors' Notes

Tom Andes was born and raised in New Hampshire and has lived in New Orleans, San Francisco, Fayetteville, Arkansas, and Oakland, California. He attended Loyola University New Orleans and San Francisco State University and has taught at SFSU as well as Northwest Arkansas Community College. His poetry, fiction, and criticism have appeared in *News from the Republic of Letters, Xavier Review, Santa Clara Review, Mantis, Bateau,* and the *Rumpus,* among other publications. A hand-sewn chapbook, *Life Before the Storm and Other Stories,* appeared in a limited run from Cannibal Books in 2010.

▪ I wrote the first draft of "The Hit" shortly after I moved to San Francisco in 2000. In part, I intended the story as an impressionistic response to the shock of moving to the Bay Area, as San Francisco was (and is) the biggest city I'd lived in. I based the character of Mickey on someone I'd met in passing: a native San Franciscan, an Irish-American ex-cop, a person about whom (a mutual friend assures me) the truth is stranger than anything I could have invented. I wanted the story to evoke the plight of the San Francisco neighborhoods that were (and still are) disappearing beneath successive waves of gentrification, as well as the schizophrenia and the greed that seem to define so much of one's daily experience in the Bay.

At the time I didn't feel any confidence in the story, so I stuffed it in a drawer. Several years later I tried expanding it into a novel, giving Mickey nearly 100 pages of backstory. But I still couldn't figure out the opening of the story, so I put it away again, and it stayed in a drawer until, in 2010, I took it with me to a residency program. Much to my surprise, when I lopped off the first few pages, the story sprang to life, and I made most of the subsequent revisions relatively quickly. I'm tremendously grateful to Ralph Adamo for publishing the story in *Xavier Review.* I'm also grateful to the Ragdale Foundation in Lake Forest, Illinois, where a two-week residency occasioned my rediscovery of the story.

Peter S. Beagle was born in 1939 and raised in the Bronx, where he grew up surrounded by the arts and education. Both his parents were teachers, three of his uncles were world-renowned gallery painters, and his immigrant grandfather was a respected writer, in Hebrew, of Jewish fiction and folktales. As a child Peter used to sit by himself in the stairwell of the apartment building he lived in, staring at the mailboxes across the way and making up stories to entertain himself. Today, thanks to classics like *The Last Unicorn, A Fine and Private Place,* and "Two Hearts," he is a living icon of fantasy fiction.

In addition to eight novels and over one hundred pieces of short fiction, Peter has written many teleplays and screenplays (including the animated versions of *The Lord of the Rings* and *The Last Unicorn*), six nonfiction books (among them the classic travel memoir *I See By My Outfit*), the libretto for an opera, and more than seventy published poems and songs. He currently makes his home in Oakland, California.

▪ "The Bridge Partner" isn't like anything else I've ever written. It had its genesis in a frightening dream—not my own, either, but that of my longtime companion Peggy Carlisle, who woke in a West Hollywood hotel out of a nightmare about participating in a play with a fellow actress who kept silently mouthing the words, "I will kill you . . ." No one else in the dream play appeared to take any notice, and the actress went on repeating the soundless threat every time they were onstage together. There was no analyzing or explaining the dream; it seemed to have no connection to anything in Peggy's past, and it neither recurred nor continued to plague her in daily life, as old nightmares so often do. I've always been grateful for that.

But it haunted me, and I kept brooding about it as a possible story notion. When I started writing, all I knew for certain was that the setting would be a bridge club rather than a little theater, despite—or perhaps because of—the fact that I know a good deal about theater and nothing about bridge. Beyond that, I was making it up as I went along, letting the characters tell me the story, which is a lazy habit of mine that I never recommend to writing students. It's just something I do, more often than not, which may be why I've never written mysteries, much as I admire and enjoy them. Mysteries require actual organization, actual planning, actual *thought.* Sounds uneasily like work—and, as I've said, I know myself to be lazy.

I'm truly thrilled to have "The Bridge Partner" defined here as a mystery, selected by the likes of Otto Penzler and Robert Crais; and if it isn't actually a mystery, I can't say what else it might be. Myself, I've always seen it in my head as a French *nouvelle vague* film, in black-and-white, directed by someone like Truffaut or maybe Chabrol, and starring Jeanne Moreau (in whichever role she wanted to take). It's most likely a one-shot—I don't know that I'll ever write anything remotely like it again—but I could be wrong. I've been wrong about a number of things in that line lately. In any case, I'm immensely proud to have it in this anthology.

K. L. Cook is the author of three books of fiction: *Last Call,* winner of the Prairie Schooner Book Prize in Fiction; *The Girl from Charnelle,* winner of the 2007 Willa Award for Contemporary Fiction and an Editor's Choice selection of the Historical Novel Society; and, most recently, *Love Songs for the Quarantined,* winner of the 2010 Spokane Prize for Short Fiction. His work has appeared in such magazines and anthologies as *Best of the West 2011, Glimmer Train, One Story, Writer's Chronicle,* and *Poets & Writers.* He teaches creative writing and literature at Prescott College and in Spalding University's brief-residency MFA in writing program.

▪ My grandmother was the original writer in the family—a reporter and editor in the Texas Panhandle for close to sixty years. In her late eighties, she was still filing three stories a week for *The Childress Index.* Her life was not an easy one—and included several bad marriages—but I always admired her fierce devotion to her vocation as a journalist. The character of Loretta is inspired by her, though what happens in the story is all fiction.

My grandfather was a skilled welder and owned his own welding shop until the day he died, in his nineties. I vividly remember those burn holes in his work shirts and coveralls and the way his skin was pocked with small heat blisters. My great nightmare—imagining his world when I was a child—was the possibility of hot steel in the eye. How a minuscule filament of metal could change the course of several lives became the guiding metaphor for the story.

Jason DeYoung lives in Atlanta, Georgia. His fiction has appeared in *New Orleans Review,* the *Los Angeles Review, Gargoyle, The Fiddleback, Numéro Cinq,* and elsewhere.

▪ "The Funeral Bill" came out of a story I heard years ago about a renter who was demanding that his landlord pay for a funeral. As in "The Funeral Bill," the funeral had been for the renter's wife, and the renter was insistent—to the point of menacing—that the landlord pay. The landlord didn't understand why he was responsible for the costs, and he never paid. I held on to the nugget of this story for years, wondering what could have been the renter's motive. I made up several, but none of them sounded true. In the end, I figured it would be a scarier story if he didn't have a reason or a clearly stated one, just a scheme for someone else to pay.

The other bit of key inspiration that went into this story comes from eyewitness accounts of lucid decapitation. That is, of freshly removed heads still blinking and trying to speak. As the story was told to me, during the French Revolution, there was such a glut of heads rolling; the more philosophical in the rabble would often ask whether these heads were seeing evidence of an afterlife. Blink once for yes, two for no. This might be apocryphal (knowing its source), but I think the idea was aptly applied to the final scene between Jeffers and RD. A special thanks goes to M. Bogan, C. Chambers, and R. Piet for your input on the final drafts of this story.

Joe Donnelly is the coeditor and cofounder of *Slake: Los Angeles*. Prior to starting *Slake,* he was deputy editor of *LA Weekly* during its Pulitzer Prize–winning heyday. He is also the former editor in chief of the influential lifestyle magazines *Stick* and *Bikini*. He is a graduate of the University of California, Berkeley Graduate School of Journalism, where he won the Reader's Digest Foundation Excellence in Journalism Award. Donnelly has won several press association awards for his journalism, and his writing has appeared in *LA Weekly,* the *Washington Post,* the *Los Angeles Times,* the *Times* of London, the *International Herald Tribune,* and many national and international magazines. Donnelly's fiction and essays have appeared in several anthologies and journals.

Harry Shannon has been an actor, an Emmy-nominated songwriter, a recording artist, a music publisher, vice president at Carolco Pictures, and a music supervisor on *Basic Instinct* and *Universal Soldier.* His novels include *Night of the Beast, CLAN, Daemon, Dead and Gone, The Hungry,* and *The Pressure of Darkness,* as well as the Mick Callahan suspense novels *Memorial Day, Eye of the Burning Man, One of the Wicked,* and *Running Cold.* His collection *A Host of Shadows* was nominated for the 2010 Stoker Award by the Horror Writers Association. Readers may contact him via Facebook or www .harryshannon.com.

▪ "Fifty Minutes" began as a fun provocation by Harry to shake me out of a bit of the writing doldrums several years ago. An e-mail showed up in my in box with the first line of the story and the terse command *Your turn.* Harry and I have collaborated on several big projects over the years, including him as my counselor/therapist on my path to sobriety and me as his counselor/therapist (though not licensed!) on his early Mick Callahan novels. So it was not an e-mail to be ignored. Harry and I wrote back and forth by e-mail over the course of a couple weeks, editing and prodding each other during the process. Having been Harry's client added a unique dynamic, though not necessarily the obvious one. I often wrote from Dr. Bell's point of view and Harry from Mr. Potter's. No doubt the cover of fiction, the friendly fire of collaboration, and our shared experiences gave us a unique opportunity to explore the dance of therapy and the depths of psychology. It was a lot of fun, and I think that shows despite the dark nature of the story. The story lay dormant on my desktop for a couple years, all but forgotten, until Laurie Ochoa, my *Slake* partner, and I were putting together issue 2, "Crossing Over," a theme that certainly lends itself to

"Fifty Minutes." Somehow, I remembered the story, dug it up, and Harry and I went back to honing it with Ochoa's steady editing hand. There must be a lesson to be found in how unlikely it is that this story ever saw the light of day yet ended up here . . . Harry?

Kathleen Ford has published in *Yankee, Redbook, Ladies' Home Journal, Southern Review, Virginia Quarterly, Antioch, North American Review, New England Review, Sewanee Review,* and elsewhere. Two of her stories won PEN Awards for Syndicated Fiction and another story was anthologized in *Cabbage and Bones* (1997). Her first novel was published in 1986. Kathleen received a Christopher Isherwood Foundation Award for 2011. She lives in Charlottesville, Virginia, where she is currently writing stories about Irish maids and the soldiers of World War I and completing a novel about the Great War.

▪ "Man on the Run" was inspired by my father's childhood. His family was populated by Irish nationalists, and many of them had taken oaths to do everything in their power to win Irish freedom. According to family lore, when Eamon de Valera visited New York in 1919, he stayed with my father's family in Brooklyn. The children were told that they had to keep their visitor a secret so no one would know when the Irish patriot (the "man on the run") had arrived. If they kept de Valera's arrival secret, no one would know which ship he'd sailed on, thereby protecting the network that had smuggled him out of Ireland.

The sheer drama of the words "man on the run" drew me to write this story, although I knew from the beginning that it would have to be a woman who was running. How I came to envision the two old ladies in their isolated house by Cayuga Lake, I don't know. I lived in Ithaca for a year, and I guess those early-morning walks in the darkness before dawn gave me the setting. I've been interested in the themes of guilt and shame ever since I began writing, and I believe that these emotions can paralyze a person just as surely as fear can. Rosemary, my old lady character, is afflicted with arthritis, but she is immobilized even more by the guilt she feels over her daughter's death seventy years earlier. Both forms of paralysis are out of Rosemary's control, or so it seems, until a battered young woman seeks shelter in Rosemary's house.

As a writer, I create characters. What I loved about writing "Man on the Run" was watching how a very old and frail character insisted on showing me the force of the human will. I'm thrilled to have my story published in *The Best American Mystery Stories 2012* and am grateful to the *New England Review,* and always, of course, to my father.

Mary Gaitskill is the author of the novels *Two Girls, Fat and Thin* and *Veronica,* as well as the story collections *Bad Behavior, Because They Wanted To,* and *Don't Cry.* Her stories and essays have appeared in *The New Yorker, Harper's,*

Granta, The Best American Short Stories, and *The O. Henry Prize Stories.* In 2011 she was a Cullman Fellow at the New York Public Library, where she was researching a novel. She is currently teaching writing at the Eugene Lang program at the New School in New York City.

▪ I wrote "The Other Place" for a very simple reason: I was afraid. I was living alone in a flimsy fishbowl house on a college campus that, as far as I was concerned, was a pervert magnet. The climatic scene of the story came to me before I had any intention of writing a story; I think it appeared in my mind because I wanted to imagine killer and victim coming right up to the crucial moment and then both walking away unharmed. At some point after that, the story formed.

Jesse Goolsby's fiction has won the John Gardner Memorial Prize for Fiction and the Richard Bausch Short Fiction Prize. His work has appeared widely, including in *Epoch, The Literary Review, Harpur Palate, The Journal, Blue Mesa Review,* and *War, Literature & the Arts.* A graduate of the United States Air Force Academy and the University of Tennessee, he was raised in Chester, California, and now writes in Alexandria, Virginia.

▪ When I was a boy, my father would take me out to shoot guns. He had a variety of weapons — revolvers, shotguns, pistols, and rifles — and we'd drive deep into the woods and fire at empty soda cans, cardboard boxes, my sister's old Barbies. One of his prized guns was a .300 Winchester Magnum, a rifle that would bruise you with the recoil if you weren't paying attention. This gun was always off-limits to me. But when I turned twelve, my father finally gave me a turn. I was shaky and nauseous as he handed me the rifle. The power intoxicated my limbs, and as I readied myself and snugged the gun deep into my young shoulder, I took aim at a helpless paper plate stapled onto a standing slab of cardboard. And then it was time. My heartbeat rushed through my ears as I took a thin breath in, and at long last I tugged the trigger and . . . nothing. I tugged again . . . nothing. I pulled back, stunned, and from behind me, my father's voice said, "Safety, son. Safety."

I wrote the end of "Safety" first, the written result being a manifestation of an unexpected fear that arose in me after the birth of my daughter, our first child: the knowledge that one day in the future I would need to be out of town, and what if trouble came on that exact day? What if I were physically helpless but acutely aware of the situation? The rest of the story was the result of me constantly asking, "How did these people get here?"

I owe a great deal of thanks to my dear friends the great writers Donald Anderson and Brandon Lingle, who helped me through early drafts. Also a special thanks to Hao Nguyen from *The Greensboro Review,* who provided the most comprehensive and spot-on editorial guidance I've received from a literary journal. Her warmth and guiding hand played a critical part in the end product.

Katherine L. Hester is the author of the short story collection *Eggs for Young America* (1998). Her fiction has appeared in *Prize Stories: The O. Henry Awards, Five Points, The Yale Review, Brain, Child,* and elsewhere. She lives south of Interstate 20 in Atlanta, Georgia, with her husband and two daughters.

▪ Like James in "Trafficking," I spent considerable time in my twenties driving back and forth on Interstate 10 between the place where I lived and the place where I'd come from. Also like him, I fell under the spell of that highway's flat tedium, its seductive neither-here-nor-thereness.

I don't have a stepbrother, much less one in prison. But that tug of war—between the place you started out and the one where you end up—is pretty universal. As are those decisions, so small and incremental, they often don't seem like decisions at all, that sometimes lead us to places we never expected.

Lou Manfredo is the author of three novels featuring NYPD detective Joe Rizzo: *Rizzo's War, Rizzo's Fire,* and *Rizzo's Daughter.* His short fiction has appeared in *The Best American Mystery Stories 2005, Brooklyn Noir, New Jersey Noir,* and *Ellery Queen's Mystery Magazine.* He worked in the Brooklyn, New York, criminal justice system for twenty-five years. Born and raised in Brooklyn, he now lives in New Jersey with his wife, Joanne.

▪ The basic concept for "Soul Anatomy" had been meandering within my subconscious since my long-gone senior year at Brooklyn's New Utrecht High School. While in science class, an incredibly gifted teacher, whose name, regretfully, I cannot recall, managed to successfully present the subject of biology in a compelling, thought-provoking manner. Much like young officer Miles in "Soul Anatomy," I found myself confronting the nuances of human existence with a somewhat conflicted view, and it remained with me.

Years later, a story would periodically materialize in various forms, all based on that long-ago class and set within the framework of some violent incident. But something was always lacking. It wasn't until my more recent personal interaction with the dismal, ultimately tragic, city of Camden, New Jersey, that the elusive missing piece of the puzzle presented itself. I rolled a blank sheet of paper into my ancient Smith-Corona and watched as the words appeared before my eyes, stigmatalike, through the dust of both long-past and vividly recent memories, and the story actually wrote itself. To date, it remains my most personal and unsettling piece of short fiction.

Thomas McGuane lives in McLeod, Montana. He is the author of numerous novels and short story and essay collections, including *Ninety-Two in the Shade, Driving on the Rim,* and *Gallatin Canyon.* His stories and essays have been collected in *The Best American Short Stories, The Best American Essays,* and *The Best American Sports Writing*. He is a regular contributor to *The New Yorker* and a member of the American Academy of Arts and Letters.

▪ Like most writers who have been honest about their craft, I've found that writing for me has to be at some stage an entirely improvisatory undertaking; that is, chance, mystery, and intuition must be given their opportunities in composition. In the case of "The Good Samaritan," I first thought the mystery lay in the relationship of the protagonist and his son, but what might have been no more than a support player, the supposedly merely irksome hired man, took over the mechanics of the story and led me on a kind of wild-goose chase that ultimately energized everything I had been trying to say in a less interesting way. It also let me embed a few beliefs about the importance of love versus the illusions of materialism. In the story decent people are cheated of their valuables and it doesn't finally matter. A father whose child has nearly slipped away from him finds a way to hang on.

Nathan Oates's stories have appeared in *The Antioch Review, Witness,* the *Alaska Quarterly Review,* and other literary magazines. His stories have been anthologized in *The Best American Mystery Stories 2008,* the seventieth anniversary issue of *The Antioch Review,* and *Fifty-Two Stories.* He is an assistant professor of creative writing at Seton Hall University, where he also directs the Poetry-in-the-Round reading series. He lives in Brooklyn with his wife and kids.

▪ I wrote "Looking for Service" as I was finishing the first draft of a novel, thinking I could go back to the beginning and add this new voice, that the novel would now have two narrators, or maybe even three, or four. What I really wanted was a release from being caught in one character's head for so long, and maybe because of that desire for release, I wrote this story quickly, finishing a draft in two sittings. This is not that uncommon for me, and sometimes after these quick first drafts the basic structure is in place, if in need of major revision. Other times the results are terrible, and I put the stories away. This story was the rarest sort: when I read it over, it seemed nearly finished. Out of the detail of the THANK YOU, GEORGE BUSH sign jammed into his front yard, the narrator's personality—his bitterness, his anger, his tenderness—was clear, and the other characters, the situation, the setting, all seemed to fit naturally around him. The only part that didn't quite work was the ending. I wrote five different endings quickly, each progressively darker, until I finally got the characters down into that room beneath the brothel, and then, with the prompting of a few readers, I got that American girl up on the stage with that whip in her hand. Then I could see what the story was really about: the divides that separate us from people—divides of age, ideology, wealth—and the persistent desire to cross those divides, to care for the people on the other side, or to hurt them, or sometimes both. After finishing the story I saw—or, rather, my wife saw—that this wasn't part of a novel but a short story. As ever, I am indebted to my parents for their seemingly endless supply of stories that have so often provided the spark for my writing.

Gina Paoli is a native of Colorado and grew up on the eastern plains, where the Rockies are only occasionally glimpsed as a purple mirage on the horizon. After completing a BA in English literature at Colorado State University, she took up residence in the university's home, Fort Collins. While she has traveled the world, she has never lived anywhere else. She has worked at various nondescript jobs, the last as a technical writer for a small high-tech company, but currently stays at home and tries to write around the schedule of her four-year-old daughter. She has been writing stories since she was very young, and while a few of her stories were published in smaller literary magazines many years ago, she has only recently begun to pursue publication again. She is now working to complete the first of a series of what can only be described as soft-noir suspense novels, while continuing to write and rework her short stories. Visit ginapaoli.com for more information and updates about her work.

▪ The central motif of "Dog on a Cow" came from a brief moment in Zora Neale Hurston's beautiful novel *Their Eyes Were Watching God*. The incident takes place during a flood of the Mississippi River, and while the cow was only a bloated carcass in this case, the dog behaved just as viciously as the one in my story. I can't say why this terrible and bizarre image stayed with me, but it surfaced years later, converging with a roadside robbery, the hypnotic nature of driving the long, empty highways of the high plains, and another, no less traumatic flood on a much smaller river. The characters revealed themselves to me very slowly; their true natures didn't come into focus until I'd been through the story a half-dozen times. It took another four rewrites for the story to reach its final state.

T. Jefferson Parker was born in Los Angeles and has lived in Southern California all his life. He has worked as a janitor, waiter, veterinary hospital emergency attendant, newspaper reporter, and technical editor. All of his nineteen novels are set in California and Mexico. He lives in San Diego County with his family. The T doesn't stand for anything.

▪ Vic Malic is a character in my 2006 novel, *The Fallen*. The protagonist of that story, an affable San Diego cop named Robbie Brownlaw, is thrown from a burning sixth-floor hotel room (while trying to rescue someone) but survives. He's addled, however, diagnosed with synesthesia, a neurological condition in which one's senses become transposed with each other. For instance, Robbie "sees" spoken words as colored shapes hovering in the air around the speaker. The guy who threw him from the hotel is a hulking and disturbed former professional wrestler named Vic Malic, whose old ring name was Vic Primeval. Robbie and Vic become friends, and this story is about what happens to Vic when he falls in love.

Thomas J. Rice was born in rural Ireland, emigrated to the United States as a teenager, and graduated from Cornell University. Along the way he's been a farmer, breeder of border collies, construction worker, tractor driver, bartender, licensed carpenter, social activist, founder of a social justice institute, and storyteller. He's also been a sociology professor at Georgetown University. His writing has been published in a wide array of journals, editorial pages, and literary magazines, from *In These Times* to *New Orphic Review*. In 2010 he published a memoir about growing up in post–World War II Ireland called *Far from the Land*. He has recently completed a collection of Irish short stories. He lives in Andover, Massachusetts.

▪ I first wrote "Hard Truths" as a chapter in my memoir. The term refers to my mother's insistence on having me immediately accept the blame for my screw-ups: no excuses! Her reasoning: people you may want to impress will usually think less of you in the short term, but you'll immediately restore self-respect and others will trust your character in the long run. The other kernel of biography in the story is that both my parents were active in the IRA resistance movement against the Brits leading to Irish independence in 1921; both were imprisoned for their roles. My mother was actually one of the celebrated "Women of 1922," a group of hunger strikers credited with bringing an end to the Irish civil war. The rest of the story is pure fiction, a drama I'd always wanted to play out with an ending that might have been. Still, I'm confident there were many women in the resistance capable of filling Kitty's shoes.

Kristine Kathryn Rusch has published mystery, science fiction, romance, nonfiction, and just about everything else under a wide variety of names. Her Smokey Dalton mystery novels, written under her pen name Kris Nelscott, have received acclaim worldwide. She has been nominated for the Edgar and the Shamus (as both Nelscott and Rusch) as well as the Anthony Award. She has repeatedly won *Ellery Queen's Mystery Magazine*'s Readers Choice Award for best short story of the year.

Kristine often writes cross-genre fiction. Her character Miles Flint, from her Retrieval Artist series, has been chosen as one of the top ten science fiction detectives by *io9* and as one of the fourteen science fiction and fantasy detectives who could out-Sherlock Sherlock Holmes by the popular website *blastr*.

WMG Publishing has the difficult task of releasing her entire backlist over the next few years (under all her pen names), as well as the next Smokey Dalton novel sometime in 2013. A novel based on her story "G-

Men," which was published in *The Best American Mystery Stories 2009*, will appear in 2013 as well.

- I grew up in Superior, Wisconsin, in the late 1960s and 1970s, moving out permanently in 1979. I visited several times, then didn't return for a long time. I was surprised to see how little of the town changed. When I finally went back a few years ago, the custodian let me into the high school to look around. The graduation list from that year was still on the office door. All of the last names were familiar—I had gone to school with their parents. While some of us moved away, most of the kids from my high school class stayed, raised their families, and lived their lives, trying to make Superior better.

I started thinking about what kind of outside murder could happen in a town like that, where everyone knows everything about everyone else through all the generations—the good and the bad. And the secrets. There are always secrets. And your neighbors always know them, even if they never discuss them. As I wrote, I vividly remembered what it was like to live in those dark, cold winters—and honestly, I'm glad I live on the breezy, sunny Oregon coast. I'm not hardy enough to go through those long winter nights again.

Lones Seiber is a retired aerospace engineer living in Morristown, Tennessee. He received a BS in engineering physics from the University of Tennessee and worked for the Pratt Whitney Aircraft Research and Development Center in West Palm Beach as an experimental engineer on the RL-10 rocket program and later on the signature elimination project for jet engines.

He began writing short fiction seven years ago and, after successfully publishing several stories, returned to the University of Tennessee to audit junior and senior creative writing courses under Professors Allen Wier and Michael Knight. Based on the stories he presented in the senior workshop, he was invited to present stories in the graduate workshop. His fiction has appeared in *GSU Review* (now *New South*), *The Pinch*, *Lynx Eye*, *The Wordstock Ten*, *Roanoke Review*, the *TallGrass Writers* anthology, *Inkwell*, *Pearl*, and *Indiana Review*. His nonfiction has appeared in *American Heritage*. He won the 2005 GSU Review Fiction Contest, the 2007 The Pinch (River City) Fiction Contest, the 2008 Leslie Garrett Award for Fiction, the 2011 Warren Adler Prize for Fiction, and the 2011 Indiana Review Fiction Contest for the story "Icarus." He has completed a novel based on "Icarus."

- I was watching the movie *Exotica* by Atom Egoyan, most of the scenes, and even the premise, somewhat gloomy, when it flashed to a golden field of grain and a cobalt-blue sky, minute figures strung along the horizon searching for a missing girl. The visual impact of that scene became the inspiration and core of my story "Icarus."

Charles Todd, of the writing team Caroline and Charles Todd, who happen to be mother and son, have published fourteen novels of suspense in the Inspector Ian Rutledge series, including *The Confession, A Lonely Death,* and *The Red Door.* The first in that series, *A Test of Wills,* was included in *The One Hundred Favorite Mysteries of the Twentieth Century.* The Bess Crawford mysteries opened with *A Duty to the Dead,* and the fourth, *An Unmarked Grave,* was published in the summer of 2012. *The Murder Stone* is a standalone, and Rutledge short stories can be found in many anthologies and in *Strand Magazine.* The fifteenth Inspector Rutledge book is in the works.

▪ "Trafalgar" began at a luncheon in Bury St. Edmund, England. One of our English friends, filling us in on the latest news from his family, added, "And the old dog died at noon that day," as if its passing were the last straw in a litany of sadness. The line stayed with us because it was an epitaph in a way, and it had a certain poetic feel to it. We, too, had cared about the old dog. That eventually gave us the first line. The rest of the story came from a house and a bookstore we saw in Dartmouth, England, home of the Royal Naval College, while on board the *Explorer,* the Lindblad/ National Geographic ship, and from a snippet of history that we hadn't heard before. There it was, taking shape, as so many things we write do, snowballing into characters and settings—and obviously turning out to be a Rutledge inquiry by its very nature. Mike Ashley had asked us to write another short story for him, this time to be included in *The Mammoth Book of Historical Crime Fiction,* which he was editing. This gave us the excuse to pursue that snowball to its logical end. As John Curran has pointed out in his intriguing works on Agatha Christie, this sort of gestation for a book or a story over a period of time is perfectly normal. What's fascinating is that given the same points of inspiration, two people can wind up at the same satisfactory conclusion without killing each other in the process. Nineteen books later, so far, so good.

Tim L. Williams's work has been published in a variety of literary quarterlies as well as in magazines dedicated to the crime, mystery, horror, and dark fantasy genres. His story "Something About Teddy" was included in *The Best American Mystery Stories 2004.* "Half-Lives" is the fourth tale featuring Memphis private investigator Charlie Raines to appear in *Ellery Queen's Mystery Magazine.* Two previous works in the series, "The Breaks" and "Suicide Bonds," garnered Shamus nominations from the Private Eye Writers of America. After years of knocking around the Midwest and the South, Tim returned to his native Kentucky, where he lives with his wife, Sherraine, and their two children, Carson and Madelyn. He is currently working on two novels, one a contemporary mystery featuring Charlie Raines, the other a historical crime novel set in a west Kentucky coal-mining town.

▪ "Half-Lives" was inspired by a drive through an industrial section of Memphis, a city that has in recent years become my second hometown. In a quarter-mile stretch I passed at least a half-dozen crumbling warehouses, all surrounded by relatively new security fences and barbed wire, which caused me to wonder what those fences could possibly be protecting and who they could be keeping out. Ultimately, the central mystery of the story, at least to my mind, is the question of why the largest sacrifices and the highest prices are demanded from those in our society with the least ability to pay them.

Daniel Woodrell is the author of eight novels and a volume of short stories. He lives in the Missouri Ozarks. He has won a couple of awards and had a couple of movies made from his novels.

▪ "Returning the River" was begun with the notion that it might become a novel, but it did not, at least for now. As I age, I am more and more aware of things that are disappearing or gone—W. S. Merwin has a line, "Show me what you see vanishing and I will tell you who you are." I live in the same neighborhood some elements of my family have lived in since before World War I, and I see little flickers of my lost dead ones all around. Some years ago we lost my grandfather's house. It sits only 200 yards away, but I will no longer go past it. I eventually realized that I felt a sort of atavistic, animalistic anger whenever I did pass, and the fact that the present owner is a scumbag who defiles my people's fine imprint on our hallowed old place did not help reduce the hostility. This is pretty common throughout the world, this broken connection to the land and one's own past, and the story was meant to give recognition to these almost presocial feelings that I seem able to access too easily.

Other Distinguished Mystery Stories of 2011

MARGOLIN, PHILLIP, AND JERRY MARGOLIN
   The Adventure of the Purloined Paget. *A Study in Scarlet,* ed. Laurie R. King
      and Leslie S. Klinger (Bantam)
MATTSON, JOSEPH
   Hamm's Toe. *Slake: Los Angeles,* no. 3

PETRIN, JAS. R.
   A New Pair of Pants. *Alfred Hitchcock Mystery Magazine,* November
PINCUS, ROGER
   Convenience. *Fifth Wednesday Journal,* Spring

RASH, RON
   The Trusty. *The New Yorker,* May 23

SANTLOFER, JONATHAN
   Lola. *New Jersey Noir,* ed. Joyce Carol Oates (Akashic)
SIMPSON, NANCY PAULINE
   The Coffin Factory. *Alfred Hitchcock Mystery Magazine,* November
SMITH, GREGORY BLAKE
   Punishment. *Prairie Schooner,* Spring
STEINHAUER, OLEN
   Start-Up. *Strand Magazine,* June–September
SULLINS, JACOB
   12 Rounds. *Georgia Review,* Summer

TAYLOR, SETH
   Ritalin. *Notre Dame Review,* Summer/Fall
TERWILLIGER, CAM
   Cherry Town. *The Literary Review,* Spring
TREMBLAY, PAUL
   Nineteen Snapshots of Dennisport. *Cape Cod Noir,* ed. David L. Ulin
      (Akashic)

URBANSKI, DEBBIE
   The Move. *New England Review* 32, no. 1

WATERS, DON
   Espanola. *Georgia Review,* Fall
WEINGARDEN, MARK
   Agent Halverson Addresses the Space Coast Optimists. *Five Points* 14,
      no. 2
WEINSTEIN, JACOB SAGER
   Golden Boy. *Popcorn Fiction,* June